GEOFFREY LEEDS

DOUBLE PLAY

Hodder & Stoughton

LONDON SYDNEY AUCKLAND TORONTO

British Library Cataloguing in Publication Data
Leeds, Geoffrey
  Double play.
  I. Title
813'.54[F]

  ISBN 0 340 42499 0

Hodder and Stoughton Editorial Office: 47 Bedford Square, London WC1B 3DP.

"When I first set out to see the world I thought it existed only in the places I was going to. I was in danger of becoming a series of deferred destinations. Now I know that travel, that 'in-between' is the time when one lives. I am going to try to turn all my destinations into part of one journey, the long journey from beginning to the end . . ."

Anthony Adverse

Contents

A Philadelphia Story

It was one of those cloying muggy days that always plague New York in summer. The racquets court on the top floor of the club was stifling, its cavernous proportions and many skylights making any effort to reverse the effects of the sun foolhardy.

From the ball-bruised mahogany benches of the spectators' gallery the two men in whites appeared to move with ease between the crimson lines of the black slate court. Though they had been pushing themselves to their limit for over an hour, the echoing chamber's majestic proportions magically slowed the 125mph pace of the small rock-hard ball, and imparted an effortless grace to their movements.

Stedman Wright had already broken the French gut on four of the special long-shafted, small-faced racquets, something which – while not unusual in tournament play – told his good friend, Wiley Travis, that something serious was troubling his opponent. The game over, Wiley asked him frankly what was eating him.

"I've got to go to Philadelphia. Suki's marrying my cousin Harry tonight."

Wiley was shocked. Until a few weeks ago Steddy had been living with Suki. They'd had a fight, but they had fought often during the two years that they had been together.

"Jesus, she's got balls. What are you going to do about it?"

Steddy shrugged. "Dance at the bitch's wedding, I guess."

Later, in the showers, as they shouted to each other over the partitions and the roar of the running water, Wiley tried his best to placate Steddy, but could only manage the usual clichés.

"It's better this happened now. You might have done something really stupid – like marry her yourself."

Steddy's deep anger and resentment exploded, and he punched his fist into the thick glass partition until the shower ran red with blood.

"Goddamned whore!" he bellowed.

Calmer now, his anger surfaced and expended, Steddy sat in the small panelled dressing alcove, sipping a cold Bass Ale from a chilled crockery mug while old Charley, the squash pro, bandaged and taped his injured hand. Wiley sprawled nearby, his legs over the arms of a big leather chair.

"You won't be able to drive very well with that hand. Want me to run you down to Philadelphia?"

"No thanks, Wiley. I'm taking the train."

"Well, at least you had the good sense not to tear up your sporting hand."

"Why? You looking for a handicap?" Steddy smiled for the first time that day.

At thirty-six, Stedman Wright could no longer be referred to as an eligible young man. A bachelor, a clubman, a champion athlete, yes, but, though the older generation liked him, they thought him too worldly, too self-centred and too unsettled, to be a serious candidate for their daughters.

He was six-foot-two-inches tall, with his mother's dark auburn hair and ease of carriage, and his father's startlingly deep emerald green eyes. Most women found the combination irresistible.

~ ~ ~

As the train jerked through the depressing New Jersey landscape of chemical plants and oil refineries, Steddy sipped a brandy and soda in the comfort of the first-class passenger car. The monotony of the bleak scene gave way to reflection, and reflection to brooding. He had just lost the only girl who had mattered to him in a long time, *but had it all been a sham from the start; had she ever really cared for him at all, and, in the end, how much did she still mean to him?* The question hung in his mind for a moment, and then drifted away, unanswered.

They had broken up three weeks ago over the usual thing – *Why couldn't he do something serious like other people? All he did was play games. When would he grow up?* The lifestyle that had become his routine since leaving college left her bored and lonely. He rose late, and normally walked to the club, where he played racquets, swam, and enjoyed a late lunch. In the afternoon, he would play a leisurely game of bridge or towie, depending upon who was available, and by four-thirty was usually back on the court. Then at six or six-thirty, he would descend to the main hall where he earned his "funny money", playing in the high-stakes backgammon chouette until eight-thirty when, if there were no specific plans, he would go back to his flat at the hotel, have a nap, bathe and if they could still find a restaurant open, take Suki to dinner.

More often than not there was a backgammon game after dinner which lasted until the wee hours of the morning when, reeking of Havana cigars and brandy, he would again find time for Suki.

He lived well enough, if not brilliantly, on the income from his trusts, but gambling held an irresistible attraction for him. It was a vicious circle. When he won, he won big, but more often than not, had a hard time collecting. When he lost, he lost big, and true to the code he had set for himself, he settled his accounts on the spot. The squeeze was ulcer-making. At tennis or racquets matches his opponents often accused him of gamesmanship when he fled the court to throw up, or joked about what he had done the night before, but some people knew that it came from the ever underlying tension of a true competitor, no matter how cavalier his superficial aspect. It was important to him never to show outwardly that he cared. His close friends knew how much winning meant to him because they all came from the same mould, lived by the same code and rarely gave any quarter.

~ ~ ~

Earl collected him at the station in his mother's car. He was the family's general factotum, whose unofficial duties had included teaching Steddy everything he had learned about cards, dice and street-fighting during a two-year stint with the Navy in the Pacific during World War II. He told Steddy that his mother was already at the club doing the place cards, and that, presuming he would be late, she had sent along his duds, and wanted him to change there instead of at the house.

Steddy shrugged and slumped into the front seat of the old Chrysler, bracing his knees up against the dashboard. The cared-for country smell of the automobile brought on a flood of warm and reassuring feelings. Earl got in beside him, tossed his cap in the back seat, started the motor and with one hand on the wheel manoeuvring the lumbering vehicle into the stream of traffic, drew a squashed pack of Camels from the shirt pocket under his jacket and lit up.

"Do you want to talk about it, son?"

"You know more about it than I do. I didn't even know the bitch was seeing him until last week when I heard about the wedding. Ain't life grand?"

"I meant the hand. Who'd you have a run in with?"

"It was with a *what*. A shower partition, to be precise."

"Jesus, son, she's not worth it, never was. You never gave two cents for her until now."

11

"Don't tell me you're on her side?"

"Hell, no. Nice piece of ass, but I never had any time for her. You're better off without her. Maybe *now* you'll meet someone decent."

"For two and a half years everyone told me how great she was. Now, all of a sudden no one can stand her."

"You never asked *me*."

Steddy grunted and changed the subject.

"Is Two here?" (Steddy was the third Stedman in the Wright clan, his father still answered to *Two*.)

"No, your dad's still in Florida."

"That bastard's never here when Mother needs him."

They drove on in silence. Steddy closed his eyes as the dusk turned to evening. His father was around less and less; it seemed he had never really known him. Earl was the nearest thing to a father he had ever had.

Steddy was dozing when the noise of gravel exploding under the fat old-fashioned whitewall tyres signalled their arrival at the club. He sat up in the car and pushed his fingers through his hair. Earl, eyes still front, put his hand on Steddy's knee as he braked the car under the porte-cochère, and said:

"Now try to take it easy tonight, Sted."

Steddy reached over with his good hand and put it for a moment on top of Earl's. The gesture was enough.

Steddy smiled remembering how as a little boy he had wanted his mother to marry Earl. He had thought it a wonderful idea and had told them so repeatedly to their indulgent laughter. Earl had never married and Steddy often noted how the two of them, Earl and his mother, had a sort of quiet way of communicating – like an old married couple, with Earl anticipating her needs at every turn. He wondered for the first time in his adult life, how deep that understanding went. He hoped for his mother's sake that she wasn't really as alone as she seemed, or as he now felt as he stepped from the car and walked into the club.

The dressing room where Steddy changed into his dinner clothes still held a sprinkling of golfers and tennis players and one or two came over to congratulate him on his mother's horse winning the Preakness the previous Saturday. Georgianna Wright had inherited her father's racing stable and instead of selling it as everyone had expected, had thrown herself into its management with a vengeance. The results had surprised the racing world, but not Steddy. He had never known her to attempt anything that she wasn't sure she could master.

He had ordered a bottle of champagne before getting into the shower and methodically drank it as he dressed. His cousin Tom, the bridegroom's brother, who Steddy had always bested at every game the club offered, approached him and seeing the half-empty champagne bottle, asked snidely:

"And what are *you* celebrating?"

The ensuing fight was short-lived, and later, when Steddy stepped out onto the terrace where cocktails were being served before dinner, he noted absently that his already bandaged hand was beginning to seep blood from the solid blow he had landed.

Georgianna Wright's eyebrow was slightly raised as she greeted her son. He sensed that behind her annoyed expression, she was secretly amused. She came from an old New York family and after forty years of living in Philadelphia, still thought of most of the locals as a dressed-up collection of pompous bumpkins.

Maisy and Stoddard Wright, Stedman's aunt and uncle had been killed in a sea-plane in Canada three years before and, though Georgianna Wright wasn't very fond of her brother-in-law's children, she had automatically assumed the role of surrogate parent, hosting her niece's debut and now Harry's wedding. The premature loss of their parents meant that his cousins had inherited very young, which Steddy suspected formed the basis for Suki's decision to marry Harry.

Suki found him on the terrace and her embrace implied that they had never been more to each other than brother and sister.

Steddy was nonplussed and said nothing when she linked her arm in his and manoeuvred him away from the receiving line.

"We must talk," she whispered urgently.

When he didn't respond, she went on.

"Darling, you knew I couldn't go on like that for ever – you'll never grow up." The almond-shaped eyes that had always intrigued him, now squinted into slits, and he wondered how he could ever have thought them beautiful. "I've told you a hundred times that I simply can't live without security, but you wouldn't change. Harry loves me – oh, I'll never feel about him the way I do about you, but . . ." Her voice faded into the background chatter. Steddy stood quite still, then turned from her as though she had never been there and strode to the bar.

Aunt Edith took his arm and steered him back out to the terrace, but not before he had got them each a glass of champagne. Edith wasn't really his aunt, but his mother's oldest and closest friend ever since their girlhood school days together in Florence. She was the daughter of an English duke and had married a Scottish earl who had been killed at El Alamein.

Steddy adored her and smiled, remembering how she had sneaked him his first champagne cocktail at a party in her hotel suite in New York when he was fourteen. Ever since then their relationship had been that of contemporaries – though nearing seventy, she was almost twice his age. When he grew older, they would lunch or dine together whenever they found themselves in the same city and exchange confidences – he, invariably about the problems he was having with his latest girlfriend and she, about how boring it was to have to go out with *creaky* old men.

"Now you're not going to misbehave are you dear boy? Your mother's quite concerned." Her opening remark brought Steddy from his reminiscence.

"Don't worry Edith – they deserve each other as far as I'm concerned. But what are you doing here? Surely you didn't come all this way to see those two insects get married?"

"Certainly not. I don't care for either of them any more than you do. I was over having a little tuck at Boston General and your mother asked me down for a few days – I don't think this little event was even in the works when she invited me. It's all rather *sudden*, isn't it?"

"Now Edith, don't *you* be naughty – you know very well that *sudden* is the understatement of the year!"

The dinner gong was sounding and a dapper, white-haired gentleman with a crimson carnation in the lapel of his dinner jacket approached to take Edith to her table. She winked slyly at Steddy.

"Now don't you do anything I wouldn't do," she said with a mischievous twinkle in her eye.

~ ~ ~

The dinner for two-hundred and fifty was in the Trophy Room, a vaulted mock-Tudor affair with paintings, animal heads and silver cups that climbed the walls in no apparent order until they disappeared into the dusty shadows of the heavy crossbeams.

Steddy was already slightly pissed when he found his table on the outer fringes of the gathering, near the service bar. It was an orphan's table made up of obscure relatives and anonymous faces. Dinner passed without incident. He talked to no one. The others accepted his silence and spoke across him as he sipped from a second bottle of champagne that he had sequestered and made quite clear to everyone, was his and his alone.

Dessert over, the last toasts from the head table were petering out, when he drew himself erect and banged a spoon on his glass for silence until he broke it.

All eyes were on him with the possible exception of Suki's and his mother's. Gripping a giant torpedo-shaped Havana in the same hand as his champagne glass and speaking with the surprising clarity that the very drunk can occasionally command, he began his toast.

"I would like to drink to Suki's family in Paris, none of whom are with us this evening and all of whom have been sorely neglected in the toasts so far this evening."

A burst of hear! hears! and table thumping followed, prompted not so much by sentiment as by collective relief that Steddy hadn't said anything to embarrass anyone.

He waited politely and then tapped another glass to indicate that he had not yet finished. The sporadic applause died and Steddy continued.

"I would especially like to drink to Suki's *guardian*, one of the most hospitable women in Paris, who it has been my pleasure to have known for many years."

Everyone was beaming at him, not noticing the dark cloud that was passing over Suki's face, or Georgianna Wright's nervous titter. Steddy continued.

"In fact, it was Suki's aunt, with her heart of gold, who introduced me to the bride-to-be some two and a half years ago in Paris. Ladies and gentlemen, I ask you to raise your glasses . . ."

A loud scraping of chairs ensued as the men stood, glasses held high.

". . . and drink to Madame Claudine, who runs the best knock-shop in Europe."

There was a momentary burst of enthusiastic applause, until what he had actually said dawned on the celebrants. In the embarrassing and ominous silence that ensued, Suki's strident shriek, "You cock-sucker!" echoed through the rafters as she fled from the hall.

A Time Aloft

In spite of twenty-four hours of abstinence, Stedman was still nursing a few very rough edges. By some miracle he had made the Air France Concorde check-in at New York's JFK with an hour to kill and after obtaining his seat assignment, was told with a Gallic shrug that the air-conditioning in the Club 2000 wasn't working. He went into the terminal and headed for the first bar in sight, a pseudo-English pub beyond the check-in where at least the Bass Ale was the real thing and was served authentically, if accidentally, warm.

The pub was cool and mercifully empty. Stedman drained the Pilsner glass and ordered a bullshot. He rationalised his behaviour at the wedding for the fourteenth time and was half way through his second bullshot when his flight was called. He paid the bill and sipped the remainder of his drink while waiting for the change. He didn't give a damn about embarrassing Suki, but his mother was a different story, especially as she had been so unbelievably understanding, with no recriminations. It was she who had suggested that he get away for a while and when he had confessed that he was broke, she had bankrolled him with the proviso that if he had to gamble, he stick to backgammon. He was smiling at the way mother and son understood one another, when the barman interrupted his thoughts to tell him that his flight had been called for the second time.

A matronly Air France stewardess showed him to the aisle seat he'd selected and, with that relaxed, drowsy feeling that comes with knowing that the earthbound tether is about to be shorn, he settled down low in his chair and closed his eyes.

Later, he would not recall whether it was her perfume – something between Mitsouko and Patchouli – or her throaty lived-in voice, that first roused him. When he opened his eyes he found her arched over him. She was as tall as he was, and in the cramped fighter-plane fuselage of the Concorde she had to bend in two in order to reach the window seat at his right. Her chestnut hair was thick and very long and brushed his face as she tried to pass. He rose from his chair too quickly to help her and banged his head on the cabin's overhead. She chuckled throatily and two dimples appeared high at the corners of her tanned cheeks.

"Wouldn't you prefer the window?" she said, back in the aisle again, still laughing over her unsuccessful attempt to climb over him.

"No, thanks. My legs don't fit unless I stick them in the aisle." She looked down at her own legs, that were every bit as long as his, and then they both laughed. She handed him an enormous duffel that she said was her bag and while he grappled with it in his hunched stance, she hung a Nikon around his neck and thus free of encumbrances, gracefully slid past him into her seat. The stewardess tried to relieve him of his burdens, but the girl insisted on keeping everything with her until somehow they managed to stow it all around them. Stedman good-humouredly feigned annoyance when she told the stewardess, "We'll keep them with us, thank you," as though it were a *fait accompli* that they were travelling together.

The *No Smoking* light went out and when she saw that Steddy was having difficulty reaching for the lighter in his trouser pocket, she lit his cigarette for him. It occurred to him that he had never met a girl who was so beautiful, and yet so completely devoid of guile.

When the steward offered them champagne, she asked for hers on the rocks and Stedman, who had always scoffed at people who did so, inexplicably ordered his the same way. Before they had finished the first glass, they were already whispering remarks about their neighbours and laughing conspiratorially. Steddy, who had felt blasé and jaded when he boarded the plane, now felt like a boy of twenty on his way to Europe for the first time. Her enthusiasm was infectious, even the aircraft held a sudden interest as he explained to her that the dial on the forward bulkhead would register when their airspeed hit Mach I, and again when they reached Mach II.

"Oh! We have to celebrate my first time at Mach II," she said.

"I'll order some more champagne." He reached for the bell.

"No, no, wait a minute. I've got some terrific coke someone gave me as a going away present and I have no intention of taking it through French customs."

"I've never had cocaine," Steddy said sullenly, but she swept right over his change of mood.

"Good, now we'll both have a first to celebrate. Have you got a hundred dollar bill?"

"Will five hundred francs do?" Steddy said, still not altogether pleased with the turn of events.

"Oh perfect. It doesn't really matter, but as it's your first time, it should be special."

Without the least effort to conceal it, she took a tiny phial and a small, round mirror from the duffel and, after adjusting the air vents in the overhead to point away from her, proceeded without a qualm to spoon out the white crystals onto the mirror in full view of anyone who cared to look. Steddy, for his part, didn't know where to look, but for some reason he was more anxious lest she notice his discomfort. He felt so silly the first time he tried the coke – bent over her lap with a five hundred franc note rolled up in his nose – that he laughed and blew a considerable amount of the stuff all over the place. She demonstrated how it was done and transformed an awkward act into something sensual, even erotic.

They skipped lunch and just had the caviar and more champagne instead. Steddy felt himself a new man, rejuvenated and, for the first time in years, unbelievably, he was sure he was in love.

She was laughing and he was nibbling on her ear when the chime ended what seemed the shortest flight of his life. He was suddenly afraid of losing her.

"You can have dinner tonight, can't you?" he asked.

"I'd love to, in fact I'm beginning to get hungry."

"Where are you staying?"

"With my mother and stepfather at the Plaza Athénée."

With growing relief and trying not to overplay his hand, Steddy asked, "Then you're not with anyone?"

She laughed, understanding the question, but choosing to ignore the point, said: "Technically, no, they don't get in from London until tomorrow."

"Well let's see, we won't get into town until about eight, so I'll drop you at the Plaza, go to my place and change and pick you up at nine-thirty."

"Make it ten in the bar, I want to wash my hair."

Steddy dropped her at her hotel and told the driver to take him on to the Ritz. She had hardly left the cab when doubt crept into his thoughts – *She was too good to be true. Something would go wrong. Maybe she was married.* He began to panic when he realised that he didn't even know her name. *What if she wasn't there? How would he find her? Maybe she wasn't even staying at the Plaza.*

He stepped from the shower, took a sip from the glass of champagne that was resting on the sink, and walked over to the window overlooking the Place Vendôme. Funny, he didn't remember ordering the wine, or on reflection, even checking into the hotel for that matter.

Her perfume told him that she was behind him.

He had reached the bar at the Plaza at nine-thirty and had spent the longest forty minutes he could remember – sipping more champagne, trying not to drink too much, but nervously not knowing what else to do.

When he spun around on the stool and saw her, for the first time in years he felt all thumbs. It was an awkwardness that he knew would not fade until he had her in his arms.

~ ~ ~

Stedman awoke with a start and a weight across his stomach, the phone had rung on his side of the bed, and she was sprawled across him talking into it. She replaced the receiver and kissed him good morning. She wore no make-up and the steady sea-blue gaze of her eyes under thick, straight, mannish eyebrows, met his with delight and humour.

"Guess what, darling. Mummy and Nubie aren't coming till this evening so we've got the whole day to ourselves. They said I could use their box at the races, so if you feel like it, we can have lunch at the track."

"And good morning to you," he said kissing the corners of her mouth. "Now don't you think it would be a good idea if we start the day by introducing ourselves at this late stage of our acquaintance?"

"What a spoilsport you are. It's so intriguing having a mystery lover, and besides, you might have a perfectly terrible name and that *would* be awful."

They kissed again and passion had stolen the place of humour when there was a knock at the door. She pushed him away, sat up in bed and pulling the sheets around her said:

"*Entrez.*"

"What the hell is that?"

"It means 'come in'."

"I know that. I mean who is . . ."

The room service waiter picked his way across the obstacle course of discarded clothing without raising one Gallic eyebrow.

She whispered mischievously. "I rang the bell while you were kissing me."

They ordered an enormous breakfast and when the waiter had left, Steddy stood formally, but still quite naked, at the foot of the bed.

"It has been a pleasure meeting you. May I introduce myself – my name is Stedman Wright."

She held out her hand with equal formality.

"I'm Theadora Boulton. Delighted."

They fell together on the bed laughing, and then made beautiful, slow, morning love until the waiter arrived. Steddy ordered a bottle of champagne to go with breakfast and they sat cross-legged on the bed eating from the table, guzzling champagne and chatting as though they had breakfasted together for years. Then Thea said, "Your name sounds familiar. Should I know it?"

"I was just going to say the same thing to you, but I know I've never met you before – there are *some* things a gentleman doesn't forget."

"Do you know my stepfather, Nubar Harkonian?"

"I should have realised when you said Nubie before, but really he was the furthest thing from my mind."

"Where do you know him from?"

"Oh here and there, we're backgammon cronies. I support myself on his losses whenever I'm in London, although, to be quite fair, he regularly skins me at bridge."

"Now I remember. He calls you Steddy, doesn't he?"

"Most people do."

"He likes you. He says you're the only real gentleman in the younger generation. You play racquets or squash or something as well, don't you?"

"Yes to all of the above. And you must be that stepdaughter he's always trying to palm off on me."

"Oh really?"

"Yes, something about a rock star in L.A., as I recall."

"You see, I told you we shouldn't have introduced ourselves."

"Never mind, no more talk. I'm going home to change and then stop at the club for a second to get some money, then why don't we take them up on their offer and have lunch at the track?"

"OK. Nubie said I could use the car as long as it picks them up at the airport at seven, so while you're gone I'll have my bath and pick you up – the Travellers, I presume?"

"I guess you've got me type-cast!" he chuckled.

Later at the bar of the Travellers, Steddy ran into Wiley Travis.

"What the hell are you doing here?"

"I might well ask you the same thing, but I've already heard *The Philadelphia Story*, which is how everyone's already referring to that little stunt you pulled."

"Christ, I'd already forgotten."

"I can assure you, you're the only person who has."

"Then let's drop it. How long will you be here?"

"I'm leaving tonight – don't you remember, I told you I was going to Germany on business?"

"Oh yeah, I forgot. Anyway, how's the action around here?"

"If you mean are there any backgammon pigeons, I can tell you there's nary a one – they're all en route to Harkonian's Schloss for his tournament."

"Is that *now?*"

"I'm surprised you didn't get the nod. I thought he was a pal of yours."

"I didn't expect to be in Europe. I imagine he'll ask me if I call and let him know I'm around." Steddy continued on his way to the door. "Will you surface anywhere after Deutschland?"

"I'll walk you out," Wiley said, following him through the doors. "I'll be in London next week."

They reached the street as the big navy blue and cream Harkonian Rolls was just pulling to the kerb of the Champs-Elysées in front of the club. The door popped open before the chauffeur had come to a complete stop and Thea leaned out to kiss Steddy, who then turned to Wiley and said:

"Sorry we can't drop you, but we're late for the races."

They lunched at the track and ran into far too many acquaintances, so they called it a day and went back to Steddy's rooms at the Ritz where they lingered under the hotel's pink silk sheets until twilight descended on the Place Vendôme. When the floodlights that bathed Napoleon's column outside the window penetrated the curtains, Thea said that she had to get back to change for dinner with her mother and Nubar.

"I'm sorry we can't be alone, but I haven't seen Mummy in almost a year. Do you mind terribly?"

"Not if you promise to come straight here after dinner."

"Oh no, I meant do you mind terribly having to have dinner with them? You absolutely *have* to come."

Nubar grinned all through dinner at Lasserre and occasionally guffawed and slapped his wife Elizabeth on the thigh. He couldn't get over it, that the two of them had met on their own after he had tried for so many years to promote a liaison. Nevertheless, Steddy could tell he was a bit miffed when, after getting a kick under the table from Thea, he had refused Nubar's invitation to play backgammon at the hotel, on the excuse that he had promised to take her dancing. He accepted, however, Nubar's invitation to fly down to Austria with them in the morning for the tournament at his Schloss.

~ ~ ~

Steddy intended for them to part company with Thea's parents at the door of the restaurant and go straight back to the Ritz, but Nubar insisted on dropping them at Régine's in his car. Thea protested that Régine's was too noisy and too much of a hassle, so Steddy suggested Raspoutine as an alternative.

"It's a White Russian clip joint, but the music's as authentic as the vodka is at twenty bucks a shot," he said with little enthusiasm.

"Do they have Gypsies?"

"Oh, yes, they're wonderful," Elizabeth Harkonian piped in. "If we didn't have to leave so early for Austria tomorrow morning, I'd come with you," she said, nudging Nubar in the ribs.

"Don't get any ideas about delaying our flight – as it is, some of your guests may have already arrived before we get there."

"My guests?" Elizabeth said archly.

"All right, my guests – but you know very well you enjoy it every year in spite of the fuss you make, my dear," and then turning to Thea and Steddy, "and don't you two stay out all night and get to the airport late or you'll find yourselves without a lift!"

When the car pulled away from the kerb, Steddy said to Thea:

"We don't really have to go in now that they've gone . . ."

"But I'd like to. I love Gypsies and I've never been to a Russian nightclub – it sounds fabulous."

They negotiated the three flights of red-carpeted stairs to the cellar until they reached the bar at the far wall of the bottom landing. The Balalaika music and the Gypsies' mournful cries that had been only faintly audible from the stairway, now precluded conversation. Steddy tried to suggest that they have *one* drink at the bar, but not hearing him, Thea followed the maitre d' down the three remaining steps into the large multi-vaulted main cellar, to a small table at the edge of the dance floor, lighted, as were all the tables, by a single silver candlestick with a fringed red silk shade.

The Gypsies were seated in a semicircle at the centre of the dance floor. The dark-skinned woman who was singing had plaited jet-black hair that was thick with oil and wore hundreds of gold chains and medals about her neck and wrists that gleamed against her garnet velvet dress. She was just finishing the solo part of "Och Chichornia", and as Steddy and Thea took their seats, the rest of the group stood and joined her for the refrain that swelled and rapidly mounted in tempo. Steddy was caught up by the music and when the captain leaned his head over to take his order, instead of asking for a bottle of champagne, as he had planned, he just said "Moscovscaya" – the Russian vodka he preferred.

When the small bottle arrived at the table encased in a thick ice overcoat, Thea raised an eyebrow and looked at him with a slightly *We are not amused* expression. He poured the icy, thick liquid into the small glass in front of her and shouted over the din.

"You wanted to go Russian tonight – that's not something you can do by half measures!"

She started to sip from the glass, but his hand restrained hers, and pointing at himself to indicate that she should follow his example, he raised his glass and knocked it back with one quick snap of the wrist. Thea picked up her glass, but hesitated for a moment until Steddy leaned over and whispered in her ear.

"If you'd rather sip it through a rolled-up five-hundred franc note, I'll understand, but I'm not sure my friends will," he said, nodding in the direction of the Gypsies who were now singing on their feet and approaching the table. Thea smiled and without moving her lips said:

"You know you're a regular little shit," and with that, downed the glass and held it out to be refilled. But the Gypsies were upon them, and Steddy stood to return their bear hugs. Natasha sat at the table for a moment and the others stood while Steddy poured them each a glass of vodka. When the regular orchestra began to play for dancing, they left, promising to play his favourite song.

"You must have spent a million dollars here over the years to get that kind of attention," Thea said.

"Not really. Years ago they had a Russian Fortnight at Annabel's in London – redecorated the whole place especially for it, and imported Natasha and her troupe to entertain for the entire two weeks – we used to take them home with us every night and they'd play until eight or nine in the morning."

"Who was your little comrade then?" Thea asked, now gingerly sipping her vodka.

Ignoring her question, Steddy said:

"Why don't we dance? Isn't that what you wanted to do?"

"A tango?" Thea said incredulously.

"Why not? Haven't you heard I do a mean tango?"

Steddy was already standing. Taking her hand, he pulled out her chair and swept her onto the dance floor. Spinning her and forcing her to lie back dramatically over his arm, he drew her to him and into the pulsing rhythm of the music. He had intended to satirise the steps of the dance to teach her a lesson, but Thea was light as a feather in his arms and responded to the sense of his body without the need for exaggerated movements. Her tall, lithe frame fitted into his as though he was the mould she was cast from, and after a few passes across the floor, the other dancers made room for them; some even stopped to watch. When the music ended they were both surprised that the applause was directed at them. They started towards their table, but the clapping continued until the orchestra began playing another tango – "Orchids in the Moonlight". Steddy bowed his head to Thea in invitation and she nodded acceptance.

This time they both became lost to the music and its sensual cadences. Their eyes were closed and the erotic aura of Thea's perfume caused Steddy's nostrils to flare involuntarily as he pocketed her earring and nibbled on her ear lobe. The vodka had done its work and freed them of inhibitions until, perspiring profusely, Steddy realised that they had to get out of there right away.

He had to drag Thea away finally, but not before the leader of the orchestra had presented her with a cassette of his music and the old woman who sold flowers had given her a bouquet of all the gardenias she had left in her basket. After paying and tipping everyone, with the possible exception of one or two of the remaining patrons, Steddy had to have the concierge at the Ritz pay the cab driver. The lights in the lobby and in the corridors were already dimmed as they made their way through them to his apartment. Thea was humming the tango, and clinging to each other, they reached his door by its measured steps. They kissed just inside and Thea began undoing his black silk bow tie.

"God, even your tie's soaking wet!"

"I haven't danced like that in years – I'd better take a shower." Then crushing her in his arms with a force that seemed to fill him, he tried to dance her towards the bathroom.

"You go ahead," she said, pulling away but kissing him gently – "I might join you in a minute . . ."

When he turned off the water of the shower, the strains of the tango that had been echoing in his head, seemed actually to be drifting through the partially opened door to the bedroom – Thea had found the cassette player he travelled with and was playing the tape from the nightclub.

He turned off the light in the bathroom and stepped over the

threshold into a very different room than the one he had left five
minutes before. Thea had draped her flowered pink silk shawl over the
bedside lamp, bathing the room in a soft dappled-rose light. The scent
of gardenias was everywhere – she had rubbed the petals into the
sheets, and the violins played "Orchids in the Moonlight" as though
they had never left Raspoutine. He drew her to him and gave himself
over completely to her and the world of scent, sound and magical light
that she had created.

~ ~ ~

By the time they surfaced, they were too late to ride with the
Harkonians to the airport, but managed, with the help of three pots of
black coffee and the Ritz's conscientious concierge, to stop at the Plaza
for Thea's things and reach the private section of Le Bourget on their
own. There, one of Nubar's agents spotted them and waved their cab
onto the field where the white Mystère could be seen gleaming on the
apron as they approached.

Evidently the Harkonians had not yet arrived as the crew was
standing in loose formation at the foot of the access stair. Thea told
Steddy that the colours of the crew's uniforms and the matching black,
crimson and gold stripes on the aircraft's tail assembly, were her
mother's, and that like her mother's title, had descended from her
Austrian forebears dating back to the Crusades. Nubar's middle-
European origins had always been something of a mystery and Steddy
suspected that this was the reason he had so greedily adopted and
preserved the symbols and trappings of his wife's ancient heritage. He
had spent a fortune restoring her family Schloss in Austria to its
pre-war glory, although Thea said she was sure that it had never
approached anything like its present grandeur in its entire history.

She was greeting the crew in her naturally friendly manner when a
truck from Fauchon pulled up, and men in surgically immaculate white
coats proceeded to unload large, exotically marked wooden cases that
Steddy learned contained hundreds of pounds of fresh caviar, truffles,
pâté and champagne. "Quite a shopping list for a five-day weekend!"
he mused out loud. "How many people are coming?"

"I think about sixty, unless they overcrowd the house."

"Anybody fun?"

"Well, certainly your gang from London, but I'm sure you'll know
everyone and have to introduce *me*; after all it *is* a backgammon
tournament."

"Don't knock it. That's how I pay my rent."

"But the prize is only a gold bar."

"It's not the prize money. That's the least of it. The big money's in the private games and the side bets."

"Will I see you at all, or will I have to enter the tournament in order to play games with you?"

"You know you're the best game in town. All you have to do is touch me with your little finger to get my undivided attention."

Just then, the navy and cream Rolls swept onto the field followed by a station car and approached the private jet with all the slow ceremony of a state occasion. The cars came to a halt as though overcome by inertia – then the driver of the Rolls smartly snapped open the passenger door precisely at the foot of the stair. Nubar was the first out and then he handed down Thea's mother, Elizabeth. It was evident by his manner that she was his most prized possession. She, in turn, appeared to delight in the court he paid her, although Steddy remembered how she had winced with disdain the night before when Nubar had repeatedly slapped her on the thigh. Her features were more delicate than Thea's, and while tall, she was small-boned and looked European. Thea had obviously inherited a lot of her lanky uncomplicated beauty from her Yankee father.

Turning to Stedman, Nubar said:

"Look who I found at the club."

At that moment Viscount Rollo Rockford stepped from the car. He was story-book tall, dark and handsome, or as half the girls in Europe called him: tall, dark and *hands*. His complexion, too sultry to be pure English, was a throwback to his Spanish grandee great-grandmother. A silky black, casually drooping moustache set off his colouring and added a satanic aspect to his overall appearance.

Steddy was genuinely happy to see his old friend and after greeting him warmly, introduced Thea.

"Dearest, this is Rollo Rockford, or as he's better known, *Roll-em* Rockford."

"No introductions are necessary. He's a legend."

Rollo flashed a brilliant smile.

"I'm flattered, but I can't return the compliment as until this moment, Nubie has carefully avoided making any mention to me of your existence."

"It seems safe enough now as it appears Steddy has her well in hand," Nubar replied, laughing.

"Where's your bride?" Steddy asked.

Rollo's face darkened visibly.

"She's down in the country, at Blyden with father and the children."

Elizabeth Harkonian sensed the tension and broke in.

"Come, let's have a glass of champagne while they finish loading. The heat is stifling."

As they climbed the gangway, Thea whispered into Steddy's ear.

"That was a rotten thing to do. You know he hates her."

"Just defining the territory, darling," he answered, grinning.

Stedman *did* know that Rollo hated his wife; who didn't? Rollo had married far beneath him against the violent opposition of his family, but his father, the Earl of Blyden, had done a complete volte-face when the children were born and now worshipped Rollo's wife and his grandsons. Rollo was nowhere.

His father's and wife's loathing of his gambling had reached a fever pitch after an incident the previous year, when Rollo had won $180,000 in Deauville and had actually left the casino and gone home.

His wife had greeted him sourly with: "And how much did you lose *tonight?*"

"But I won darling – $180,000!" Rockford had replied, still full of the thrill of his coup.

"Did they pay you?" she hissed.

"Well no, I took their marker – didn't feel like waiting for a cheque."

"Well you march right back there this minute and get one."

He had gone back to the casino and while waiting for the cheque to be drawn, looked in at the now almost empty baccarat table. Forty minutes later he departed again without the cheque, this time leaving behind *his* marker for $200,000. She had left him and moved in with his father at Blyden.

Stedman knew that the loss at roulette had broken Rollo utterly, but assumed as did everyone that Nubar had been bankrolling him ever since. Nubar liked Rollo enormously, but more important, he was impressed with Rollo's family and the fact that he would one day be one of England's premier earls.

There was a thump and the aircraft jiggled as the door closed behind them and the noises of the airport were replaced by the faint strains of Vivaldi.

The interior of *Flying Cloud*, as Nubar had christened the aircraft, smelt and looked like the inside of a good limousine. Walls, chairs and settees were upholstered in tobacco-coloured leather. The tables were made of burled walnut veneer trimmed with polished nickel, and the deep leather steamer chairs had been cleverly fashioned to appear so heavy that Stedman wondered how the aircraft was able to gain its element.

As they taxied to the runway, the steward – now in a crisp white jacket – poured champagne into enormous crystal balloon glasses and gave them each a menu card printed with the date and a tiny map showing the route to Salzburg.

Harkonian touched the side of one of the tables and the spring-loaded top flipped, revealing a backgammon board on the other side. Stedman threw his head back and laughed.

"Christ, we've been conned. It's a flying casino."

"Beware of Harkonians bearing bloody gifts," Rollo echoed.

Nubar smiled. "Well, I've got to make this little toy support itself somehow. Would you gentlemen care for a brief chouette before lunch?"

~ ~ ~

The approach road up to the Schloss seemed familiar to Steddy, but he realised that his déjà-vu was prompted by old war-time newsreels of Mercedes-Benzes speeding up the steep incline at Berchtesgaden to a rendezvous at Hitler's "Eagle's Nest". The path was so narrow that the gate-keeper had to telephone up to the Schloss to ensure the way was clear before passing the Harkonian Rolls onto the steep, alpine road that climbed to the house through the dense forest of fir trees.

Stedman's ears popped halfway up and he was still distracted trying to clear them when the car reached level ground at the summit. The panorama before him was not at all what he had expected. Instead of a large gloomy house clutching a rocky promontory, a broad open plateau surrounded by snowy peaks spread before him. In the middle was a great black serpentine glacial lake that drained the blue from the sky and reflected the puffy white clouds as in a black mirror. The Schloss was on a gentle rise beyond the lake and as the car entered the main allée that led on a straight axis to the entry court, a black, red and gold standard broke from a flagstaff on the principal turret. It would have been very difficult not to have been impressed; even Rollo whose family house, Blyden, was one of the grandest in England – gaped visibly. Gardeners and gamekeepers in traditional alpine uniforms uncovered their heads as the Rolls swept by them through the deep blue-grey gravel.

At the entry, the butler and a staff of at least forty were lined up for review. Stepping from the car, Stedman felt as though he had slipped through a time warp into the Edwardian era.

Elizabeth Harkonian asked Thea to show Stedman to his room which was reached by means of a tiny round, blue silk-lined lift that rose inside of one of the corner turrets. On the small stone landing, Thea pushed open a low oak door into a pie-shaped room with stone walls and a high vaulted, wood-beamed ceiling. The bed was an austere Napoleonic campaign bed covered in red velvet with a vicuna cover – the rug and chairs were vicuna as well and a fire burned in the grate.

"The bed isn't much, but the rug looks terrific. What are you doing for the rest of the afternoon?"

"I'm free for a little while before I have to help Mother, but I have a better idea."

Stedman looked downcast as Thea turned from him and walked over to two large doors at one side of the room.

"Will you help me push these apart? They haven't been opened in years."

"If you're sure you wouldn't rather stay here."

Beyond the doors was a canopied room that contained the most enormous bed Stedman had ever seen. Thea never ceased to surprise him.

~ ~ ~

She stood in front of a picture window that had been hewn from the stone walls of the turret. Stedman lay in bed transfixed as he watched Theadora dress. It was all so unreal. Only a week ago he had been in Philadelphia, totally demoralised and now he was high in the Austrian Alps with a girl who in a few days had become an inextricable part of him. Beyond her he could clearly see the snow-capped Alpine peaks. She stopped to step into her chemise and the profile of her body made him shudder. He understood all at once, and for the first time, what it meant to love someone so much it hurt. Still, he was afraid to show or attempt to express what he felt, afraid of suffocating her, afraid he might jinx what they already had – he felt so clumsy and boorish in the presence of her delicate grace. Then she bent over and kissed him and a curtain of auburn hair closed out reality. Her perfume had become for him a Pavlovian aphrodisiac. She gently broke loose from his arms.

"Darling, I must go. I promised Mother I'd help her. Come down when you're dressed and we'll put you to work."

She slid through the door and then still holding it, poked her head back inside. Her eyes sparkled with the reflected mountain light and everything that was lively. "I love you, you know."

Without waiting for a reply she was gone, and the door clicked shut behind her.

Stedman was still in bed reflecting on Thea's exit, when the ring of the telephone from the room next door jarred him from his reverie. It was Nubar asking Steddy to join him in his study for tea. Steddy said he'd be right down, knowing full well that with Rollo out riding and none of the other guests due until the following day, it was backgammon, not tea Nubar had in mind.

He was actually on his second cup before the fact that he was ten points behind sufficiently roused him to concentrate on the play. They continued for an hour or more, and by the time his hostess interrupted and told them it was time to get dressed for dinner he was well ahead. Entering the circular lift, he was rather pleased with himself. He had $5,000 more to play with than when he had arrived.

The doors between their rooms were still open, and her smell enveloped him. He whistled and she called to him from behind an alcove where he found her soaking in a sunken marble tub that was big enough to accommodate an entire Japanese family. She splashed him until he undressed and as he sank into the warm scented water, he began to wonder if with her he might not be able to accept happiness.

The next morning, they went riding after breakfast. They rode in the park that extended for about a mile and a half behind the Schloss to the edge of the plateau. It was like being in a Disney production of *Heidi*, suspended amongst the mountain peaks with nothing to mar the natural perfection of the surroundings or the glory of the day.

When they returned, the drive at the front of the Schloss had been transformed into a motor show. Elegant cars of every conceivable mark and colour were arrayed on the gravel forecourt like a metallic bouquet with brigades of servants swooping on them like vultures – picking them of their contents and leaving them for the grooms to drive round to the garages to make room for the new arrivals that still streamed up the mountain road.

Taking in the sight, Steddy and Thea were about to turn and ride off again, but a groom was already at the bridles of their horses and Nubar had spotted them.

"Steddy, come over, won't you. There's someone I'd like you to meet."

Thea was already looking dejected.

"Well, I guess now I won't see you for three days and nights."

"Don't be silly, darling, but I do have to try to earn enough to keep you in the style to which I am so rapidly becoming accustomed."

The baronial hall was full of guests milling about the central table where name cards with room assignments were lined in alphabetical order. Elizabeth Harkonian was threading her way through the crowd with a footman in her wake carrying a tray of glasses and a bottle of champagne. Steddy knew about fifty per cent of the people and was standing with Thea on the edge of the crowd, pointing out to her anyone he thought she might find interesting, when Elizabeth reached them.

"Now, one glass of champagne, and then off you go and change out of those riding things for lunch. I want to get this horde seated before they get lost all over the house, and I'll need both of you to help me round them up."

Stedman was about to refuse the champagne, but taking another look at the crowd, gulped down a glass, and taking Thea by the hand said:

"Come on, darling, there's a small matter I'd like to take care of before lunch."

"You said it, I didn't," she parried.

~ ~ ~

The toast Stedman gave that night at dinner was a far cry from the last one he had proposed in Philadelphia, and a good deal less startling. The guests were in high spirits and the toasting continued in a jovial vein until at last Nubar rose, welcomed his guests and commenced the Calcutta – the auction to sell the players in the tournament.

It was generally assumed that Steddy would fetch the highest price in the bidding, but when an Arab paid £12,000 for Rollo – £2,000 more than Steddy had brought – it came as a surprise and started the whole room buzzing. Thea whispered to Steddy that Nubar had told her Rollo had asked him to invite the fellow on his guarantee, as a personal favour.

The two-day tournament was scheduled to begin the following afternoon with playing time limited to the hours between lunch and dinner, leaving plenty of time for private high-stakes games in the evening.

After a polite glass of champagne with the ladies, Stedman joined the chouette already in progress in the study with Rollo, the Arab, who was called Omar, Jack Pilkington, an English film producer; and, of course, Nubar. After about an hour's play, Rollo had won a few games as part of the chouette, but lost two 8 games in the box and was behind £6,000. He suggested raising the stakes to £1,000 a point with automatic doubles – an astronomical amount. Steddy, Nubar and Omar stayed in, but Pilkington dropped. Rollo was in the box with Steddy playing for Nubar and Omar.

The game opened with two automatic doubles. It was a scenario that Rollo relished, a chance to recoup his losses and take an early lead in one grand stroke. He moved swiftly into a back game – his favourite position – establishing Steddy's one and three points. In the next series of passes, Rollo rolled everything he needed, closing his own board, but for his six point. His next toss brought up a builder from Steddy's three point, allowing him to pick off one of Steddy's men on the way, which he slapped loudly on the bar.

Steddy's next roll didn't get him in. Rollo grinned and though his six point was still open, and he had left a blot behind on Steddy's three point, he slid the doubling cube across to Steddy with the 8 showing. Steddy polled his partners. He wanted to take, Nubar wasn't about to back off, and Omar accepted without expression. It fleetingly crossed Steddy's mind, that if Omar *was* bankrolling Rollo, he was really just hedging his position. Steddy took the cube and nodded his acceptance. Rollo rolled double threes – the worst possible combination – he couldn't cover the blot, or make his six point.

Steddy rolled a six/one, came in on Rollo's vacant six point and dropped a man on his own three point, removing Rollo's blot in the process, leaving Rollo two chances of getting in – Steddy's one point, where Rollo still had two men, and the three point where Steddy had left a man exposed in taking him out. But it was not to be. Rollo's next toss didn't play.

Steddy redoubled to 16, and produced a pair of sixes which proved to be the start of a streak, as he continued to throw fives and sixes turn after turn. The game became a rout when Rollo, whose back-game had disintegrated, realised that he was in danger of being backgammoned – the name of the game, though rarely allowed in England – and fled for home to avoid the triple game. As it was, he lost a double game, 32 points to each of the other players.

It was late and they agreed to continue again the following night after dinner. Rollo's losses were £102,000 for the evening.

It didn't surprise Stedman that Rollo wasn't the least perturbed at the turn of events – he was a master at maintaining his English sang-froid, but knowing his financial straits, Steddy was now sure that staking Rollo must have been the price that Omar had paid for admission to the house party. Steddy didn't care. He was up £34,000, and for once, there was every chance of getting paid.

Later in their room, Thea, who had been one of the silent spectators, said that seeing him compete in the last game was the first time she'd really grasped the excitement of high-stakes play. Steddy said:

"I hope I can keep it up so we can really paint the town in London."

"You didn't invite me to London."

"The tournament at the Clermont is in two weeks. You will come won't you?"

"Of course I will, but you don't have to impress me you know. Back home I live on a ranch."

"I can just imagine," Stedman replied cynically.

By the time the dinner gong rang the next evening, Stedman had advanced to the finals of the tournament, besting a Greek shipping tycoon handily. Rollo had also reached the finals after an easy win over Nubar. Thus the final match for the tournament's prize – the gold ingot – scheduled the next day after lunch, would be between Steddy and Rollo.

Later, when Stedman and Thea came down for dinner, the decibel level of the sixty guests' conversation at cocktails seemed twice that of the previous evening, and much more animated.

"They're making side bets on tomorrow's game," Steddy explained to Thea. "Excuse me, darling, while I try to pick up some of the action."

He left Thea at her mother's side and, threading his way through the crowd, was only halfway across the room when Omar clasped his shoulder.

"Who are you backing tomorrow?" It was a fair question – players often laid off bets against themselves in a tournament.

"Rollo's under pressure, but I'm feeling lucky."

Omar's eyes narrowed. "I think you're the better player, but on the other hand, I think Rollo's due for a winning streak and judging from his easy win over Harkonian, he may have hit it." The Arab's voice had a shrill whining pitch. Steddy responded to his probing.

"Well, I'm always delighted to back the man I believe in. What did you have in mind?"

"Perhaps you'd like to make a small sporting wager?" Omar grinned showing his noticeably small teeth – "Say, ten thousand?"

"I was thinking more in terms of twenty-five," Steddy parried.

Omar's sardonic smile didn't change, but when Thea came over to take Steddy's arm into dinner, and it became clear to him that Steddy had no intention of waiting for his answer, he quickly said "done", before even acknowledging Thea's presence. Stedman was still smiling as they walked into the dining room.

"You look positively delighted with yourself. What did you do to that poor Arab?"

"Let's hope he's anything but poor. I just accepted a wager on tomorrow's game."

"Who did you back?" she teased.

"Me. Who do you think?"

"Oh, I don't know, I just wondered. I've often heard Nubar talking about laying off bets. Isn't that the clever thing to do?" she replied, the picture of innocence.

"Not when you're hot, darling, and I've never been as hot as I've been since I met you."

"That's sweet, but just how hot have I made you?"

Stedman's hand which had been gently resting on her knee, started to slide up under the sheer chiffon of her dress.

"Not that kind of hot!" she said smiling over clenched teeth. "I mean how much did you bet?"

"Twenty-five thousand."

"Twenty-five thousand dollars!" she said, truly shocked.

"No, darling – pounds."

"Dearest, I hope you're not doing this for me." Concern was written over Thea's face. "I really don't care about the money and I'd feel dreadful if it was my fault that you lost so much – it would ruin everything."

Stedman's expression softened. He took her hand.

"Darling, this is the way I would have played whether I'd met you or not. The only difference is that now – because of the way I feel about you, this has all become a game – I *realise* it's just a game. It's the first time I think I've ever seen it in perspective. Until now, I've never had anything or anyone else that mattered enough for me to see it for what it is. Oh, I still care about winning – I want to win more than ever. But if I lose, it won't really matter. I don't know if you can understand that, because I'm not sure that I do myself, but that's why – for the first time in my life – I'm absolutely sure that I *will* win."

Thea nuzzled his ear and whispered:

"Just when I think it isn't possible to be this much in love, you say something like that and I love you more."

~ ~ ~

The library where Steddy, Nubar and Rollo gathered unhurriedly after dinner had once been the billiards room. The original green silk damask still covered the walls, but along them, interspersed between crowded trophies of stag and boar, new mahogany bookcases filled with coloured calf and morocco bindings now soared to the ceiling. The old billiards lamp with its large pleated silk shades still served as the room's chandelier and hung directly over the backgammon table that was already prepared for the next day's final – spot-lighting it in contrast to the shadowy recesses around the room.

While the combatants fixed themselves brandies and selected cigars, the other guests drifted in by twos and threes. They sensed that a mortal blow was about to be dealt and that tonight's private game, rather than the next day's final, would be the true auto-da-fé. It was the scent of blood that had drawn them, but, with the silent respect that aficionados at a bullfight display when the matador takes up the sword for the kill, they kept their distance and did not crowd the players or disturb the hush imposed by the stately room.

The principals moved into the circle of light and took their seats. Their black evening clothes seemed to accentuate the sobriety of the occasion. Each man threw a die to determine who would first hold the box, the staccato clatter on the ivory playing surface stilled the whispered chatter and brought the room to attention. Not one of the remaining guests was absent.

Steddy won the box, accepted an early double and took the first game and four points. The next game with Rollo playing opposite him, opened with one automatic, then, with one man on the bar, Steddy accepted a double. He came in with double fives, took one of their men off and closed his board. Rollo eventually got in and home and they were in a race to bear off. A timely pair of threes gave Steddy the eight game – another £16,000. The next game he lost a two and the box passed to Nubar who quickly won a double, a single and then lost a two.

When Rollo took over the box he was already down £102,000 from the night before plus £5,000 more so far that evening. He took a double game off Steddy and another double when Nubar sat across from him.

Later he dropped at sixteen, conceding the box to Steddy who had tried to double him to thirty-two.

Stedman's dice were hot. The next game, against Rollo, opened with two automatics. He was up eleven points so he accepted Rollo's early double to eight and beavered to sixteen. Then Rollo, true to form, worked his way into a back position and took out two of Steddy's men when he only had seven left to bear off. Rollo doubled to thirty-two. Steddy didn't get in on his next turn, and when Rollo rolled he was able to shut Steddy out. One of Steddy's men came in when Rollo cleared four men off the six point with double sixes, then Rollo rolled double fives, leaving a blot behind on the four point. Steddy rolled double fours, knocked Rollo's man out, and headed for home. The dice and the players' hands became a blur – Rollo was in and out again with double fives, passing Steddy on the way, Steddy was bearing off again and the onlookers, unable to contain themselves, crowded closer to the table.

When Steddy rolled double sixes they gasped – he had two men left, one on his five point and one on his two. Any high combination would have won Rollo the game, but his next roll left him with one man on his two point and one on the one point – a slight advantage to Steddy's remaining two men on his five and two points. It was Steddy's roll, he could be wiped out with a bad toss. He looked Rollo in the eye, picked up the doubling die, turned it to 64 and with three fingers extended, calmly pushed it towards Rollo and Nubar.

This was the game played at its best – on the edge, using guts and the doubling die when luck wasn't enough.

If Nubar dropped – and Steddy was banking that he would – Steddy had hedged a possible loss of 64 with a win of 32.

Everyone in the room knew that they were witnessing a game that would be replayed on both sides of the Atlantic for years to come. Whatever the outcome.

The room was hushed, and no one missed Nubar's quiet reply to the challenge:

"Drop," he said, and sat back in the chair.

Rollo's answer hacked the stillness and reached every corner of the room.

"Roll-em!"

A roll of five and two would have been adequate, but Stedman threw a pair of sixes, consistent with his performance the whole evening.

It was Thea who broke the tense stillness that followed. The applause started when, in a burst of enthusiasm, she ran to Steddy and hugged him – even Rollo had got up from his seat and clapped him on the back in what Steddy knew to be a genuine act of good-sportsmanship. Rollo had just lost £64,000 on one toss of the dice.

"It was your bloody Yankee Cavalry to the rescue yet again!" he roared, in a good-natured attempt at bravado.

"And lucky for the poor Yank too!" Steddy countered, smiling. "I had an awful feeling all evening that Rockford's red coats were waiting up your sleeve to sweep the field."

Nubar saw to it that everyone had a full glass of champagne – even the servants had stopped circulating during the last minutes of play – and a round of toasting commenced.

Later, when they were alone, Thea told Steddy that an unsmiling Omar had put down his glass untouched and left the room.

~ ~ ~

The final of the tournament the next day was sheer anti-climax. Rollo had been so soundly beaten that even though he tried to put up a good front, his heart clearly wasn't in it.

Stedman took him easily in three games and afterwards accepted the solid gold brick worth £25,000 that Nubar ceremoniously presented to him as the traditional first prize of the tournament. The £10,000 cheque that Rollo received was little consolation.

Directly after the presentation, in front of the full complement of guests, Omar walked up to Steddy and handed him a cheque for £25,000 drawn on an obscure but solvent London bank, covering his side bet with Steddy on the outcome of the tournament. Then, with something of a flourish and a total lack of discretion, he handed Steddy a second cheque covering Rollo's losses. Now everyone knew for a fact what had up to then been only speculation.

Stedman was deeply embarrassed for his friend and went straight to Rollo and offered to take his marker. Rollo turned him down flat.

"Take his cheque old boy. He owes me that and more."

Unpleasantness aside, Steddy was over the moon. In four days he had cleared £202,000.

That night in bed, Stedman made up his mind to celebrate in earnest. He turned to Thea, who was the one person in the world with whom he wanted to share his good fortune.

"Darling, I'm feeling very rich and we've got a week before we have to be in London. Where would you like to go? Anywhere in the world."

Steddy had never been able to say that to anyone ever before and the thought exhilarated him. She replied:

"I'd just like to be alone with you. I feel as though I've been living with a soldier who commutes from the front."

"How about Marakesh? There wouldn't be anyone there at this time of year."

"I couldn't stand another hotel; after all, this place might as well be one. I want to make breakfast and dinner – that sort of thing."

"I know someone with a house in Jamaica I can use, but once word got out on the bush telegraph that we were there, we'd be swamped with people."

"Don't worry about it, darling. It doesn't really matter. I just thought . . ."

"I've got it! Do you have any woollies with you?"

"Being alone with you is one thing, but don't you think the North Pole is going too far?"

"No, no joke. A friend of my mother's – she's like an aunt to me – has one of the most beautiful places in Scotland. It's remote and she has a few cottages that she lets friends use. They're quite a way from the castle and she never goes up herself until August. She's always asking me to stay. I'm sure it would be all right and it'll be fabulous now. A little cold, but you'll have your wish – there won't be anyone around for miles and miles of the grandest country you've ever seen."

"Oh Steddy, can we leave tomorrow? Nubar and Mummy are staying on for a few days, but I'm sure they'll let us use the plane just to go to Scotland."

"I'll have to call her first, but we could make an early start and call her from the plane . . . I assume there's a phone on the plane?"

"Natch."

"Somehow I find it awfully difficult to give credence to your protestations of being a simple country-girl, when you seem to adapt so easily to your present surroundings."

"If we fly commercial, we'll lose the whole day changing planes in Vienna, anyway. Just get me to the Highlands and buy me a pair of walking shoes and I'll make an impression on you, you won't soon forget."

~ ~ ~

It was almost midnight when the train pulled into King's Cross Station. During the six days they spent in Scotland, they had become so in tune with the simplicity of their surroundings that they preferred the gentle return to civilisation provided by a six-hour train ride to the inevitable hassle of dealing with airports. Even so, they were grateful to see the station man from Claridge's on the platform, who helped immeasurably to cushion the shock of re-entry.

The lights in the lobby had already been dimmed when Steddy and Thea arrived. Steddy was glad it was late as there was less chance of running into anybody – if only for one more day. He was signing the register when, from behind him, he heard:

"Where the hell have you been?"

Steddy turned and faced one of the few people in the world that he could have been happy to see at that moment – Wiley Travis.

"Wiley, you old fart. It's great to see you." And then, turning to Thea, "You two met in Paris."

Wiley, who was in dinner clothes, said:

"You S.O.B., you know very well there was no way you were going to introduce us in Paris." And then turning to Thea, he clicked the heels of his patent leather shoes and bending from the waist said: "I am happy to meet you at last. No thanks to this bum."

Thea was amused and liked Wiley at once. He had strikingly blond hair with darker eyebrows and the minted, even features of a head on a Roman coin. She could tell he was at once sophisticated, but still the sort of American who could live abroad forever without becoming Europeanised.

"Come on," Wiley said, "let me buy you both one for the ditch. I want to hear about your Austrian coup from the horse's mouth."

Thea turned to Stedman and said:

"Not me, darling, but you go on. I've got to wash that train out of my hair."

"OK, I won't be long."

As Thea stepped into the lift, Stedman and Wiley went into the hall and took a table opposite two Arabs, who were the room's only other occupants. Wiley ordered a stinger and Steddy had the same.

"Jesus H. Christ, Steddy, you really pulled one off. Everyone in London's talking about it. I just had dinner at the Griffins who don't exactly move in the fast lane, and you were the sole topic of conversation. I'm so bored with hearing the story, I left early. I even heard about it in Munich."

"There were a lot of Germans at the Schloss."

"Come off it. What's the real poop? Rollo, of course, still hasn't recovered. I gather he's been losing badly at roulette and that that wife of his is back with him, giving him no end of shit about Austria."

"Screw that. It's not my fault. I told him he didn't have to pay me right away, but he insisted that I keep the Arab's cheque."

"What Arab?"

"Some creep called Omar that Rollo had in tow. I didn't really want to take his cheque because he made such a bloody show of giving it to me to cover Rollo. Everyone saw it – he made sure of that. I'm surprised you didn't hear about that, too."

"Not a word, but I have heard about the Arab – none too appealing from what I gather. People seem to think he's a little sinister."

"Well I hope to hell his cheque clears. Come on, here're the drinks, let's change the subject. Tell me *what* and *who* you've been up to?"

"Not so fast. Where the hell have you been? Everybody's been asking me how to get hold of you. George even called me from Paris."

"I'm not telling you where I've been. It was so perfect that just talking about it would be an intrusion."

"The man's in love!"

"I admit it unabashedly."

"I'm glad for you, after all the shit Suki put you through."

"Suki who?"

"You lucky son of a bitch. Is she as terrific as she looks?"

"Every bit of it. She is the only woman I think I have every *really* loved."

"Have you set the date?"

"I haven't even asked her. I don't want to crowd her."

"Women don't get *crowded* by proposals."

"She's different. But maybe you're right. We think so much alike I sort of took it for granted that she knew how I felt. Listen, I'm bushed, but let's have lunch tomorrow. I really want the two of you to get to know each other – say, one o'clock at Wilton's?"

"OK with me, but if you're getting married, I'm buying – even if you are the man who broke the bank at Monte Carlo."

~ ~ ~

The following evening was the kick-off dinner and Calcutta at the Clermont for the London gambling club's annual backgammon tournament. Stedman and Thea sat with Rollo, his wife, Nubar and Elizabeth, and Wiley, who was with the English girl he had brought to lunch that afternoon. Stedman fetched the highest price in the auction even though for once he didn't buy part of himself, but he did buy a piece of Rollo to make sure he went for a respectable amount. Jackie,

Rollo's wife, bitched all through dinner about his gambling, his drinking and his friends, caring little that most of them happened to be at the table. Stedman had yet to see Thea display a temper or act rudely, but he was sure that if he didn't get her away, she would do as she had threatened and punch Jackie in the nose.

The minute the auction was over, Stedman got up and announced he was taking Thea downstairs to Annabel's for a dance. On the dance floor they ran into some friends from New York and sat with them for about an hour or so when the page from the Clermont appeared, sent by Wiley to get Stedman. Steddy said he'd be up as soon as he finished his drink, but the page whispered that he had better come straight away.

"What is it, John – is anything the matter?" Steddy asked.

"It's Lord and Lady Rockford, sir. They're having a terrific row at the roulette table."

Steddy rose from the table and excused himself from the others. "What is it, darling?" Thea asked him.

"Evidently Rollo and Jackie are brawling. I'd better go up and try to get them out of here. Why don't you stay, I won't be too long. I've become something of an expert at breaking up their knock down drag-outs."

"No, I'll come with you."

When they reached the hall of the Clermont, the Rockfords could be clearly heard shouting at each other from the bottom of the spiral stair. It was like a scene from *Who's Afraid of Virginia Woolf?* Halfway up the stair Stedman could see Rollo's face – it was crimson from drink and anger. His hair – usually slicked to his scalp – was rumpled into devil's horns and his eyes were wild and bloodshot. He was literally foaming at the mouth. The sight of him made Stedman's stomach go clammy, and he didn't even feel it when Thea's fingernails dug into his palm.

Jackie, in contrast, whose face couldn't have been more than an inch from Rollo's, was as cool as a cucumber – not a lacquered hair out of place. She answered his shouts in her high, shrill, phoney aristocratic voice which only worked to anger him more. Stedman was sure that Rollo would either burst a blood vessel, or have a heart attack.

As they climbed closer to the appalling scene, Stedman spotted Wiley, his face white and pinched, in the front row of the semicircle of spectators that had formed along the railing. They reached the landing and were threading their way through the crowd when Steddy heard Jackie shriek gratingly:

"You bastard – you gamble because you can't get it up. You can't screw me so you think you can prove something by trying to screw the house and your friends."

Rollo's face went from red to black. He raised his joined fists in the air as if to strike her. Steddy found himself wishing that he would. The moment froze in suspended animation. Then – with a great gasp of air rushing from his lungs – Rollo's two fists smashed into her chest with all his strength. Jackie shot over the banister without making a sound, then came the hideous thud when she landed on the marble floor of the foyer below. Stedman was overcome for a second, by an irrational mixture of emotions – horror and elation. Then his adrenalin flowed and an automatic response to events took over. He was the first to break from the stair and reach her side. Her head had caught the last step, and though he had never seen a broken neck before, it was clear from the exaggerated angle of her head what had killed her. He heard a mass of keening from above, and when he looked up, saw Rollo standing behind him. Visibly shaking and quite pale now, Rollo asked:

"Dead?"

"I'm afraid so, as far as I can tell."

Without another word, Rollo strode past him into the hall and out the front door to the street. Steddy followed, but by the time he reached the pavement, Rollo had already put his navy blue Aston Martin into gear and was accelerating out of Berkeley Square.

~ ~ ~

Stedman awakened with a premonition of doom.

It was nothing specific, nor could he blame it on the greyness of the day or on the rain that relentlessly pelted the roofs and the terra-cotta chimney pots which were the only bright spots in his view from the hotel's sixth floor. He just wanted to shut the telephone off and stay in bed. But Thea's customary exuberance when she arose and ordered breakfast, forced him to stop catering to his mood and follow her example.

His resolve was short-lived. The morning tabloids that arrived on the breakfast table dramatically gave credence to his original foreboding.

The British press were having a field day exploiting the fall from grace of a peer of the realm, labelling what Steddy considered to have been an accident, as out and out murder, and splashing lurid characterisations of "The Rockford Set" – which included Steddy, Nubar, Wiley, and half a dozen others – all over the front pages, representing them as dissolute gamblers and "idle sports".

Reading the articles while Thea bathed, he made his second mistake of the day since deciding to get out of bed when he answered the telephone.

A Chief Inspector Allsloe of Scotland Yard was downstairs and wanted to come up to see him.

The man Stedman admitted to the sitting room was bullying and rude, and immediately made it clear that were it in his power to do so, he would have arrested Steddy for leaving the scene of the "crime".

"Abetting", and "material witness", were words he liberally employed during that early-hour interview, until Steddy remarked casually that he wasn't aware a "crime" had been committed, as what he had witnessed had surely been an accident. But Allsloe refused to rise to the bait, and coldly informed him that there was to be an inquiry conducted at the Clermont that afternoon at four and that Stedman and Thea were required to attend.

Wiley telephoned as the inspector was leaving and suggested that they meet for lunch.

"I hear the street outside the hotel is swarming with reporters."

"Why don't you come here and we'll order from room service?" Steddy suggested.

Wiley looked shaken. He tossed an extra edition of the paper over to Steddy. The headline read: ROLL-EM ROCKFORD CRAPS OUT. Rollo's Aston Martin had been found in a remote area by the Dover Cliffs; the implication was that he had thrown himself into the sea. A search had begun, but so far no body had been found.

The paper, citing "reliable sources", said that Rollo had been heavily in debt from gambling and concluded that this, combined with his hand in his wife's death, formed a compelling motive for suicide. They went on to report that the police had not rejected the possibility that the car had been abandoned at the cliffs as a purposeful ruse, and that Rockford was still alive somewhere in Britain.

"The fool," Steddy said. "Now that he's run, he looks as guilty as that inspector seems to think he is."

"That becomes academic if he *is* at the bottom of the Channel."

"I don't think he's the type . . . but on the other hand, I've never seen him in the state he was in last night. If I had only been able to catch him at the door, it could have all been cleared up then and there. He was justified in striking her. The fact that she fell over the banister was an accident."

"But surely he must have realised that, Steddy," Thea said.

"I'm not so sure, darling. He was very drunk you know, and then, not that he wasn't provoked, I think he wanted to kill her when he struck her. I don't think he meant her to go over the railing, but I do think that in a moment of uncontrollable rage, he very much wanted her dead."

"So, then, might he not have killed himself when he realised what he had done?" Thea speculated.

"No, I don't think so. Even if he did drive to Dover with that in mind. I'm sure that by the time he was halfway there, he would have figured out some sort of scheme. He'd need help, but I can't think who he'd go to – certainly not his father; the way Blyden felt about Jackie, he probably would have turned him in. For that matter, the way the police are behaving, I'm not so sure he was wrong to run," Steddy added pensively, and continued: "That man Allsloe is acting as though this is a personal vendetta!"

"Do be serious, darling."

"I am, darling, but you didn't hear that S.O.B. from Scotland Yard. He acted as though he would have cheerfully hung *me* on the spot, given half a chance. I just hope for Rollo's sake that whatever he may have decided to do last night, he gets himself one helluva good lawyer. This whole thing is getting out of hand!"

"He might have called Nubie. He often did when he needed advice. You two order lunch while I call Mummy and see if she's heard anything."

It was half an hour before Thea came back into the sitting room.

"Any news?" Stedman asked.

"No, we were just talking about the whole thing. Mummy hasn't seen Nubar all day. He went out before she was up. She's been trying to reach him, though, to let him know about the inquiry."

~ ~ ~

Omar was at the inquiry, although no one recalled having seen him at the Clermont dinner. When he offered to walk back to Claridge's with Thea and Steddy afterwards, Steddy didn't object as he was curious about this strange man's relationship with Rollo . . .

In clubs, backgammon is a gentleman's game, but outside the clubs' walls, it often attracts an odd assortment of wealthy middle-aged groupies to its fringes. Omar fitted neither mould, and lacked the passion for the game that was apparent with most of the big-time punters who often backed a brilliant player just for the privilege of getting close to the action. No, there was definitely something more there, and Steddy aimed to find out what it was.

He let Omar squirm for a bit in the hotel lobby, and then, in spite of Thea's less than discreet signals, allowed the Arab to wheedle an invitation up to the suite.

It was almost nine when Wiley showed up. He seemed surprised to see Omar, but a raised eyebrow from Steddy aborted the question on his lips. It had been a long day, so they again decided to order dinner in the suite.

What had become crystal clear during the proceedings, though nothing specific had been said, was that the police were investigating a murder, and that Allsloe, the inspector in charge, was out for blood – preferably blue blood. He didn't like people like Rollo and his friends.

The late editions of the papers that Wiley had brought back with him, now printed the general speculation that Rollo was still alive and still in England.

Though they tried to avoid the subject that had just been re-enacted at the Clermont for four hours, it was the only topic at dinner. Omar, as usual, was a silent observer.

At ten-thirty, Thea's mother called to ask her to spend the night at the house in Belgrave Square. Nubar had been called out of town to negotiate a labour dispute, the servants were already down in the country, unaware that the weekend had been cancelled, and she didn't want to be alone in the house. Thea agreed to go as soon as dinner was over.

"Nubar didn't say anything about leaving town at the inquiry," Wiley said.

"Mummy said it came up at the last minute or they would have gone to the country. I know he tries to make it look effortless, but you can't run a big conglomerate without some problem cropping up every minute. He just doesn't go on about them."

"He was out early this morning too. Wasn't he?"

"What are you driving at, Wiley?" Thea asked with a tinge of annoyance.

"Well, it just seems to me that if Rollo was going to call anyone, it probably would be Nubar. Who else does he know who has two jet planes, umpteen houses, agents all over the world, and most likely bags of cash?"

"If he had called Nubar, Nubar would have made him go straight to the police – accompanied by the best attorney in London. Don't you agree, darling?" Thea looked to Steddy for support.

"All I know for sure is that Nubie values his British passport more than anything in the world – I'm sure he wouldn't do anything that would jeopardise it."

Omar spoke for the first time since he had arrived.

"Sometimes the very rich think themselves above the law," he chanted in his high sing-song voice.

"Do you feel that way?" Stedman asked, sharply turning inquisitor, remembering why he had got the man up to his suite.

"Oh, where I come from, I'm not very rich. In fact, I'm considered rather middle class."

Steddy was warming to the subject and was about to ask Omar just where he *did* come from, when Thea interrupted and said that she had better go.

He walked with her to the lift. It was the first time that they had been separated since they had met. They both realised it at the same moment and felt foolish making so much of it.

"They say absence makes the heart grow fonder."

"It's not possible," she replied simply.

"I'm going to miss you desperately, you know . . . will you call me from your room when you get to bed – no matter how late it is?"

"Yes, darling, I promise."

They were almost in each other's arms when the liftman opened the door, leaving her no choice but to get in. She waved forlornly as the door closed. He hadn't even kissed her goodbye.

Steddy was already feeling blue by the time he got back to his suite. He almost relished the fact that he *could* feel that way. It hadn't been so very long ago that he had been incapable of feeling anything. The thought cheered him a little.

There was a bottle of cognac on the chimney with the manager's card leaning against it. So far it had remained unopened. Steddy peeled off the seal and drew the cork.

"Who'll join me in a brandy? It looks as though this has turned into a stag party."

"Delighted, if you'll join *me* in a few games of backgammon," Omar replied.

"Sure. Why not?" A shadow crossed his face when he recalled that the man didn't actually care for the game. "You in, Wiley?"

"No thanks, Sted – not at your stakes, but I will have a brandy and then I'm for bed. It's been a long day."

"Oh hell, I haven't got a board," Steddy remembered between gulps from his glass.

"I have one in my room. We could play there if you like."

"Thanks, Omar, but I'm expecting a call. Why don't you get it or ring down and ask the hall porter to fetch it and bring it up?"

Omar left to get his board while Steddy and Wiley sipped their drinks.

"That guy makes my skin crawl," Wiley said, the moment he heard the door close.

"Maybe you're just not used to being around Arabs – they're completely different from us. You'd seem just as strange dressed in a burnouse, sitting in Jedda or Abu Dhabi or wherever it is he comes from," Steddy said, refilling his glass.

"That's just it, Steddy, he's never said where he comes from – never talks about what he does or anything. He never talks at all, for that matter, but he sure does listen. He didn't volunteer a word about Rollo all through dinner even though we all know he's been bankrolling him for months."

"Why do you think I let him invite himself up, and agreed to play backgammon with him? I want to find out what makes him tick – you can learn a lot about a man when he's playing for money."

"All I know is that he gives me the creeps and I'd be very careful what I say around him if I were you."

At that moment Omar let himself in. He was carrying two matching attaché cases.

"Why two boards – superstitious?" Steddy asked.

"Not at all my dear fellow. One contains money. I like to settle my obligations with cash."

"Are you planning on losing?"

"Oh no. It's just a habit. Tonight I feel lucky."

"Well, if that's the case, I hope you won't be offended if I have to give you a cheque."

"No, no, my dear friend," he oiled, accepting the tumbler of spirits Steddy pressed on him. "It's just that where I come from, we always use cash, that way we can't lose more than we can afford and there are no problems later."

"That's very sensible. If we had to do that *here*, no one would ever play at all!" Steddy laughed, and then, still smiling, he raised one eyebrow and asked: "I wonder that you didn't pass on some of that advice to Rollo, instead of letting him go so far over the top?" Steddy's pointed question went unanswered as Omar busied himself with setting up the board. Steddy glowered and looked at Wiley who shrugged his shoulders, as if to say, "This is *your* party", so he continued: "Then why don't I limit myself to what you have on you?"

"That would be £50,000 sterling."

Wiley whistled softly and interjected:

"And I thought this was going to be high stakes! Good night, fellows – I don't even want to watch this."

Stedman drained his glass and poured out another.

"You sure you won't stay and watch the fun?"

"No way, José. I'll see you tomorrow and buy you lunch. You'll probably need a free meal. Good night, Omar."

Steddy refilled Omar's glass from the almost empty bottle. He noticed that Omar had brought an identical bottle back from his room.

"I see we are both recipients of the manager's largesse," Steddy said.

They played two or three games and drank an equal number of brandies. Steddy was appalled at the ineptness of Omar's play with no partners to help him as he had had at Nubar's Schloss.

The telephone rang and, knowing it would be Thea, he went into the bedroom to take the call. As he shut the door behind him, he suddenly felt very drunk.

"Darling, I miss you terribly," he said when he heard her voice.

"So do I, darling. I've got Mother to bed and it only just occurred to me – I don't know why you didn't come too? I mean she wouldn't have minded, in fact, it would make a lot more sense to have a man in the house if anything happens. Now it's too late because she's already set the bloody alarm system and I don't know how to turn it off – I think you can only do it from her bedroom."

"Yeah, and I'm playing backgammon with Omar anyway."

"That's not very flattering. I thought you'd be miserable and missing me."

"I am, darling." He choked between hiccoughs. "I'm only doing it for Rollo."

"You're drunk! I leave you for two hours and the wheels fall off. I know those Arabs, I'll just bet he's got three or four bunnies from the Playboy Club on their way over right now – God, men are predictable!"

"Ooh, wouldn't that be fun," Steddy sniggered.

"Oh, darling, you really are loaded. How is it possible in two hours?"

"Sheer misery. It heightens the effect."

"Listen, darling, try to take care of yourself. Get rid of Omar and get into bed – and no monkey business. I'll be back first thing in the morning, as soon as Mummy turns off the alarm."

"Nag, nag, nag. So this is what married life is going to be like. I have a good mind to withdraw my proposal."

"I wasn't aware that you had."

"Had what?"

"Proposed."

"Oh . . . In that case, will you marry me? Please, darling – see how miserable I am without you?"

"You don't sound miserable at all – just blissfully drunk and glad of it! Ask me tomorrow when you're sober, and don't think I won't remind you. Now get rid of Omar and Go To Bed!"

"If you think I'm drunk, you should see him. When last observed, he was drinking straight from the bottle."

"I can't believe it. You're all like children. Where's Wiley?"

"He left hours ago."

"He's the only one with any sense. I'm hanging up now, so say goodbye and please go to bed."

"Good night dearest – I love you. Do you remember that first night with all those lovely gardenias . . . ? "

"Now I mean it. I love you, but good night."

Steddy felt drunkenly forlorn. He couldn't tell if Thea had been really angry or only amused and teasing. A pull at his brandy didn't clear up the quandary, but he did realise that he'd left Omar alone for rather a long time.

He found his backgammon opponent had passed out in a wing chair and tried to awaken him. Having no success, he lifted Omar's feet onto a chair and, in a drunkenly protective way, tucked him in with a blanket from the bedroom.

Steddy poured himself another brandy and then, seeing the diminutive Arab wrapped up like a Cherokee, became convulsed with laughter with the realisation that the Prophet had obviously known what he was doing when he forbade alcohol to true believers. Still chuckling, he managed to get himself back to the bedroom and take off his clothes. He was asleep before his head hit the pillow.

When the telephone rang, the noise had the jarring effect of a freight train running through his room. It was, in fact, Thea and it was 9 a.m. She called to say her mother was not yet up, so though dressed, she still couldn't get out of the house. She didn't comment on his behaviour the night before, but *did* say that the phone had rung "at least twenty times" before he had picked it up.

Stedman called down for a pot of black coffee, and then, remembering that Omar was probably still there, added another pot to the order. He opened the door to the sitting room, and through the curtained gloom, was able to discern Omar's legs still stretched out on the chair as he had left him. My God, is he going to be stiff, he thought to himself and decided to let him sleep a bit longer while he showered.

He had just put on a white shirt and was buttoning the trousers of an old glen plaid suit when he heard the knock at the door of the other room. Steddy signed the bill at the door and took the tray. He poured a cup of coffee, and walked with it to the window and drew the curtains – flooding the room with light. Turning to Omar, he said,

"Come on, Sleeping Beauty – wake up, it's time for brekkers."

The appalling sight that the daylight revealed caused Stedman to drop the steaming cup into Omar's lap.

It didn't matter – Omar couldn't feel it – not with the entire back of his head missing.

He was slumped as if dozing, still wrapped in the blanket as Stedman had left him only hours before. The only noticeable difference in his appearance was a small black spot on the bridge of his nose, which, for all Stedman knew, could have been there hours before when he had drunkenly covered him. That thought and the pungent odour in the room that mingled with the wholesome aroma of the coffee, paralysed him. He had smelt that smell before in the bullrings of Spain. It made him gag and feel weak in the stomach as it had then. At bullfights he had attributed his reaction to the heat, the dust and the smell of cheap cigars and sweat, but now he recognised it for what it was . . . it was the smell of blood and guts and brains and death and he knew he would never mistake the odour again.

The phone rang. It was the hall porter.

"Chief Inspector Allsloe and two detectives from Scotland Yard to see you, sir. Shall I send them up?" he asked, crisply.

Steddy panicked.

"I'm just in the shower. Ask them to wait ten minutes and then send them up, would you?"

"Bloody Hell!" he shouted to the empty room as he slammed down the receiver.

Allsloe would never believe him – the bastard hated him!

The imagined headline screamed before his eyes – ROCKFORD'S PALS SHOOT IT OUT IN WEST END HOTEL. It had been so easy to decide what *Rollo* should have done, but now the shoe was on the other foot, and he had to get away and get away quickly.

He ran to the wardrobe and tore the jacket of his dinner suit from its hanger and then, shaking uncontrollably, he fumbled at pulling a black bow tie through the collar of his white shirt. He tore the top sheet from the bed, trembling fiercely all the while and after folding it, wrapped it round his waist, covering his plaid trousers like an apron. With the black, silk-lapelled jacket on, he looked like a waiter, and thought he could manage to get down the hall without arousing suspicion.

There was a sharp rap at the door.

The panic that swelled and grew inside him, turned his trembling into racking shakes, and the sound of his heartbeat almost drowned out the knock when it came a second time.

He saw his strange reflection in the mirror over the chimney – he couldn't let them find him like this – nothing he could ever say or do would convince them that he wasn't the killer. Irrationally he ran to the window seeking a way to escape and looked down hopelessly at the traffic six floors below.

An idea, wrested from his desperation and fuelled by adrenalin came to him.

In one step he was at Omar's side, and with the strength of the terrified madman he had become, he picked up the body, still swathed in the blanket, and without breaking stride – heaved it through the window as far as he could into the rush-hour traffic on Davies Street. He didn't wait to see the havoc that resulted, but took up the breakfast tray from the table and opened the door. Raising the coffee pot in front of his face, he gestured hysterically at the startled men in the hall – screaming in broken English:

"The window – the window . . . I try to stop him . . ."

They were past him like a shot, straining to see out the gaping window, blinded by the billowing net curtain and then tearing it from its support. Stedman could hear the horns and screeching brakes, and almost before he realised it, the men were past him again, on their way to the elevator and the stairs. Steddy didn't know what to do first – they'd be back in seconds! Get out of the room – Get out of the apron – Get your passport – Get some money – Money! He only had twenty pounds cash – not enough for anything – shit! He switched jackets for the one that matched his trousers, tore the bow tie from his neck and stuffed a tie from the wardrobe and his passport into his pocket. As he ran for the door, he spotted the second of Omar's attaché cases – it had been hidden before by Omar's body and the blanket. Steddy plucked it up as he ran from the room and down the stairs that led to the ground floor. He slowed his pace on the last flight where it widened into the grand stair that spilled into the centre of the main lobby. His caution was unnecessary – everyone in the building had rushed out the side entrance into Davies Street to join the commotion. Steddy strode out the unattended front door into Brook Street and feeling a thousand eyes at his back, walked the two blocks to Bond Street and hailed a cab.

"Where to, Guv?"

"Uh, uh, the Zoo, please."

Hopscotch

Why had he picked the London Zoo? He'd never even been there. *Hell, one place was as good as another to collect his thoughts and call Thea. God, Thea, what would she think? Damn,* he wished he hadn't had all that brandy. Serious doubts began to torment him. *Why the hell had he run? Had he overreacted? Had he allowed fear to paralyse his reason?* Now that he was calmer, he could see nothing to justify his behaviour, but how could he go back and face the music after heaving Omar's corpse out of the window – it was disturbingly macabre and the thought of it made him shiver. Men had been hanged on much less damning evidence.

He distracted himself by opening Omar's briefcase, vaguely remembering that he had said it had money in it – there was nothing vague about the neat piles of banded twenty- and fifty-pound notes that filled it to the top. Now it came back to him – Omar had said he had £50,000 with him, but somehow it hadn't registered before. There was a notebook as well – a small brown paper one, the kind that fits into a breast pocket. Steddy flipped through it – there was a lot of writing – but it was all in Arabic. At least he assumed it was.

The cab pulled up at the Zoo. The driver was not at all happy to give change for a twenty-pound note. *That was my first mistake as a fugitive,* Steddy thought. It wouldn't take Scotland Yard very long to trace him now. He would have to move away from there on the double, at least as soon as he had called Thea – if he could still catch her at home and he prayed that she would be there.

She answered the phone but he forgot to push the coin into the box to complete the circuit. Damn! When he rang back the line was busy. He was still so shaken that he dialled three wrong numbers before it finally started to ring again. Ten times and still no bloody answer. He was sure he had the wrong number again but was afraid to hang up for fear it was the right one. He was about to slam down the receiver and try again when a voice answered. It wasn't Thea's.

"Double three, double one."

"Could I speak to Miss Theadora, please?"

"She's just gone out sir. I just passed her on my way in."

"It's terribly urgent. Could you try to catch her?"

"Well, I'll look out the window if you'll wait just a moment."

Steddy was apoplectic. If he missed her now, he'd never get her. They would surely be watching her. Damn the waiting. He had to put another coin in the call box. He heard footsteps coming to the phone.

"Well, I hope it's important sir – I had to call her back all the way from the corner."

"I assure you it's very important."

Thea was breathless and curt when she took the phone, but her tone softened when she realised it was Steddy.

"Couldn't it wait five minutes? I had one foot in the cab."

"Darling, I'm afraid it's very important and I don't have much time." Thea sensed from his voice that something was wrong.

"What is it darling?"

"Thea, Omar was murdered in my suite last night when I was asleep."

"Oh my God, you poor thing . . . Who did it?"

"That's just it, I haven't any idea, but I'm afraid I bolted . . ."

"But why darling? They couldn't possibly accuse you."

"I'm afraid the evidence was rather convincing and then everything I've done since has only made things look much worse."

"What did you do?"

"Darling, there just isn't time now. Please don't ask any questions and just listen. I've got a lot to tell you and very little time – I've got to get out of town fast and . . ."

"But where will you go?"

"I don't know dearest, but what's important now is that they'll be watching you so we have to figure out some way of communicating that they won't be able to trace."

"Please go to the police Steddy – look what happened to Rollo because he panicked."

"It's out of the question."

"But listen . . ."

"It's too late for buts. You'll understand when you read about it in the papers. That's why I have to be able to call you and tell you what really happened."

"Darling, don't do this to me. You must tell me what has – "

"You're wasting time. I may only have a matter of minutes. Now just listen. OK?"

"OK, but . . ."

"Tomorrow, I want you to go to the Savoy and have a drink in the bar, as though you are waiting for someone. Don't arrive a minute before six – I don't want them to have time to trace the call or anything."

"Will you meet me then?"

"No dearest, but I'll call you there at five minutes past and . . ."

"But what if there's some reason you can't? Oh Steddy, what do I do if they're following me, or questioning me and I can't get away?"

"Listen Thea, you've got to stay calm. You'll be my only way of communicating with the rest of the world. I may not be able to get to a phone on time – we have to plan now for every possible screw-up."

"Steddy, don't do this, please . . ."

"When I call you tomorrow, the first thing I'll tell you is where and when I'll call the next day. That'll be safe, they won't be able to trace it that quickly."

"And if you don't call, or I'm not there?"

"Then we have to have a back-up, some restaurant or something."

"How about Drones? It's always crowded."

"That's fine, but only if we haven't connected – then you go there at noon the following day. Got it?"

"I think so, but darling this is all so unnecessary. You didn't do anything so why should you run? You're not English – you'll stick out like a sore thumb and you won't even know where to go. They'll catch you right away and then you really will look guilty . . ."

"Listen, I know my chances aren't great, but if I went to the police now, they'd lock me up and throw away the key . . . I've just got to buy some time. Maybe it will all just straighten itself out."

"If you insist, then I'm coming with you. I'm so worried . . ."

"Don't worry, I'm not going to get hurt. If they catch me, I have no intention of doing anything stupid – I'll go with them like a lamb. Now I've got to go darling, they may have traced my taxi by now. And please, darling, try not to worry – I love you so much."

"I love you too. Be careful and . . . Oh wait! Steddy, is it Claridge's at six tomorrow?"

"No dearest, the Savoy . . ." and then, "At Five Past . . ." he screamed into the phone, but the money had run out and the line was already dead.

~ ~ ~

There was a kiosk next to the telephone booth that sold sweets and postcards for tourists. Steddy bought an A-Z map of London and a small guide to Great Britain. He knew that he had to get away from the Zoo without taking another traceable cab. He knew that he couldn't stay in London, but he now realised that he couldn't show his face at Victoria Station or Heathrow.

The map showed that Luton was the first major town on the railway line to the north. He could get there by Green Line bus. The nearest stop looked about a half a mile away, so after buying a supply of sweets and biscuits, he set out for it at a brisk clip. The military surplus store that he passed on the way had an anorak in the window. He bought it plus some trousers, underwear, hiking boots and a money belt that caught his eye. He wore the anorak and stuffed everything else including the money, into a second-hand rucksack, and disposed of Omar's gaudy leather case in the first dustbin he passed.

He only waited five minutes at the stop for the bus to come, though it seemed five hours. At Hampstead he got off, hid the anorak in the rucksack, and put on the black knitted tie that he'd stuffed into his pocket. *Not very professional*, he thought, but it might put them off the scent and gain him valuable time. Time was very much on his mind as he nervously stared at the face of the clock in the church tower for the twenty minutes that crawled by before his next bus came. It seemed a week had passed since the telephone's harsh jangle had awakened him to a nightmare. In less than three hours since that moment, he had become a fugitive on the run, and he didn't even know where he was going.

Well, at least if I don't know where I'm going, Scotland Yard certainly doesn't either.

On the bus, he studied the small guidebook's map of Great Britain. From the moment he'd realised that his passport was useless and he couldn't leave the country, Scotland had been hovering in the back of his mind as a possible destination. Having just been there with Thea, he thought of it as a refuge – a place where one could get lost and become part of the scenery, as they had for those six days. But no one had been *hunting* them. An American on his own, with no reason to be there would be very noticeable.

His finger traced the names on the map . . . Aberdeen caught his eye. He knew that there had been a lot of Americans there because of North Sea oil, and he'd read how the Scots resented the American invasion from the off-shore rigs – turning Aberdeen into their private playpen/ pigpen. He couldn't remember when or where he'd seen that piece, but he knew it had been a long time ago, and wondered if the Americans were still there in droves. It might be the place to get lost. Hell, he'd only be one more ugly American.

The bus trip to Luton took about forty-five minutes and Steddy was able to find the station without having to ask directions. He had determined from the map that the safest way for him to go north was to take a train to York where it looked as if he could change to a direct line to Edinburgh and there catch a train to Inverness – the end of the line, from whence he planned to make his way circuitously to Aberdeen.

From the timetable he picked up at Luton he learned that in order to get to York he had to change at Sheffield. The train for Sheffield left in fifteen minutes. He had just enough time to change clothes in the men's room, cram the money belt full with Omar's cash, and buy a ticket. He hoped that the anorak, hiking boots and rucksack would make him look more or less the inconspicuous tourist.

The two-and-a-half-hour ride was uneventful and he made the connection with enough time to search out an empty compartment – he would arrive at York in time to catch the 4:01 to Edinburgh. But just before the train pulled out, a mother and son took two seats opposite him. He buried his nose in the Scottish guidebook to avoid conversation, and tried to concentrate on the pages, but the compartment was very hot and in spite of the tension, he had to fight to keep his eyes open.

A policeman had him by the shoulders and was shaking him. When he opened his eyes, he realised it was the guard. The train had stopped, the compartment was empty, and they were in a glass-covered shed.

He froze with fear.

"This is the end of the line, and unless you've a mind to spend the night in the shed, you'd best be on your way."

"Where are we?" Steddy asked.

"Newcastle. We've been here for twenty minutes."

Steddy gathered his things and left the train. The station clock read 4:45, and the timetable told him that there was an express to Edinburgh at 5:08 – he would arrive in Edinburgh ahead of the train he had missed from York. *Was he lucky or just plain stupid?* He had tried to go unnoticed, and now, if asked, the guard was certain to remember him.

He found a compartment with only an elderly lady in it, too late noticing that the overhead racks were full of gear. He started to leave, but the lady told him sweetly to take a seat as there were two free. There was nothing he could do then but comply. He was stowing his rucksack when four young men dressed in hiking clothes, noisily entered the compartment and shut the door behind them. Steddy could tell immediately that they were Americans, and by the time the train had left the station he had learned everything there was to know about them – short of whether or not they still had their wisdom teeth. Within ten minutes they were grilling him as to where *he* was from in the States and where he was going in Scotland and wasn't it grand that they were all going hiking.

It hadn't occurred to Stedman that he would need an alias, so when they introduced themselves, he was hard put to come up with a name – Wiley's was the best he could think of at short notice. It turned out that all four of them were from Colorado and were in the Army, stationed together in Germany. They were on a two-week furlough and were bound for Scotland to climb Ben Nevis and hike through the Grampians.

Steddy invented a lectureship in Marine Biology at Rutgers University for himself, and said that they had sponsored his trip to study plankton in Loch Ness. He had no idea whether Rutgers offered such a course or if plankton was part of the curriculum, and Loch Ness was the only Scottish body of water that came readily to mind, but they didn't seem to notice, and kidded him about the monster, which Steddy conceded he hoped to get a glimpse of. Fortunately they were too excited about their own trip to ask any searching questions about his.

They had bought Cornish pasties, pork pies and beer at the station and insisted that he share their meal with them, and after the second beer had muffled some of the brandy-clatter from the previous evening, Steddy found to his surprise that he was enjoying himself – almost believing he *was* going to Loch Ness – wishing that he was really on his way to climb Ben Nevis with them and not a fugitive on the run from Scotland Yard.

The trip to Edinburgh was just under two hours. He would arrive at 7 p.m., just missing the last train to Inverness. The hikers already had the address of a hostel where they would spend the night. When they asked Steddy where he was going to stay, he said the hostel sounded like a good idea.

~ ~ ~

Chief Inspector Allsloe was not amused. He had never before been seen by his fellows with a loosened tie and an unsprung collar. He was one of the few men in London who still wore separate collars – not through any desire to be eccentric or for that matter smart, but rather because he wore the same shirt three times during a given week, limiting himself to two fresh collars.

He had a wife and a char, and a laundress once a week, but still persisted in maintaining himself like a first-former from a bygone era. He affected to be neither middle class nor upper class, but was simply a middle-aged survivor of *second-son* limbo. Uncomfortably bright for his allotted profession, he had nevertheless persevered and found his own dusty niche, ultimately reaching that sleepy cerebral standing at the Yard where he was normally only called upon to judge the work of others. There wasn't one man of the fourteen who crowded his room a few hours after the discovery of what they had already labelled "The Brook Street Murder", who didn't know this, yet they all sensed with the Rockford case, an awakening in him, a change from passive to active. There was no doubt in their minds that this was to be very much *his* show.

Allsloe naturally possessed all the theatrical accoutrements required to portray a brainy pedant or an arcane history professor; the worn, lovat-green tweed jacket, the fuming meerschaum and the noble but battered, brown fedora. In his right hand, he constantly clicked and rolled two glass marbles – a habit that had earned him the nickname "Queeg". (Though Allsloe had shattered many an immy long before Wouk put pen to paper.) The hand that held them had a rumpled, chalky, scholastic look that was in harmony with his general appearance. In contrast, his startlingly red eyebrows popped out as if they were surprised by the dull, colourless eyes that they framed.

As his annoyance grew, the modulation of his voice did not change, only the more urgent clicking of the crystal balls in his wizened paw signalled his mood.

"When I briefed you all some days ago, I told you only what I felt you needed to know, fully confident that you would be able to perform the tasks assigned to you. Today, you will notice dispersed among you a number of unfamiliar faces."

No one looked round – they had already marked the strangers.

"These gentlemen are from another branch of government service and will, for the time being, be monitoring our briefings anonymously."

The marbles were now resounding a high-pitched ping, until one fell to the carpet in front of the ornate Victorian desk, and rolled beneath it.

"Till now I did not deem it prudent to brief you further than was necessitated by the scope of your duties with regard to the surveillance of Stedman Wright and the Arab known as Omar. You were all aware that this work pertained to the Rockford case, but you did not know until now – and I might add, until each of you signed the Official Secrets Act, ten minutes ago – that I have been selected to head a joint team made up of ourselves here at the Yard and certain gentlemen from MI5. I can only say that a grave matter of national security with international ramifications, is involved. You were led to believe that

Wright and the Arab were the sole targets of our investigation; now you know that that is not the case."

Murmurings filled the room.

"I would like to remind you again that you have all just signed the Official Secrets Act."

Allsloe's unfocused gaze panned the ceiling above the suddenly taut, nervous faces, as he spoke.

"Any one of you not wishing to be involved further in this investigation may absent himself *now*." He lowered his eyes and met the frozen, but steady stares that returned his, as he fixed each of them individually.

"I said this was to be a joint operation. Allow me to elaborate. Some time ago, it came to our attention that our brothers in the secret branch sought to eliminate a certain Arab operative. The whys and wherefores are unimportant, suffice it to say they had their good and valid reasons. We occasionally stumble upon what the secret chaps are up to and *normally*, we don't interfere. However, in this case, due to the closeness of their target with our ongoing investigation, an unusual opportunity seemed to present itself and we were able, through channels, to convince the minister that, in this particular operation, a collaboration of the two services would be in everyone's best interest." He turned his back to the room, and surprised the gathering by asking:

"Could one of you please find the marble I just dropped?"

The sudden request brought everyone in the vicinity of his desk to their knees.

He left them to it for a minute, and then abruptly told them to let it go. It took a moment for them to settle down; no one wanted to abandon the search unsuccessfully.

"Now I'd like you to imagine that the lost marble is Lord Rockford." No one questioned his hypothesis with so much as a raised eyebrow.

"He has *rolled*, if you'll pardon the pun, from sight and, just as the transparent crystal marble I dropped takes on the colour of the carpet and is rendered almost invisible, so too is Lord Rockford capable of becoming invisible against the multi-coloured carpet of these British Isles, scattered as they are with the dwellings of his influential friends, who – it would appear – are only too glad to hide him.

"The fall of the marble was silent and unobserved, making the finding of it much more difficult – we don't even know in what direction to begin to look. Rockford's disappearance – though far from silent – was unobserved, and so far, no one with any information has willingly come forward. *They* don't believe he has committed a crime . . . I know he has, and I believe he is still in this country, but with every day that passes, his chances of escape by yacht or private aircraft increase dramatically."

A blond inspector in the front row raised his hand.

"Do we have any leads or anything at all to go on, and how does Stedman Wright fit in?"

"I told you of a combined operation with our clandestine brethren. This was launched the very night of the Clermont murder which is why I was not able to brief you to the extent that I would have wanted from the outset. Let us hope that this excessive caution over security between our services has not cost us the entire operation." He fixed the liaison officer from MI5 with an accusing stare and continued. "The American, Stedman Wright, is our one possible direct thread to Rockford – a thread that we took great pains to spin. I cannot emphasise too strongly the importance of finding him and keeping him under constant surveillance before *he* slips through the looking glass as well."

Allsloe paused – allowing what he had said to sink in – watching their faces from beneath his red brows for their reactions. Then, slowly raising his right hand above his head, he held out the second glass marble between his thumb and index finger. It was red and he displayed it as if it were a jewel of great price.

"You will remember that I referred to the first marble as Lord Rockford." Everyone nodded to signify that they did. "Well here gentlemen is Mr Stedman Wright, American."

The red glass marble tumbled from his fingers in much the same way as the first had, except that this time twenty-eight eyes followed its slight, silent bounce and gentle roll under the desk.

"Now do you think one of you could retrieve Mr Wright for me?"

Holbrook, the blond chap who had spoken before and was closest to the desk was first to his knees and in a moment had the marble in his hand. He did not immediately rise, however, but took a minute to scan the vicinity where he had located it and was rewarded by finding the Rockford marble, transparent and almost invisible, nearby, behind the foot of the desk. Holbrook stood and handed them to Allsloe. The significance of the click of the *two* crystal balls, once again united, was not lost on the others.

"So Wright is just a pawn to lead us to Lord Rockford, sir?"

"Essentially, yes. Although Rockford himself is far from the most important bag in this particular shooting match."

"How so?" Holbrook queried.

"There are others involved – foreign agents that we know about and perhaps some that we may not, and vital documents that may involve some highly placed individuals in this country. We're not at all sure how deep this thing goes."

"But, now that Wright's given us the slip, we're back to square one?" It was an officer from the back of the room.

"As far as Wright's giving us the slip, that remains to be seen. *He neither slipped away quietly nor unobserved.*"

The reference to Wright's explosive departure from Claridge's, accompanied by Allsloe's waggling finger, provoked a burst of laughter which dissolved the tension that had been steadily building, but the chief inspector brought them quickly back to the subject.

"We should be able to get a line on him fairly soon through *standard* police work." He glared again at the man from MI5 and continued. "Remember, he's not the transparent marble that can fade into the woodwork as Rockford did. He's the bright one – red, white and blue, if you like; an American who will stand out and be remembered by anyone he comes in contact with the moment he opens his mouth.

"We do have a few leads though. We know that, like Rockford, Nubar Harkonian is his most influential friend in England – someone he might naturally turn to for help. He's also carrying on an open affair with Harkonian's stepdaughter and is bound to try to contact her. He can't have much money on him – as far as we know, he never carries more than a few hundred pounds in cash, and if he tries to cash a traveller's cheque or use a credit card we have circulated his picture and description to all the usual sources with strict instructions to notify us, but do nothing. He left the hotel with only the clothes on his back, and we'll have a description from a cabby or a busman very soon – we haven't found his passport, but if he's foolish enough to try to use it we'll be waiting for him. As with Rockford, we can expect no help from his friends.

"Unfortunately, throwing the Arab out of the window was an effective diversion – no one at Claridge's saw him leave the building – and it causes some problem for us. It was always a long shot, but we *had* hoped to set him running without any undue public attention – don't want some high-minded British subject doing their duty and turning him in.

"So far, the press are playing ball with us and trying to make the Arab's death look like a suicide, but I don't know how long we can hold them. You all know what they're like.

"Thank God Mr Wright doesn't have any *more* bodies to toss around," he said, ending on a note of levity. But no one saw that his fingers were crossed behind his back.

~ ~ ~

Nervous about Steddy's warning not to be too early or too late, Thea had nevertheless arrived at the Savoy a quarter of an hour before the appointed time. She paced the lobby, trying to detect whether she had been followed and worried over the discrepancy between the time on her watch and that of the clock on the wall. When it occurred to her that Steddy never wore a watch, she hurried into the bar.

With the London season still in full swing, the small room was packed and there wasn't a table to be had. Only by flirting with two men standing at the bar was she allowed to put an elbow between them. Most of the crowd were Americans from the mid-west, talking animatedly about the dollar, the tennis, the racing, or the theatre, or the prices, or a mixture of everything at once. When one of the men bought her a bullshot, she was too distraught to even thank him, but she did manage to tell the barman that she was expecting a call. The telephone rang on two occasions, but both times the cashier spoke briefly and replaced the receiver. *What if someone else gets a call first?* she wondered, and felt like screaming.

The third call was from Stedman. He wouldn't tell her where he was.

"But there's been nothing in the papers except a small piece on the second page about an accidental fall from a window at a West End hotel. They didn't say it was Claridge's or mention your name. It could be just a coincidence." She spoke quickly, breathlessly, not letting him get a word in. "No one from the police has even called me and I'm sure I'm not being followed. Maybe you were mistaken about Omar being dead . . . Steddy, this is all so silly, *please* come back."

"Darling, he had better have been dead," he replied almost inaudibly. "You see *I* threw his body out of the window." He heard her muffled gasp, but, conscious of the time, continued. "They want you to think nothing's happened so that you'll relax your guard and lead them to me."

Thea was so appalled by what he had just told her that, for a moment, she was speechless. Then, ignoring it as if she had never heard his words, she went on.

"But maybe they don't even know you were there. You could have been out."

"Sure. I answered the phone when you called and spoke to the hall porter when he announced the cops."

"But . . ."

"And besides that, they will have found out by now from the autopsy that half his head was blown off and he was dead on arrival when he hit Davies Street."

"Oh, darling, I've got to see you. I can't make any sense talking to you this way – I have to whisper. I'm leaning over the end of the bar and the place is jammed."

"Listen, they're probably tracing the call by now or at the very least listening in on the line. I've got to go. Goodbye darling, I love you."

"Oh Stedman, I'm so afraid."

"Don't be. Just remember I didn't do anything wrong – it's just got to sort itself out. Now goodbye darling."

Thea was about to hand the receiver back to the barman when she heard Steddy scream on the line, "Oh damn! I forgot. Did you have *lunch* at the Connaught?"

"With whom?" she replied totally nonplussed.

"The Connaught!" he screamed with frustration.

"What? . . . Oh God yes, the CONNAUGHT!"

Steddy realised that she had at last understood where and at what time they would liaise the following day, and gingerly replaced the receiver as though it had suddenly become very hot, but was too delicate – or dangerous, to drop.

~ ~ ~

Stedman stepped from the stale, reeking call-box and made his way through the beer-brown haze, to the bar of the seedy Aberdeen pub. The fear that the call might have been traced made him want to run, but he gritted his teeth and ordered a pint of lager from the landlady – resigned to await the time and charges. When his beer arrived he hunched over it to avoid being drawn into conversation with his burly fellow patrons.

The night before, he had left the train at Edinburgh with the hikers, finding their hail-fellow-well-met attitude both refreshing and somehow reassuring. Their excitement was infectious and Steddy was quick to realise that their company provided excellent camouflage. They had gone straight to the hostel to leave their gear, and then they had insisted that he come with them to the pub next door, where in the hour left before closing, they drank too much beer and swore eternal friendship.

Steddy felt dreadful the next morning and was shocked that in his position with half the police in Great Britain after him, he had behaved so irresponsibly.

They had parted at the hostel, promised to meet again, and five minutes later he was at the station. He had no stomach for the trip to Inverness, and everything it would entail. No longer concerned with laying a false trail, he decided to wait the two hours for the direct train to Aberdeen – to wait and be spotted he thought morosely.

He could hardly credit the number of stupid amateurish mistakes he had made in the last twenty-four hours. Then again, he thought – *I am an amateur at this, thank God!* The thought was of little comfort, though he had prided himself all his life on retaining his amateur status in everything he had ever done – probably from some unformed fear of becoming pigeon-holed as a professional anything. This was one time he regretted his standing.

Wiley – one of the few friends who understood how he suffered after sustaining a big loss, especially a gambling loss, once asked him if it was possible that people like Rollo and he didn't sometimes subconsciously precipitate spectacular losses in order to affirm publicly that they played for the sport, not the money, but Stedman had never replied.

The loud clanging of the telephone behind the bar, jerked him rapidly from the past to the present, and as the landlady approached, he downed what was left of the beer and reached for his change.

"That'll be £1.10, dear," she said, including the telephone charges with his lager.

Steddy mumbled his thanks, pushed the change across the bar and exited into the street to hurry the few dank, decrepit blocks to the hotel/flop-house, where he had secured a bare cubicle with an iron bed.

Instead of lifting his spirits, speaking to Thea had only made him more aware of his shortcomings and how little he deserved her.

~ ~ ~

Inspector Holbrook knocked and entered Chief Inspector Allsloe's room at the Yard.

"Well, Holbrook, what's happened?"

"Miss Boulton's led us a bit of a chase all over town and ended up at the Savoy where she hung around in the lobby for a bit, seemed nervous about the time – Jones and McHenry were sure he was going to show – then she went into the bar where two chaps bought her a drink."

Allsloe cocked an expectant eyebrow.

"No sir, our men checked them out. They were just Yanks, out for a bit of fun; but she did take a call at the bar."

"Did they get a trace or monitor it?"

"'Fraid there wasn't time for that either. She was on the phone for less than two minutes."

"They questioned the barman?"

"Yes sir. She gave him her correct name and said she was expecting a call."

"Was it a man on the line?"

"Yes, the barman was sure of that, but he didn't recall whether it sounded local or long distance. All the noise in the bar, you know."

"It had to be him. He must still be in the country – if he'd been calling from abroad, I'm sure the fellow would have noticed and remembered," he said, willing it to be so. "What did she do then?"

"She left right away, went by cab straight to Claridge's and met Wright's friend Wiley Travis in the hall. Do you think she could have been talking to Travis on the phone sir? To rearrange their rendezvous. Possibly they were to have met originally at the Savoy."

"I suppose it's possible," he reluctantly conceded, "but it's easy enough to check out."

"Sir?"

"Get through to Claridge's and find out if he made any calls to the Savoy. You have the precise time, I presume?"

"Certainly sir."

"Well, if he called, they would have had to charge him, and there'd be a chit."

Holbrook started towards the door.

"And, Holbrook . . ."

"Yes sir."

"If you can't determine that Travis made the call, I want a man on permanent duty at the Savoy switchboard and one in the lobby."

"Yes sir." He again turned to the door.

"And make arrangements with the G.P.O. for a rapid trace from the Savoy and Claridge's."

"Claridge's is already in place, sir, but I'll see to the Savoy right away."

"And Holbrook."

"Sir?"

"Is she still at Claridge's with Travis?"

"No sir. They went by foot to Mark's Club in Charles Street. 'Fraid we can't get in there, sir, without making a fuss, so Jones and McHenry are staying with it outside."

"Quite right. Those two flatfoots in Mark's Club would really set the cat amongst the pigeons."

As the heavy oak-panelled door clicked shut on its polished brass hasp, Allsloe wondered if he had underestimated his man. The plan had been for them to throw a scare into Wright and leave him an opportunity to escape – a controlled operation – but Wright's unexpected, ruthless reaction had taken them completely by surprise and had ruined the scenario. Allsloe had had his men stationed all over the ground floor of the hotel, every means of egress had been covered. He really couldn't blame them for leaving their posts to a man when the body had splattered all over Davies Street; then it had taken fifteen minutes or more for them to identify the corpse. They had known there was a body in the suite – they should have noticed sooner that it was missing.

No, Wright's irrational, or perhaps very clever behaviour, had simply bowled them over. *God save us from amateurs,* he thought, *or could this American really be something more than the dissolute playboy they had taken him for?* The file they had compiled showed him to be an athlete. That didn't really go with the drinking and the gambling, he thought, but there it was. Some people had the luck of the devil. No military service other than a private troop for privileged boys – not even any business training – nothing, in effect, to indicate that he would be prepared to handle this sort of situation. Yet it was now over thirty hours since he had disapppeared and all they were sure of was that he went to the Zoo and bought a map of Greater London – then nothing.

Allsloe had no misguided affection for Stedman Wright, but he did hope for Wright's sake, that the Yard would get back on his track before the Arabs did.

~ ~ ~

Thea asked for Wiley on the house phone in the small booth by Claridge's main entrance.

"Well, back at last, eh? I've been calling and calling – I was sure that the two of you had pulled a disappearing act on me."

"Wiley, I'm downstairs."

"Where's Steddy?"

"Could you please come down?"

He sensed a tremor in her voice.

"Sure. I'll be right there – get a table in the hall."

That S.O.B., he thought as he replaced the receiver. *One night on his own and he's already screwed up. Plus ça change . . .*

He had sensed that she was upset, but her pallor surprised him. She was usually so vibrant, so vital, that it was almost impossible to imagine her going to pieces. She wasn't at all the sort he would have expected to weep on "the best friend's" shoulder. She had too much pride.

Thea got up when she saw him and he found himself returning her hug with the strength that she seemed to need to draw from him. His cheek was wet when they drew apart.

"Thea. What's happened?"

"How much do you know?"

"Only that I haven't been able to reach either of you since yesterday. I thought you'd gone off again to be on your own someplace."

"What did the operators say when you rang the suite?"

"No answer, no answer, no answer, when they were polite. Usually they just left me on the line ringing an empty room. I even asked Mr Bentley."

"What did he say?"

"Oh, just that he'd had no instructions from Steddy. You know – they're used to him taking off for a few days or even a week without saying anything."

"Wiley, will you order us a stiff drink, please."

"OK, Thea, but listen. I'm sure he's all right. You know he was quite drunk the other night when I left. He could easily have gone off with Omar – they're probably holed up playing backgammon in Antibes or somewhere. It wouldn't be the first time he's pulled a stunt like that."

"Then you don't know about Omar?"

The waiter, dressed in formal livery, unchanged for over a hundred years, did not notice Wiley's disturbed expression when he arrived to take their order.

"Could you let us have two Gordon's martinis, very cold, straight up with a twist of lemon please." Wiley spoke without consulting Thea.

"Right away, sir."

The Gypsy orchestra started playing "Fascination". The clock had stopped half a century ago at 7 p.m.

A little less sure of his ground now, Wiley asked:

"What about Omar? He checked out yesterday."

"He certainly did!" Thea laughed nervously.

"What's so funny about that? They told me he'd checked out when I tried him yesterday to see if he knew what had happened to Steddy. That's why I thought they might have gone off on a toot together."

"He checked out all right – right out the sixth floor window."

Tears started to roll from her sea-blue eyes and her strong straight brows seemed especially severe against her pale pinched face. Wiley realised he was seeing Thea at the age of eleven or twelve, momentarily stripped of all sophistication and completely vulnerable.

"Thea, get hold of yourself, the drinks are coming." Wiley cringed at public displays of emotion, under any circumstances.

They drank for a while in silence while Thea pulled herself together. After a time, she calmed and her colour returned. Wiley ordered two more drinks.

"Theadora. Do you know where Steddy is?" Wiley had inherited his father's habit of addressing people by their full Christian name to bring them to their senses when they were, in his opinion, *out of control*.

"No I don't, damn it – not exactly, that is . . . I did just talk to him."

"So he's all right."

"I think so."

"Hell, Thea, I can't help if you don't tell me what's going on."

"Wiley, could we go someplace less public to talk? We may be being watched."

"Come on, Thea, don't you think you're being just the slightest bit melodramatic?"

"You'll understand when I tell you everything. Please, just trust me until then."

"OK, listen." Wiley gulped down the last of his second Martini and rose from the table. "You stay here and finish your drink while I go upstairs and call Alexandra . . ."

"Oh, Wiley, I'd forgotten you had a girl here. I didn't mean to mess up your evening."

Wiley rolled his eyes.

"Don't worry, I can always meet her later, she'll understand . . . I hope."

Thea smiled wanly, and Wiley raced on before she could change her mind. "Is Mark's OK with you? We can walk over, and it's a club, so no spooks can get in unless they're members."

"Fine."

They cut across Berkeley Square on foot in the now warm evening. Neither of them spoke, but Wiley knew that she would talk when she was ready.

He opened the unmarked door of the discreet club for her and signed the register in the hall. They climbed the small circular stair to the tiny bar at the top of the first landing, where Wiley steered her to the chintz-cushioned window seat at the end of the bar that was just big enough to accommodate both of them. Thea asked for a daiquiri straight up, and Wiley had one too. The waiter brought them with the menus. The atmosphere had a comforting effect on Thea. It was more like a cosy Edwardian residence than a club.

An hour and a half and two daiquiris later, they still hadn't ordered, but now it was Wiley who was ashen while Thea was flushed from relating her story.

The only evidence she could show him was the small shred of newsprint torn from the second page of the *Daily Mail*, but Wiley knew before reading the report – which named no names – that Thea was telling the truth, at least the truth as *she* knew it.

"It's all really too fantastic, but I believe you – only don't get annoyed if you catch me looking for traces of blood on the pavement on our way back to the hotel."

"God, Wiley, I'm so relieved. I had to tell someone and there isn't anyone else I can talk to."

They agreed not to speak on the telephone about anything to do with Steddy, so Thea suggested that they meet the next day for lunch, and said she would collect him at the hotel at noon. That would give them plenty of time to walk the few blocks to the Connaught for the one o'clock rendezvous with Steddy.

~ ~ ~

Steddy awakened in his dreary, box-stall room without any idea of the time of day. He lay in bed thinking, staring at the peeling ceiling and the unlighted bare bulb suspended over his head. The constant grey light of the northern summer morning gave him no hint of the hour.

Forty-eight hours had passed since he had stepped into Brook Street and taken a cab to the Zoo, and from that moment all of his waking hours had been spent on the run, striving to maintain his freedom. *But to what end?* He had argued with Thea that he was running to gain time, *but for what? Maybe she had been right; perhaps he should have stayed. Why should they think he had killed Omar? He had hardly known the man.* On the other hand, it was obvious that the inspector from the Yard had a low opinion of him and would probably have assumed that they had argued, gambling. Not a bad motive, *but then where was the gun?* For all he knew there *could* have been a gun somewhere in the suite – he certainly hadn't thought to look for one – but if someone had wanted to frame him, surely there would have to have been a gun.

Someone had tried to make it look as though he had killed Omar!

That was the crux of the whole thing. The thought that had been nagging at the back of his mind finally took root. He had been set up!

It couldn't have been a fluke or a coincidence – he had been deliberately set up. But by whom, and why?

It hadn't been robbery – all that cash in the money belt, now wrapped around his waist, proved that.

No, it must have been deliberate. So what other motive could there be?

Then there was the police showing up like that out of the blue. *Why would they have come unless someone had deliberately tipped them off? Or had they simply come to ask more questions about Rollo?* Certainly not at that hour in the morning. After all he was just an innocent bystander in the Rockford affair . . . . *Rollo again!* And why hadn't anything been released to the papers yet? They surely knew by now that Omar hadn't died from the fall.

No, it was all too fishy. Either they knew Stedman hadn't done it, or they were *sure* that he had and wanted him to relax and assume that they thought him innocent.

Omar, of course, was still the big question mark. If anyone had ever heard his last name, no one remembered it. They had all accepted him at face value on Rollo's introduction . . . *Rollo again;* it *all* seemed to have *everything* to do with Rollo – the son of a bitch, or poor devil, depending on who was feeling sorry for whom. *But why am I being dragged into it whatever it is?*

Stedman got up and poked his head out of the window to get an idea of the time. The Granite City looked pretty grey and rundown in this part of town, which, judging from the name of the pub across the street, was the perfect neighbourhood for him. It wasn't called the Bonnie Prince Charlie, or the Caledonian, but rather, in bold red, white and blue letters, the sign above the door proclaimed – the Yankee Go Home Saloon.

He had once read how irritated the Aberdeeners had been over the invasion of their city by swarms of American red-neck oil riggers, and wondered if – since the boom had gone flat – his countrymen had followed the command offered in the pub's name.

The big clock in the tower tolled 8:30 – time to get moving. He pulled on his trousers and shirt, grabbed the single, threadbare towel from the night stand and padded barefoot down the hall to the door marked Bath.

It certainly *was* the American neighbourhood – if there ever had been a bath, it had been replaced by two shower stalls – decidedly un-British, though an antediluvian W.C. with enormous shiny brass pipes and a varnished mahogany and porcelain water tank of equal scale, remained.

Undressing, Steddy found there were no hooks for his clothes. The floor was awash, so he hung his shirt, followed by his money belt and trousers on the fulcrum of the lavatory pull chain.

It was the first wash he'd had in almost three days and he was thoroughly enjoying it when a red-haired, embarrassingly fair-skinned, bearded, Incredible Hunk of a man, came in. He was covered incongruously, by a dainty terry cloth wrap-around that barely joined about his extraordinary girth. The giant grunted by way of acknowledging Steddy's presence. Steddy grunted back and began to rinse the soap out of his hair. A minute or two later there was a terrific banging that penetrated the noise of the shower which made Steddy jump so that he crashed his head into the low-mounted nozzle and was then scalded when the cold water was diverted to refill the tank of the loo. He heard the man grumble, "Oh shit," and then the shower next to him joined the cacophony.

When Steddy finished, he saw the cause of the commotion – his clothes had fallen when the clot had pulled the chain of the W.C., and now, money belt on top, lay sodden across the loo. "Thanks a lot fella," Steddy muttered angrily.

"Anytime ass-hole," was the brusque, unconcerned retort of his countryman.

By way of farewell, Steddy pulled the chain on his way out and was gratified by the resulting scream that he heard as he closed the door to the hall behind him.

He dressed quickly in the rumpled but dry things from his duffel, descended the impossibly canted stairs through clouds of smoke from frying fat and managed to avoid alerting the landlady who invariably poked her pin-curled head out of the door of her small front room. He wanted no part of the breakfast she offered, preferring the Buttery at the station where he could at least read the London papers. That was where he headed after stopping to buy a cheap plastic digital watch.

There wasn't a word about him, or Omar for that matter, in any of the papers, but there were a few items about Rollo – mostly a rehash of his ancient family heritage, his gambling and his girlfriends. His wife had been interred in the family crypt at a private service. Steddy didn't imagine anyone would have gone even if they'd been asked.

~ ~ ~

When Wiley returned to his room after his tête-à-tête with Thea at Mark's, he was still troubled by her revelations, and, with the help of half a bottle of Black Label, he had mulled the problem over until finally, at 2 a.m. – 8 p.m. in the States – he had decided to put in a call to his boss. However the number he had given to the Claridge's night operator wasn't that of Skinner, Hart & Crowley, the New York Publishers, but was preceded by a Washington, D.C. area code, and eventually, rang directly through to a private exchange across the Potomac, in Langley. Wiley had left his name with the telephonist, poured himself another drink and settled down for what would prove to be a long wait before his call was returned.

When Holbrook awakened him at 7:30 a.m. by telephone, to arrange for him to meet with Allsloe at 9 o'clock that morning, he had had only two hours sleep – and the hangover didn't help.

~ ~ ~

It was the damn rain. Steddy blamed it for all his frustrations, including the crossed lines and short tempers that were making it impossible for him to get through to London – as if it wasn't bad enough to have to make the call from a pub.

He was in the Yankee Go Home Saloon, a ridiculous establishment that had once catered almost exclusively to the red-neck Americans enjoying time off the rigs in the North Sea. Now, though the old Scottish pub had reverted mostly to local clientele, the music that blared at weekends was right out of the American southwest, as were the rough looking customers on Saturday leave off the rigs who crowded the bar. They were the hard core who had stayed behind, and Steddy spotted the red-haired hulk from his boarding house, standing among them.

Steddy was across the room in an alcove, adding cigarette butt after cigarette butt to an already overflowing tin ashtray in front of him. The call to the Connaught finally came through. The crisp familiar tones of the hotel operator's voice – a direct connection to normality – made him feel even more distant and remote. He asked the barman to be put through to Thea, and while he waited, jealously savoured the sounds of conversation and laughter in the background. Then Thea was on the line and the resonance of her voice made the cords in the pit of his stomach go sloppy, like loose guitar strings. She sounded a million miles away – so unattainable, yet so familiar.

For a moment he felt a terrible resentment that deafened him to the meaning of her words. He was mesmerised by the sound of her voice, trying to match it with the memory, staring blindly at the black and red numbers on the dial of the telephone as though it were a Rosetta Stone that would bring clarity to the meaningless palaver that she was spouting about newspaper headlines and murder.

The surprise of hearing Wiley's voice, startled him.

"Damn it Steddy, listen to me. I've got to see you. I may be able to help – but we have to sit down face to face and talk it out."

"Shit, Wiley, what can *you* do? I don't need a pep talk. This isn't a club squash meet, and I'm not turning myself in, so don't waste your breath, and if you want to buy an exclusive on the publishing rights, you'll just have to wait till the hero gets the girl in the last chapter and everyone goes to the seashore."

"Cut the crap, Steddy. I don't want you to turn yourself in. I've got friends who can help, but you've got to let me talk to you."

"So talk."

"Not here and not now – it's got to be face to face."

"No can do Wiley."

"Listen partner, don't say no. Just promise me you'll call tomorrow – I'll know more then and maybe you'll listen to me."

"Hey pal, I need all the help I can get, but I can't risk anyone knowing where I am, they're probably trying to trace the call right now."

"Will you promise to call tomorrow? Please, Steddy."

"Thea will know where and when."

"OK then."

"Put her on."

Thea grabbed the receiver as though it were a ratline to the last lifeboat on the *Titanic*.

"Darling, you've got to let me meet you. If I were with you, I could stand it somehow."

Steddy looked down at his watch.

"Sweetheart, it's been almost three minutes. Are you dining with *David* tomorrow?"

"David? . . . Oh, *David*, well, I think so (recovering quickly), but I haven't heard from him yet. I did say I'd meet him in *the boss's* suite around seven, so I guess it's still on."

Steddy understood right away. "The boss" was the nickname that Thea called her father, Grover Boulton. He kept a suite all year round at the Dorchester – the hotel the D in David had stood for. She had offered it to Steddy when they had first come back from Scotland, but the oddly proprietary feelings he had where she was concerned had made him decline.

"Well, give him my best, darling. You can't know how much I love you."

"Me too," Thea said, feeling inadequate and at a loss for words.

The phone clicked loudly, crackled and then went into the grating continuous rattle of the dial tone.

~ ~ ~

"That's really the jackpot! They were on the phone for over three minutes in a public bar and you didn't get a trace? I simply can't believe it."

Allsloe was pink with rage.

"I put two men on foot and two in a mobile unit on both the girl and Travis, and still they manage to carry on a three-minute conversation in public with the most wanted man in the British Isles – under your very noses. It really is the limit."

Holbrook tried to stare into the eyes of the portrait of one of Allsloe's predecessors that hung on the panelled wall directly behind him, in a vain attempt to appear bravely to be facing the music, but he found no solace in the cold glare that the picture returned. Glumly, he allowed his gaze to bypass his chief's as it descended once again to his large, brown, unpolished shoes.

"Well sir, they just strolled over to the Connaught from Claridge's – even stopped first in that Persian rug shop on Mount Street, next door, so it really seemed as if they were only going to have lunch. They had just ordered a drink when the barman went right up to her – he must have known her – and called her to the telephone. It didn't seem at all planned."

"Listen, Holbrook, these people are obviously not the silly asses we took them for. He's the bloody devil incarnate. From now on the minute that girl walks into a hotel – any hotel – I want a man on the switchboard and the G.P.O. notified immediately. Have you got that?"

"Yes, sir, but really there was no way we could have . . ."

"STOP. From now on, be it hotel, restaurant, bed and breakfast or brothel, get through to the G.P.O. on the double. Even if she goes into

Harrod's! They think they're diabolically smart, but they're really just smart alecs and we'll get them, by God, but only if we're on top of them every minute."

Holbrook nodded his agreement. Under the circumstances, he just didn't know what else his men could have done, but he didn't defend them, fearing that anything he said would bring another diatribe, and, with his tail between his legs, quietly left the room – bested by amateurs, and *American* amateurs to boot.

~ ~ ~

The lifeline was severed again – at least for another twenty-four hours. Being alone in a crowd took on a new meaning for Steddy as he returned to the Klondike gold-rush atmosphere of the saloon. He was feeling bloody-minded, desperately in need of the company of his fellow man. Instead of cowering off in a corner to wait for the time and charges, he went straight up to the bar, found a spot he could get an arm through and ordered a shot of Black Jack with a Coors chaser, the first he'd had since the summer of his Junior year when he'd worked for one of his father's friend's oil companies in Oklahoma. The taste was welcome and familiar, and because he was as taut as an overwound alarm clock, the powerful bourbon quickly went to work on the cords of his neck and shoulders, and made him feel as if he'd just had a two-hour massage.

When he ordered his third, he realised that he couldn't recall having ordered the second and only knew that he had from the glasses lined up in front of him. A tattooed and bearded giant with extraordinary plumage in the band of his wing-brimmed stetson insisted on buying him a fourth and by the fifth, Steddy was buying drinks for at least six of the drillers at the bar and had told them he was a stringer for *Newsweek*, doing a story on the local effects of the oil glut on Aberdeen.

The landlady gave him the charges on his London call which prompted a few questions from his new best friends, so he told them that he had met a stewardess from London on the plane on the way over and that he was hoping to see her on the way back before he left. He told Bill the same story on the train up to Scotland. The conversation rapidly turned to the local talent, and finally to comparisons between the Scottish kilted lasses and the tight-jeaned honeys of the Southwest. Downing another neat shot of Bourbon, Steddy toasted the cowgirls and swore that no one on earth could compare with them, although he allowed he had only been in Aberdeen a few days and had no way of forming a first-hand opinion.

By unanimous acclaim, it was decided that this was a situation that could not go unremedied for another minute, and with a great many Whoops, Yeehas and Yahoos, bills were settled, numerous full bottles of Jack Daniels found their way across the bar and almost the entire company (including the hulk from the boarding house, Steddy noticed through a Bourbon haze), exited into the street with Steddy leading them singing another chorus of "Up Against The Wall You Red-Necked Mother", at the top of his lungs. They headed down towards the docks to a destination unknown to him, but frankly he didn't care. He had ceased to be a fugitive for a while, and was happy, trusted and loved by his fellow man.

~ ~ ~

Wiley left Thea after lunch, on the excuse that he had some errands to run, but promised to have a drink with her later so that they could make plans to meet for Steddy's call the next evening without being followed.

She had walked him to the corner of Grosvenor Square where he left her to cut across the park in the centre of the sedate Georgian enclave, past the black-bronze statue of F.D.R., to the American Embassy, a clumsy modern monstrosity that time could not mellow.

He entered the building at the side through a glass door marked Visa Department and identified himself to the girl on duty at the reception desk, who directed him behind the counter to a lift down the hall. The Marine guard posted there punched out a three-number code in the wall unit by the door that allowed him access to the security area of the lower basement.

Wiley knew from experience that the C.I.A. didn't burn agents unnecessarily, and other than the men who had been processed and briefed with him for six weeks at the *Farm* in Virginia, fifteen years ago when he had first joined up, his sole contact was Pete Register – the man who had recruited him at Princeton.

One never, never met a field operative. After all, Wiley wasn't one of the Agency's *spooks*, as they were often called in the books he really did publish. His only role was to absorb information and contribute to the daily stew of world wide intelligence/gossip that he assumed nobody ever read or paid any attention to.

Another Marine guard was stationed outside the lift when the doors opened at the lower level, and with only the word, "Sir", he escorted Wiley down an unpainted sheetrock corridor to a grey metal door. A similar security unit with buttons was mounted on the wall to the left of the knob, but the guard didn't use it – instead he rapped discreetly three times with his white-gloved hand, turned smartly and quick-marched back from whence he had come. Wiley waited, but it wasn't until the sound of the retreating Marine's footsteps was almost inaudible that the door finally opened.

The room was carpeted, but the colour was indiscernible. There was very little light – just two old-fashioned tin-shaded goose-neck lamps on a military-issue, metal desk at the far side of the room. In front of the desk stood two similar green-grey steel and vinyl armchairs.

A disembodied Camel-smoker's voice came to him from behind the door.

"Good afternoon, Mr Travis. Thank you for coming in."

"How do you do!" Wiley said, turning towards the voice.

A second voice came from the darkness beyond the lights on the desk.

"Don't turn around, Mr Travis, if you don't mind, just come over here and take a chair. Make yourself comfortable."

Wiley did as he was bidden, even though he found the ritual somewhat melodramatic. As he took his seat, he heard a light tread along the periphery of the room – the man behind the door was joining his colleague.

"Forgive us, Mr Travis, if these precautions seem obsessive, but you will appreciate that it takes many years and a great deal of money to place undercover agents in the field, and it would be irresponsible to expose their identities, even within the *family*, unless it was absolutely necessary."

"Burn them, you mean?"

"I see *some* of the Company's terminology hasn't escaped you."

"I learned most of it from reading the manuscripts of the books we publish. I never really took much of it too seriously. Till now."

Wiley could hear the other man sitting down.

"Well now, to get down to cases. You seem to have got your control back at base pretty excited over this Stedman Wright business."

"I just told him what I knew and asked if there wasn't some way we could help him."

"State is the agency that goes to the aid of American tourists who get in trouble abroad – why didn't you go to them?"

"Steddy's a really good friend of mine and I thought that Pete . . . er, my control, might be able to get to someone here in British Intelligence who could intervene."

"It seems that there are other circumstances involved here. Perhaps we should start at the beginning."

"Well, I ran into Steddy in Paris at the Travellers Club . . ."

"Was that the first time you'd ever met him?"

"I've just told you, he's my best friend – I've known him all my life."

"Well then let's start again *there* – if you don't mind."

Wiley heard a tape recorder being restarted.

During the two hours that Wiley spent in that basement room, his nameless, faceless interrogators were very thorough. Periodically, they would leave the room by a second door to confer, he supposed, or consult with someone else. They seemed reasonably satisfied that his account of Steddy's patriotism, politics and moral fibre tallied with the report that had probably been flashed from Washington, although they accepted it somewhat grudgingly, as it appeared that they didn't entirely approve of Steddy's lifestyle.

The Camel-voiced fellow re-entered the room and sat down.

"Do you think you could get him to call you at a secure phone here at the Embassy?"

"I really doubt it. He was adamant that he wouldn't take a chance on anyone tracing his call."

"We can guarantee that the call won't be traced. The number we'll give him is in Washington and connects directly into the Government Audibon system. The call is then scrambled and rerouted via satellite directly to the descrambler unit on the ambassador's desk."

"Who should I say wants to talk to him?"

"Well don't say C.I.A. over a land line, whatever you do."

"I'll have to say something or I won't be able to get him to do it."

"Just say that you're a friend of the ambassador's and that it's the only way you can have a *secure* conversation with him – and that you think you can help him."

"Can I?"

"That will depend largely on your friend."

"Do you think you might at least tell me what this is all about. He's my best friend and I'd like to know what I'm getting him into."

"*You* haven't got him into anything. But he may have already got *himself* into a highly sensitive situation, especially as the host country is our closest ally."

"Wouldn't the British cooperate if you just told their people what this is all about?"

"Mr Travis, you have a great deal to learn about intelligence operations, and this is neither the time nor the place for an introductory course."

"But for Christ's sake, I'll have to say something. What the hell has he done?"

"We hope, nothing; in which case this whole thing could be straightened out fairly easily – that's why you're not cleared to know any more than absolutely necessary."

"Do you mean that the whole thing could turn out to be nothing and we could just bring him in?"

"We sincerely hope so, but I don't want you to get the wrong idea, because it's vital that you impress upon him for his own protection, the urgency of calling in. He could be playing hard ball with three very dangerous elements. They're the new breed, the kind who've thrown away the rule book."

"God, but how? I know Steddy's never been mixed up in anything like that in his life."

"Does he know you're with the Company?"

"Of course not."

"Well, if your positions were reversed I'm sure he'd swear that there was no way you could be involved with the C.I.A."

"Are you suggesting he's a *hostile*?"

"Probably not. It could simply be a matter of being in the wrong place at the wrong time – or having the wrong friends, or it could be an attempt to make a quick buck."

"He'd never do that."

"I don't think there's any point in further speculation."

The nicotine-stained fingers that were attached to the Camel-smoke voice slid a small white pad across the bare linoleum top of the desk.

"The top number's for you to reach me when you've set up the call, and the bottom one in Washington is for him to use – tell him to call collect."

"Who do I ask for when I call?"

"Just tell them your name, that'll get me. Oh, and by the way, I'm putting a man on you and on the Boulton girl – just in case."

"Just in case of what, for God's sake?"

"If any of those guys I mentioned are looking for your buddy, you two would be the best place to start."

~ ~ ~

It was seven when Wiley arrived at the Harkonians' cream-coloured house in Belgrave Square. Thea came to the door, and he was struck by the sheer simplicity of her beauty.

Her hair was long and liquid as though floating in water. She wore a man's pink shirt with the tails knotted at her waist – there was a monogram over her left breast that Wiley knew was Stedman's without the need or desire for confirmation. Her feet were bare and her blue jeans looked as if they'd ridden a lot of fence somewhere out west. Yet in spite of her outfit, she was surprisingly at home amongst the elegantly gowned eighteenth-century ladies in the full-length Gainsboroughs that graced the walls of the hexagonal black and white marble entry hall.

"Let's go into the study. I've got the news on."

Although his interest in pictures was largely limited to British sporting paintings, he couldn't help but be impressed by the Van Gogh that completely dominated the small, well-proportioned room. He had seen it before, of course, in virtually every art history book he had ever perused, but the real thing was something else.

It was the portrait of a peasant woman seated in profile – rigidly at attention as if posing for a tintype. Her face was brutally mannish, starkly set off by reddish-brown hair gathered in a knot at the top of her head. In contrast to her dour visage, the colours were electric – the background a brilliant emerald green, her dress an equally bright royal blue and crisply folded about her shoulders was a warm yellow flowered shawl that she clenched at her bosom in both her gnarled hands.

The walls of the room were the same vibrant yellow ochre of the shawl and glowed with the depth of sheen of hand-rubbed lacquer. Two over-stuffed divans covered in a deep royal blue velvet flanked the picture and the chimney. Thea was casually sprawled on one of them in a nest of rumpled newspapers. The television was turned on behind her with the sound off, and a telephone was perched precariously on a fat yellow silk cushion at her elbow.

She looked up and caught Wiley just as he realised that his mouth was open.

"She affects everybody like that the first time."

"Gosh," was the most sophisticated comment Wiley could muster.

"She's so powerful, isn't she?" Thea said.

"It's just that she's so much more alive than any of the reproductions I've ever seen."

"Nubie has a few other great things scattered about. I'll show you around after the news is over, if you like?"

"That will have to wait. We've got a lot to talk about."

Thea was immediately alert.

"Have you found anything out?"

Wiley knew he would have to tread very cautiously where Thea was concerned; she didn't miss a thing, and he had been put on notice by the men at the Embassy to tell her as little as he could get away with.

"A little."

Thea now sat up with her legs crossed under her.

He started slowly.

"Well, I went to see a friend of mine at the Embassy after I left you today, and he thinks Steddy could be accidentally involved in something pretty serious."

"Like what? Do they think he murdered Omar?"

"No, no, nothing like that. It's just that the murder did happen in his suite and he could have inadvertently got involved with some rough customers."

"You mean like the Mafia or something like that?"

"No, I don't think so. They really wouldn't tell me very much because it may all be some sort of nasty coincidence – in which case there isn't a thing to worry about."

"Oh, what a relief. I know he wouldn't be purposely involved with criminals."

"Well, it isn't quite as simple as that."

"What do you mean?" Concern raised ridges on her forehead and crinkled her eyebrows.

"It's these other types, you see. They may think he is involved in the murder or even something worse."

"But what could be worse?"

"I don't know. They wouldn't tell me. It's on a need-to-know basis."

"But what on earth could it be? Except for that one night, I've been with him constantly since he arrived in England – or even in Europe for that matter."

"Thea, they just wouldn't say any more and that's a good sign, because it means that they really don't think he is involved."

"Not very reassuring," she observed testily. "And anyway, why are the Americans involved? Are they working with Scotland Yard?"

"No, and we're not to tell the British that we've even talked with them."

"But none of this makes any sense. Who did you talk to anyway?"

"Hold on Thea." (She was getting away from him.) "They really do want to help, and I think that if we can establish that Steddy's not part of any of this, they can fix the whole thing with the British."

Thea started to interrupt again. Her avid mind was racing to questions and conclusions that Wiley was anxious to avoid.

"Listen Thea, this is what they want us to do." And he told her about the special satellite hook-up.

"Do you think we can get him to call? You heard how he is."

"It'll be perfectly safe and we'll be able to talk openly for as long as we like. The Embassy boys can ask their questions and maybe then we can put an end to this – we've simply got to convince him to do it when he calls tomorrow. It's the only way he's ever going to get out of this. He can't just hole up somewhere forever. He probably doesn't have any money, and what if the British police get hold of him – just look at that headline." Wiley pointed to the tabloid that had fallen to the floor.

WRIGHT DONE HIM WRONG

"They've already convicted him."

"I know. It's a nightmare."

"Listen, it's no good whining about it. Let's try to keep ourselves occupied with practical things that can help him. For the moment, we're the only lifeline he's got."

"What can we do?"

"First off, we've got to make a plan for tomorrow – we've got to get ourselves into that suite at the Dorchester without being followed."

"Are we sure we really are being followed? I haven't noticed a thing. Have you?"

"No, but there's something I forgot to tell you."

"Ugh." She clenched her fists.

"They have assigned each of us a watchdog for the duration."

"You mean like Secret Service?"

"Sort of, but I think they're a little more secret than that."

"But why? We're Americans – don't they trust us?"

"It isn't that at all. It's just that if there is anything to this, they think that the men who'd be after Steddy could try to get to him through us."

"Oh Christ," she said, pressing her hands over her eyes and then up through her hair. "But then shouldn't we be glad to have them around – if only for protection?"

"I think it's only fair to Steddy that until he agrees to go along with them, we play the game by his rules."

"OK, but how do we manage it?"

"Normally I'd say we should split up and divide them, but in this case, we know for a fact that there's at least one man following each of us and you can be sure they're good. Scotland Yard probably has a man on each of us, too – at least we should assume they do – so that makes four; I can't begin to speculate about the others and there isn't much point in trying, but I do think we have a better chance of being sure we've lost them if we stick together – four eyes being better than two and all that. Also if we're apart, there's a greater likelihood that one of us wouldn't shake all of them and that would blow the whole show."

"You mean *me*," she said accusingly.

"No, no. But at least if we're together and we know we haven't pulled it off, well then we can be quick on the phone and set up the next rendezvous. What do you think?"

"The logic's sound." Thea looked at him as though she were seeing him for the first time. "Wiley you don't seem the type – how do you know so much about this sort of thing?"

"Oh, I guess just from reading the bad spy books we publish, but listen, we've got to think of a place that we can lead them to and lose them. Any ideas? My knowledge of London is pretty much limited to hotels, restaurants and theatres."

"You mean someplace where we could go in one door and out the other sort of?"

"That's the idea, but it would have to be really fast before they caught on and no place obvious like a hotel that runs through a street – they'd be sure to cover all the exits."

Thea looked pensive.

"You know, about ten or twelve years ago during the queen's Jubilee, there was a big reception and . . . well, I was at the hairdresser. It was pretty late I remember because it was almost impossible to get an appointment what with all the Royals in town and . . ."

"Thea do get to the point."

"Well, I hate that sort of thing, but I was in London and Mummy insisted that I go – she'd bought me a dress in Paris especially and said my hair had to be just so – you know, up, with flowers and jewels, ich! I don't honestly think I've been to a hairdresser since."

"Thea!"

"Well Grace and Caroline were there too and there must have been a hundred newspaper men and photographers in front of the door – I had to really fight my way through them to get in . . ."

"Um hum." Wiley was beginning to get annoyed.

"So anyway, I was finished at the same time they were and as we were about to leave, the lady downstairs told them – Grace and Caroline I mean – that she had sent someone to tell their driver to go around to the mews entrance at the back."

Wiley's interest picked up markedly.

"Grace was very grateful and I asked the woman if I could leave that way too – you know the press were so rabid, they really didn't care who you were, they just pulled you to pieces until they found out . . . Anyway, we went out into the mews, the big Roller was already there with flags flying and there wasn't a soul around and they were very sweet and gave me a lift home."

"Where is this place?" Wiley asked, his interest now fully primed.

"In South Audley Street, right at the top of Mount Street. You must have seen it – it's the shop with the striped canopy."

"Sure, I know the place you mean. I always thought it was a bakery."

"I suppose in a way it is."

Wiley ignored her attempt at humour. "It could be perfect. How long does it take you to have your hair done?"

"Gee, I don't know any more."

"Come on, be serious – this is important."

"Anywhere between an hour or two, depending on what you have done."

"You mean if you asked for one sort of thing, it might take an hour, but if you were going to a ball it could take two?"

"Listen, I know some people who spend the whole day – three times a week. They have the works, a facial and a manicure and then . . ."

"Hey, hold it. Timing this thing is critical. Do you realise that it's less than a minute's walk from that mews to the Dorchester?"

"Why do you think I brought it up?" Thea said, and the look that she gave Wiley made him feel like a chastened two-year-old.

~ ~ ~

The pain. Only a shattering scream can attempt to convey and give form to real pain to make others grasp the full extent of its presence.

The pain was everywhere. His eyes felt as if someone had carefully placed a baseball over each one and proceeded to smash them one at a time with a sledge hammer.

Stedman wasn't sure which had surfaced first – the pain, or consciousness. Probably it had been consciousness of the pain. It was daytime, he knew. The light was too bright for him to open his eyes; when he tried, tears ran down the sides of his face and formed wet pools in his ears. He discovered that it was agony to turn his head when he tried to get rid of the water, and only succeeded in passing out.

When he came to again, the pain was still there and he knew better than to move a muscle. He just lay there trying to remember, trying to concentrate above the pain.

Thea was the first image to break through. He had talked to her from a bar, but where? The taste of Bourbon still strong in his mouth brought it back – The Yankee Go Home; he remembered the men he'd been · drinking with, but the pain; this couldn't just be a hangover, not in a million years. He tried to peep open one eye, but the sharp needles of light exploded inside his head and mercifully knocked him out again.

The next time he awoke, the pain seemd to ebb and flow from mild to excruciating, like an afternoon tide that gently lapped at the edges of his sanity. Fear of not knowing where he was and speculation as to where he might be, finally overcame his fear of the pain and he opened one eye.

The first thing he focused on was the bare light bulb suspended from the ceiling, glaring at him. He averted his eyes – the general illumination from the window seemed softer than it had before. He was enormously relieved to find himself in his room. From the condition of his body, he had been sure that he would discover himself in Scotland Yard's worst security cell or, during the wilder flights of his tortured imagination, in a dungeon in the Tower of London.

The pain hadn't dissipated, but he was able to move a little – he was literally punching through the agony – desperate to know what day it was, horrified that he might have blown the whole telephone arrangement with Thea and broken the chain – his physical and emotional lifeline.

Crossing his arm over to read his watch made him curse the Japanese technology that required a button to be pushed in order to read the date. He had to repeat the painful exercise over and over until he was able to comprehend the A.M., P.M. and day sufficiently to determine that it had been less than twenty-four hours since he had last spoken to her.

When nausea welled up inside him he closed his eyes until he could get it under control and then tried to determine, by running their last conversation over and over in his mind, how much time there was before the next telephone rendezvous. Bit by bit, it came back to him. He recalled talking to Wiley, but wasn't absolutely sure he hadn't dreamt it. There was no time for further reflection – if his watch wasn't as bruised as his body, he had only two hours to make it to a phone.

Getting to the mirror to determine the extent of his injuries became his primary goal and the way he felt, two hours might just be sufficient time to accomplish the trek across the room.

First, legs over the side of the bed – *Oh God, the pain* then, thanks to the cheap iron bed, he was able to use the bars at the head to slowly pull himself upright. He was sure that his ribs were cracked, and his eyes felt as if they had been carefully sanded with a fine-grade paper – and he couldn't decide which was the more agonising.

Upright, holding to the bars so that his knuckles were white from the pressure, he almost fainted again. He was sick to his stomach and painfully swallowed like mad, trying not to retch. The cold sweat that ensued in the now shaded room, made him shiver. As he stood there shaking, he sensed almost more than saw, the familiar square-shaped bottle of Jack Daniels at the side of his bed. That was when he knew for sure he didn't have any kind of king-sized hangover. Somehow seeing the poison made him realise the relatively minor role it had played in the drama that his body was staging.

He snatched at the bottle and managed to hang on to it. It was unopened, and cracking the export seal that surrounded the top required a supreme effort. It hurt swallowing the pungent liquor and burned fiercely going down, but in the hurt there was help, and he clenched his gut, waiting for the spasm to pass, until he could have another pull from the bottle.

There was a large old-fashioned water jug on the bedside table and in spite of the pain that each gulp brought to his ribs, he greedily swallowed half of it. The next fifteen minutes seemed like hours as he alternated pulls from the jug and the bottle. He could move a bit, thanks to the liquor– a few more swallows and he could stand without holding on. His eyes were still mostly closed, but his hands were now free to clutch the two sources of his returning strength. He knew he was in no danger of getting drunk – the pain was consuming the alcohol.

Snatches of memory came back to him; the wee lass in the upstairs parlour of the whorehouse who had turned out to be an old pro imported from Zurich. He remembered sitting with her on a black, Victorian horsehair settee, and how she had tried to put a condom on him while he had tried to concentrate on playing with and slurping on her big, pendulous Swiss tits. Every time she had succeeded in getting the thing on, he had whipped it off with a flourish and thrown it over his shoulder, leering with drunken disdain.

He recalled that the unpopular game had gone on through a series of erections and deflations until he became as bored as the girl had looked when he had first arrived. He had given her a twenty-pound note from his money belt, told her to go fuck herself and headed downstairs.

The money belt – Oh shit, where was it? How big a fool could one man be?
That was when he remembered the Incredible Hulk from the

boarding house coming for him in the alley. He had been too drunk to even take a stab at defending himself. He must have been beaten almost senseless and, from the feel of his ribs, kicked after he had gone down. But before he'd blacked out he remembered a shadowy figure creeping soundlessly through the haze of the alley, and then his attacker crumpling on top of him.

Steddy took another big swig from the bourbon and the last of the water. Eyes open – streaming, but open – he took in the totality of the room at last. His clothes were neatly folded over the chair. *How had he managed that?* With a stab of pain he threw them on the floor. No money belt.

He looked under the bed and as he bent over, the pressure in his head increased like a depth-charge fast approaching detonation.

Another pull at the bottle – no water now, but none necessary. He could actually stagger to the mirror and was amazed by what he saw. There wasn't a visible mark on him. He was red here and there, but there was no blood – no bruises. He must have been worked over by a real pro. On the sides of his chest where there wasn't any hair, he could see some inflammation and swelling, and when he gingerly pressed on his rib cage he could tell they were at the very least, fractured. There was no doubt about it, he'd been royally rolled.

Steddy smiled a crooked smile at himself in the mirror – happy to see his teeth were still intact – and thought, *Ain't life grand?*

After another slug from the bottle, he fell across the bed and for the first time since the whole mess had begun, indulged himself in the hopelessness and despair of his situation.

Then he found the money belt intact under his pillow.

Steddy allowed himself a few minutes to ponder the mystery of his clothes piled neatly on a chair, the unopened bottle, the money and the diary still there, the shadowy figure in the alley who must have been the good Samaritan who had got him home – but none of it made any sense. *Who was his benefactor and why had he done so much for him? And if he had gone to so much trouble, why hadn't he taken him to a hospital? Luckily he hadn't or he would have awakened in a police station. And how had the man known where he had lived?* How much easier it would have been to fathom had he remained sober. Had he remained sober there wouldn't be anything to fathom.

There was no time to analyse it further. He only had an hour to get to a phone and call Thea.

~ ~ ~

It was 6:15 when Wiley crossed South Audley Street and took the few paces that would bring him to the tented canopy that marked the entrance to Rene of Mayfair.

He knew he was being followed. He had spotted one car that he was sure of, although it wasn't the same one that he thought he'd seen earlier in the day.

He'd met Thea for lunch at Fortnum's Fountain and keeping to the plan they had carefully developed the night before, they went upstairs afterwards where Wiley sat affecting a bored countenance – without too much difficulty – while Thea modelled one evening gown after another. At 3:15 he made a big show of looking at his watch and saying she'd be late for the hairdresser. She quickly opted for the first dress she had tried on and they left the shop in a hurry and hopped into a cab in Jermyn Street. Wiley dropped her off at Rene's, paid the driver and then walked the few blocks back to Claridge's, where he napped restlessly until it was time to change into black tie and fetch her.

Wiley walked back to South Audley Street in a fine English summer rain. He took his time – ostensibly looking in the numerous shops that line both sides of Mount Street – but he was really trying to mark the two men on foot on opposite sides of the street who he didn't think were out for a stroll. As he pulled open the glass door of Rene's, he thought he saw reflected in it a signal of recognition pass between one of the men who had followed him and a man on the corner across the street from the shop. Probably one of Thea's watchdogs he thought to himself as he entered the hairdressing salon.

She wasn't down yet, but then he was ten minutes early. He asked for her at the desk and the girl rang upstairs and told someone in French that there was a gentleman waiting for Mademoiselle Boulton, *la fille de la Baronne Harkonian.*

He cooled his heels walking around the reception area looking at the dramatic photos of painfully thin girls modelling the latest hairstyles.

At exactly 6:30, the door of the small lift opened and Thea stepped out – at least he thought it was her. Only her height and the fact that she walked straight to him and kissed him confirmed her identity.

She was ethereal in a diaphanous Grecian, off the shoulder, sea-green chiffon dress that barely dusted the floor. Her hair had been swept up and was the main contributor to the dramatic change in her appearance. It was braided and intertwined with tiny pale green orchids and two lacy, diamond clips that must have had each stone mounted on a separate spring, because they shimmered at the slightest movement of her head.

The play had started and they both knew their lines.

"Hello darling. Did I keep you waiting long?"

"Not a bit, in fact you're right on time. I was a little early."

Then for the benefit of the staff.

"We've got plenty of time now to get down to Kent and still make it to the Johnstons' for cocktails before the Stricklands."

"Let me just sign the bill and we can leave."

Thea went to the counter, signed the bill, said *bonsoir* and taking Wiley's arm, started for the door. Then, stopping as though she had remembered something, she turned back to the desk.

"Mademoiselle, I wonder if we could go through the mews? I left my car parked there and with the weather outside – well the less slogging about in the foggy, foggy dew, the better the chances of your fabulous coiffure arriving at the ball in one piece."

The effusive compliment served to allay any question of not complying with Mademoiselle's wishes.

"Mais, bien sûr, M'selle!"

They followed her through a small stock room where a door was unlocked and, after Thea thanked the receptionist profusely in her native tongue, the door was gently closed behind them, leaving them alone in the silent damp cul-de-sac.

~ ~ ~

In spite of the crowds in Aberdeen Station at quarter-to-six that evening, Steddy was the sole occupant of the long mahogany bench opposite the telephone exchange.

Dressing had been an agony, but nothing compared to negotiating the three flights of stairs at the boarding house. On impulse, he'd stuffed his few possessions into the duffel and taken them with him – spooked that someone he didn't know, knew where he was.

Communicating his destination to the cab driver had been an unexpected trial – when he tried to use his voice for the first time, he found that it didn't work, and only after endless throat clearing had he been able to utter "Station". He wondered what Thea would think when she heard him or even if he could carry on a conversation.

With one eye on the clock, he began to flip through the evening paper. At first the caption at the bottom of page three hardly held his attention – he was looking for an update on his own story which the press were finally using to sell papers. Then something made him turn back and study the headline more carefully.

DEAD MAN FOUND IN DOCKS ALLEY STILL UNIDENTIFIED

His physical senses grasped the story before his brain did, cold sweat materialising on his neck and spine, his stomach queasy. From the description of the corpse, it had to be the Hulk from his boarding house.

The body had been discovered at 6:45 that morning, and the time of death had been estimated at approximately 1 a.m. What really got to him was that the cause of death, "originally assumed to have been a heart attack," had been ruled by the coroner to be death by misadventure when the autopsy uncovered a bloodless wound at the base of the skull that penetrated five inches into the cerebral cortex. Death had been instantaneous, they said, and the weapon would have resembled an ice pick.

The old town clock striking seven brought Steddy out of a state of mental arrest. He had been sitting, staring sightlessly at the station clock when the alarming toll zoomed it into sharp focus. Seven o'clock! He hadn't even placed the call to Thea!

Incapable of running, he shuffled as quickly as he could across the aisle to the telephone office, but a man was ahead of him. Steddy reached past him for a scrap of paper and pencil, found the London directory on the counter and carefully wrote down the number of the Dorchester. Blessedly, by the time he had finished, the man was departing for a booth, but the girl behind the counter was the only attendant and she was busy getting his number.

He stood there with the paper quivering between his fingers – his mind still locked like the overheated gears of a burnt-out Formula One racing machine. He had been present at the scene of two murders in less than ten days, the country was being scoured for him as the prime suspect in the first case and it wouldn't be long before they placed him at the scene of the second crime. He was beginning to think about giving himself up to face the music before something else happened. *But what else could happen?* he asked himself.

The attendant's voice came to him from a great distance.

"If you want this call, sir, please go to cabinet number two."

Steddy looked at her as though she was mad.

"That's cabinet two, sir. You do speak English?"

Steddy looked down at his hand and saw that the bit of paper had been taken from him and, like a sleep-walker, made his way to the booth.

He lit a Players while he waited for the connection. The rough smoke clawed at his throat and when it reached his stomach, he had a flash of nausea. It passed and left him a little high.

"Thea?" Steddy croaked to the girl's voice on the line.

"This is the Dorchester, sir. May I help you?"

"Miss – I mean Mr Boulton's apartment please."

"Putting you through."

The phone had hardly rung when Thea's voice came on the line.

"Steddy?" And when there was no immediate reply – "Steddy, isn't that you?"

But all he could do was keep nodding his head – yes it's me, come and get me and never . . .

"Wiley, I hear breathing but no one says anything. Steddy? Steddy . . ."

Wiley took the phone from her hand.

"Hello, hello. Is anybody there?"

The sound of Wiley's voice shook Steddy out of it.

"Is that you Wiley?" he rasped.

"It's me." And hearing Steddy's voice, "But is that really you?"

"Don't be an ass hole."

"That's you all right. What the hell's the matter with you?"

Thea pulled at the receiver.

"All right, all right, Thea wants to talk to you, but stay on the line. I've got to talk to you and we've gone to a great deal of trouble to make sure that the phone's not tapped – so don't worry about the time. OK?"

"Wiley, I don't give a shit anymore. If they're listening, I'll tell them where I am right now and save them the trouble of tracing it."

"Just don't do anything until I talk to you. Promise."

"OK, OK, just let me talk to Thea."

"Darling, what's the matter?"

"Just a bad cold," he lied, all of a sudden feeling silly – the sound of her voice made him want to be strong.

"But it sounds terrible. Where are you? Please let me come. You can tell me now darling; I swear there is absolutely no one on this line."

"Thea darling, you know I can't tell you – it wouldn't be fair; what could you do, ring me up to say goodnight, or come to meet me and become an accessory? Try to be sensible darling. You must know I need you just as much; especially now. You're all I've got – and only for three minutes a day."

"But that's just it, Steddy. Wiley thinks he can fix it."

"How do you mean?"

"Well he's been with the ambassador and all sorts of big shots at the

Embassy and, well, I'll let you talk to him, but don't hang up when you finish."

"Darling, the only reason I'll talk to Wiley is if it might mean that there's a chance we'll be together again sooner . . . I love you."

"Oh darling and I love you. Now here's Wiley, and listen to what he has to say, and do exactly what he tells you," she said, nodding the phone at Wiley. "In case you've forgotten, he's a really good friend of yours."

Wiley took the phone.

"Steddy, what Thea said about the Embassy and all is essentially true, but first . . ."

"I knew there'd be a 'but'."

"Now hold your horses. Simply put – if you haven't done anything, you've got no problem."

"Listen kid, I certainly know I haven't done anything and you fucking well ought to know that too, for Christ's sake . . ."

Steddy started coughing from the strain of yelling and Wiley had to repeat himself.

"Let me finish, will you! Jesus, you'll never change. Now will you please hear me out?"

"OK OK."

"OK, it's like this. No one in our government seriously thinks that you had anything to do with any murder . . ."

"So then what's the problem?"

"The only problem is that there are other factors . . ."

"Such as?"

"Will you *hold on*?"

"Shoot."

"Evidently Omar was mixed up in something pretty high level and secret and he wasn't alone in it because three other governments besides our own are involved in it too."

"What is *it?*"

"Listen, who do you think I am, J. Edgar Hoover? That's just the point. They don't want any of us to know what it is, which is why they're worried that you could have got yourself involved, either by accident or by design – now don't get huffy – they don't think you're a spy or anything. They just want to know what you know – if anything."

"Wiley, there's been another murder. I don't think it's related – but it sure has me spooked."

"Jesus Christ, Steddy, are you shitting me?"

"The only shitting I'm doing is in my pants – I'm scared to death."

"Where did it happen?"

"Well, I was bombed leaving this cheap local whorehouse – hey, don't say anything to Thea – and I got jumped by this brute who was staying in the same boarding house I was – I'm certain he saw my money belt, so the motive is pretty damn clear and . . ."

"Where did you get a money belt? Thea said you hardly had any money at all."

"Ya, well, Omar had quite a lot on him and I didn't figure he'd mind in the condition he was in when I last saw him."

"So it was self-defence – the guy who jumped you, I mean?"

"Wiley I didn't lay a hand on him. I was so drunk, I could barely stand."

"Shit, Steddy. Can't you at least try to stay sober? You're in enough trouble!"

"Shut up, Wiley. Not in front of Thea."

"OK, so who killed him?"

"Well he gave me a pretty good beating . . ."

"So that's why you sound so lousy."

"Yeah, and all I remember before I passed out – listen it was very misty – so all I remember was this sort of shadow of a man behind the big guy who was pounding me. Then, all of a sudden, the big guy collapsed on top of me without a whimper. That's how I think my ribs got broken."

"So the guy behind sandbagged him and he didn't wake up."

"No, no, it's definitely murder. It's all over the papers. He was punctured in the brain by some sort of ice pick, or something; they didn't even notice the puncture until the autopsy – there wasn't any blood."

"You noticed that there wasn't any blood when you came to?"

"That's the weird thing that's really got me spooked. I came to in my own bed feeling as though I'd gone a few rounds with King Kong, but other than that, my clothes were all neatly piled on a chair by my bed and I know I couldn't have done that in my condition, my money belt was still there – which really screws up the motive, and even the bottle of bourbon I had with me was on the night table. I tell you I can't figure it out. It's really got me going."

"How much was in the money belt?"

"The better part of fifty thousand pounds and Omar's diary. I just don't get it."

"You have Omar's diary?"

"Well, it looks like a diary or an agenda or something – Christ! It's probably his betting book for all I know."

"Didn't you read it?"

"It's in Arabic – I think."

"Wiley, let me talk to him. What's all this about?" Thea interrupted.

"Hold on Thea. This is very serious." And then into the phone: "Now listen, Steddy. I want you to take this telephone number down now, in case we get cut off or anything. It's very important – have you got a pencil?"

"No but . . ."

"Get one!"

Steddy reached out of the booth, painfully stretching on the receiver and its cord and grabbed a pencil and a slip of paper from the counter. The girl was reading a magazine and didn't even notice.

"OK, I've got one."

"Now what ever you do, don't lose this number. I don't care if you have to have it tattooed on your backside – don't forget it."

Wiley dictated the Washington number to Steddy.

"OK, now, when they answer at that number, if you identify yourself with my first name, they'll accept the charges, no questions asked, from anywhere in the world. Your call will be switched by secure tie-line to a location in Virginia where it will be scrambled and transmitted by satellite to the safe phone on the ambassador's desk, here in London. At 4 p.m., tomorrow, I will answer that phone and you had better be on the other end of it. And listen, if you get into anything you can't handle before then, you can still ring the number and a duty officer or the ambassador will pick up. You can talk to them as you would to me – minus the x-rated crap. Is that crystal clear?"

"Smells a little C.I.A. to me, old boy."

"Steddy, I don't give a shit what it *smells* like to you. You do it!"

"If I'm still a free agent."

"Steddy, you've got to give me time to talk to these guys – you don't have any idea what you've got yourself into, and believe it or not – I don't either. But I'll promise you one thing, I'm going to go over there right now and find out."

"But if you think it was Omar's diary they were after – why didn't they just take it?"

"I don't have any of the answers Steddy. I'm sorry – I know that doesn't help. All I do know is that you're possibly in the company of some of the most dangerous agents in this hemisphere and it appears that one of them has taken a shine to you."

"A sort of fallen – Guardian Angel," Steddy said without mirth.

"He may be the best protection you have until we talk tomorrow. Now be good, and for God's sake, stay sober!"

"Not in front of Thea, you jerk!"

"Here she is."

A Guardian Angel

London 08:00 hours

Allsloe's first announcement at the Combined Ops a.m. briefing accounted for his sunny disposition – a big change from the night before when he learned that *both* teams had lost Wiley and Thea. Today he was positively ebullient. Stedman Wright had been traced, through standard police work, to an Aberdeen brothel where a Swiss prostitute had positively identified him from a photograph, placing him near the scene of another murder – this time not staged – precisely at the hour the coroner had adjudged to be the time of death.

The meeting had been convened for over an hour, when Allsloe asked Major Lowson of MI5 if he would care to add anything on behalf of his department.

Lowson – whose physical stature and bearing could have singled him out as the archetypal Guards' officer – rose from his chair. He wore a double-breasted grey chalk-stripe suit, stood six-foot-six inches in his stocking feet, and had never observed anything or anybody except down the full length of his nose.

"As regards the actual murder, our branch is quite familiar with the perpetrator's particular m.o."

His tone was more than slightly condescending and one could easily tell that he was both uncomfortable and unhappy speaking openly about secrets his department had carefully garnered – and in front of a room full of men he so clearly dismissed as clots. Nevertheless, he had been ordered to collaborate, so he continued.

"Though we haven't had the opportunity to do more than a preliminary study of the autopsy report, there can be little doubt that Chelak was the assassin."

The room was silent. The name meant nothing to most of those present. Allsloe, not wanting to ask and trying to maintain his dignity as well as his control of the Combined Ops group, said:

"Major, I wonder if you would mind elucidating on Mr Chelak for the benefit of those present who are not already acquainted with his activities?"

Lowson, still standing, clasped his hands behind his back and unconsciously came to parade rest.

"I wish I could say we were certain that Chelak *is* a male, though we have no reason to conclude that he is not . . . Quite simply put, we know very little about this most effective agent, except that he is employed by the Israelis; he is ruthless and unpredictable, and he is one of the most dangerous operatives that we have ever come up against."

Allsloe's cheeks flushed as if he had been slapped. Lowson anticipated the question before the inspector could utter it.

"It's the wound, you see," Lowson drawled. "The victim is invariably struck from behind in precisely the same spot as your victim in Aberdeen. The weapon is always the same. We will match a cross section of the wound from the Aberdeen corpse with a dozen x-rays in our files, but it isn't really necessary to make a positive I.D."

Holbrook broke in:

"What is the weapon?"

" 'Fraid no one's ever survived to tell us, but from traces on the bone material, our technical boys say it's made of platinum. They think it's probably a surgical pin – the sort they nail ageing aristocrats' broken bones together with."

The room filled with the buzz of conversation until the voice of another of Allsloe's men was heard above the rest.

"But what have the Israelis to do with all of this?"

Allsloe cleared his throat loudly and interjected:

"I think I had better answer that one Major. Thank you."

Lowson took his seat.

"I will now tell you what up until this minute only the prime minister, the major and his chief, as my opposite number, have been aware of. The Israelis have *everything* to do with this operation."

He paused waiting for the room to quieten and then continued.

"Till today, for the strictest reasons of security, I have been compelled to keep this information on a need-to-know basis. Now, largely due to the good major's swift and astute identification of the killer as an Israeli agent, all that has changed. It seems the Israelis have got the jump on us and we will have to double our efforts to locate Wright."

Lowson rose slowly again, to Allsloe's annoyance.

"Yes Major?"

"I think I should just add that, essentially, the game has changed. Not only will it be played out at a faster pace, but having a foreign power running an assassin on British soil changes the entire complexion of the operation."

The innuendo of the major's comment defined what he felt was *his* territory, and was not lost on Allsloe, though the inspector chose to ignore it.

"Yes . . . thank you Major." Allsloe composed himself, riffled his papers, and continued. "If the Israeli is as clever as the major says, he will not wish to impede Wright from reaching what is in fact, our *common* goal. Nevertheless, we must get there first, and without the Israelis knowing of it."

"But, sir, aren't we allied with the Israelis?" Allsloe's man asked.

"When it comes to military secrets, politics very often take a back seat. For a while we even wondered whether Wright might not be an American agent, but nothing in MI5's records or, for that matter, in his background, points to that."

"Do you mean, sir, we're up against the *Americans* as well?"

"No, surely not *against* them; in fact as far as we know they aren't aware of this . . . shall we say . . . opportunity – and we'd like to keep it that way."

A number of hands were raised, but Allsloe, with a quick gesture of dismissal, caused them to disappear.

"Hold your questions for the moment and let me tell you what you must know. We have to get on with this; the Aberdeen chief of police was flown down here on a military aircraft and has been waiting outside for almost an hour.

"Some time ago, Lord Rockford befriended one of the military attachés at the Israeli Embassy here – not an altogether unlikely liaison – the man was a womaniser and liked his backgammon. In other words, a perfect companion for 'Roll-Em' Rockford. They met at a weekend house-party and continued to meet regularly and play backgammon in the Israeli's flat. There were always girls present on these evenings, so the arrangement suited Rockford to a tee, giving him a place for his extra-marital trysts that was far removed from his normal circle of friends. It seems he valued discretion in such matters, and the only cost to him was giving the bloke a few games of backgammon at harmless stakes.

"We became aware of this budding friendship between a British peer and an Israeli military attaché, because Special Branch keeps tabs on Embassy personnel in London as a fairly standard operation." Then he added: "The romantic dalliances of the aristocracy are no concern of ours," as if to show that his interest in Rockford's private life was purely professional.

"Now this is where it starts to get interesting. Round about the same time, Military Intelligence picked up a rumour of a new Israeli Strategic Plan for the Middle East. Of course we had been fully briefed by the Americans on the Israeli Army's contingency plan in the event of war, which was just that – a *contingency* measure – planned retaliation to every possible attack any of their neighbours might institute against them. At first we thought the rumours just alluded to the plan that we already knew of from the Americans, but recent developments have bolstered MI5's suspicions that the original plan has been superceded – that a new plan, code name White Star, does exist – a plan whereby the Israelis are preparing to *initiate* a full scale aggressive action, not just a surgical, hit-and-run air strike, or the sort of brief incursion over their borders that we have become more or less accustomed to expect.

"The mere possibility of such a development made Whitehall exceedingly jumpy – exceedingly jumpy indeed, especially since the feelers we've put out to the Americans lead us to conclude that they haven't the foggiest notion of this new strategy – they *can* be very naive at times – which is why it became vital for us to get hold of some hard evidence.

"Now Israeli Intelligence is known for their razor-sharp vigilance – which has become even more sensitive since Mordecai Vanunu leaked all over *The Sunday Times!* They're efficient, professional and ruthless – witness their unabashed kidnapping of Mr Vanunu – and they're not anxious to have a repeat performance, I assure you.

"We had to find a weak link!" His hand slapped the desk for emphasis.

"After months of surveillance and weeding-out possible candidates by our people around the globe, we fixed on the attaché here at their Embassy. His speciality is search and destroy commando missions behind enemy lines, and we believe he was a contributor in the formulation of White Star. He's pushing sixty and has a young wife who didn't come to England with him, ostensibly so that their child she's carrying would be born in Israel. But our informants tell us that the marriage has been rocky for some time, and we know that the baby was only an excuse to cover up what was really a trial separation. I say cover up, because if the Mossad had suspected the slightest instability in someone as privy to sensitive material as he is, they would never have approved his posting abroad which he desperately wanted for the additional money – hush money for an extravagant wife.

"From then on, after reviewing his file and factoring in the women and the gambling, everything pointed to Rockford as the logical means to get to the Israeli, and to acquire the plan." He then raised his right hand and ticked off on his fingers as he explained.

"One: he was seconded to intelligence when he did his national service in the Army, where, it may surprise you to learn, he did rather well and had a reasonably high security clearance.

"Two: his family's ancient and illustrious history of service and loyalty to the crown.

"And Three: Rockford loved intrigue – everything was a game to him, or should I say still *is?*

"As I understand it, his former colonel called him in, and softened him up with a chat on patriotism and duty, then he made the intro to the MI5 boys. After that, they took over.

"Well he went for the idea like a shot and was in fact quite helpful in mapping out the strategy. He told them frankly that he never played backgammon flat out with the fellow, or for very much money, as the benefits he derived from the use of the flat, et cetera, more than made up for his trouble.

"The plan was simple. As Rockford had already inadvertently lulled the man into an inflated sense of his own backgammon acumen, all Rockford had to do was increase the stakes, 'to make the game a bit more interesting,' and then, pour on the steam. When he had got him sufficiently into his debt, he would lower the boom. And that is exactly what he did.

"When Rockford threatened the Israeli with public exposure if he didn't pay up . . . well knowing what desperate financial straits Rockford was in, the Israeli took him at his word. He would have done anything to prevent a scandal ruining his career, which would also mean the loss of both his salary and pension. Rockford, meanwhile, was making regular reports to his control at MI5, and in the middle of May, reported that the chap had agreed to get hold of White Star and turn it over to him in settlement of the debt – Rockford had rationalised the deal by convincing him that Great Britain was a friendly power, an ally, so her possession of the document wouldn't make much difference in the grand scheme of things.

"The next thing we know the fellow had made a trip to Israel and back – presumably to fetch the plan. How he managed to get his hands on it, we never discovered.

"They met briefly at the flat – he and Rockford – the evening he returned – the same evening as, and just prior to, the Clermont dinner, which of course was when everything fell apart. The Israeli disappeared – Mossad, we understand from the major's sources." He nodded at Lowson who squeezed his eyes shut in acknowledgment. "And we all know – or rather, *don't know* – what happened to Rockford.

"With the benefit of hindsight, it's clear Rockford had already arranged a double-play, and would have disappeared once he'd peddled the material to the highest bidder. What other business could he have had with Omar Khyat, a known Palestinian operative, and how else did the Syrians find out about the operation?" He did not pause for an answer, but rushed ahead.

"The unfortunate death of his wife only forced Rockford to move more quickly than he had anticipated, in order to avoid having to stand trial against a charge of manslaughter – an inconvenient delay that would have eventually forced him to turn the document over to us." He paused for a moment, then continued more slowly.

"The murder *could* have been premeditated . . . though I doubt it . . . But then running from a manslaughter charge after *accidentally* killing one's wife *does* stand in better odour in this country than being had up for treason.

"That's it in a nutshell, except that we believe the plan is still out there somewhere – most probably in Rockford's hands. Otherwise the Israelis – and by that I mean Chelak – wouldn't now be looking for him."

Allsloe started to gather his notes, preparing to go on to his next meeting.

"Wasn't Rockford a buddy of Harkonian – as in Harkonian Industries et al?"

"Yes. Harkonian may be mixed up in this somehow. He could be hiding Rockford out of friendship or could even be the agent for the sale of the documents. He's one of the few private people in Britain who could field a play that requires the kind of contacts and resources that this operation needs. But let me add that apart from his friendship with Rockford, we don't have a thing on him. I've raised the question at the last ministerial conference and was shot down the minute I named him as a possible suspect. He's a personal friend of at least two members of the Government and they won't hear a word said against him without first producing some hard evidence of his involvement."

"But how can you produce any evidence without launching a full scale . . . ?"

"There's many a way to skin a cat, and our recruitment of another of his protégés, one Mr Stedman Wright – albeit unbeknownst to him – could provide us with all the proof we need.

"Now, gentlemen, if there are further questions, I'm sure that Major Lowson will be happy to provide any information he feels is appropriate and germane to your duties. I really must see our colleague from Aberdeen. I've kept him far too long."

With that he swooped up his notes and, like a harried Oxford don, hurried from the room.

Washington 03:00 hours

At virtually the same moment that Allsloe was bringing his meeting to order in London, a weary Peter Register arrived at the White House for an urgently summoned 3 a.m. meeting with the president's chief of staff. The routine report he had filed on his conversation with Wiley Travis had for some reason set alarm bells going in the upper echelons of government, and as he negotiated the anti-terrorist concrete barricades that blocked the entrance, he wondered just what kind of a mess Wiley had tumbled into. He had known the man he was on his way to meet both socially and professionally for many years, but nothing in their terse, one-sided telephone conversation had allayed his fears. Something was very, very wrong.

The officer inside the door of the small white guard house checked the picture on his credentials and then his name against the clipboard roster. When he matched the name, he carefully double-checked Register's face, returned the identity card and courteously waved him through. As always, there was a hum of activity about the place and as he followed the page down the ramp leading to the executive offices, he noted that a number of them were in use. But this was not unusual; in fact, it was reassuring – no crisis frenzy – just people quietly and efficiently going about their work as if on the night shift in a hospital.

"How the hell are you, Pete?" he was greeted through the open office door by the White House chief of staff. "It's been a dog's age, but as you can see, this job of mine doesn't leave much time for socialising." The tall smiling man stood in his shirtsleeves while stacks of documents, folders and newspapers were piled all around him covering the floor, couch and chairs, leaving only his desk curiously devoid of clutter.

"Here, let me make some room for you," he said, picking up two fat stacks of papers in his enormous hands and carefully placing them crosswise on top of two other piles on the floor. "The president says that if I don't get this place cleaned up by next week, I'm fired." He was grinning, nevertheless, confident of his indispensability.

"I don't imagine you called me in to help you tidy up?" Register said wryly, accepting the steaming mug of black coffee that the White House chief poured from the percolator behind his desk.

"If only you could. I've got four secretaries out there and even they can't help – I've got to go through all this shit myself."

Register gingerly picked his way through the path of papers and took the seat that had been cleared for him. His friend sat on the corner of the desk.

"I'm sorry to get you out at this hour, Pete, but the president is vitally interested in the report you made about your operative in London this afternoon . . ."

"The president!" Register interrupted. "Since when has he started reading routine Agency memoranda?"

"He hasn't. It was brought to his attention by the director . . ."

"But why's he interested in a spoiled kid who's got himself in a jam – I was going to turn the whole thing over to Ed Ulmann at State."

"You didn't, did you?" Concern furrowed the chief of staff's brow.

"No, not yet. I didn't think it would hurt to let him stew for a few days. What's this all about?"

"Is he a spoiled brat? Never mind, we don't have anything on him yet, but that's not what matters here. He's into a situation that we've been desperate to get a line on. We've called in your man Travis – he's being interviewed in London as we speak – it appears things have already escalated considerably since your last conversation."

"What do you mean *you* called in my man? Who called in *my* man and *why* wasn't *I* aware of it?" Register's flash of anger coloured his face a deep crimson.

"Keep your shirt on. The president ordered it and the director arranged it with your own people. We couldn't reach you and the boss wanted immediate action taken. You're here because the president wants me to take charge of this thing personally and I've asked permission to have you head up the field operation. You recruited Travis, didn't you?"

"Yes, but . . . what operation? What the hell is this all about? Travis isn't *really* an operative, he's a feeder – a listening post, that's all. If this is something really serious he couldn't possibly handle it . . ."

"That's why there's an Air Force jet warmed up and waiting for you at Andrews. You can be in London in under three hours."

Register put his hands in his jacket pockets, slid down in the chair and crossed his legs. "Don't you think you'd better tell me what this is all about?"

"I'll give it to you short and sweet. You'll be fully briefed by your own people in London." He walked around behind his desk, poured himself some more coffee and perched against the windowsill.

"For some time now we've been aware that the Israelis have formulated a new strategic plan for the Middle East – it was your people who first got wind of it a couple of months ago, but since then they haven't come up with a thing. State's useless, they don't believe Israel would make any major policy shifts without consulting us. You know what the *gentlemen* over at State are like," he added with unconcealed disdain. "When did the Israelis *ever* consult us, except to ask for more? Even then, they line up their Congressional lobbies *before* approaching us!"

Register grunted agreement, while the chief of staff continued.

"The president's wild on the subject; he's in the middle of some delicate negotiations with the Saudis and Hussein and is damned if he'll get caught with his pants down if they pull any more surprise monkey business like when they took out the Iraqi atomic plant with our planes and our missiles. Every time they act unilaterally like that, the Arabs scream bloody murder. They won't even talk to us for six months at the very least, and then we have to start from scratch with an agenda that's twice as long as the one we were halfway through. Spying on Tel Aviv is political dynamite, but we can't go on negotiating in the dark.

"Until this afternoon, we haven't had a single lead. Now news of a document has surfaced in London. It's their new strategic blueprint and we've *got* to have it!"

Register's eyes were on the coffee cup he held in his lap as he began to comment.

"I understand the problem, but do you seriously expect a rank amateur with no more experience than a six-week field course he took fifteen years ago, and a spoiled brat who's never done a lick of work in his life, to solve this for you without the whole thing blowing up in your face?"

The chief of staff's eyes narrowed, so that his thin smile did little to mask the underlying threat of his words.

"No, I don't. The president is counting on *me*, and I'm counting on *you* to bring this baby home for us."

"You realise, of course, that I haven't run an operation in the field for more than twenty years."

"Listen, I don't expect you to get your hands dirty – just orchestrate from the wings. You'll have everything we can bring to bear at your disposal, all you have to do is pull the strings."

"You make it all sound so easy when even under the best conditions . . ."

"Don't get me wrong. I know it's a tough assignment . . ."

"And what about the British, are they aware we'll be operating on their turf?"

"I thought I'd made it clear that this operation carries the highest priority."

"You mean they don't know?"

"They know the document exists, they don't know we do – and that's the way it's got to stay or the plan won't be of any use to anyone. Their service is riddled with leaks – how the hell do you think we found out about this? If *they* get hold of the document it would be worthless within five minutes and we'd be back in the dark where we started. If the documents are going to be of any use, it's vital that the Israelis don't find out we've got them until *we* decide to use them. Only then will we have an effective lever."

"I guess there's nothing more to say – I'd better go home and get my toothbrush," Register said wearily.

"Here." The chief of staff leaned over and extracted a fistful of new toothbrushes from a bottom drawer of his desk. "What's your favourite colour?"

London 16:00 hours

Eight hours later, Register was seated in the American ambassador's office in Grosvenor Square waiting for the call from Steddy that Wiley and Thea had arranged. The ambassador was not present. He couldn't be a party to a covert operation on British soil and besides, his security clearance wasn't adequate.

The night before when Thea and Wiley had finished talking to Steddy, they had sat for an hour nursing large whiskies, planning what to do next.

Thea was adamant that she would go to the Embassy the following day for Steddy's call – what she had gleaned from Wiley's side of the conversation alone had been enough to convince her that Steddy was in mortal danger. Wiley tried to dissuade her, and said that once they went back to their respective abodes, they'd never lose their trackers again, and that if they were both seen going in and out of the Embassy by the British it would complicate matters and make it more difficult for the Americans to help them.

Thea would not be put off.

"In that case, why don't we both stay here?"

"You mean at the Dorchester?"

"Why not? No one knows where we are; there's a closet full of Pop's clothes that will fit you at least as well as your own," she said, tugging at the floppy lapel of his baggy suit. "And anyway it would only be for one night or two at the most."

Wiley ran the possibilities over in his mind. Once again, it seemed, Thea had come up with the solution. From what Steddy had told him on the phone, it looked as though he was up to his neck in this business – C.I.A. business, and that meant that the less either of them were seen going in and out of the Embassy, the better. If they stayed where they were, he could brief his contact that evening by telephone without fear of it being bugged, and then they could both go to the Embassy tomorrow at four without being followed. After that, they could probably set up some means of making contact without having to go to the Embassy or maybe by then the whole thing would be settled.

At 8:30 he called the London number his contact had given him and was surprised when the Camel-smoker's voice answered on the first ring.

He reported that the appointment for Steddy to call the Embassy was set for four o'clock the next afternoon, and then, almost as an afterthought, he told him that there had been another murder.

The fellow became very agitated and asked Wiley where he was.

"I'm at the Dorchester in Thea's father's apartment talking on his private line, but there's no need to worry – we gave everyone the slip."

"You think you're pretty clever, I suppose."

"It was necessary . . ."

"Listen, shithead, two of those men you gave the slip were mine and they're not very happy; and in case you can't tell from the tone of my voice, neither am I."

"Whoa, Tex – in case you don't know it, I don't get paid to do this, so whoever you are, you can . . ."

"Can it. Is the girl with you?"

"Yes."

"OK. You're about to find out who I am, or at least what I look like. Call me back in fifteen minutes."

There was a click and the connection was terminated.

~ ~ ~

They met at the little Italian restaurant in Curzon Street.

It wasn't very crowded and Wiley had no trouble locating his man who, as arranged, was engrossed in a copy of the *Financial Times*.

They greeted one another as old friends. The man was lanky with sandy hair that might have been shot with grey if he was fifty-five, or just as easily might not if he happened to be ten years younger – it was hard to tell. The smoker's voice had a slight Texas softness to it and he dressed as though he had either been educated in the east or had been in London long enough to find a decent tailor.

"Those men were there for your protection. Don't ever pull a stunt like that again."

"I had to talk to Steddy long enough to convince him to call in tomorrow. He would have hung up in three minutes if I hadn't been able to give him my word that we hadn't been tailed. As it turns out it was lucky I did – he gave me quite an earful."

Tex didn't look convinced or impressed. The waiter came and Wiley realised that he hadn't eaten all day, so he ordered ravioli, followed by a veal picatta with a bottle of Barola. Tex, who just wanted to get on with the business at hand, was gritting his teeth, but ordered a spritzer for himself. *A reformed drinker,* Wiley thought. The waiter left them, and Tex said:

"You're a real prize. Jesus! How the hell do we get people like you?"

"I know you won't take it personally if I remind you that we managed to lose two of your best bloodhounds this evening – how the hell do you get people like them?"

They were off to a good start.

Wiley related verbatim his conversation with Steddy.

Tex said nothing until Wiley mentioned the way Steddy had described the murder weapon.

"So he's in Aberdeen," Tex said pensively.

"What makes you think that? He didn't tell me where he was."

Then, as if talking to himself, not looking at Wiley at all, he said:

"We had a flash about that earlier today."

"Why a flash? Steddy said it was in all the local papers."

Tex looked at Wiley as though he were a child.

"We don't read *all* the local papers. You'd better just sit tight here for a minute. I've gotta go out and make a call."

Without further explanation, he got up and left the restaurant.

The waiter came and asked Wiley if he wanted the bill. Wiley told him he was a guest and that his friend would be right back.

Tex grudgingly paid the bill when he returned, and when the waiter brought the change he asked for a receipt and then hustled Wiley out the door and into a small, nondescript automobile that smelled of wet dog. They drove in silence (Wiley figured there was no point in asking where they were going), eventually parking in Knightsbridge. From there, it was just a short walk in the then insistent rain, to a narrow house at the back of Brompton Square. It had been converted into flats and they climbed three flights of stairs before reaching their final destination.

It was a typically dreary service flat – Wiley's New York publishing company had installed him in plenty of them until his private income rose sufficiently to permit him to spring for the tab at Claridge's.

Two nameless men waited there in front of the electric fire that filled the chimney. When Wiley walked in, one went into the next room and shut the door. Wiley was then asked to repeat, word for word, his conversation with Steddy. When he finished, the two men exchanged places and he was told to repeat the whole thing over again.

He never questioned them or complained. Only once did he depart from the script and ask if he could call Thea to tell her he was all right. Permission was not granted, but they told him they would get a message to her immediately.

They kept him all night, frequently leaving the room to confer or make calls, always in tones too low for Wiley to overhear.

At first light, a greasy plate of ham and eggs was brought to him from some beanery next door in Knightsbridge. He left it untouched until noon when he gingerly picked at the ham.

At about 12:30, they took him to the Embassy. He and Tex entered with the rest of the lunch-time crowds through the Visa entrance at the side. He was allowed to shower and shave in the Marine's basement locker room, given a Bologna sandwich in the staff cafeteria, and then left to cool his heels until 2:30, when he was escorted up to the ambassador's office, where to his great surprise, he was greeted by Pete Register – the man who had recruited him for the CIA at Princeton, and who he had talked to on the phone in Virginia after Thea had first told him the story.

"Hope you weren't waiting long. I got here as fast as the Air Force could manage."

~ ~ ~

Steddy looked up at the station clock and saw that it was 7.30. He had talked to Wiley and Thea for half an hour and almost regretted not hearing the police siren that would signal the end of the whole affair. He was still in pain, so he headed for the small chemist's shop near the entrance. There were four boxes of Veganin on the counter by the till. He took them all and then asked the assistant for an elastic bandage, hoping that if he taped his ribs it might ease the pain when he moved.

The men's room seemed miles away – he had to get some of those Veganin down where they could do some good. When he got there it was full of people so he locked himself in the nearest stall and collapsed onto the seat using the rough toilet paper to mop at the perspiration that was pouring from his brow, neck and underarms. He tried to swallow one of the tablets, but without water it started to dissolve in his throat and made him gag and sweat all over again. He could hear loud conversation outside the stall – people were still coming and going, so he pulled himself up, hung his duffel on the hook behind the door and began the painful process of removing his shirt. It was difficult not to cry out; the jabs of pain were intense as he wrestled with the sleeves. *The booze must be wearing off,* he thought as he unwrapped the bandage and began to wind the first turn tightly around his chest, under his arms. He had to lean against the marble wall of the stall to recover between each rotation. The cold stone was a relief against his sopping, pounding head. It took forever to complete the operation. When at last he fastened the clip at the end of the bandage, time had become irrelevant and the elastic was already soaked through. The thought of using the cubicle for the purpose it was intended crossed his mind, but the idea of sitting down and standing up again dissuaded him. His mother's words came to him. *You never know when you'll have another chance.* He really *didn't* know when he'd have another chance – so for once mindful of good advice, he unhitched his trousers and sank to the seat.

Mother! Good God! She must be frantic. He had to get word to her right away, but how? He couldn't call her directly – the way Wiley had painted the picture, even *her* phone could be tapped. He'd have to reach her indirectly some way . . . Aunt Edith. Why hadn't he thought of her before? She was right here in Scotland, or she certainly should be by now, as the shooting season was due to start any day. It seemed light years away since he and Thea had escaped to her house after Nubar's tournament. Could it really have been only two weeks ago? Edith could relay a message to Philadelphia, but it wouldn't be fair to get her involved in his mess even though it was right up her alley. She had once told him that during the war, by staying awake while her daughter, who worked in Churchill's war room, talked in her sleep, she had been the first civilian in Britain to know the time and place of the invasion.

Steddy stood up and fastened his trousers. The washroom was deserted now, so he ran the cold water and using his hands as a cup, managed to swallow four Veganin. The cool water felt so good on his face that he doused his whole head and combed his hair. Looking in the mirror, he was amazed that none of the beating or the pain showed in his face. It almost wasn't fair, but drawing attention to himself, and sympathy, were two things he didn't need at present.

As he shuffled from the men's room back into the bustle of the station, it occurred to him that he had no place to go. It was well after 8:30, and he couldn't spend the night there – airports and train stations were the first places the police looked for a fugitive.

There was a pub winking at him across the way and he strode towards it as best he could. At the threshold he remembered his fallen guardian angel and paused to look back over his shoulder. He saw no one there, but the hackles stood up rigid on his neck.

~ ~ ~

The station pub was dreary, and the people who patronised it were dreary station people – all browns and greys. Steddy sat at the bar, ordered a drink, and waited for the alcohol and codeine to work their synergistic wonders.

Gazing into the grimy mirror behind the bottles, it was impossible to conceive that any of the pedestrian types reflected there could be his sinister protector. Of course he had no idea what to look for. He didn't even know the man's nationality or anything about him. *Well, that's not quite true*, he thought. He did know that whoever he was, he had to be extremely lithe and athletic to have done what he did with such ease and accuracy. He had to be strong too – he'd got Steddy home and up three flights of stairs which was no easy feat with a thirteen stone dead weight. Of course he must have had an accomplice. *But how could he have fingered me, how could he have picked up my trail so easily when even Scotland Yard hadn't been able to, and what the hell does he want from me? He doesn't want to harm me or he would have already, and he can't want anything I've got or he would have taken it. Maybe that's it, maybe he found out I don't have what he wants, and he's gone and left me, left me with my bottle of bourbon as a token of farewell. Certainly it was a possibility that he wasn't being followed at all any more.*

The alcohol and the drug were beginning to have their effect. He was feeling mildly euphoric.

But Wiley said that this man would follow me if he could, and that he might prove to be the best guardian angel I could have . . . What the hell . . .

Steddy's thoughts were getting muddled. The stilling of the pain was accompanied by a dulling of the brain. He had no facts, ergo he could reach no conclusions. *Well*, he thought, *if he's the only protection I've got, here's to him.*

He raised his glass to offer a mock toast over his left shoulder and found himself looking into a grinning, vaguely familiar face.

Fear of being recognised and a hundred other fears blurred his mind in the fraction of a second before Steddy realised that the smiling, uncomplicated face in front of him was friend not foe – but he couldn't place him.

It wasn't until he noticed the trio in the background and realised that they were calling him Wiley, that he remembered Bill Meyer and his companions from the train – the hikers he'd spent the night with in Edinburgh. He couldn't recall ever being so happy to see anyone in his whole life. He felt as though the Marines had landed.

"Hell, we never thought we'd run into you again," Bill said.

"Yeah sport – Did you see that monster?" another interjected.

"Monster?" Steddy went blank. *The only monster he'd seen was now safely in the Aberdeen morgue.*

"Loch Ness. The monster?"

It came back to him – he had told them he was a marine biologist. "No 'fraid not, but it really is good to see you – all of you! How was your climb and what are you doing here?"

"Fantastic! The mountains were great. Of course, by the time we got any altitude the weather was so bad we couldn't see a thing and almost froze our nuts off, but it was really worth it."

"Did you come straight here by train?"

"Hell no. We camped along the Spey, on the Whisky Trail. Ever heard of it?"

"No, but if there is one, it would have to be in Scotland!"

"Well, just about all the malt distilleries are clustered in this one area – I think it's because of the water in the Spey. Ever heard of Glenfiddich and Glenlivet?"

"I see you got an education as well as a snootfull. 'Tis Glenfiddich that I hold in me hand," Steddy said, raising his glass with a flourish. "You'd better all have one."

"We'd better stick to beer," Bill interrupted. "We spent so much money on malt whisky to bring back to the base that we're just about broke."

"Hey. It's on me. After all, this is a celebration – a reunion. Besides, I can't swear that I remember much about that night in Edinburgh, but I don't think you guys let me pay for a thing."

"Well, thanks a lot."

Steddy ordered the drinks, as Bill went on with his story.

"You wouldn't believe it, all these distilleries let you drink as much as you want for free – of course, each one had a shop and we all bought a lot, so I guess it works out. But I swear every time we tasted the malt at a new distillery it was better than the last."

"I'm not surprised," Steddy said, laughing for the first time in recent memory. They were so full of enthusiasm, it would have been impossible not to climb aboard their high.

"Don't tell me that with all that whisky in you, you walked all the way to Aberdeen?"

"Nah, Tom here sprained his ankle, so we took the train from Elgin and here we are, just in time for a drink!"

"Well, Tom, that makes two of us," Steddy prevaricated. "I had a nasty fall down a river bank, so I'm a bit battered too."

"Are you coming or going?" Tom asked.

"Just got in from Inverness," Steddy said, not liking to lie to these decent fellows.

"Where are you going to stay?" asked Bill who was obviously the spokesman.

"No idea."

"Well, you're sure welcome to stay with us. We heard about this great beach with a campsite south of town – lots of action with French and Scandinavian chicks, unless the guy who told us was a bullshitter."

Steddy felt as though the silent prayer he didn't remember offering had been answered.

"That'd be great, but I haven't got any camping gear – just a sleeping bag."

"Hell, we've got two big tents – U.S. Government issue and all the whisky you could drink in a year. What else do you need?"

"Frankly I can't think of a thing. I accept."

"Fantastic." They all whooped and slapped him playfully on the back. Steddy ordered another round and they drank together to celebrate the camaraderie of the open road.

"The only problem," Steddy said, "is how are we going to get there? I'm as bad as Tom when it comes to walking – if not worse."

"We thought we'd hitch a ride," Bill said. "It's not supposed to be too far, but it's definitely too far to walk on a bum ankle."

"I tell you what," Steddy said. "We could rent a car." And then hushing their objections. "Don't worry about the money. I don't have to pay for it anyway – the University will, that's part of the deal."

"Well in that case . . ."

Steddy cut Bill off. "There is one problem though."

"What's that?" Bill asked.

"When I fell in the river, I lost all my papers – driver's licence, credit cards, the works."

Their faces all hung in unison.

"But I do have plenty of cash that wasn't on me when I took the plunge, so if one of you has a driver's licence, I can give you cash for the deposit."

"That's no problem. I've rented cars before over here with my military licence – as long as you've got the money. There's a place right over there that looks like it stays open late." Bill pointed outside, across from the pub.

Steddy had been fiddling with the money belt inside his shirt, his hand covered by his parka, so that when he pulled out a bundle of notes and counted out the money, it appeared to have come from an inside pocket. He handed it to Bill:

"Better take £250, just in case."

"By God, you may never see me again," Bill grinned, fanning himself with the wad.

"Listen Bill, if you'll organise that – and be sure to get the biggest one they have 'cause I can hardly bend – we'll order your dinner for you while you're doing it. All on the old Alma Mater, you understand."

"I'm beginning to feel like an alumnus."

They gorged themselves on Aberdeen sausage, a hearty meat roll made of minced beef and ham that Steddy had been virtually living on for the past few days, and washed it down with bumpers of thick, dark beer and raucous conversation. Bill had no trouble renting a comfortable Rover and, as darkness comes late during the northern summer, it was still light when they piled into the car in the car park behind the station.

The rental agent had marked a map for Bill, so he had little trouble finding the coast road where they turned south along the shore in the lazy lingering dusk.

The first two campsites they reached were full, and as they continued south the warm gold glow of the late evening sky gradually coloured the clouds and stretches of sand with the full spectrum from rose to violet.

Throughout the drive Steddy painfully twisted his neck round to see if they were being followed, but the continual bends in the road made ideal hiding places for a pursuer, and with the sky so bright there was no chance of sighting the telltale cut of a headlight's beam.

Eventually, in the gathering gloom, they spotted the glow of campfires and this time there was a place for them.

114

The camp was populated almost exclusively by Finns and as Steddy and Tom – the invalids – built a fire and Bill and the others erected the two clumsy, field-grey tents, their neighbours approached to welcome them, tall and golden in the flickering firelight, conjuring up ghosts of their Viking ancestors, invaders of those very beaches a thousand years before.

Of those who came by, three girls and a tall gangly boy lingered by the fire until the work on the tents was done. Bill brought out a bottle of his precious malt and invited them to join in round the fire. The boy accepted for them – he was the only one who spoke English and happily turned out to be one of the girls' younger brother. They had brought a bottle of Aquavit, but Bill wouldn't hear of it, making the boy literally translate: "When in Rome . . . ," which totally confused the issue and left them all rolling with laughter. Things got even sillier when they discovered that the statuesque redhead next to Bill was Danish and had some difficulty communicating with her own companions although not, it appeared as the evening progressed, with Bill.

The girl sitting between Tom and Steddy had impossibly long shapely legs. Here name was Kirsten and she was staggeringly beautiful with straight, white-blonde hair that fell to the top of her cut-off jeans, and ice-blue eyes that were softened by her skin's browned-butter tan.

The signals Steddy got from her transcended the language barrier.

She saw that he was stiff with pain and by gesture offered to massage his neck. Not to hurt her feelings, Steddy tried to explain that it was still too tender, and when she understood, she captivated him with a smile that caused the corners of her mouth to crinkle up and two tiny white dimples to materialise at either side.

Steddy never noticed when the brother and sister left, nor did he see Tom leave after Bill and the Danish girl drifted off. They had been alone together with their thoughts for some time – thoughts that they read in each other's eyes that sealed a covenant of nature.

She stood and extended her hand to Steddy. He took it, rose to her side and followed her into the darkness beyond the perimeter of the fire's light.

The smallness of her fitted the palm of his hand like the warm trusting head of a tiny animal. She held his beaten body to her and offered a healing tenderness that, in helping him, seemed to fulfil some basic need in her. For a long time the familiarity of their intimacy was enough.

When it came, the transition from warmth to passion was as

imperceptible as the faint wisp of smoke that precedes spontaneous combustion.

~ ~ ~

By the time they surfaced the next day, the entire campsite seemed to be lunching under awnings extended from their campers or at tables set up alongside their tents. The August sun was warm and the note that Steddy found pinned to Bill's tent said that they'd decided to take advantage of the weather and were across the road on the beach. When Steddy and Kirsten found them, they were sprawled like so much flotsam, washed up on a shore of khaki army blankets. Bill raised himself up on his elbows, not wanting to disturb the lovely Danish redhead who was apparently asleep beside him, using his washboard mid-section for a pillow.

"Well, we were just about to send out the reserves to see if you were still in the land of the living," Bill quipped good-naturedly. "You missed breakfast, but you didn't miss much."

"That's OK. I've got to go to town to make a phone call and we can pick something up then," Steddy said looking at his watch. It was almost two o'clock and he'd promised Wiley and Thea that he'd call them at four.

Steddy asked Bill if he had the keys to the car.

"Listen, as far as I'm concerned, it's your car," Bill replied. "But what if you get picked up without a licence? Maybe I'd better drive you."

"I didn't think of that, but I don't want to ruin your day – this is probably the best weather you've had since you've been here."

"No sweat."

"No really . . . but if you lend me your licence, I probably won't have to use it and we have pretty much the same vital statistics . . ."

"Sure, that's OK. Just don't do anything that'll land me in the stockade. I've only got six months to go in this man's army and I'd like to keep it that way."

The Scandinavians had finished their lunch and the seashore was filling up with uninhibited Finns, Swedes and Danes frolicking in the surf au naturel. Sweltering in the heat, Steddy made up his mind that it was no time for misplaced modesty. Kirsten helped him strip off his shirt and began gently to unwrap the elastic bandage that covered his entire torso.

"Holy Christ!" Bill exclaimed, after a low whistle.

"Why not? Everyone else is bare-assed," Steddy remarked, undoing his trousers.

"No man, it's not that, but look at yourself! Shit, you really did have a bad fall. Have you seen a doctor?"

Steddy looked down and examined himself. He had turned every colour of the rainbow.

"No, it's just bruises and a few cracked ribs. A dip in the ocean is just what the doctor ordered."

It was too cold to stay in for very long. Steddy was soon numb from the waist down – the water's temperature having solved the mystery of how the Scandinavian men remained oblivious to the half-naked smorgasbord of stunners that surrounded them – and had no further qualms about leaving the water.

They dried each other with a big towel that Tom lent them and put their clothes on, preparing to go to town.

"Why don't I get a big steak and some wine in town and we can have a real piss-up dinner tonight," he said to everyone.

"Great idea!" Tom answered enthusiastically.

Then the young Swedish boy – the brother of the girl who now seemed to be with Tom – said:

"That would be a wonderful farewell party for us, no?"

"Are you leaving?" Steddy asked.

"Ya."

"All of you?" he asked again.

"Ya Ya, tomorrow morning."

"Kirsten too?"

"Ya, Kirsten too," the boy said smiling in the sunshine like a snapshot of a forgotten summer.

Steddy was now frowning and, using his hands to mimic the wings of a plane, asked Kirsten if she was really leaving the next day. She understood and nodded her head, yes.

"Well, in that case, we'd better make it a proper gala. Have you got something we can cook the steaks on Bill?" he said, feigning enthusiasm, but depressed at the thought of her leaving.

"Don't worry about a thing. You get the food and leave the cooking to the army."

At 3:15, they rounded a low hill and descended into the town of Stonehaven, nestling at the foot of a magnificent valley that spilled into the sea where it formed a horseshoe cove that was full of sailing boats and fishing craft.

It was further than some of the towns they had driven through the night before, but the map the rental agent had given Bill showed that

Stonehaven was the nearest big town, and Steddy didn't want to run
the risk of calling from a small fishing village that might have only one
telephone with no privacy.

Throughout the silent fifteen-minute ride with one arm round
Kirsten, Steddy tried to analyse the powerful sense of loss he felt at the
news of her leaving. What they had together seemed so natural.

The sight of a red telephone kiosk by the harbour arrested his
meandering thoughts. He parked the car by the quay, and looking at
his watch, decided there was time to do some shopping before placing
the call. The first place they went into was a sporting goods store and
Steddy bought a sturdy pair of hunter-green corduroy trousers, a few
shirts and an oilskin slicker with a hood. He tried to get Kirsten to pick
something out, but she wouldn't, so he got her three microscopic
polka-dot bikinis in assorted colours. In the small market next door
they ordered two thick porterhouse steaks, and while they were being
cut, Steddy selected the wine to go with them from the bins. When he
noticed that it was quarter to four, and the steaks were still not ready,
he gave Kirsten a fistful of money and made signs to her that he would
be outside on the telephone.

He got in the booth and realised that there was still a good ten
minutes before he had to call. Worried that someone would come along
and need the phone just at the wrong moment, he picked up the receiver
and pretended to talk into it to forestall anyone who might come along
until it was time.

Unlike public phones in town, an operator came on the line and
asked him for the number he wanted. In a totally reflex action, he found
himself asking her for directory enquiry for Perthshire. When he
realised what he had done, he told himself that it wouldn't be a bad idea
to have Edith's number handy – just in case. Then when the operator
asked him if he would like to be connected, he thought – *Well, I'll just
ring and see who answers*. It was an enormous place and she rarely ever
answered the phone herself, but this time she did.

"Edith? What are you doing answering the phone?" he asked
idiotically.

"You mean you rang me and you didn't want to talk to me?"

"Well yes – I mean no, I mean . . ."

"Where are you Steddy?" she said imperiously as though addressing
a child who's stayed out beyond his curfew. "We've all been dreadfully
worried."

"Edith are you alone?"

"Blissfully so. I've had a house full of people who, thank God, left this morning. I can't imagine why I answered the phone. I've taken to my bed with a boiled chicken and left strict orders not to be disturbed.'' Then, exasperated: ''Now (Deep breath,) where are you?''

''I'm not far, but I don't think we should talk on the telephone – someone may be listening.''

''On my telephone? Don't be an ass. Why would anyone listen in on my telephone?''

''Because they're looking for me, or haven't you been reading the papers?''

''Of course I have . . . and your poor mother . . .''

''Have you spoken to her?''

''Yes, and she's worried sick. How could you do it?''

''But I didn't do it,'' he answered wearily.

''I never thought that you did, what I meant was, how could you neglect calling your mother? She's been on to the White House, the ambassador and every senator and congressman she knows – she's simply frantic – she's even called some democrats.''

''It isn't a game, you know. I was framed and I'm trying to figure out why. None of it makes any sense.''

''I'm afraid for once I agree with your mother – you've been running around with the wrong people.''

''Edith, please. Don't *you* start.''

''All right, but you had better come straight here before you get into any more trouble – and then I can call Georgianna and at least put her mind at ease.''

''Don't do that, whatever you do. A friend of mine is going to call her through a direct line from the Embassy in about half an hour.''

''Is everything all right then?''

''No, nothing's all right.''

''Well, then you had better come here until it is.''

''But I can't get you involved . . .''

''Well that would be a first! Now just you listen to me Stedman,'' her tone was commanding. ''We can hide you in the old keep if it comes to that, and . . .'' Stedman started to interrupt. ''Hush, I say! Now, we can hide you in the old keep – heavens – they hid dozens of Catholics there in the sixteenth century and no one ever found them – and you'll be very comfortable – Harry's father had it all done up in the nineties as a hideaway from his wife and her parties – it hasn't been used since the War and I doubt if any of the servants – except Karesin and Cook – know that it exists. So what do you say to that? Eh?''

''I don't know what to say.''

"Well then, that's settled."

"But how can I arrive without the rest of the staff seeing me?"

"That's easy. I'll send Karesin into Scone to pick you up. As long as it's after ten in the evening when everyone's gone to bed, no one will see you arrive at the house."

"But, Edith, I really . . ."

"There'll be no buts about it," she said emphatically. "This is what we'll do. Karesin goes down to the pub in town occasionally for a pint, the one in the square; well, I'll let him take the big car tonight so you can't miss it. Just hop in the back and wait for him. Can you be here between ten and ten thirty?"

"I can't, it's not possible, it's already . . . Oh my God! It's already after four – I'm late for my call."

"All right then, we'll see you tomorrow night. Same arrangements. Now do try to stay out of trouble."

There was a click on the line. She'd rung off before Steddy could say another word.

Getting onto the overseas operator was surprisingly quick and when the number answered in Washington and the operator said she had a collect call from Wiley – the charges were accepted immediately.

Steddy glanced nervously at the big clock on the corner through the glass panes of the kiosk – it was nearly ten past. He lit a cigarette and prayed that Wiley would still be by the phone. He heard it ring once and then:

"Steddy?"

"Yes, Wiley, it's me. Sorry I'm a little late but it couldn't be helped."

"No sweat. Now listen, Steddy; I've been here all night being briefed, and an associate of mine has just been flown out from Washington in a fighter plane to take charge here – which will give you an idea of how seriously everyone's taking this thing – I've know him since Princeton and I'd trust him with my life. I want you to trust him too, Steddy . . ."

"You sound like a doctor, introducing a terminal patient to the surgeon."

"That would be a pretty fair analogy, except that in this case the patient *isn't* terminal."

"Glad to hear it," Steddy said, sounding unconvinced.

"Now trust me, Steddy – I'm not walking away from this, but Pete's in charge and he'd like to brief you personally – that's his name,

120

Pete – Pete Register. Now I'm going to put him on the phone and I want you to listen to him, and when he's through, I'll come back on the line and answer any questions you have. Then I'll get Thea for you. She's in the outer office now, but we don't think she should be in on this phase of . . . well, Pete, will brief you on all that."

"Listen, Wiley, there's one thing you've got to promise me that you'll do the minute we're through."

"If I can do it – you've got it."

"Call my mother on that fancy phone of yours and tell her I'm all right."

"I can't do that officially, but . . ."

"Wiley, cut the crap. I wasn't born yesterday. I know you're C.I.A. or something, but just you remember that we go back a lot longer than you and Uncle Sam. So call her. Call her unofficially – just as my friend – and tell her I'm OK and that we're in touch and not to worry. If you won't do that, I'm hanging up right now."

"Steddy, I didn't mean that I *wouldn't* call her. Of course, I will. I just meant that I can't make any statements on behalf of the Government, but don't worry. I was going to call her anyway, after I talked to you – she's been calling the ambassador every day."

"OK, Wiley. Now what's this guy's name again you're putting on the phone and exactly who the hell is he?"

~ ~ ~

When Wiley had left the Dorchester to rendezvous with "Tex", Thea undressed, put on one of her father's pyjama tops and got into bed to watch television and wait for him. She was rather pleased with herself for the way she had orchestrated their escape and felt more at ease after speaking to Steddy.

A little after midnight, she became concerned that Wiley hadn't returned, and leafing through old issues of the *Tatler* and *Harper's and Queen* only added to her nervousness. At 1 a.m., she poured herself some wine. At 1:30, a voice on the telephone informed her that her *friend* was all right and would see her the next day at 4 p.m. He told her to go to the main entrance and the receptionist would direct her. With that the connection was terminated before she could ask, "the main entrance of what?"

After that she tried to sleep, but couldn't. She hadn't had any dinner and it was too late to get anything decent from Room Service. All there was in the fridge was a tin of pâté which eventually she ate with a spoon.

The next day, tired and irritable and unable to wait any longer, she left for the Embassy at 2:30 in a cab, even though it was less than a five-minute walk. The receptionist at the main entrance sent her straight up to the ambassador's office where she was greeted by his secretary and told to have a seat. She asked for Wiley periodically, and was told that she would simply have to be patient.

At 4:30 the door to the ambassador's office opened, and Wiley poked his head out and told Thea to hurry in if she wanted to talk to Steddy – as though *she* had been late, she thought, as she brushed past him.

The room was standard Embassy stuff – white walls, deep blue carpet and red leather chairs. A silver-haired gentleman, who Thea assumed was the ambassador, rose from behind the desk and proffered the red hand-piece of the telephone. Wiley pushed an armchair behind her, and as she sank into it, she began to speak.

"Steddy, dearest, is it all over?"

"Not quite darling, I'm afraid."

"You sound so subdued, so serious, what's the matter?"

"I'm not really sure yet," and then, trying to be cheerful, "I think Wiley's friends seem to have everything in hand, but it's still going to take a little time."

"But darling, if it's just a question of time, we can wait together."

"It isn't quite that simple . . . it wouldn't be safe for a bit."

"What you mean is, they haven't done a thing!" she said, rapidly flushing with anger, her eyes darting like a cornered animal between Wiley and Register.

"Dearest, talk to *them* about that; let's not waste the time we have, arguing."

"But I can't take this another minute. Not knowing anything, being followed, wondering if you're all right. Steddy, if I can't be with you, I'm going home and try to forget you – I mean it, darling."

Her threat broke his resolve.

"Darling, why don't you go to your friend *Edith's* for a bit until all this blows over . . ." he prayed she understood his meaning, for though the line might be free of Scotland Yard bugs, there was no guarantee that the Yanks weren't recording it.

"Yes, darling, but how long will it take?" Thea disguised her exuberance and made it sound like despair.

"Oh, I'd say no more than *two* days." Steddy tried to tell her when he would be there.

"Yes, darling, if you really think so."

"And remember, whatever you do, be careful darling – no matter who you lost yesterday, you've got them back on your tail as of now."

"I know. I promise."

She was doing a good job convincing the listeners in the room that Steddy was talking her into being patient.

"Just be careful then. If *these* people are after me, they could be after you too."

"Of course I will darling."

Wiley and Register were getting nervous keeping Steddy on the line for such a long time. Register was no happier about the job he'd been forced to accept – running an agent within the borders of America's oldest ally without their knowledge – what worried him most was the unknown quantity, Stedman Wright.

He'd read Wright's dossier, of course, and Wiley had sworn up and down on his friend's behalf, but he still had no sense of the man – even after talking to him and briefing him with as much information as he dared, Stedman hadn't given him an answer. He hadn't agreed to cooperate. He said he'd let them know and wouldn't even tell them where he was – wouldn't even tell Wiley – his best friend. How could they work like that?

Still and all, Wright was in their camp and if anyone had a shot at locating Rockford and the plan, it had to be him. The Israelis were no better off or they wouldn't be shadowing him . . .

Thea's voice interrupted his thoughts.

"Thank you for letting me use your phone, Mr Ambassador."

Wiley cut in. "Thea, I'm sorry, but we didn't have time before – this is a friend of mine from Washington, Mr Register," and turning to Pete, "May I present Miss Boulton."

They exchanged greetings and then Thea opened with:

"Now I would like to know just exactly who the hell you are and what you're really doing for Steddy?"

~ ~ ~

Steddy broke the connection with his finger, but kept the receiver to his ear and continued to act as though he was still engrossed in conversation. He could see Kirsten, not fifteen yards away, sitting on the bonnet of the car with her face to the sun, and needed a moment to gather his thoughts and compose himself.

Register's briefing had been too much for him to digest all at once, except for one bit of news that had burned through the mists with the bite of a surgical laser – *Chelak*.

The shadow, his fallen guardian angel, now had a name which made him more tangible; he had a reputation – they had pulled no punches and told Steddy everything – which made Chelak more frightening, but worst of all, he still had no face – Register could give him no clue to help him spot the man.

Slowly pivoting in the booth, Steddy scanned the landscape for this phantom. The people he saw in the streets were local types: fishermen, shopkeepers and housewives; the tourists were all still at play in or on the sea. No one except perhaps himself looked in the least bit out of place, but then why should this man – a master of subterfuge – look out of place and how could Steddy hope to mark him when no one else had ever been able to?

He could no longer allow himself the luxury of assuming Chelak wasn't there. Not after what Register had told him, and now that he was committed to meet Thea at Edith's he had to be damn sure that no one followed him. But how would he know for sure that he had lost him when he wasn't even sure he was there at all? No, if one tenth of what Register had told him about Chelak was true, he would have to assume that he was there. *Hadn't the man already killed to ensure that Steddy survived until he led him to Rockford?* The only possible edge he had was that Chelak probably didn't know that Steddy was aware of his presence. *Maybe somehow he could take advantage of that and make it work in his favour . . .*

Enough! He wasn't going to think about it now. If he was out there then he already knew where Steddy was staying. No, there was nothing he could do now and Kirsten was leaving in the morning; there would be time enough then.

He replaced the receiver, stepped from the shade of the booth into the sun, and walked to the car where a smiling Kirsten awaited him.

~ ~ ~

They could see that the GIs and the girls were still on the beach when they passed on the way to the camp to park and unload the provisions. Kirsten took the salad things she had bought and, while Steddy lay down on the blanket next to his sleeping friends, continued onto the shore to wash them in the ocean.

He crossed his arms under his head and closed his eyes. The heat, held by the sand, penetrated the blanket and gently eased the pain in the muscles of his back. Dozing, he wondered whether Chelak ever slept. *Could he slip away in the middle of the night or did the Israeli keep a constant vigil? He must surely have a car, but would he use it if Steddy left in the black of night on foot and give away his presence, or would he abandon it and take to the road after him? How can I guess what this man will do? How do I lose a man*

124

who might not be there? How do I solve this problem without the main piece of the puzzle?

"So you're back. Have any trouble with the car?" Bill had woken up and mercifully broke into his muddled train of thought.

"Not a bit."

Then, looking around and seeing that Kirsten was by the sea: "Get hold of your girl?"

"Who?" Steddy looked puzzled. Surely he hadn't drunkenly told them about Thea?

"The stew in London." And when Steddy didn't spark. "The one you met on the plane on the way over."

"Oh, sure, she's expecting me tomorrow night."

"That's perfect 'cause we've got to leave tomorrow too – we can all drive to the airport together and turn in the car."

"That'd be great," Steddy replied unenthusiastically. He realised that this was just one more problem; he had no intention of going back to Aberdeen and didn't yet know how he would explain it to them. Changing the subject, he said:

"We've got one hell of a steak for dinner and Kirsten's preparing the salad. I hope you guys can really rig a grill."

"Hey, don't worry about a thing, but maybe we should get started setting it up. C'mon, Tom, we've got work to do."

Steddy went with them to keep his mind occupied and his thoughts from dwelling on Chelak. Tom found an old refrigerator rack that someone had abandoned and with two bricks left from levelling a departed camper, they had the makings of a fairly professional grill.

They busied themselves gathering wood while the girls helped Kirsten invent a dressing and mix the salad in a big plastic garbage bag.

As the steak cooked over the driftwood fire, Steddy borrowed Bill's army knife and drew the corks from the eight bottles of Margaux he'd bought in town, splurging with his ill-gotten largesse. *Nothing's too good for these chaps*, he thought, as he started to hand them out, one to a customer. Then Bill stopped him.

"Hey, let's save that for the steak," he said. "This is our last night together and I think it only fitting that we share a dram to honour Scotland before eating the fine dinner our host has provided."

A bottle of malt whisky appeared from Bill's bottomless duffel and after he poured a drop in the sand, "for those who passed before," it was duly passed from mouth to mouth, and even though Steddy was busy turning the steak and rolling the potatoes on the grill to keep them from burning, he was not allowed to miss his turn.

As if timed by a master, the bottle of whisky was finished precisely as the steak was taken from the fire. The meat was carved with a commando gravity knife, honed razor sharp, and consumed from a rainbow of plastic plates; it was unquestionably the finest steak any of them could recall ever having eaten.

As the light faded from the sky, the debris of bone and bottle quickly disappeared into the pit that Bill's men had dug and was covered over with sand. Kirsten and the girls had gone off to clean the plates and now returned with the bottle of Aquavit they had offered the night before. This time no one turned it down and as they settled in around the fire, Kirsten found a place in the crook of Steddy's arm.

"That was one hell of a dinner," Bill said passing the Aquavit to Steddy. "Best I can remember in a long time."

Though the ladies didn't retire, the fact that not one of them spoke English had the same effect, and, as is customary with gentlemen the world over after a fine dinner with fine drink, the conversation quickly deteriorated to the telling of the crudest jokes they knew. They howled and hooted with laughter until tears rolled down their cheeks, and the girls were caught up in the hilarity – even people from nearby campers drifted by to see what was going on, but the circle of comrades was to remain unbroken that night. There was a fraternity about them that precluded the invasion of strangers. Soon, however, the party began to break up. Kirsten stirred on Steddy's shoulder and whispered in his ear what he took to mean that she was going to prepare for bed. He held up the last of the Aquavit to say that he would be along in a minute and when she left, only Bill remained. Steddy took a swig from the bottle and laid his head back on the duffel, staring at the extraordinary show in the heavens, when Bill surprised him by reaching over and taking the bottle from his hand – he had thought he was asleep. Bill drank deeply and then spoke very softly:

"Who are you really, Wiley?"

The question didn't startle him. Steddy had even forgotten that they knew him as Wiley. He was totally relaxed and at peace for the first time in two weeks – and he was suddenly tired of lying.

"I'm called Stedman Wright. How did you know?"

"Oh, a lot of different things. Is it serious – the trouble you're in?"

"The worst I've ever had."

"Would it help to talk about it?"

"It would if I could, but I can't really. Even though I've accidentally become the lead character in this show – it isn't my story to tell."

"Are the cops after you?"

"I guess I can tell you some of it – the part that's in the newspapers anyway. You'd have read it yourself if you hadn't been on top of a mountain."

Steddy then told Bill how it had begun – how he'd been framed and how he was being pursued by the police and others.

Bill's face registered belief and genuine concern.

"Why don't you just turn yourself in at the Embassy in London?"

"There's more to it than that. A friend of mine's been in touch with them – that's who I went into town to call – and they want me to play along with it; continue like this. I can't say any more about that and you wouldn't want to know, but you see, they know I'm innocent, but they've asked me to be a sort of Judas Goat and stick with it."

"Are you going to?"

"I haven't decided. I told them I'd let them know – you see there's a girl involved and I don't want her exposed to anything violent like what happened in Aberdeen."

"You mean you hadn't just arrived there when we ran into you?"

"No, I was getting the hell out – you guys were a godsend."

Steddy then told him about the murder in the alley adjoining the whorehouse and – without identifying Chelak – about the man who had saved him and was, even now, pursuing him.

"So that's how you got beaten up; I knew that didn't happen in a fall the minute I saw the bruises. That was one of the things that tipped me off."

"Well, anyway, that's where I'm at now."

"Will you go along with the government people?"

"All I know is that I'm not going to make up my mind until I lose this guy and see Thea – that's my girl."

"Is she in on this too?"

"I'm afraid she is by association, whether I like it or not, and I'm not going to decide anything until I'm sure she's safe. I'm supposed to meet her in a few days, but I can't, not with this guy on my tail – if in fact he is. But I've got to *assume* that he's following me. I don't have any other choice."

"Maybe we can help you with that."

"Hell, you don't need this, and anyway I think it would be better just now if the other guys didn't know – not that I don't trust them – but with a thing like this, I just can't take any chances."

"They won't have to know. I'll give them some story. Don't worry, they'll go along with me."

Steddy knew that what he said was the truth. In spite of his calm quiet ways, Bill was a born leader.

"If there was only some way we could draw him off with the car and leave you behind. That way, by the time we got to the airport in Aberdeen and he realised that you weren't with us, you could be well away from here. You could even keep my driver's licence if it would help; I could just report it lost when I got back and . . ."

"Shit, I'm sorry I forgot to return it," Steddy interrupted, reaching into his trouser pocket.

"No sweat."

"I hope you don't think . . ." Bill cut Steddy off.

"Fuck that. Let's try to think of a way we can make this work."

They lay back again, staring at the heavens, as if the stars held the solution. After a while Steddy said:

"A friend of mine once told me a story about being alone with an old native guide out in the bush in Kenya. They . . ."

"Is this just a story, or something to do with our problem?"

"No, no, it could be the answer," Steddy replied. He couldn't help but like the way Bill had said *our* problem.

"So what happened?"

"Well, the guide spotted a swarm of tsetse flies coming their way. Peter – that's my friend – he said he thought it was just a dark cloud until he realised how fast it was moving. Evidently, when there are that many of them swarming, the bites will kill you, so they buried themselves in the mud of a river bank and used hollow reeds to breathe."

Steddy finished and waited for Bill's reaction.

"How does it apply?"

"Well maybe I could bury myself until you'd drawn him off with the car. See what I mean?"

"Yeah, you could use one of those big reeds we've been lighting the fire with."

"That's what made me think of it, but how could we pull it off and be sure that he hadn't seen us do it? I've got to be sure that he falls for it, otherwise I'll never know if he's behind me or not."

"I'll tell you what we could do," Bill said after a while, leaning forward on his elbows. "We could dig a shallow trench inside the tent and bury you in it just before we took it down. If we changed clothes – what with all the confusion of breaking camp and loading the car – well if he is watching, he won't be close enough to tell whether it's you or me and he won't be counting us because he won't expect one of us to disappear into thin air."

"That's perfect, but we'd have to play it out until the very last minute. We could dig the hole ahead of time so I could make a lot of trips out to the car and really be sure he knew what I was wearing and then you'd have to become a quick change artist so he wouldn't notice anything fishy."

"I think we could pull it off," Bill said. "But can you take it that long – being buried for fifteen or twenty minutes? You don't get claustrophobic do you?"

"Do I have any choice?"

~ ~ ~

Kirsten's tent smelled of musk and verbena from the scented oil that burned in the lantern on the ground by her mat. She was lying on her side, reading. Her white-blonde hair spilled from between her fingers and fell to the pages of the book like a waterfall.

When he unzipped the tent flap, she seemed startled by the intrusion and hurriedly covered her nakedness. Perhaps she was blinded by the light and couldn't see who it was beyond the lantern. Whatever it was, the sudden recognition of fear in her eyes, and her beautiful vulnerability, triggered a primal reflex in Steddy and unleashed a demon within him.

He took her brutally as if by right. She fought him with a strength that approached his, but could not equal it. She tore at him fiercely until that too became part of what he was taking from her and was all that she could withhold from him, but she realised it too late and it was over as quickly as it had begun, leaving him spent and unconscious at her side so that she could barely believe what had passed.

They parted the next morning after breakfast. He had awakened in the middle of the night with a terrible thirst, to hear her sobbing softly beside him and only then did the memory of what he had done come back to him. They had no common language so Steddy was unable to communicate his sorrow and shame. Only when his own tears of genuine grief and frustration fell on her shoulder, did she respond to him; then they had clung to each other in the dark, like children who had carried a joke too far, and cried themselves to sleep.

They had said their wordless goodbyes, and now walked together to the road and the car where her friends were waiting. Steddy handed her into the back seat of the little red Volvo piled high with equipment and kissed her tenderly through the open window. As it drove away he stared unblinkingly after her, until the ice blue of her eyes vanished against the morning sky and the wind drew tears from his eyes.

~ ~ ~

It was barely seven in the evening when they called down to Room Service and ordered supper. Neither Wiley nor Thea had eaten or slept very much in the last twenty-four hours and they were both tired and hungry.

Thea went through and took a bath the moment she had finished ordering and returned just as the food was being wheeled in, wearing the top of a pair of her father's pyjamas that hung down to her knees.

They ate in silence, each absorbed with their own thoughts; Wiley trying to digest everything he had learned at the briefing, most of which Thea *wasn't* privy to; Thea planning her escape to Scotland. She didn't like not telling Wiley, but she knew he was under strict orders not to let her out of his sight, and Steddy had been emphatic that she did not let *anyone* know where she was going.

After dinner they watched television for a while, grateful not to have to converse, guarding their own secrets, until Thea said she was going to bed.

"Me too. I'm exhausted. Have you got an extra pillow and a blanket?" Wiley asked.

She went into the bedroom, returning with the bottom half of the pyjamas she had on, and tossed them over to him.

"Here, put these on and come to bed inside. It's a big bed and we're both adults. Unless of course you snore?" she taunted.

Wiley protested and said that the couch would be fine, but Thea pointed at the spindly wood-framed settee.

"Don't be silly, Wiley, that thing's too small for you. You wouldn't get a minute's sleep."

He acquiesced when she made him feel prudish not to, and went into the bathroom to shower. When he opened the door to the bedroom, the lights were out and Thea was already asleep. He left the door open a crack so that he could negotiate his way to the far side of the bed, and got in gingerly, not to disturb her. Being in bed with Thea, enveloped by the sensual yet woody aroma of her perfume, distressed him more than he had bargained for.

He lay there for what seemed hours, hands clasped behind his head, waiting for sleep to rescue him from his wildly wandering imagination. *Yes,* he thought grimly, *we* are *both adults*.

Thea moved into him like a gentle breeze on a sultry night. Her head nuzzled against his naked chest and her long silky hair fell over his belly like a mist. He was sure that she was still sleeping and was afraid to breathe lest she awaken and spoil his fantasy. The silence gradually became oppressive. His arm, as if acting of its own will, reached round and held her to him. Eventually she stirred and raised her enormous eyes. He arched over her and kissed her with a soul-borne passion – and in a lightning flash of realisation Wiley knew that he had loved her since the day he had first seen her with Steddy outside the club in Paris.

~ ~ ~

The grave, as Bill insisted on calling it, had been dug and though considerably shallower than the real thing, gave Steddy the willies when Tom and the others joked about it.

They had decided by the campfire the night before that the best time to make the switch was at dusk when visibility would be poorest, so they spent the afternoon lolling about on the beach awaiting the late northern evening. At about five o'clock, great thunderclaps drew up on the distant horizon like warships forming a line of battle, so they gathered their things and went back to camp to begin their preparations.

Steddy moved the car near the side of the tent, ostensibly to facilitate the loading, but really so that their comings and goings would be partially sheltered from the high rocky hills that surrounded the cove. By eight o'clock, all that remained to be done was to strike the tent.

Though it would normally have still been bright, the threatening storm had caused an early dusk to fall, and though Steddy might have liked to put off his entombment, there was no reason for further delay. He took one last load to the car for the benefit of his phantom watchdog, and then, the moment he returned, began tearing off his clothes, tossing each article at Bill who was already undressed in readiness. Steddy put on the new things he had bought in Stonehaven and finally wrapped himself well in his rubberised slicker and tied the hood securely around his face. They said goodbye and Steddy thanked Bill warmly for everything he had done before lying down like a mummy in the shallow trench.

Tom and the others were already outside pulling up the tent poles, when Bill knelt beside Steddy, tucked the slicker in tightly, and began methodically to cover him with sand, starting at his feet and smoothing it as he went along until he reached Steddy's neck.

"Well, so long fella. You be careful, ya hear."

"If I make it through this, I can make it through anything," Steddy replied, beginning to have second thoughts. Then he added more cheerily, "Don't forget to call me when you get stateside."

"Will do. I don't want to miss the end of *this* story!"

Bill then placed the bottoms of the three large reeds they had tested into Steddy's mouth and covered the remaining exposed part of his face with his handkerchief. When he had finished tamping the sand around Steddy's head and smoothed the residue over the whole area, he scattered more broken reeds over his handiwork so that it was impossible to tell that the ground had been disturbed.

As Bill finished, the sides of the tent started collapsing in on him and he called out to Steddy.

"Wiggle the reeds if you can breathe all right."

They jerked reassuringly.

"Well, adios amigo – hasta la vista."

With that, he and Tom pulled out the last two remaining collapsible tent poles, folded the sodden canvas and loaded it all into the car.

They left quickly, so that even in the shadows of the gathering clouds they would not long be observed.

~ ~ ~

As her father's brown Bentley sped north at a steady seventy miles per hour, Thea relaxed and enjoyed the first peace and tranquillity she'd had in a long time.

She had left the hotel at four in the morning, wearing a big great coat and an old, snap-brim Lock's hat pulled down over her face. Taking a circuitous route – by taxi, underground and foot – Thea had circled back to the enormous car park that lay underneath Hyde Park, opposite the hotel where she had started. The key for the old Bentley Continental was in her pocket, but it took the better part of an hour for her to find it amongst the countless cars stored there.

The next hour was spent driving in circles through the empty early dawn streets; at last sure that she was not being followed, she worked the car up to the Edgware Road and finally onto the A1, where she pointed the flying B on the bonnet northward, to Scotland and to Steddy. Thea tried to think of the last time she had been alone, a free agent; the answer didn't come to her right away and it suddenly seemed important to remember.

She had been sixteen when her parents divorced, and had gone to live with her mother and Nubar in London where they had put her into the last real finishing school to survive the War. It was a far cry from Foxcroft, the Eastern Establishment boarding school where her life had been ruled by the bugle and revolved around military drill and horsemanship, but the discipline she learned there had seen her through, and she had endured the starchy post-war English food, cold baths and lack of central heating without a whimper. When she learned that she was to be presented to London society that was the last straw. She flatly refused. Not yet eighteen and still a tomboy, she didn't want to make her bow to a world that she neither understood nor wanted to be part of. There had been fits and fights until Nubar and Elizabeth had finally got their way.

Elizabeth tried to get her into the swing of it, and took her to Balenciaga in Paris where she bought her almost the entire collection – minus the wedding dress – although she would have liked to have had a reason to order it as well. That summer was when Thea first began to realise that she wasn't altogether ugly.

Cristobal Balenciaga had personally asked her to model his clothes at a charity gala at Versailles. That launched her. Previously she had always judged her looks against her mother's fragile, petite beauty and found herself wanting. Her five-foot-eleven frame she thought skinny and maladroit; her long, liquid, dark chestnut hair, formless; her eyebrows too thick, and her size seven feet out of the question; but she had been critically analysing the individual parts without ever addressing the whole. Balenciaga had no such prejudices.

She stopped the show and stole it. For the rest of their stay, she was lionised by Parisian society and the press. Paparazzi waited outside both entrances of the Ritz to record her comings and goings and, just when she thought she had escaped them, invariably a restaurant owner or shopkeeper telephoned her whereabouts so that they were waiting for her when she left.

Eileen Ford, the head of the model agency, saw her picture on a contact sheet that a photographer from French *Vogue* showed her in New York, and cabled London to offer her a job if she ever wanted to work as a model in Manhattan. The timing was propitious. The cable arrived during another tearful session with Nubar and her mother who wanted her to make her New York debut in the fall. She decided to go along with them, just to get there so that she could accept the Ford proposal and stay on and work. It was the first totally independent thing she had ever done and now, as she sped north on the A1, she wondered if it hadn't also been the last.

New York had been fun then. No one else called the tune. For the first time she had her own apartment and had decorated it herself with things that *she* liked, with money she had earned. It was that wonderful moment in life when it seems that the piper will never have to be paid. She had a date every night and could easily be in El Morocco or Le Club until four in the morning without showing or feeling the slightest fatigue at an 8 a.m. sitting the following day.

Then she had met Philip Wilmette, the acerbic New York theatre critic, and she found herself swept into a different world – his world – where she began mixing with a coterie of intellectuals and artists, and felt she was learning something and growing every day. Soon she was accepted into Wilmette's circle as a celebrity in her own right and was politely allowed to occasionally contribute to the incestuous conversation of the writers, actors and journalists. Eventually she moved in with him.

She gave up modelling, spending more time at home, but soon after discovered that he was temperamental and boorish. He despised her friends so she started seeing less of them, and then only on her own for lunch. It was two years before she realised that she had become little more than his servant and left him.

In the ensuing years, she had lived with other men, but as she sped through the green English countryside, Thea realised that *she* had always compromised, melted into their lives, adopted their friends, their likes and dislikes, as though she had no personality of her own. Only Steddy had made no such demands of her. He was socially at ease wherever he went and seemed to like to be with her because he truly enjoyed her company. He was a man of her own background – they had things in common – and at the same time a bit of a bounder. She liked that quality in him – he wouldn't allow himself to become blasé and seemed to *try* to stay on the outer edge of propriety. That was why she was in love with him.

He had mentioned marriage and even though he'd been drunk, it had started her thinking seriously about it for the first time. She felt that she needed Steddy desperately, but was it him that she needed or just someone to give form to her life? And then, she thought, if she was really in love with Steddy, why had she led Wiley on last night? She admitted to herself that she had done it on purpose, knowing that he was in love with her even though she had stopped things in time.

Well, one thing was sure. Right now Steddy needed her, and that would have to be enough for the time being. She would play out the hand.

~   ~   ~

Time did not fly swiftly for Steddy. From the very beginning of his interment, his jaw began to ache from grasping the reeds; and soon it was all he could do to fight the onslaught of claustrophobia. Under the circumstances, it was difficult to maintain shallow breathing when the capacity of the reeds was so small, and he had continually to battle the gremlin of panic in his head that kept telling him to sit up and breathe before he suffocated.

He tried to follow Bill's advice and count out the minutes in military fashion – one one-hundred, two one-hundred, but he kept losing his place when panic overrode logic, even for a second. It seemed like days since he'd heard the car's motor start and the noise that the bite of its tyres transmitted through the sand. He tried to sing in his mind to have some handle on the time that was passing, but he couldn't think of a song to save his life. He knew that all he had to do was sit up if things got really bad and he'd be able to breathe, but he *knew* in his heart that that was not truly an alternative – not now that Thea was already on her way to meet him. He couldn't put her in harm's way by leading Chelak to her.

Suddenly, he was aware of an intermittent drumming sound – nothing he could put his finger on, but it seemed to be growing louder and more regular. It might be a car driving towards him, or worse, *over* him. He was ready to use any excuse to break from his confinement and this seemed like a good one; then a great roar of thunder told him that it was rain he was hearing.

Water seeped into the hood of his slicker, into his ears and trickled down his nose, making him want to sneeze. Panic again raised its ugly head and he felt as if he was drowning. He counted to twenty-five promising himself that that would be long enough and then, when he reached it, he started over again – counting as quickly as he could, going on to fifty and starting again . . . Then he felt a sudden pressure on his feet. Someone was walking on top of him. It couldn't be one of the campers out for a stroll in the storm, he rationalised; and anyone just arriving would wait in their car until it passed.

The weight was now firmly planted on the middle of his chest, making his breathing that much more difficult. He was terrified that whoever it was would feel the rise and fall of his lungs under their feet. The reeds jammed violently into his cheek – he could taste blood in his mouth – then, as if it had never been there, the weight was gone.

It was the fear that finally calmed him. Not the illogical, panicky fear of claustrophobia, but the very real terror that Chelak might have found his hiding place . . .

Could he possibly have noticed Steddy's absence from the group in the departing car? In an attempt to focus his thoughts, Steddy tried to analyse the odds in a rational way. It worked for a time, but the crazed monkey in his mind kept surfacing, telling him that he was an ostrich with his head buried in the sand, and that the rain had washed away the rest of his covering, leaving him lying there, exposed for all who passed to see. He continued to do battle with his own wits until he could stand it no longer. Then, his decision to get up made, he counted to one hundred with deliberate, torturous slowness as Bill had taught him.

At one hundred he sat up as quickly as the encumbrances of sand and slicker would allow. The reeds fell from his mouth before he could get his arms up, and took a bit more of the tender inside of it with them. It was still raining hard and the force of the water peeled the sand-weighted handkerchief from his face. All was blackness.

A car approached, surreally silent along the meandering course of the shore road, its motor muffled by the rain's pelting wall of noise. A strobe flash of its headlights as it rounded a bend showed him that his legs were still buried and had not been exposed by the force of the water. He stood up and retrieved his duffel from where it had lain under his feet. The rain seemed to be coming from all directions now like a six-nozzle shower, and breathing was almost as difficult as it had been through the reeds. But the weight was lifted from his mind and he stood rejoicing – holding his arms heavenward as though beseeching the Deity – while the water washed the caked-on sand from the slick surface of his oilskin.

The glowing red read-out of his watch told him that he had been under for forty-five minutes. To his surprise he had exceeded his goal. He raised the duffel to his shoulder, hobbled through the darkness and sand to the road and set out down it to the south with nothing but the occasional faint glow from the well-worn dividing line to guide him.

Only one vehicle passed him in the hour and a half that it took to walk in to Stonehaven, and it turned out to be nothing more than an ancient flat-bedded truck.

It was ten-thirty. The rain had abated and the rising moon glimmered through the shredding wisps of cloud.

He waited at the edge of town until the loud boozy voices of the last people to leave the pub had ceased to echo in the empty, wet streets. As he made his way along the quay the rebellious squeals of his newly exhumed shoes were magnified by the silence of the buildings whose shadows absorbed his own.

The red telephone kiosk stood in front of him. It made him think of Edith and he realised that at that very moment Karesin was waiting for him outside the pub in Scone. Steddy was afraid to call her – the kiosk was as bright as a beacon and his whole plan depended on at least getting through Stonehaven, unnoticed. It would be the first place Chelak would look when he realised that Steddy wasn't in the car when it arrived in Aberdeen.

On the other hand, if he didn't call Edith, she'd get worried and then there was no telling what she might do.

Steddy entered the booth, uncradled the receiver and waited for the operator to come on the line. While he gave her the number, he used his cap to unscrew the bulb above him. She answered the phone on the first ring.

"Aunt Edith, it's me."

"Haven't you found Karesin? I've been waiting up for you."

"No, I'm afraid I haven't made it that far yet."

"Well how long will you be? He won't wait all night you know."

"I'm still fifty or sixty miles away – I can't make it before tomorrow."

"Well how long *will* it take you to drive here?"

"I don't have a car."

"Then how are you planning to get here?"

"It seems that I'll have to make it on foot."

"That's perfectly ridiculous – it will take you weeks!"

"I can't risk renting a car."

"Well then stay put and I'll send Karesin to fetch you in the morning."

"It won't do, Edith. I've got to get out of this neighbourhood before morning and . . ."

"Then, let's fix a place for tomorrow where you can meet. Where shall it be?"

Steddy wanted to avoid drawing any attention to himself, but the prospect of a sixty-mile hike in wet clothes was becoming less and less appealing and it was also true that the sooner he got off the road, the less exposure he'd have – there was still Scotland Yard to consider.

"Are you still there?"

"Yes, Edith. I just have to get a map out. Hang on."

He pulled the car rental map out from under his slicker and with trepidation, tightened the light bulb in order to see its contours. He was momentarily blinded and felt as though he was on display in a department store window.

"There's a town on the A94 called Brechin – looks about twenty miles from here which would put it about forty miles from you. I could make it there by about four in the afternoon."

"All right, let me get a pencil. All right now, what's it called – Blechin?"

"No, it's Brechin, B-R-E-C-H-I-N!"

"All right, Steddy, see you tomorrow . . ."

"But wait Edith . . ."

"Yes."

"How will we find each other? I don't know the town."

"Well, it can't be very big as I've never heard of it. I'll just tell him to park in the town centre – that's always marked – so you won't miss him."

"Well, then, you'd better tell him that I'll signal him to follow me until we get someplace where there aren't too many people."

"All right Steddy. Now GOODNIGHT . . . and be sure you're there on time; Karesin will have been waiting for you half the night in Scone and won't be very happy about it. You really should have called earlier; you know he's not as young as he once was."

As he left the booth, Steddy could picture her perfectly, sitting up in that enormous bed of hers, under a satin coverlet with her hair wrapped up in a turban and a book or tray across her knees. He knew there would have been little point in explaining that he would have called earlier had he not been buried alive at the time.

~ ~ ~

The car Edith sent was a custom-built, long-bodied tourer that would have turned heads in Berkeley Square; in Brechin, it dominated the centre of town and might as well have landed from outer space.

Karesin was leaning against one of the big, chrome P 100 headlamps of the forest-green motorcar wearing a beat-up pair of tweed plus fours with a khaki shirt, open at the neck. His white hair glistened in the sun as if competing with the polished metalwork of the car.

Steddy elbowed his way through the throng of admiring children and motorcar buffs until he caught Karesin's eye and cocked his head to indicate the road that led down the steep hill, out of town. Minutes later, the big car lumbered past him, until it disappeared round a bend.

They had their reunion just beyond, at a lay-by near a copse of wood.

Karesin was pretending to tinker with the motor when Steddy came abreast of him.

"Couldn't you find anything bigger in the garage?" Steddy greeted him.

"Could a done, but I thought this'un would do for you," Karesin was quick to reply.

"Guess you didn't think you'd see me again so soon," Steddy joked, alluding to his previous stay over a month before when he'd been up with Thea.

"Tell you true, I didnae think on it at all," he replied, his eyes smiling all the while. "And I'll thank you to keep your appointments in future. I had to drink in the pub till after closing last night." The smile round his eyes crept down to the corners of his mouth.

"That must have been a real hardship for you," Steddy replied, laughing.

Karesin looked him up and down, taking in his sunburnt, unshaven face, mussed hair and general dishevelment.

"You're a fair sight. What have you been up to then?"

"Got cold cocked in an Aberdeen whorehouse, haven't had a bath in four days and just walked almost thirty miles in wet clothes," Steddy said, not expecting sympathy from his old friend and not getting any.

"Do you good – want a bit of toughening up you do." Then, with a degree of concern, "Hop in the back and lie down flat before somebody comes along."

"Did Thea arrive yet?" Steddy asked before getting in.

"Not before I left. Why, was she supposed to?"

"Yes, but I don't know when."

Steddy climbed into the car's womb-like passenger compartment. The smell of the leather and wood was as reassuring as a first class ticket home, and the carpet – as thick as Devonshire cream – was the softest thing he'd lain upon since his abrupt departure from London. He opened the bar and took a swig of whisky from one of the cut crystal decanters. Karesin heard the click of the cabinet,

"Now, don't you be drinkin' up all her ladyship's whisky. Here, take this, Sook sent it to you special," he said, passing a large basket over the divider. "But don't eat and drink it all up, 'cause you'll have to stay in the car until after ten when everyone's gone to bed, and there'll be no more when that's done. And mind you don't make a mess back there, I just got through sweeping it out."

The hamper Karesin gave Steddy was wicker and inside it, wrapped in a red and white checked table cloth, were three big sandwiches – one of beef, one of ham and one of cheese – all on thick-cut homemade oatmeal bread, slathered with butter from the dairy, accompanied by two pints of beer, an orange and his favourite chocolate cake. He offered Karesin a sandwich and a beer, but he said he'd already eaten, so Steddy, famished, combined the ham and the cheese and wolfed it down, interspersed with shots of whisky from Edith's decanter, with beer as a chaser.

The alcohol and a full belly soon had their effect, and with the sun's flickering warmth through the big plate glass windows, the comfort of the carpet under him and the gentle sway of the three-ton vehicle, he was sound asleep before they had gone ten miles.

~ ~ ~

A strong beam of light awakened Steddy from a dreamless sleep that had become a torpor.

"Come on, get out of there sleeping beauty," Karesin intoned in a hoarse drill sergeant version of a stage whisper.

"Where are we, Karesin?"

"I'm at Castle Lynde, but I think you're still at the feather ball. Now wake up and get out of there – and keep your trap shut so we don't wake anyone up."

Steddy followed the puddle of light in a trance, still punchy with sleep. He could sense rather than see the cavernous dimensions of the coach house that had been his favourite place to play when visiting as a boy, and recognised the familiar smell of damp and motor oil. They made their way past ghostly silhouettes of tarpaulin-covered motor-cars, some so tall that a big man could get into the back wearing a top hat without stooping. These represented a history of the Lynde family's love affair with the automobile since its inception.

Steddy would have tripped on the cross-piece of the small door cut out of the garage's big double doors, but Karesin caught him. He heard a muffled oath and then the light was extinguished. They were out in the chill Scottish night with just enough light from the moon to guide them. The gravel of the drive gave way to a narrow stone path that cut through some hedges and then down three steps into what Steddy recognised as the kitchen garden at the side of the house. Suddenly they were in darkness again; he looked up to see the crenelated tower of the original castle's keep, blocking the moon. Karesin held his arm and guided him up the broad balustered stone stair that led to the south terrace. They crossed it and went in through an open french door into

140

the vast panelled library – part of the Georgian wing that had been added in the eighteenth century. The flashlight was on again and its beam pierced the stately gloom as Steddy followed it through an endless number of sitting rooms and picture galleries. He was beginning to think they were going in circles – crazily passing through the same rooms like a dream sequence from a Fellini movie – when they crossed a broad stone saddle and entered the heart of the house, the great hall – part of the original fifteenth-century structure.

Steddy had his bearings now, the great hall was the main entrance of the house. They had come in from the most distant point at the back, working their way through generations of additions that the centuries had piled up against the ancient tower as memorials to the changing lifestyles of the preceding earls and barons. The hall's lantern, the size of a small lift cab, was extinguished, and in the dimness of the sidelights the epic staircase elled up to the first landing and slowly vanished above them like an invitation to a lost dimension.

He followed Karesin across the many carpets scattered over the stone floor, to a large Flemish tapestry that hung in a recess under the stair. Karesin pulled on a cord behind it and the tapestry drew to one side revealing a small, very solid looking, oak door. He opened it and flipped a switch illuminating a steep spiral stair that descended into the bowels of the keep.

"You should be able to manage from here," Karesin said, handing Steddy his duffel and indicating the stair, "and turn off the stair light from the switch at the bottom."

Steddy, somewhat surprised at his rather abrupt dismissal, crouched in order to clear the low door, when Karesin stopped him.

"Well, welcome home, and I'll see you tomorrow – oh, and be sure to lock the door at the bottom behind you and don't open up for anyone, save me, Cook and her ladyship."

"Where is Aunt Edith?" Steddy asked.

"Gone to bed and she'll see you in the morning. Now get yr'self down there – y'll find it comfortable enough."

When Steddy reached the bottom of the narrow stair he turned the iron ring handle and pushed open the heavy door that was embedded in the side of the granite wall . . . Karesin's odd behaviour was immediately explained by the pervasive scent of Mitsouko that made Steddy's pulse swell, his ears ring and inspired other, equally Pavlovian manifestations.

Thea had arrived and her scent proclaimed her presence as strongly as if she were standing at the door to greet him.

Steddy threw his duffel into the room ahead of him and, when there was no exclamation of welcome, stepped anxiously across the threshold.

The apartment was not the cold, bare dungeon he had expected, but rather a warm and welcoming hideaway. The stone walls were covered in a deep scarlet felt and the wall-to-wall carpet was a cheery rendition of the Lynde family tartan. The furnishings were simple and unpretentious; a big brass bed with a fur cover, a marble-topped dresser, and a desk and two small tufted leather sofas. But there was no sign of Thea other than the lingering scent of her perfume . . .

He was about to turn and reclimb the stair to get Karesin and find her, when a door he hadn't noticed, camouflaged as it was with the same felt as the wall, opened, and she stepped into the room. The towel that she was using to dry her hair, covered her face.

Steddy's breathing stopped – he was frozen in place, watching her as she stood outside the bathroom door, bent over, rubbing her long hair between the folds of the towel. She moved towards him unwittingly, still not aware of his presence, humming the tango they had played over and over again in Paris. When Steddy could no longer keep still, he started to hum along with her, but it came out as a croak that startled her. She threw her head back – they were inches apart now and Steddy was grinning at her surprised expression.

"You bastard . . ."

"Aren't you happy to see me?" Steddy asked, hugging her tightly around the waist.

Thea held him off with both hands at his neck.

"And just how long have you been here?"

"About half an hour," Steddy lied, knowing how long it took her to wash her hair.

"Karesin was supposed to buzz me before he went to get you from the car . . ."

"When did you get here?" Steddy asked.

Her hands released his neck, but she turned her head and answered while he kissed her behind her ear.

"I drove up – arrived this afternoon." Steddy paused and looked her in the eye, his face suddenly lined with concern.

"Are you sure you weren't followed?"

"I'd just like to meet the man who could have followed me!" she answered cockily. "I'm only sorry about Wiley – I didn't even tell him. I just wanted to surprise you."

"You did darling, you did."

As they embraced, the towel fell from around her and Steddy started to edge her towards the bed.

"That's far enough, Buster," she said, grasping his ear firmly and pulling him painfully towards the bathroom. "You smell like a goat."

Still holding him by the ear, she made him take off his clothes and marched him into the shower. It was an old-fashioned one, a gazebo-like structure with fat brass pipes and nozzles pointing from every direction. He pulled her in after him in spite of her cries that she had just dried her hair, so she got back at him by scrubbing him from head to toe with a stiff Scots bristle brush until his skin tingled. Then, when he wouldn't let her out, she gave him a proper welcome until the hot water ran out.

"I've always liked a cold finish after a hot shower, but that was a bit of a letdown," he quipped.

"Well, let's just see if we can't warm you up again."

They dried each other and climbed into the big metal bed. He reached for her, but she held him back tenderly this time,

"Do you want to tell me about those bruises, first?" she asked quietly.

"Not tonight dearest, but you will be gentle with me, won't you?"

~ ~ ~

Steddy was awakened by the insistent buzzing of the intercom.

"Well, dear boy, I'm glad you decided to make it. All in one piece I trust?"

"Yes, thank you, Edith," and then looking at Thea. "Thank you for everything – say, this is really swell down here – all the comforts of home and I never knew it existed."

"That's just the point, no one does; and by the way, I'd like to keep it like that. It comes in handy once every hundred years or so."

"Don't worry Edith, we'll keep your *keep* a secret," Steddy laughed.

"Good God, levity as this hour of the morning. How revolting. Now put on some clothes and come up here – Theadora will show you the way – I've had some breakfast sent up and I'd like to have a look at you."

"OK, we'll be right along." He replaced the receiver. "Come on darling, rise and shine, breakfast is ready and Edith says you know the way."

As Steddy lay back in bed with his arms crossed behind his neck, waiting for Thea to finish in the bathroom, he wondered how he could have ever doubted the true depth of what they shared. In fact, their forced separation seemed to have brought them even closer together.

In the shower, Thea was musing much the same thing when Steddy interrupted her thoughts.

"Hey, in there, hurry up – I'm starving."

Steddy followed Thea up the same stair he had descended the night before and then up a further spiral he hadn't noticed. After opening another heavy oak door, Thea triggered a spring-loaded panel that was part of the decoration in an alcove between Edith's bedroom and boudoir. Thea motioned him to stay quietly where he was while she went ahead into Edith's bedroom to make sure that she was alone.

"Good morning Theadora. Where's Stedman?"

Steddy heard her and crossed the threshold.

"You don't look nearly as bad as Karesin said," she noted after looking him over. "Why, you've even lost your casino pallor and got some colour. I have to think this sort of thing agrees with you."

Steddy approached the substantial, canopied bed and stretched across it to kiss the cheek she proffered. Her hair was still in a turban, but lipstick and powder – the only makeup she ever wore – were already neatly applied. In spite of the early hour, her aristocratic features, combined with the elegant cut of her frogged velvet bed jacket and her impeccably varnished, bejewelled fingers, imparted the air of a formal levée, to the occasion.

"Theadora. You had best run down the hall to your room and muss the bed or the servants will think it very queer that you didn't sleep there."

"All right, Lady Lynde."

"I thought we agreed that you'd call me Edith. After all we are rather partners in crime, I suppose – thanks to this naughty fellow," she added, arching an eyebrow in Steddy's direction.

Thea left the room.

"You mean the staff know that Thea's staying here?"

"Well, of course they do. She arrived during the middle of lunch so what was I to do? Anyway, what difference does it make? They could all see that she was quite alone when she came, and no one but Cook and Karesin know that *you're* here."

"She swore that she wasn't followed, so I suppose it really doesn't matter," he replied pensively.

"Now Steddy, will you please stop playing Sherlock Holmes for a minute, or is it Professor Moriarty – I'm still not sure which role you're cast in – and explain to me exactly, what *is* going on . . ."

144

Steddy sat down at the foot of the bed and patiently told his story. Thea returned and sat quietly beside him, occasionally clarifying a point here and there about Wiley or the men at the Embassy.

"We are going to have to call Wiley," Steddy thought out loud. "He really stuck his neck out for me." Then, looking at Thea. "Well, really for both of us, and it's not fair to leave him in the dark like this without even a words of thanks."

"Well, I don't think you should call any of them. After all, why should you risk life and limb in this affair when it appears to have absolutely nothing to do with you?" Edith observed.

"I haven't said that I would help them, Aunt Edith. But I do owe Wiley at least the courtesy of telling him what I do decide."

"Steddy, now you listen to me. After all, I feel somewhat responsible to your mother while you're under my roof and . . ."

"I don't think that I could help them, even if I wanted to."

"Well, that's all the more reason to stay here where you're safe, until we can figure out a way of getting you out of here and back to America."

"I can't spend the rest of my life in your dungeon – posh though it may be – now, can I?"

"Maybe I could though . . ." Thea's voice trailed off pensively.

"Spend the rest of your life in a padded cell?" Steddy asked, amused and smiling incredulously.

"Don't be silly. Maybe I could help," she answered.

"Now *you're* being silly my girl . . ." Edith interjected, but was promptly cut off by Steddy.

"Darling, you've done enough. I will not have you getting involved any deeper in this thing. It's far too dangerous – these people aren't fooling. And in any case, I'm the one in trouble and I doubt if *I'm* going to stick my neck out any further for those bastards – so why the hell should *you?*"

"Darling, as long as you're involved, I'm involved. As long as you're in prison, I'm in prison, and you know, darling, what I said to you from the ambassador's office in London wasn't just talk . . . I really have had it. If I can't be with you, I'll be without you. But for good."

"Is that a threat? Because if it is, God damn it, I consider the threat – the very real *physical* threat that hangs over me, and thereby over you, of much greater consequence than anything . . ." Steddy was beginning to steam when Edith interrupted him.

"Children, children, be still! There can be no more question of Thea involving herself any further in this sordid business than of you carrying on with it," she said, glaring at Steddy. "You're as safe as houses right here, and here you'll stay until I can come to some arrangement with the authorities."

"Now, Edith, *that* is definitely out of the question! I don't intend to rot in an English jail until I'm sixty any more than I do in your keep . . ."

"That's just it, Steddy," Thea interrupted. "We've got to try and find Rollo and make a deal. Don't you see? It's the only way to end this. They've got you in the middle and they're not going to let you go until they're satisfied one way or another, and in spite of what you said, I think I *am* very much a part of this – and not just because I happen to love you."

"What do you mean?"

"If Rollo does have these documents and is being hidden somewhere."

"Well?" Steddy coaxed her, perplexed.

"Well if he is still alive – don't you see? There's only one person in all of England who could hide him . . ." Thea paused, her hands apart expressively, waiting for the realisation to hit Steddy.

"Nubar," he said, under his breath.

During breakfast they sat head to head, quietly discussing the new possibilities Thea had raised, while across the room Edith bantered on the telephone.

"You know I'm sure you're right, Thea. That's what Wiley said from the beginning – remember, it was just after the inquest, back at the hotel. Omar was there too," Steddy said.

"I remember, and I remember I got very huffy when Wiley suggested Nubie might have had something to do with hiding Rollo – I said that if Rollo were still alive and went to Nubie, that I was sure he'd get him the best lawyer in London and send him packing straight to the police to turn himself in."

"Well, it seems now that everybody is convinced he's still alive and if that's the case . . ."

"That points a finger straight at Nubar." Thea finished the sentence for him, looking at Steddy with a hint of satisfaction over her deduction.

"Well, I can't just call him and accuse him, can I?"

"You could, but you wouldn't get very far. On the other hand, if I called him, he wouldn't be able to wriggle out quite so easily. I've got a few things on him that he wouldn't want my mother to know about – we've never discussed it – but he knows I know."

"Thea, if he is involved in this, it's a lot more serious than a little back room slap-and-tickle. If he's involved in this, I doubt that anything you could say would get it out of him."

"You only see the suave, relaxed side of Nubie, but I assure you, beneath that well dressed, portly aplomb lies a socially insecure, quivering mass of jelly who's terrified of my mother. Once you know her, you'll find she's just the opposite; beneath her delicate exterior lies a backbone of pure iron. She can be damn tough when she wants to be, and besides that, Nubar's terrified of anything that might ruin his social ambitions; he always pays the two dollars rather than risk a confrontation that might offend a potential stepping stone on the social ladder."

"But Thea, none of that could make any difference here. This is much too serious – he could go to jail if he helped Rollo."

"Not Nubie, he'd produce banks of lawyers and psychiatrists and somehow come out smelling like a rose. He may be jelly when it comes to Mummy and an easy mark for his social pals, but he's a street fighter when he's cornered. No, you just leave Nubie to me."

Later, upon reflection, Steddy realised that that was when he lost the ball. When he'd agreed to let her *handle Nubie* he handed over the helm to Thea, and nothing would be the same afterwards.

"Handling Nubie" meant calling him, and when Steddy told her that she couldn't call from the house or it would be traced right back to them, she said she would go to Scone after lunch and place the call from there through a third party – "a friend in Paris," she said. Her enthusiasm had railroaded him, though in retrospect he wondered how he had agreed to it.

He'd gone back down to lunch alone in the "dungeon" which without Thea had lost its charm, and, apart from providing the opportunity for a reunion with Margaret, the cook, was singularly boring. Thea was forced to eat in the dining room with Edith and some of the local gentry for appearance's sake and never had a moment alone with her to tell her she was going to town. She slipped down briefly to the cellar to say goodbye before setting out to make her call and when he had objected again to her going at all, telling her that it was dangerous for her to be seen, she said that no one would be looking for her in Scotland, kissed him on the nose and merrily went on her way.

That had been hours ago and with every minute that passed, Steddy's cabin fever, after two nights in the open air, got worse.

At 5:30, he became concerned when she still hadn't returned. At six, she had been gone over three hours. Steddy put down the book he was reading and examined the intercom. The base had a row of small buttons next to corresponding, but faded, labels. He selected the top one and hoped it would ring Edith's room. She answered.

"Oh, hello Steddy! What is it?"

"Have you seen Thea?"

"No. I thought she was with you."

"No, I haven't seen her since she left."

"Left. What do you mean?"

"She went to town to make a call from a pay phone, just in case your line is tapped."

"I wish she'd told me. There's a telephone in your room left over from the war. It still works, and there's no record of it – I don't even get a bill!"

"Damn!" Steddy cursed.

"Well, it's only just six. I shouldn't be too worried. The shops are open until five-thirty and it is a twenty-minute drive. I'd give her another half hour, she might have taken a wrong turning."

"God damn it, I told her not to go, but she wouldn't listen."

"Give her half an hour more, and if she hasn't come by then, come up to my room, but buzz first in case I'm not alone."

"OK, but I'm really getting worried."

Steddy replaced the receiver and began to pace out the diagonals of the room, his athletic stride cramped to a nervous shuffle by the confines of his quarters. He was like a young lion in a small, unfamiliar cage.

At 6:30, he picked up the phone to buzz upstairs again, but there was already someone talking on the line.

". . . yes, I see. Well if you'll just drive into town and see if you can find her, Karesin – she's probably just lost her way, but she is well overdue and we're getting rather concerned."

"Yes, milady."

"Hold on there, Karesin. I'm coming with you!" Steddy cut in.

"Stedman, you know it's rude to listen in on other people's conversations. Now put . . ."

"I just picked up the phone to ring you. Karesin, wait for me, I'll be right up."

"You'll do no such thing! Karesin, get along with you. Now, Stedman, you are not going to jeopardise everything we've accomplished especially as there's every likelihood that Thea's had a flat or taken a wrong turn and will probably be home before Karesin. Now put down that phone and come upstairs where I can keep an eye on you."

He knew that she was right, but he resented it bitterly. Hadn't he said the exact same thing to Thea not four hours before? If only he hadn't indulged her!

As he mounted the stairs to Edith's apartment Stedman had to remind himself that so far *nothing* had happened.

The thought was of little comfort.

~ ~ ~

"Allo. Qui?"

"Cristina! I don't believe it. It's Thea."

"Theez-zee, darling, how wonderful! Are you in Paris?"

"No. I'm calling from . . . Well, no I'm not."

"Then you must be coming. It's been ages."

"No I'm not – not just now anyway – but I've been trying to ring you for hours. First there was no answer and then it was constantly busy . . ."

"I was talking to Gerard – he's on assignment in New York. You won't believe it, but I just gave him your number out west, he's doing a cover story for . . ."

"Cristina – I'm sorry, but I don't have much time – I need you to do me a favour."

"Anything, if I can."

"Would you ring Nubar for me in London – it's very important . . ."

"But where are you darling?"

"That doesn't matter, but there is a good reason why I can't call him myself, so if you wouldn't mind . . ."

"But are you in some kind of trouble? You know I'll do anything I can . . ."

"No, it's nothing serious – all I need you to do is call Nubar for me – here, I'll give you the number in London, it's . . ."

"I have your number in London, but what do you want me to say? He'll ask me where you are."

"He won't, because I want you to give him a message and hang up the moment you're sure he's understood it. Is that clear?"

"Yes Theez-zee, but . . ."

"Just tell him that I said to be sure to be in the office at one tomorrow. I'll call him there. Oh! And be sure . . ."

"But Thea, you are in trouble. Can't I . . ."

"Cristina, please."

"Yes, of course, darling, but please, isn't there anything I can do?"

"No, just do as I say, and I'll be eternally grateful."

"All right, but will you call me again tomorrow? I'm very worried by all this."

"I'll try, but don't worry – it's nothing serious – I just have to talk to him when I'm sure no one else will be listening in."

"If you're sure, but please try to call me tomorrow . . . I'll ring him right now and I'll keep trying until I get him."

"Thanks a million, and please don't worry about me. I'll let you know how it all turns out."

"All right, darling, but Theez-zee, please be careful."

"I will and I'll talk to you very soon."

With that, Thea broke the connection, left the booth and went to the desk to pay for the call. It was already five-thirty – Steddy would be worried – but she didn't dare call him. She collected the coins from the counter and rushed from the hotel.

The change in the weather was dramatic; only two and a half hours ago she had driven into town from the castle under a glorious blue sky – that same sky was now black as night. As she gathered her cardigan around her shoulders against the chill, a clap of thunder exploded overhead and rain started to fall – just a few drops at first, but each one would have filled a tea cup. By the time she reached her father's car where she had parked it across the square, Thea was soaked to the skin.

The old automobile was still warm inside from the sun. Even so, at first it wouldn't fire until she put aside her impatience and remembered to gently coax it to life, the way she had learned on the long drive north.

She picked her way carefully out of town – even the piercing beams of the car's powerful headlamps were of little help against the blinding rain. By the time she gained the narrow road lined with low, stone walls, that led into the valley, the rain had become so fierce that it was sheeting off the windscreen and she found she could see better with the wipers turned off. Her impatience got the better of her – she pushed the flat chrome stick shift into third and felt the big car surge forward. She knew Steddy was worried about her, but more than that she was anxious to get back to him – anxious to prove to him what she could accomplish. How clever she had been to tell Nubar to go to "the office", when no one listening in would know that that was how he always referred to the Clermont – his gambling club. Steddy would see that she was now a full partner with him in his troubles, and no longer just a soothing voice on the other end of a telephone line.

As she piloted the car into the entrance of the valley, a flash of lightning bathed it in an eerie daylight, silhouetting the craggy stone ridges against the black sky and imparting a purple phosphorescence to the heather on the moors. The strobe flashes of lightning grew closer to the thunder until they occurred simultaneously. The storm was overhead. She began singing to herself, but could barely hear her voice over its raging. She pushed the car through a bend, expertly clipping the corner when, in the next flash of lightning a grey sedan materialised directly in her path, blocking the narrow gap between the stone walls.

In the split second that fear and adrenalin stretch into a lifetime, she thought she saw a flashing light off to the side of the road, but she was only yards away and there was nothing she could do – only her natural reflexes jammed the brake pedal to the floor activating the powerful hydraulic servos. The car slewed sideways and slammed broadside into the obstruction, virtually demolishing the lesser vehicle, dragging what was left of it for yards against the stony embankment until the sparks created by their transit were doused by the rain and darkness, and the sounds of the storm were all that remained.

She never even heard the hurrying footsteps on the gravel as they approached the wreck.

~ ~ ~

Wiley and Pete Register dined early at the Connaught Grill and went to a show to take their minds off things. The chain of command from Washington had convinced Register to stay on in London for the rest of the week and await developments. Register didn't have to convince Wiley to stay – Wiley was already deeply concerned about his friend's welfare, if a little confused as to his own motives when it came to Thea. The circumstances of their last evening together at the Dorchester had become distorted in his mind over the last four days by wishful thinking, and now his handsome blond head was crowded with fantasies that were only natural but nevertheless alien to the nature of his loyalty to Steddy.

The phone rang just as he was getting into bed. It was Steddy.

"Wiley, I'm sorry I didn't call you before this, but I've been trying to sort things out for myself and . . ."

"Damn it, Steddy, do you have any idea how many people have been sitting around in London waiting for word from you – and then Thea goes and pulls a disappearing act too – makes me look like a real horse's ass and . . ."

"Wiley, hold it please – can you get up here right away?"

"Shit Steddy, you've got to be kidding. First no word for days and then you want me to meet you right away – I don't even know where you are."

"Thea's been kidnapped." Steddy had spoken very quietly, but the impact of his guilt-ridden words were not lost on Wiley, whose response was suddenly equally quiet – the quiet of a disciplined, if forced calm. "Are you sure she was kidnapped? Do you know who did it?"

"The note wasn't signed, but I'm sure it was Chelak."

"Where are you?"

"The phone's probably tapped. I'll call you in fifteen minutes where we had dinner after Wimbledon, two years ago."

"Steddy, this is no time for . . ."

There was a click and the connection was severed.

Wiley was furious that Steddy should so casually take his compliance for granted, but his concern for Thea didn't allow him the luxury of even considering an alternative.

The code they had been using – based on common memories – though lightweight, had so far served to stump Scotland Yard and was in fact as uncrackable as anything the C.I.A. had to offer. Steddy had been clever to recall that particular dinner; it had been Wiley's birthday and Steddy had taken him to the men's final at Wimbledon and invited a group of friends to celebrate afterwards at the Clermont. It had been a surprise and Steddy knew that Wiley wasn't likely to forget where it had taken place.

The Clermont was the private gaming club over Annabel's where Rockford had knocked his wife down the stairs – in fact, where the whole damn mess of the last ten days had begun. Wiley reflected on this as he walked the few blocks down Davies Street to the club in Berkeley Square. He wasn't worried about being followed – as it was a private club, anyone on his tail would have to make a hell of a stink to get in and hopefully by then he would have finished the call. Anyway, he really didn't give a damn any more.

As he entered the club's premises, the porter at the desk greeted him.

"Good evening, Mr Travis. We've just had a call for you – let me just see if it's still on the line."

The girl who answered the phones confirmed that it was.

"Shall I ask who's calling?" she said politely.

"No, that's all right, I was expecting it."

Wiley walked to the booth at the end of the hall and picked up the receiver.

"Hello."

"OK, now pay attention, because I'm only going to say this once."

Wiley said nothing. He was resolved to abdicate the direction of his actions, for the present.

"Take the 7:30 morning express from King's Cross to Edinburgh – swear you won't tell anybody . . . SWEAR . . ."

"I swear."

"And make sure you're not followed. I don't care how you do it, but be damn sure."

"OK."

"You get in at 12:34, and you'll be contacted at the station when the person who's picking you up is satisfied that you are alone – Thea's life depends on it. Please be careful."

Before Wiley could comment, the dial tone replaced Steddy's voice. He left the booth and headed for the front door. The porter interrupted his thoughts.

"You won't be gaming with us this evening, sir?"

"No, I don't think so, but on second thoughts I think I will go upstairs for a drink," Wiley said, shedding his raincoat.

He realised that he needed a few moments to collect his thoughts before launching himself headlong into he didn't know what. The small bar was empty.

"Good evening sir. Whisky and water?" The barman spoke attentively, a polished glass held poised between two fingers.

"Not tonight, George, just a Coca Cola please."

He would need to have his wits about him this night – and it promised to be a long one.

Steddy was sitting on a small satin boudoir chair, pulled alongside Edith's bed. The telephone was still balanced on his knees.

"Do you really think it was wise to have called him, Stedman? The note was very specific."

"I know, Aunt Edith, but I've got to have someone on my team who I can trust and who knows something about this murdering maniac."

"I told you that I'd be happy to call old Loxton-Peacock – he was the head of intelligence during the War; I'm sure he'd help."

"I'm sure he would," Steddy said to mollify her, "but the Americans are already deeply involved in this, so it wouldn't do any good having them against us at this point, and besides, at least *they're* not after me for murder."

"I just hope you're doing the right thing; after all Thea's life is at stake. I've grown very fond of her and I'd . . ."

"Damn it, Edith – I'm in love with her! Don't you see, this is the only way to do it? The Americans *know* what this man is after, and maybe even how to get hold of it for him – that's the only way we'll ever get Thea back. I've just got to play ball with them, there's no other way. At least with Wiley between me and them, I've got a chance to find out what they know and use it to get Thea back – damn the consequences! If I went to the British, I might end up straight in the slammer and then how could I help her? This Chelak thinks that I'm the key to something he wants – that's why he took Thea. Only Wiley and his people know what that is, so you see I really need him."

"Well there's nothing more that either of us can do tonight so you'd best be off down to bed and get some rest. I'm sure you're going to need every bit of strength you can muster before this is over – I know I've had a bit more excitement than I bargained for and I doubt if tomorrow will be any better."

Steddy warmed for a moment; Edith looked measurably older under the stark light that the bedside lamp threw into the shadowy recesses of her canopied bed. He bent over and kissed her on the cheek.

"I'm really sorry, Edith. I never wanted to get you involved in all this. I did try to warn you . . ."

"Even if I'd believed you I still would have done the same thing," she replied. And then, cheering up a bit: "Now to bed wi' ye, as Cook would say and try not to worry too much. This sort of thing just doesn't happen to nice people."

But Steddy was beginning to suspect that perhaps it did.

~ ~ ~

From the description Steddy had given him, Karesin had no trouble recognising Wiley. His height made him tower over his fellow passengers and his ash blond hair stood out like a beacon in the grey morning mist.

On Stedman's orders, he had hung back to determine if anyone displayed more than a passing interest in Wiley. Although his only training in matters clandestine still came from motion pictures, his inborn country suspicion helped him size up the various types loitering about the station, while Wiley, knowing that he would be watched, did his best to stay clear of crowds by casually wandering about looking into shop windows, studying the arrival and departure boards, buying a newspaper and finally, out of frustration, when he felt that more than enough time had elapsed, going into the railway pub and ordering a Pimm's with an extra measure of gin.

Karesin, meanwhile, decided the coast was clear and made his move to the pub. He took a stool beside Wiley and ordered a lager. After a few sips and more than a few furtive glances about, he caught Wiley off guard by almost bellowing in an untrained stage whisper. "Would you please follow me out, sir."

Wiley's surprise caused him to choke on a mouthful of Pimm's, but he recovered his equilibrium and indicated his assent by pushing some of his change on the bar towards the barman and pocketing the rest. Greatly relieved that his one line in the play had been delivered, Karesin calmly finished his beer before leading Wiley to the car park and the beat-up Land Rover that he had borrowed from the game-keeper for the mission.

The ride to the castle took an hour and a half and was conducted in sticky silence once Wiley realised that none of the answers to his questions would be forthcoming from the mute Karesin who, mindful of the responsibility of his commission, was busy watching the rear view mirror. In any case, Wiley was grateful for the opportunity to get some sleep, after having spent the entire night running around London trying to ensure that he had lost his tail.

They crossed a lake-like moat and drove through the single narrow portal into the forecourt where the dourness of the massive, worn grey stones was uncharacteristically relieved by geometric patterns of white-washed flower boxes that overflowed with multi-coloured blooms.

A signal had evidently been sent ahead from the gate-house because the front door opened at their approach and Wiley saw a tall, elegant lady in a periwinkle-blue afternoon dress, standing at the threshold, flanked by a liveried footman. He stepped from the car and she came forward to meet him, her arms extended in familiar greeting.

"Wiley, dear, I'm so glad you could come after all." And then turning to the young footman at her right: "Edward, will you see to Mr Travis's bags; he's in the Chinese Room."

Wiley was flabbergasted, having never laid eyes on this woman in his life. She held him round the shoulders and extended first her right and then her left cheek to be kissed, and dutifully, he did what was expected of him.

Karesin brought the footman up short when he approached the Land Rover.

"There's been a mix-up with the bags milady, but they'll be coming along later."

"Oh dear, what a bore for you, Wiley; still, at least you've arrived in time for a well deserved drink before lunch . . . but what am I thinking of – Karesin? I'm sure Mr Travis would like to wash after such a long time on the train. Will you show him the way, and Edward, would you fetch the drinks trolley to the terrace and bring plenty of ice for our *American* guest."

With that she turned on her heel and disappeared into the depths of the house, leaving Wiley completely in the dark and once more in the hands of his silent warder. He followed Karesin across the great hall, past the tapestry that could not be drawn in front of the other servants, up the stairs and through Edith's bedroom where he activated the panel in the boudoir and motioned Wiley to precede him through it. Wiley stopped when he saw the steep stone stair that spiralled below him.

"Listen here, Karesin, or whatever your name is, I don't have to wash up, but I do have to get some answers out of you."

Karesin's expression registered nothing, not even the slightest hint that he had even heard Wiley as he snapped the panel shut and swung the heavy inner oak door closed with a resounding clank that echoed eerily down to the bottom of the stone shaft.

"Now where's Mr Wright? These schoolboy dramatics have gone on quite long enough."

Karesin stepped ahead of him and began to descend the stair.

"Just follow me, sir – you'll find the answer to all your questions at the bottom."

From behind, Wiley could not see the effort Karesin was exerting to keep himself from roaring with laughter.

Below, Steddy had heard the door close and was waiting for them at the foot of the stair.

"God, I never thought I'd be so glad to see you," Wiley exclaimed, relief smoothing the wrinkles of concern from his face. "I was beginning to think I'd fallen in with a bunch of lunatics."

Steddy greeted him warmly, smiling for the first time since Thea had disappeared.

"Don't tell me Karesin here's been giving you a hard time?"

"Why, sir, I was just following orders – doing like you said – keeping a sharp lookout and all that." He had stopped trying to control himself and his beaming smile and twinkling eyes lighted up his whole face. Then he and Steddy exploded with laughter over how the country mouse had put one over on the city slicker, and, try as he might, Wiley was unable to keep from joining in.

Steddy finally put a stop to the merriment.

"Enough of all this. We don't have much time and there's a lot of ground to cover."

"Well I'll leave you, sirs – just be sure to show the gentleman out through her ladyship's bedroom, and mind you're not more than twenty minutes; he's expected at lunch."

Steddy gave Karesin a military salute and said:

"Yes sir, Mr Karesin. And by the way, thanks for everything."

Steddy then steered Wiley into his subterranean world and sat him down on one of the leather couches.

"Well there haven't been any new developments since I spoke to you, but here's the note that was given to the gate-keeper last night."

He handed Wiley a small, innocent looking, pale blue envelope that had typed on its face:

> Stedman Wright, Esq.
> c/o The Countess Lynde
> Castle Lynde

"It would appear that your kidnapper has a copy of Debrett's."

"Wiley, I'm worried sick – you can't imagine – when I think that I put Thea in this terrible spot. If anything happens to her, I swear . . ."

"Calm down, Steddy, and let me have a look at this note."

Steddy mixed them both a gin and tonic and handed Wiley one when he had finished reading and put down the sheet of blue paper.

"Well what do you think?" Steddy asked anxiously.

"It seems pretty straightforward, wouldn't you say? He wants the documents in exchange for Thea, and he's reminding you about Aberdeen so that you'll realise that if you don't play ball – the same thing will happen to her as did to the man in the alley."

"But how does he know that I know anything about the papers? After all, I *didn't* know anything about them until your friend briefed me the other day, and that was on that trick phone of yours that, supposedly, no one can tap."

"Well it could have been tapped at your end."

"No way. I just stepped into a pay phone at the last minute – there wouldn't have been time."

"Listen, Steddy, I don't claim to be any expert, but there are all sorts of sophisticated devices that he could have used to listen in from quite a way away. Of course, that would only allow him to hear *your* side of the conversation."

"And I wasn't doing much talking that day, just listening." Then something clicked. "But he could have heard me agree to let Thea meet me again and then have had someone follow her up here."

"That's a possibility, but if he was that close to you, he would have just followed you himself."

"Christ, no matter how you look at it, there's no one responsible for what happened to Thea but me."

"Let's not try to lay the blame – let's just figure out a way to get her back – OK? We have to assume that either he doesn't think you know exactly what he wants, or, even if you did, exactly how to get your hands on it. If he did, he would have taken *you* long ago and never bothered with Thea. For some reason, he sees you as the key to all of this – which isn't unusual because our people look at you the same way. They want to force you to do their work for them, as if they're sure you know something, even though you may not be aware of it yourself, and . . ."

"But will he honour the exchange?"

"Not if he can help it – at least not if she's seen him. Hopefully he used someone else to take her; then it wouldn't matter to him, as long as he gets what he wants. But don't worry – there are ways to make sure that both sides stick to the bargain – that's just a question of craft. The crucial thing here is, can you get your hands on the papers?"

"Wiley, be serious. How the hell would I know how to get hold of a top secret Israeli battle plan?"

"Did you tell Thea about the documents?"

"Hell, no. I never even heard of them until a few days ago. Then I didn't have time – I hardly saw her and then she was taken. Oh Jesus!"

"Calm down, Steddy. Now do you know where Rollo is?"

"Wiley, I *swear* to you that if I knew the whereabouts of that son-of-a-bitch, I'd kill him myself. Christ, after what he's put us through . . ." And then, as if what Wiley had said had only just sunk in: "You're *sure* that he's alive, aren't you?"

"No, not sure."

"Then what the hell do we do if he *is* dead?"

"It wouldn't really change things much unless we could prove that he had the file with him when he went over the cliff."

"But that's impossible without a body. The police mounted a massive search – so what hope would we have?"

"That's why we'd better just pray that he's still alive – and all my instincts tell me that he is."

"I agree. He'd never kill himself – no matter how drunk he was – not as long as there was one roll left – but how can *I* find him if nobody else can?"

"It seems the British, the Americans, the Israelis, the Palestinians and possibly even the Russians have every confidence in your ability to do just that. I even heard some talk about the Syrians: it looks like everyone else thinks you can do it."

"But that's absurd. I don't have a bloody clue. You believe me don't you?"

"I believe that you don't *think* you know where he is, but of course you haven't been trying to find him, have you? And that's what everyone was counting on."

"What the hell's that supposed to mean?"

"Look, Steddy, we're pretty sure that you were set up with that thing at Claridge's with Omar and all . . ."

"Don't tell me the goddamned C.I.A. did that to me?"

"No, no, calm down, it wasn't us . . ."

"So you admit you're C.I.A. – God, and I thought I knew you, and all the time you were a fucking spy and you never told me."

"Steddy, I *was* working for *our* country. I wasn't spying on you, and anyway I've never really been a spy – just an unpaid, glorified listening post."

"Well if the C.I.A. didn't set me up, then who the hell did?"

"We don't know, but it was probably the Israelis."

"But shit, I don't know where Rollo is! Christ, what have I got Thea into?"

"You can't blame yourself Steddy, you've been manipulated all along. The trouble is, you've been *too* resourceful."

"What do you mean?"

"Well, the way we figure it is that when they set you up, they thought that as an American in England, on your own and running in the same crowd as Rollo – you'd probably run in the same direction, but you didn't, did you?"

"Isn't that a little far-fetched – a hell of a long shot. I mean what made them so sure I'd run at all? What if I'd just turned myself in?"

"They probably would have scared the shit out of you and allowed you to escape, with the same end result."

"God, it's all so Machiavellian . . . hey, wait a minute Wiley, if I *had* turned myself in, it would have been to the police – the British police – not the Israelis!" He paused, massaging his temples with both hands, and then looked up at Wiley, questioningly.

"Wouldn't it have had to have been the Brits who set me up?"

"That's a good point. Believe me, no one has discounted the possibility that the British are behind this. It just goes to show you how desperate everyone is to get their hands on this file."

"But where the hell did they think I'd go?"

"If they knew that, we wouldn't be sitting here right now. You'd probably be off in the sun some place with Thea, and I'd be sweltering in New York, reading manuscripts and fighting my way to Long Island every Friday night."

"Stop it, Wiley! I just don't know what to do – maybe if I met this guy and told him the truth . . ."

"Do that and you're both dead."

"So, what do I do – give up?"

"Hell, no. Your Uncle Sam has a few ideas even if you don't."

"I can't take the chance. Oh God, you didn't tell them about this, did you?"

"Steddy, I gave you my word."

"Forgive me, Wiley – I'm not myself," Steddy said, cupping the palms of his hands over his eyes and then drawing them back through his hair.

"Steddy, can't you see that you have to throw in with us? Who else are you going to trust?"

"It's too risky Wiley – you read the note – they'd kill her if they knew I had anything to do with the C.I.A. Don't you give a damn about her?"

"Of course I do, but I don't think you realise what's at stake here from the various governments' points of view. You're not even a speck of dust in their eye when it comes to something as hot as this. You've got to have protection or they'll steam-roll you."

"But can't you see that that's just it? None of them – and that includes the C.I.A. – give a shit about Thea and me, and the only way I can even try to protect her is to hang onto as many cards as I can."

"Steddy," Wiley said with renewed patience. "Alone, you just don't have the means or resources to . . ."

"I've got the means, kiddo, but you've got to tell me what buttons to push – like for a start telling me what your C.I.A. pals thought I would have done."

The intercom interrupted them. It was Edith.

"Steddy, whatever can you be thinking of, keeping Wiley with you so long? The servants will think he disappeared into thin air. Get him up here at once."

Steddy mumbled a reply into the receiver and turned back to Wiley.

"You've got to get back upstairs pronto, but first tell me your theory about Rollo."

"Steddy, now it's my turn to think this one over. It's a pretty serious matter to go against the Company and take matters into my own hands – it's not like the movies you know."

"What's that supposed to mean?"

"Just that I'm going to think this one over before I decide what to do. I'll let you know after lunch."

"Is that your final word?"

"My word will be final after I've had a chance to think it over. I'm not making any more spur-of-the-moment, rash decisions, and whether you believe it or not, *I* care a great deal about Thea and yes, even you, when it comes down to that, and I won't let you bully me into doing something that in my best judgment will eventually prove harmful or even fatal to either one of you. I intend to think this one out."

"Just promise you won't do anything until we talk again after lunch – that much you owe me."

"Steddy, I'm not sure at this point that I owe you anything, but don't worry, I'll come back and tell you what I've decided."

~ ~ ~

"Actually, I've only just read the note."

Wiley was trying to control himself in the face of a barrage of questions that Edith hissed at him every time the servants left them alone for a moment on the terrace where they were having lunch.

"But surely the C.I.A. intends to take some sort of immediate action?"

Wiley was shocked. After fifteen years of perfect cover, it suddenly seemed as if the whole world knew he was C.I.A.

His answer was tentative, but when Edith snapped that if the C.I.A. didn't intend to do anything, she certainly could call on old friends in British Intelligence from the War, he quickly cautioned her that any action of that sort could put Thea and Steddy into the greatest peril.

Wiley realised that Edith would be an important ally in convincing Steddy to do the right thing and told her as much.

"He's simply got to play ball with the C.I.A. To bring in anyone else at this point could prove fatal – and as I'm *already* involved, I really don't see what difference it can make."

"But as you said yourself, the note was quite specific – and of course we're all being watched, so any more people would . . ."

"That's just it. I am here. No one else knows I have any connection with the C.I.A. – that is except for you and Steddy. I don't think Thea ever knew, although she might have guessed. You see, I can act as an intermediary so that we'll have their full support without any obvious presence. It's really the only way."

Wiley realised as he was talking that he had made his decision and that he would have to make Steddy see it his way, for everyone's sake.

"Even if he were able to get hold of what this fellow wants, without our help – which I very much doubt – the odds of his successfully completing the exchange without proper back-up are very slim. I don't think either of them would survive."

"You've convinced me, Wiley. Now let's go and convince him."

They left the table and entered the house. Edith led him upstairs to her bedroom where she locked the door and called down on the intercom for Steddy to join them.

Wiley did not hesitate to use his trump card. He blamed Steddy for leading Chelak to Thea in the first place whereas, had he let the C.I.A. take care of her in London and let them send someone else up to Scotland to handle Chelak, she wouldn't be a captive at all.

Steddy shrank visibly, suddenly realising that ninety per cent of his belligerent behaviour was due to the guilt that he felt – he wasn't being objective. At last he sat down on the sofa opposite Edith – defeated, but not ready to give in entirely.

"Well, Steddy do you agree that I can call Pete Register and put him in the picture?"

"On one condition."

"And what's that?"

"That you, and you alone, are my only direct contact with them and that you agree to stay with me at all times and make no effort to contact them other than by mutual agreement."

"Don't you think that's going to hamstring them to the point that we might as well not have them?"

"No I don't. What I *do* think is that this bloody Israeli has eyes at every point of the compass. As you pointed out, I've had some very unpleasant brushes with him, and I will not take any more chances with Thea's life if one of your cronies gets spotted contacting you or vice versa. They can keep an eye on us from a safe distance – and I mean *safe*."

It was Wiley's turn to sit down. This was turning into more than he had bargained for. He had never actively worked in the field before and while he had taken the basic training course and a refresher every year or so, he was not by any stretch of the imagination a seasoned agent. Now, if the Company agreed to Steddy's ultimatum, he would be pitted directly against one of the most ruthless operatives in the world. It would be a baptism by fire.

"Well, Wiley, wasn't that just what you wanted?" It was the first time Edith had spoken during the discussion.

"In spades, I'm afraid. In spades."

"Well, I'm glad that's settled. Now you both had better get out of here. I've got a fitting in ten minutes."

Back in his room Steddy poured a drink of whisky from the decanter on the sideboard and cocked the crystal tumbler at Wiley. Wiley didn't really feel like a drink, but he sensed the ritual and knew that it was an important unspoken gesture of the reaffirmation of their friendship. Steddy handed him the glass and poured himself one, then he flopped on the old leather chesterfield, suddenly feeling the full weight of the physical strain and emotional drain of the past weeks. It was a relief to have another shoulder to bear some of the burden.

"I guess if you're going to call them, Wiley, there's no time like the present. The phone's behind you and don't worry about it being tapped. Edith told me that it was put in during the War for some secret stuff and there's no record of it. She doesn't even get a bill. If only I had known about it before . . . Thea could have used it to call Paris and none of this would have happened."

Wiley had a sip from the glass, put it down on a table and went over to the telephone. As he picked it up he spoke softly and evenly.

"Steddy, we're doing the right thing, but in any case, I want you to know that I give you my word not to do anything without telling you first."

"Wiley, we're all in this together now. In every sense of the word – we are *trusting* each other with our lives. You're on my side now and I'm glad, it's been pretty lonely."

Wiley dialled the direct code for Washington, mulling over what Steddy had just said. The full extent of their isolation hit him like a cold shower. He felt chilled to the bone and reached for his glass of whisky.

Trained professionals exposed themselves to these sorts of risks every day for their country, but they did it by their own choice. Now he was being drawn into a deadly business by a friend, with no way of extricating himself. Was he doing it for his country or was he really doing it for himself – to fulfil his own need to prove something basic? Up until now he had allowed himself the luxury of believing that what he did for the C.I.A. was the real thing and imparted nobility and purpose to what was otherwise an unexciting superficial existence. Now, he had the feeling he was about to find the answer to a lot of questions he had avoided asking himself in the past, and he was afraid and thrilled at the same time by what he might discover.

The operator in Washington came on the line and Wiley told her his name, making use of the channel they had set up for Steddy that would raise the senior C.I.A. man on duty at the Embassy. He was not surprised when Pete Register answered on the first ring.

"I knew you'd call and it's about time too. Where the hell are you? You know these disappearing acts aren't making you very popular with the local boys – and by the way, that goes double for me."

"Listen, Pete, I'm with Steddy and there have been some new developments . . ."

"I asked you where you are."

Wiley pressed on, ignoring Register's question. "Steddy has agreed to play ball with us, but there are certain conditions."

"Do they include you not telling me where you are, 'cause if they do, I don't want to hear them."

"Pete, listen. Chelak has made his move and Steddy's just taking precautions, which might not be a bad idea in the long run."

Wiley took the silence at the other end of the line as a tacit agreement that he should continue. He started to speak, but then looked over at Steddy whose eyes were riveted on him. He made a calming gesture with his hand. He wasn't going to break his word.

"He'll go along with us, but only if I'm the sole contact with you and then only by secure phone – no direct contact with you or any other agent."

"Did you go along with this?"

"Yes. It's the only way he'll agree to cooperate, and in view of what's happened, I think he's right."

"First of all, are you saying this for his benefit, and secondly, what has happened?"

Wiley looked Steddy directly in the eye and answered.

"No I'm not saying this for his benefit, and I cannot tell you what's happened until you agree to his terms – and I want your own personal word to me on that."

Register didn't hesitate for a second.

"You've got it, but I hope you have some small conception of what you're getting yourself into."

164

"I do, but I think you had better give your word to Steddy directly. I want him to accept it personally – then I'll brief you."

"Put him on."

Steddy didn't require the double assurance and he told Wiley so, but Wiley insisted, so he took the receiver.

Register repeated himself to Steddy.

"Are you sure you really understand what you're getting yourself into without a lifeline, 'cause in case Wiley hasn't told you, he's little more than a top-secret gossip columnist!"

Steddy didn't reply.

"You still want my word of honour?"

"Yeah, and crossed fingers don't count."

Register ignored the sarcasm and gave Steddy his word. Steddy passed the phone back to Wiley who covered the mouthpiece with one hand and asked Steddy if it was all right to go ahead. Steddy nodded in the affirmative.

"Chelak's taken Thea Boulton as ransom for the plans."

"Oh that's just great. I was expecting something bad, but not this bad. God damn it! You guys are really a bunch of amateur jerks. How the hell can I help you with a thing like this with my hands tied behind my back? Don't you realise that that girl's life is at stake? Put that moronic, punch-drunk playboy friend of yours back on the line. We can't go on like this with that girl's life in danger for one more minute."

The second note from Chelak arrived by the same means, shortly after they had finished briefing Register. He had raved and ranted, but Steddy had stuck to his guns and Register had to agree in the end to play it their way as long as he was kept informed of developments on a minute to minute basis.

The note instructed Steddy to go to the ruins of the original twelfth-century castle, which was about half a mile across the estate, at the top of a hill. The meeting was called for midnight.

"I don't think you should go alone," Wiley said.

"You read the note – it was very specific."

"Nevertheless, if I'm going to be of any use I can't just sit around waiting to react only when something happens to you. It would be too late."

"That's not very encouraging."

"Maybe not, but it would be a good idea to get him used to the fact that I'll be around helping you – right from the start."

"Yeah, maybe, but I don't know how good an idea it would be at this first meeting. Seeing you might just scare him away."

"Tell him that I'm your oldest friend and that as the police are after you, you'll need someone to do the leg work for you."

"That makes sense, but I still think it's risky to take a chance on blowing the first meeting."

"Steddy, we've got to have a safety net. These people are not averse to using torture, kidnap and murder. If I'm there, or somewhere nearby, the chances of him trying to take you are at least marginally reduced."

"Maybe if you came part of the way with me and then waited where I could signal you with a flashlight if I needed you?"

"That's a good idea, but let's make it that unless you signal me to stay where I am, within say five minutes, I'll come ahead. That way I'll know that you're all right."

"OK."

"Do you know if there's a gun in this house?"

"I should think just about any kind you want. This is one of the finest shooting estates in Scotland."

They asked Karesin for a revolver and two flashlights and then Edith volunteered two of the walkie-talkies that the gamekeepers used on the estate.

"We may try to maintain the old ways here," she said, "but we don't live in the dark ages."

With forty-five minutes to kill before leaving for the rendezvous, they returned to the discussion of Rollo, Nubar and the file. It appeared from what Wiley said, that the C.I.A. had come to the same conclusion as Thea; that if Rollo was still alive, the only person who could possibly have helped him was Nubar.

"There are no two ways about it, Wiley. We'll have to get Nubar up here and put the screws on him to find out if he knows anything. The trouble is, how do we contact him? That's what Thea was trying to do when . . ." his voice broke off. "I'm sure his phone is tapped and anyway, even if we do get through to him, how can we make it seem natural for him to come up here without drawing attention to ourselves?"

"Contacting him should be no problem. That's something my people in London should be able to handle without much difficulty, but as for a reason for him to come . . ."

"I think I can provide an excellent excuse, gentlemen," Edith said. "Do you boys have any idea what the date is?"

They looked blankly at each other and then at Edith.

"Well, for your information, today is the tenth of August."

The light of comprehension still did not dawn on their faces.

"Well, if today is the tenth, in two days it will be the twelfth . . ."

There was a pause and then they both blurted out simultaneously:

"The *Glorious Twelfth!*"

"Exactly, and in case you've forgotten, the opening of the grouse season on the twelfth of August is the biggest thing that happens in Scotland every summer. It wouldn't seem the least bit out of character for someone like this Nubar – at least as you've described him to me – to come for the opening of the season. In fact if he's the sport that you say he is, it would be positively odd for him not to."

"Edith, you're a genius," Steddy exclaimed. "It's perfect, no one would give it a second thought – but have you got an open gun?"

"Of course not. What do you think, two days before the most important shoot of the year? All my guns were invited and confirmed six months ago."

"Well, but it would look odd if he came all the way up here and he couldn't shoot," Wiley said pensively.

"I'll have to give up my gun – that's all. There have never been more than nine guns on this shoot and I'm not about to change that. No, he can have my place and I'll double-bank behind someone else. I've done it before, although never on the opening day."

"But that's a terrible sacrifice for you," Steddy said.

"Don't speak of trifles. It's settled now, just be sure you can get him up here; a few of my guns are arriving tomorrow evening, so he can come as soon as you like. In fact the sooner the better – I'd like to get to know him before everyone else arrives. Does he have a wife? Oh, of course, he does – Thea's mother. Do you think he'll bring her? It would make a difference what room I put him in and with the table placement – I did them ages ago for all the meals, now of course I'll have to redo them . . ."

Steddy grinned at Edith's priorities, knowing it was just her way of hiding her excitement and the fact that she was enjoying herself tremendously.

"Wiley, we still have almost twenty minutes before we have to go, do you think you could get the ball rolling in London?"

"I don't see why not, but you realise that we're going to have to come down on him pretty hard – about Thea and all – in order to convince him to drop everything and come."

"Of course you will, there's no alternative. If he doesn't come, we've lost the whole shooting match."

Wiley got up to go to the telephone and Edith called after him:

"Don't forget to have them find out if he's bringing his wife."

The waning moon was high in the sky when Steddy and Wiley set out across the low hills to keep their rendezvous. They made their way quietly, using the flashlights from time to time to expose the gullies and deep burns that crossed their route. It was only then – trekking through the wet, fragrant gorse – that Steddy realised that he was actually about to come face to face with Chelak, his phantom. The thought was oddly comforting – he wasn't feeling brave or reckless – it was just that at last things were coming to a head, there was a plan, and he felt more in control of the course of events. Now that Wiley was with him, he couldn't imagine how he would have ever got through it on his own.

They crossed a narrow pony track and then climbed a steep rise that brought them to the ancient, rough-cut, stone road that spiralled the last hundred yards up the hill to the ruin. Steddy illuminated his watch – it was two minutes to midnight. Perhaps the dark was for his own protection; they'd told him that no one had ever seen Chelak's face and lived to describe it. He turned to Wiley and said with a note of regret:

"Well pal – I guess this is where we part company."

"OK *Bogey*, but first check that you've got your radio on stand-by." Wiley chuckled, surprised by his own levity.

Steddy felt the switch and said, "Right. Now give me ten minutes to signal you. Two flashes if you've to come up and one if you're to stay where you are."

"And if I *don't* get a signal after ten minutes I'm coming up anyway. Understood?"

"Yeah, and the radio's just in case of an emergency."

"Good luck," Wiley whispered, "and for God's sake, stay calm and don't get excited."

~ ~ ~

At half past midnight Edith was still sitting up in the library of the castle with Karesin fussing over her in order to keep her company. Wiley had told her before leaving that he doubted that Pete Register would call back before they returned, but that if he did, just to say they were unavailable for the moment and would call back as soon as possible.

In any case neither Edith nor Karesin had the least intention of going to bed before "the boys" got back.

At five minutes to one, the telephone did ring and although Karesin was first to reach it, Edith exercised her prerogative and snatched the receiver from his hand. She stood up straight, raised the instrument to her ear and in her most regal voice, that registered somewhere between Queen Mary's and Eleanor Roosevelt's, intoned, "Lady Lynde speaking. Who is that please?"

There was a moment's silence, a throat readjusting itself from the unexpected salutation and then:

"Good evening. Could I speak with Wiley Travis please?"

"Who is that speaking?"

Another pause.

"This is Peter Register, ma'am, and I hope I haven't disturbed you at this hour."

"How could you possibly disturb me when I'm staying up to see them safely home?"

"*Them*, ma'am?"

"Wiley and Stedman, of course. Somebody has to look after their welfare as it certainly doesn't appear that the C.I.A. gives a hoot!"

Register couldn't believe his ears. *How could Wiley have been so irresponsible as to confide in an old lady?* He chose to ignore her remark.

"You say they're out, ma'am?"

"That's right, they're out there in the dark meeting that horrible Israeli who kidnapped Theadora – doing your job for you, I'll wager. I think it's simply dreadful that you spies find it necessary to involve decent young girls and boys in your nefarious goings-on. Why in my day . . ."

"Excuse me, ma'am, but I don't think this sort of talk is going to help any of us just now. How long ago did they leave?"

"Didn't they tell you what they were doing when they called you about Nubar Harkonian?"

At the mention of Nubar's name, Register became apoplectic.

"Madam, you'll forgive me but I don't think any of these matters are appropriate for us to discuss. I do not know you and you have not been cleared to have knowledge of this information."

"Not cleared? Not cleared? I like that." And then aside to Karesin, "Imagine the nerve of this puppy! Young man I'll have you know . . ."

"Were you talking to someone else in the room, ma'am?"

"Certainly. My manservant, Karesin. I suppose you think that he's not cleared – you have a nerve. I'll have you know that I was given the highest security clearance in the kingdom by his majesty's Government in 1940 – why I even knew the date of the invasion before the king did, and as for Karesin, *as for Karesin*, his people have worked for my people for over three centuries and fought side by side for this country all over the world, and the only war we ever lost was for the American colonies which is evidently what's the matter with you. Not cleared, I like that! You could take a lesson or two when it comes to . . ."

Register couldn't get a word in edgeways. He was anyway mute with surprise. When at last she appeared to be running out of steam, he tried to compose himself.

"I think you can appreciate that we are not going to gain anything by continuing in this vein." He waited for another stream of invective and when it didn't come, he continued. "Now believe it or not, all of us here are vitally concerned with their safety." (Actually he was thinking that he would cheerfully shoot them if they were standing in front of him at that moment.) "And will do everything we can to help and protect them, but they must consult us before going off half-cocked, or there's nothing whatsoever we can do."

"I agree with you absolutely, of course. After all, didn't I help Wiley convince Stedman to cooperate with you in the first place?"

"I didn't know that ma'am."

"Well of course I did, and I must say I'm surprised that they didn't tell you about tonight's meeting, but they're both so worried about Theadora and, well you know, boys will be boys."

"Yes ma'am." The about-face in her attitude convinced him that she was a raving lunatic. "Now when did they leave?"

"Well the rendezvous was at twelve and it's a fifteen-minute walk from the castle – I'd say they left at 11:45, or thereabouts."

"So they've been gone for a little over an hour?"

"That's right. I'm frightfully worried, but still, what with coming and going, that's not so terribly long, do you think?"

"I don't know, but if they're not back by 1:30 – no matter what deal I made with them – I'm sending in a team."

"You'll forgive me for saying so, but don't you think that's what you should have done in the first place?"

"Would you please have Wiley call me the minute they get back?"

"Certainly. Is there a special number you'd like him to call?"

Register was now beyond anger.

"He has it. Thank you, Lady Lynde, and good night."

"Hold on a moment. What about the Harkonians?"

"Well, what about them?"

"Well, are they coming to my shoot or not?"

"Lady Lynde, the C.I.A. is *not* a social secretarial agency," and then – defeated, "but to answer your question, the baron will be arriving on his private jet at 8 a.m. tomorrow morning. I hope that will be convenient."

"It couldn't be less convenient, but we all have to do our bit don't we?"

"Yes, I guess we do."

"At least he'll be in time for the first drive, but you didn't tell me if the baroness is coming with him."

"The baroness?"

"Yes, Baroness Harkonian. I must know if she's coming – for the table placements and the rooms, don't you know."

"I'm afraid I don't know whether or not she's accompanying him."

"Well do find out and get back to me, won't you?"

Although one of the toughest negotiators in the Agency, Register knew that he had finally met his match.

~ ~ ~

Steddy knew the ruin of the old castle well. He had played there as a child with Edith's children, and, during the shooting season when the weather was fine, the shoot lunch was always laid in the lee of the towering stone wall that had once made up part of the original keep. As he carefully picked his way up the steeply winding road, he could see that wall looming above him, silhouetted against the sky like a snagged tooth jutting from the soft mossy ground.

At the top, the structure came alive and took on its own eerie character – resonating a melancholy melody orchestrated by the wind, and back-lighted by the racing moon that cast it in deep undulating shadow one moment and pitch blackness the next.

He crossed the great worn stone that had once been the threshold to the castle's interior, and his flashlight's beam picked up the charred indentation of the hearth, directly opposite. He advanced halfway towards it and then pivoted slowly, shining his light on the low, decaying walls that defined the perimeter.

The woody timbre of the voice when it came was so thoroughly in harmony with the windsong that Steddy wasn't startled by it. He merely continued to scan the ruin, seeking the source of the disembodied words.

"You will not find me in the light of your torch." The voice spoke in clear, distinct English without the slighest trace of any accent, although the use of the word torch instead of flashlight told Steddy instinctively that the man's training had been British.

"Before we come to the business in hand, would you kindly explain why you disregarded my instruction to come alone?"

Steddy hadn't expected the question so soon.

"Let's just say he's my oldest friend in the world and likely to be concerned if I disappeared. I also thought that in case I get picked up by Scotland Yard, it would be a good idea for you to have somebody else to deal with so that we can still get Thea back safely."

"I have no desire to harm anybody."

"I don't know what it is you want. If it's money – I have quite a lot of cash . . ."

"I am well aware of how much cash you have, Mr Wright. If I had wanted money, I would have taken it in Aberdeen. You forget that it is only thanks to me that you still have your money not to mention your life."

"So it *is* you I have to thank for that?"

"Don't mention it . . ."

"I suppose I also have to thank you for the mess I'm in. Why did you murder Omar and pin it on me?"

"Alas, that was not me, Mr Wright. A very messy business, not at all my style. I think you will have to blame that one on your friends, the British. Not so civilised as they like one to think, are they Mr Wright?"

"But none of this makes any sense. Why would they go to such lengths to frame me? And if you don't want money, what do you want? I don't understand any of this."

"Your friend, Lord Rockford, has what we *all* want."

"But he's dead."

"That is doubtful."

"If you don't want Wiley to come up, I'll have to signal him now. He may already be on his way."

"Then by all means do so, and take your time, Mr Wright. We have plenty of time . . . tonight."

Steddy retraced his footsteps over the threshold to the edge of the track and signalled down in the general direction of the spot where he and Wiley had parted. There was no answering flash, so he signalled again and this time got a reply right away, but from much closer up the path than where he had left him. *He's already started up*, Steddy thought, as he turned back to the ruin, glad he had caught Wiley in time.

172

"Mr Wright," the voice seemed to be coming from the chimney. "If you will just shine your light to the right of where you are standing, you will find a snapshot that I'm sure will be of interest to you."

Steddy aimed the beam in the direction Chelak had indicated and almost at once the light picked up the glint of the photo against the dull mossy stone. It was a Polaroid of Thea.

"When you get back, you will be able to compare the London *Times* that Miss Boulton is holding in the photograph with yesterday's edition. (It's now past midnight.) You will find they are the same, but don't conclude that the photo was taken in London, or even England for that matter – as you know, *The Times* is sold the same day, all over Europe."

Steddy stared at the picture of Thea under the flashlight. She was sitting upright in a chair, her long hair, untypically, covering one side of her unsmiling face. *How strange it is that the more one loves someone, the more impossible it becomes to conjure up their features from memory,* he thought, *and how appropriately, ghoulishly ironic if this picture were to become the only image he would ever have to remember her by.*

"Come come, Mr Wright. Let's get on with this. The picture is yours to keep."

"But what will happen to Thea if Rockford *is* dead?"

"I have told you that Rockford is not dead. He contacted someone after the time that he was supposed to have thrown himself into the sea."

"Well, wouldn't whoever he contacted be better able to find him than I? I don't have the slightest idea where he is."

"I'm afraid that the only person we know he contacted was the man you so blithely threw from the window of your hotel room, which should prove to you that I had nothing to do with his demise."

"I have his notebook – it's in Arabic or something, but maybe it could tell you something."

"I had an opportunity to look that over in Aberdeen as well. There was nothing in it of any value, although Lord Rockford appears to have been in greater debt to him than I had supposed."

The sound of the wind through the ruin increased to a howl and brought with it big drops of water. Steddy became impatient.

"Look here, the only thing I'm interested in is getting Thea back safely, as soon as possible. Now suppose I *am* able to locate Rockford – what then?"

"You have but to tell me where he is and once we have recovered what is ours, Miss Boulton will be returned to you."

Here Wiley had coached Steddy very thoroughly and he was grateful that he was prepared.

"I'm afraid I couldn't agree to that. How could I be sure that you would return her once you had what you wanted? No, we would have to work out some sort of exchange."

"I commend you on your prudence Mr Wright. I am sure we could work something out provided you can obtain what we want."

"And what *is it* that you want? If Rockford is alive, I'm not going to turn him over to you so that you can do to him what you did to that man in Aberdeen."

"I told you I have no interest in harming anyone, all we want is what is ours. Lord Rockford has certain documents in his possession that are rightfully the property of my government. They are in a yellow envelope which is sealed with sealing wax. Identifying marks are stamped into the seals. The envelope must be returned to me with the seals intact – or Miss Boulton's life will be forfeit."

"But what if they've already been broken?"

"I do not believe Lord Rockford would have done that as their value would be lost if they were opened."

The rain was pelting Steddy in earnest now.

"Well, I'd better get to it then," he said, wanting to bring this interview to a close. "How will I contact you when I learn something?"

"You cannot. I will contact you. We will meet here tomorrow night at the same time."

"But what if I discover something and have to leave to find him before then? I don't want you to think that I ran out on you."

"That would be most unwise – for Miss Boulton's sake."

"That's just what I meant. Will you be nearby the whole time?"

"I think you can appreciate that I have no intention of answering a question like that. But you will be watched, if that's what you mean."

"No, it's not that. It's these walkie talkies; we can make contact in case of emergency." Stedman wrestled the unit from under his jacket and held it up by the flashlight. "The keepers use these on the estate; they have a very long range because there are booster antennae all over. I think they're good for about ten miles and they're synthesised so we can set them to work on whatever frequency you like."

"You are full of surprises, aren't you, Mr Wright?"

"Just being prudent as you said before. Wiley has the other one and if you pick a frequency – I could leave this one here for you and match the setting on Wiley's."

Steddy stood in the driving rain for some minutes before Chelak answered.

"What frequency is it set on now?"

Steddy examined the digital readout of the synthesiser as Karesin had shown him.

"It's set at 440.050, for Wiley and me. We changed it from 440.025, which is the frequency the estate uses."

"Then leave it as it is and place it where you found the picture."

Steddy walked back to the wall and placed the transmitter under the stone shelf.

"Now, Mr Wright, we shall maintain a radio watch . . . shall we say for fifteen minutes every two hours, starting at 8 a.m.? If you have a message, transmit at those times and you will be contacted."

"That will be fine with me, and if anything goes wrong with the radios, I'll be here at the same time tomorrow."

"Then good night, Mr Wright."

Steddy stood still for a moment, but there was no further sound save the wind reclaiming the ruin.

The Glorious Twelfth

It was precisely 8.00 a.m. when the tiny wheels of the white Mystère alighted on the tarmac of the small airstrip outside Perth. The cabin door containing the stair opened as the jet came to a halt. Karesin drove the lumbering old shooting brake onto the apron and parked alongside the aircraft. Nubar was out of the plane with Elizabeth hurrying to keep up with him before the steward had a chance to secure the hand-rail.

Harkonian neither waited for Elizabeth nor acknowledged Karesin who held the Bentley's weather-beaten wooden door for him as he climbed in – he was obviously in no mood to display the courtesy people thought was second nature to him. He sat in the back, fists clenched and face like a thundercloud, oblivious of the activity around him as Elizabeth entered the car, and two small cases were placed in the rear compartment by the steward. When the car had gained the main road back to Scone, Karesin addressed him.

"Her Ladyship's compliments, sir, and I was to tell you that the party was gathering in the forecourt at 9:30."

"Party? Party? What party?" Harkonian appeared to have been awakened from a dream, and the trace of an accent suddenly tinged his normally flawless English.

"Why, the shooting party, sir," Karesin replied.

"Shooting party? Are you mad? I've come all the way up here to see Mr Wright on very urgent business." And then, genuinely confused, he asked, "Isn't that where you're taking us?"

"Yes sir."

"Then what's all this about a shooting party? Is this some sort of a joke? Because if it is you can turn . . ."

"No sir, it's just that her Ladyship thought it would be safer for you to meet during the shoot – what with all the guests about the castle."

Nubar was fuming. "This is preposterous and who is this lady anyway?"

"Countess Lynde, sir, and I think it would be best if her Ladyship explained everything to you when we get to the castle."

Edith was in the hall greeting and directing arriving guests either to their rooms, if they were staying the night, or into the dining hall where

176

an enormous shoot breakfast had been laid. She was prepared for the Harkonians when they appeared; she was getting quite used to treating perfect strangers as long lost friends, and had no trouble recognising them in their fashionable town clothes in contrast to the comfortably worn country tweeds of her other "guns".

"My dears!" she exclaimed, walking forward to meet them as they entered the hall. "I'm so glad you could make it. It's been an age," she gushed, kissing Elizabeth on both cheeks. "Let me take you to your rooms so you can get changed."

Noting their puzzled expressions and to avoid any embarrassing questions, she took hold of Elizabeth's elbow with a force that was surprising in a woman of her years and directed her in a no-nonsense manner towards the stair – presenting them to a royal duke and a newspaper tycoon on the way.

"I can't think why you've stayed away so long," she could still be heard cooing from below as they ascended the great stair.

The obvious importance of the castle and of the position that his hostess appeared to command in the social order of things helped to calm the troubled waters of Nubar's temper, for though he loomed large in the power structure of Europe's financial capitals, and moved with ease amongst a glamorous circle of friends, he was a snob and the smell of old *titled* money and the opportunity to shoot at the elbow of a royal duke was still the stuff that filled his fantasies. Edith had a gut understanding of his weakness and intended to exercise the full weight of her privilege to force his hand.

"I do hope you'll be comfortable in these rooms. They were the king and queen's favourites – they used them quite a lot during the War."

The sitting room she had shown them into was circular with the palest blue and white panelling that fused with the Scottish sky through the big curved windows overlooking the park.

"The bedroom is through there," she gestured to where a footman had disappeared with their cases.

"Oh it's splendid, isn't it Nubar?" Elizabeth replied with genuine admiration.

"Yes dear, and the countess seems to have tamed the Scottish climate."

"I wish I could take credit for the weather, but if I could, fine days like these wouldn't be so few and far between."

The footmen bowed their way out of the room and closed the door. Edith turned to the Harkonians in earnest.

"I apologise for the sham performance, but it would seem awfully

177

odd to everyone if I invited *total strangers* to shoot on the most important day of the year."

Edith's manipulation of Nubar was artful. In one sentence she had taken him on as an intimate, a confidant, and a co-conspirator, while in the next breath she had put him in his place – clearly beneath hers. But Elizabeth Harkonian could no longer restrain herself, her face revealed the undeniable strain she was under.

"Countess, we were told rather brutally by a perfect stranger using Stedman Wright's name, that my daughter had been kidnapped, was in grave danger and that only by coming here could we help her, but now it appears that Steddy and Thea have been playing a very ugly joke at our expense, and that we've really been brought here for a shooting party – I assure you we would have been delighted to come without these melodramatic cloak and dagger shenanigans and . . ."

Edith warmed to Elizabeth, and admired her bluntness.

"My dear, I wish I could put your mind at ease; I've become very fond of Theadora while she's been with us and I can't tell you how worried we all are."

Elizabeth's eyes grew larger and glistened. She seemed visibly to shrink under her cape as she crumpled into the overstuffed chair by the chimney that made her look even smaller and more vulnerable. Edith sat on the arm of the chair and took her hand.

"Now my dear, tears won't . . ."

Nubar strode over to them; his wife's distress had galvanised him into action.

"This whole thing is absurd. I demand to know exactly what's going on."

There was a knock at the door – Edith was glad of an excuse to ignore Harkonian's rude remark.

"Come," she ordered sharply.

Karesin entered the room having changed back into the charcoal grey jacket he wore in the house.

"Yes Karesin, what is it?"

He eyed the Harkonians suspiciously, hesitant to speak in their presence.

"Come, come, what is it?" she repeated.

"There's a gentleman from the police to see you, milady."

"Can't you see this is no time to entertain the local constabulary? Send him away."

"But milady, he's not a local. The only thing Scottish about him is that he's from Scotland Yard! He asked for Mr Wright."

"God, it must be that awful Also, or whatever his name is," Harkonian interrupted.

"Allsloe, I believe sir," Karesin replied, proffering a card. Harkonian groaned.

"What did you tell him?" Edith asked.

"I said that we didn't know a Mr Wright, and then he said Stedman Wright. Well I said we knew him, right enough, but that we hadn't seen him in some time. Well, milady, then he asked to see you, or if you weren't available Mr Travis. Everyone in the hall was getting curious like, so I put him in the library and came up to fetch you, milady."

"You did the right thing Karesin, now go back down and tell him I'll be along directly." Edith spoke nervously now, glancing at the clock on the chimney. "We've never started a shoot a minute late and I am determined that today will *not* be the first time. I had better go down and see to this policeman."

"Would you like me to come with you?" Nubar volunteered without enthusiasm.

"No thank you. Why don't you both relax for a bit and I'll let you . . ."

"But what about Thea?" Elizabeth exclaimed. "And where's Steddy? Is it true he's not here?"

"My dear, I will send Steddy to you the moment I've got rid of this Scotland Yard man. Now do try to calm yourself and order some tea." She pulled the bell cord for a maid as she left the room.

Wiley was waiting for her on the landing.

"I gather that bloody Allsloe is here."

"Yes, I'm just going down to see him. They must have followed you when you came up."

"I really don't think so," Wiley defended himself, "but they seem to know that Steddy's here as well."

"I think he's bluffing; otherwise they would have paid us a visit long before now. Now you go through to my room and tell Steddy that the Harkonians have arrived but that he has got to stay hidden until the inspector goes – and make sure no one sees you."

"Will do."

They parted to carry out their individual missions.

Edith was surprised by the appearance of the person she found waiting in the library, for the man whose dull gaze greeted her as she entered the room was certainly not in the mould of a chief inspector of Scotland Yard, at least not in the mould cast by her imagination.

Here was a simple gentleman, not undistinguished, with thinning ginger hair and startlingly red bushy eyebrows that could have marked him as a Scot. His clothes didn't give him away either. Wearing a well-worn tweed suit and clean unpolished brogues, he could have been one of her guests for the shoot, or at the very least one of her gentlemen tenant farmers.

Comfortable was the only description she could think of – he did look rather comfortable – like almost any one of her old friends.

She straightened her back and approached him to introduce herself as one of the footmen in the hall closed the door behind her. She had the oddest feeling that she was intruding on *him* in *his* library – she forced it from her mind.

"I'm Lady Lynde, how may I help you?"

"Good morning Lady Lynde, I'm Inspector . . ."

"Yes I know," she interrupted him, holding his card out for him to see. "Can't whatever it is wait till another day? It is the twelfth of August, my shoot starts in twenty minutes – and as you can see I haven't dressed yet."

"I'm sorry to incommode you and don't wish to make you late, but I'm here on a very grave matter."

"Have no fear of making me late. I don't intend to allow it. This shoot has never begun late in over a hundred years and today will be no exception."

"If you'll just take me to see Mr Wright, then you can get on with your shooting – you certainly have a lovely day for it."

"My man told me you were looking for Mr Wright, and that he told you he is not here. I'll save you the trouble of asking again for Miss Boulton – she is not here either." Edith felt better that at least half of what she had told him was the truth.

"I may as well tell you now that I have a search warrant."

"And how could that possibly affect what I say?"

"Let's leave that for the moment . . ."

"Yes let's do that," she said – her tone chastising him for questioning her veracity. He seemed not to notice.

"And Mr Wiley Travis is not here either?"

"Mr Travis is one of my guests. Would you like to see him?"

"That would be most helpful."

Edith started towards the door. "I'll have Karesin try to find him for you, but now I really must change. Will you look after yourself till he comes? There are some books over there that might interest you – my husband collected mysteries." And then at the door: "Would you like some coffee?"

"That would be very nice, thank you."

"I'll look in on you before we leave." She closed the door behind her, gave instructions about the inspector's coffee and hurried up the stairs with Karesin at her heels.

Karesin had trouble keeping up with Edith as she swept up, her peignoir trailing behind her.

"I want them all out of the house Karesin – do you hear me? I will not be caught out lying to the police – and can you imagine the cheek – bringing a search warrant!"

"Yes, milady."

"Now go down to Steddy and get him into some clothes so he looks like a loader – he can load for Harkonian. I'll go and get them into something suitable for the field."

They reached the top of the landing,

"And be quick about it." Then, as an afterthought: "And *damn!* You had better get one of the men to set back the courtyard clock a half hour and be sure no one sees him. I will not start this shoot late."

She charged into the Harkonians' living room without knocking and found them in the same positions as when she had left them.

"Now there is very little time and you must do exactly as I say. I'm arranging for you to meet with Steddy, but that policeman has had the nerve to bring a search warrant and I can't have him find you and Steddy in the house, especially as you say he knows who you are. Now please follow me."

She wheeled and left the room before they had a chance to question her and followed her down the hall to where a small mahogany door led off a vestibule. She addressed Nubar over her shoulder as she opened the door.

"This was my late husband's dressing room; he was about your size and you will find everything you need to wear in the field in the cupboards."

"Not this bloody shooting again. Can't you see my wife is half mad from all these charades?"

"Please do as I say. There is no time to explain except to say that Steddy will be your loader and you'll have plenty of time between drives to talk in complete privacy. You can shoot, can't you?"

"Yes, of course I can shoot, but . . ."

"Then please be quick getting dressed – here, wear this." She threw a tweed suit from one of the cupboards at him and said to Elizabeth: "You come with me."

Elizabeth walked meekly behind her through a connecting door into

Edith's adjacent dressing room where her clothes were laid out on a chaise and her maid was awaiting her.

"Harriet, I shall dress myself. You help the baroness find a skirt and a sweater and some more appropriate shoes; if she can't wear mine, get her some wellies from the boot room, but do hurry."

There was a knock from the wall behind her that hid the secret door to the keep. Young Harriet, her lady's maid, looked very puzzled.

Edith barked at her, "Go on, quick, quick, down to the boot room with you." Harriet scurried from the room, totally confused but too frightened to question her mistress's orders. When Edith heard the bedroom door close behind her maid, she exhaled a deep sigh.

"Oh God, what can it be now?" Elizabeth watched her in total bewilderment as she sprung open the panel to reveal a red-faced out of breath, Wiley Travis.

"I hope I did the right thing coming this way, but Karesin told me that Allsloe is still in the hall."

"Not in the hall, but in the library waiting for you."

"You can't be serious, what did you tell him?"

"Aside from perjuring myself left, right, and centre, the only true thing I told him was that you were here – not that he didn't know already."

"But what shall I say to him?"

"Frankly, Wiley, I don't give a damn! I've got a shoot to run. You're C.I.A., I'm sure you'll think of something, but he seems to have an awful lot to say himself. Why don't you just try listening to him?"

Nubar came in through the adjoining door without knocking and immediately spotted Wiley.

"Wiley! What do you know about all this? No one else here has managed to tell us anything."

"Wiley has to go straight down to the inspector before he comes looking for him, and if you don't mind, you're in a lady's boudoir and most unwelcome. We'll fetch you when we're dressed which will never happen if you don't both leave – *now!*"

Karesin was rehearsing Steddy in his duties as a loader while he dressed him in an odd assortment of borrowed tweeds, worn tattersall shirt and wool tie. Fortunately, with plus fours there was no need to make allowances for Steddy's height – they simply became plus twos. Steddy was a little put out at Karesin's patronising attitude.

"You know very well that I had to load for my father for years before I was ever allowed to shoot," he said, defending himself.

"That's not to say you remember. We can't have that foreigner shooting up the local gentry on the first day out – give the shoot a bad name."

"Don't worry, I'll keep an eye on him. He's a pretty good shot, but I'm not sure if he's ever killed grouse before."

"If he's never shot grouse it might as well be the first time he ever shot a gun as you well know – still, I drew a pair of Bosses from the gun room for him – Kinear has them, he'll give them to you in the courtyard."

"I guess I'll have to go out with the rest of the loaders and the beaters?" Steddy asked.

"You'll be going with the other loaders and Duncan – he's one of the new underkeepers, old Will's boy – you'll remember him. The beaters are long gone – they have to get on the ground early, they're beating the tops at Buchowrie for the first drive, but you'll know some of the loaders. I told Kinear to tell them not to let on to their guns that they know you – said you were playing a practical joke on the foreigner."

"They must have thought that was a little odd?"

"When it comes to foreigners, they don't think anything's odd – they're all good chaps. They'll play along with it."

Karesin sneaked Steddy out to the courtyard through the kitchens, where everyone was in such a flurry of activity getting breakfast out and preparing the lunch to be served in the field, that no one gave him a second glance.

Kinear, the head keeper, gave Steddy as big a hello as a Scotsman ever does and handed him the pair of Bosses in their sleeves and the cartridge bags he would need. The last to arrive, Steddy was piled into the back of a long-wheelbase Land Rover with the other eight loaders. He sat next to Duncan, who had often loaded for him over the years.

"We heard you were having a bit of sport at a foreigner's expense. Must be an important fellow for her Ladyship to give up her gun on the first day." The first part of the charade had begun.

~ ~ ~

Nubar and Elizabeth were at Edith's heels when she corrected the duke who suggested that they were starting a bit late and took him by the arm to lead the party out to the courtyard. He changed his watch when he saw that the clock over the stables read 9:25. She took a small, worn leather slip-case from the pocket of her tweed jacket. It held the nine numbered ivory counters that would be drawn for position.

"All right, everybody, please draw a number." The nine men who were shooting crowded round her and drew one of the small staves from the pocket that concealed its number.

"We'll be shooting Buchowrie for the first drive – they're beating the tops now. There's a lot of canny old cocks up there that I want killed, so let's see your best shooting. Oh, and for those of you who've never shot with me before – please advance two numbers after each drive. We'll have three drives before lunch and two after – now who's drawn five?" The duke raised his hand.

"Oh grand Beaky, you've got the hot seat – now do your best – those old birds played havoc with my breeding this spring."

"I'll try not to let any of them by, old girl."

Edith had kept her thumb over the end counter till everyone had drawn but Nubar and then offered it to him. It was number nine and for the first drive, it would be the last butt at the top of the ridge – where he could do the least harm and would have the fewest shots.

Karesin held the door of the tan Bentley shooting brake open for his mistress, and at precisely 9:30 she and her guests got into the two matching vehicles that would take them out on the moors.

Elizabeth was sitting in the back seat of Edith's car between Nubar and the duke.

"Has your husband done much grouse shooting?" the duke asked with a royal mixture of genuine curiosity, courtesy, and enthusiasm.

Nubar answered for himself.

"No sir. I've never killed grouse before, but I do a fair amount of shooting – mostly in Austria and Czechoslovakia."

"I used to shoot in Czechoslovakia every year with my cousin, till those damn reds finally got the better of me. But I believe you know my cousin Ferdinand – he's spoken of you often – says your woods are riddled with game."

"Yes, of course, sir – the prince comes to shoot with me frequently in Austria."

"Well, grouse shouldn't give you too much trouble – they're a lot faster than pheasant but there isn't much wind this early in the season. Now you've really got to watch these old birds on the first drive, though – they haven't lived this long because they're stupid and they'll jink if they spot you. The best advice I can give you is to keep as still as possible and take your time." He then turned to Elizabeth. "Well,

Baroness, you're in for a treat. Edith doesn't usually allow observers in the butts – you must be greatly in her favour."

"I've always wanted to see a grouse shoot," she replied, somewhat unenthusiastically.

"Just remember to get right down behind the wall and stay down if you feel you're being peppered – you'll be all right."

"Thank you for the advice, sir. I'll certainly heed it. I'm only staying out for the first drive, but I'll join you in the field for lunch later."

"That will be a great pleasure," he said, smiling warmly at her. He than asked Nubar: "What number did you draw?"

"Nine."

"Well, that's good for your first time out. You won't get much action, but at least you'll get a chance to get the hang of it – couldn't be more perfect if it was planned that way."

It was a beautiful day and the drive across the moor – purple with heather and dotted with sparkling burns and streams – was exhilarating.

After about fifteen minutes, Karesin pulled the car up alongside some scrub and pinewood where the pony men in kilts held their animals, laden with large panniers to hold the bag after the drive. The loaders were already at their butts as Kinear, the head keeper, had radioed the draw ahead.

Everyone regrouped by the cars and Edith turned to speak to Nubar.

"Baron, you had better start hiking. It's a long steep climb and you'll need a few minutes' rest before the drive reaches us. Freddie, will you show them the way – you're number eight aren't you?" The last sentence was addressed to a tall man of about sixty called Colonel Blake-Williams.

The red-faced colonel jovially took them both in hand and led them over the plank bridge across the deep burn that ran alongside the road. They followed the rude stony path cut through the heather and bracken, and climbed the steep hill to the ridge at the top – passing the eight other butts along the way and listening to the colonel's shooting stories. He was a neighbour and had shot every opening day since the War, and had, it appeared, a tale for each butt. He wished them good luck as he joined his loader in number eight and they continued the gruelling climb till they reached number nine which was dug into a hollow below the ridge and, like the other butts, built of stones and sods. A grim-faced Steddy, looking very much the local, awaited them.

~ ~ ~

Wiley had little choice but to follow Edith's orders and present himself to the inspector in the library. He still had no idea what to say when he arrived and shut the door behind him. Allsloe was standing across the room looking out of the window.

"Hello, Inspector. What brings you to Scotland?" Wiley spoke with all the nonchalance he could muster.

Allsloe replied without turning. "Mr Travis, you know very well why I'm here, and as time is not on our side, I think nothing will be gained by beating about the bush." He slowly wheeled to face Wiley.

"I know that Stedman Wright is here with you and I know that Miss Boulton is missing." He paused for effect, but the gaze that Wiley returned was as blank as his own. He continued.

"Please bring Mr Wright to me immediately – nothing will be gained by searching the house and disturbing Lady Lynde any further."

Wiley was shocked to hear that Allsloe knew about Thea. *Where was the leak?* he thought, but his face remained devoid of emotion.

"I'm afraid I don't know what you mean."

"That simply won't do, Mr Travis. I have the authority to take you all into custody if you don't cooperate – and that includes Lady Lynde and all her influential guests if need be. Think of the scandal! Now once more, where is Mr Wright?"

"I can honestly say that he's not here," Wiley said, still trying to stall.

"Look here, young man, I know that you're doing what you think is right, but you have no idea of the gravity – life-threatening gravity – of the situation in which Miss Boulton and the rest of you have become involved."

"I only know that none of this would have happened in the first place if you hadn't set Steddy up and then pinned the Arab's murder on him."

Now it was Allsloe's turn to be taken aback, but ever the professional, he did not allow his surprise to show.

"Whatever do you mean?" he asked quietly.

"You know very well that you arranged the Arab's assassination in Steddy's room, hoping that Steddy would run and lead you to Rockford." Wiley realised that in mentioning Rockford he had probably said too much and silently cursed himself.

"Now where would you get an idea like that?" Allsloe parried, feeling for firmer ground.

Wiley decided on his tactic: his best defence would be a good offence.

"Look here, Inspector, I thought you said that there wasn't any more time left for playing games?"

"So I did."

"Well, then why don't you play straight with us and we'll play straight with you, but just remember that *our* only interest is in getting Thea back safely and putting an end to this whole mess."

"And what makes you think that my motives differ from yours?"

"Because you're after White Star, and don't give a damn about Thea or any of us for that matter."

He had said it and felt better for it, even though he knew it meant his head back in Washington.

"Maybe we had better sit down," Allsloe said, looking suddenly very tired.

~ ~ ~

At Buchowrie, the first drive, Steddy and his fellow loaders waited where the narrow road cut the line of butts between numbers one and two. Numbers two to nine crossed the moor and were staggered in a straight line up the steep rise that defined it, carefully placed under the stony striated terraces that faced the drive, to a point just below the top of the ridge. Each of the men carried a matched pair of twelve-gauge guns that were the product of Britain's finest gunsmiths. They leaned them casually in their protective sleeves against the low stone wall that separated the road from the deep burn while they waited until Donald, the underkeeper, got their butt assignments over the walkie-talkie from Kinear who was still at the castle.

Steddy had the longest climb to reach the number nine position, so he and the loader for number eight, set out first to allow plenty of time for the ascent. One of their duties was to see that the keepers had put the butts back in good order after the winter. If they weren't it was their job to police them so that all would be in readiness for the guns when they arrived.

Steddy had yet to decide how to handle Nubar – so much had transpired that morning, especially with the inspector showing up, that he just had not had time to compose his thoughts. He bid his companion good luck when they passed number eight and concentrated on climbing the treacherous stony track to number nine.

When he reached it, he leaned the pair of Bosses against the front wall of the butt, put his cartridge bags on the low seat in the corner that was fashioned of sods, and began to even out the top of the front wall with extra sods of peat that were left for that purpose. As he laboured, his thoughts turned to what he would say to Nubar. No one really knew for a fact that he *was* hiding Rollo, and from what Wiley had told him, it seemed that even the C.I.A. was only guessing – just as all their friends in London were guessing – nobody really knew anything; Nubar was simply the prime candidate, the only one in their group with the means to have helped Rollo, had he wanted to. Steddy knew Nubar would have helped Rollo if he could, he always had – at least with money . . . But then there was this other thing that complicated matters – White Star. It seemed as if everyone knew about the documents. But did Nubar?

Nubar would never let himself get involved in anything like that; he valued his British passport and his growing position in the establishment too much ever to take such a chance. He even bragged that he was proud to pay his taxes, Steddy reasoned . . . Unless, of course, Rollo had something on Nubar and was using it – something that was so damning it would finish him in England . . .

The sun was hot and he was perspiring in his tweeds as he bent to the work of arranging the sods around the butt. Below him, he could just make out the shooting party setting out across the moor, and Steddy redoubled his effort to psyche himself up for the confrontation. If he showed that he doubted Nubar's involvement for a moment, he'd never get anything out of him. *Of course, there was more than mere gossip; there were a lot of very serious people who believed that Rollo was still alive. The Israelis had even gone so far as to kidnap an American in Britain, and the C.I.A. were also operating clandestinely under the nose of a friendly power. What about them? What about the British? It seemed almost a fact that they were the ones who set me up in the first place, maybe they knew something that the others didn't; after all they had been responsible for the operation to find Rollo's body. Maybe they knew for a fact that he wasn't dead and were withholding the information to keep the others off the track.*

He shook his head hard, as if to clear his mind of all the convoluted possibilities, and took his position in the butt to await Nubar's arrival. He was no longer mesmerised by the beauty of the day and the glory of the moor, but once again, fully a part of the nightmare he'd been living – grimly determined to make an end of it today – to clear away the smoke, find Thea and get her back – whatever it took.

It was a grimly resolved countenance that greeted Nubar and Elizabeth when they reached the top of a great flat stone and saw Steddy slightly below them through the opening of the butt.

Nubar slipped on the weather-polished surface and almost tumbled headlong into the enclosure, while Elizabeth gingerly picked her way around it and entered the butt, composed and frowning in the bright sunshine. Nubar was winded from the climb and tossed the cartridge bags to the floor so that he could collapse on the sod bench and catch his breath. Elizabeth started to question Steddy almost immediately, but Nubar, still unable to speak, flagged at her with his hand to be quiet until he was ready.

"I'm very grateful that you could come so quickly," Steddy said, looking at Elizabeth.

"We had no choice – the way that man spoke to us," Elizabeth said.

"I'm sorry if he was rough, but I assure you it . . ."

Nubar interrupted. "Where is Thea?" he gasped.

"She's been kidnapped by a foreign agent," Steddy replied, not sure how much detail he should go into.

It was Elizabeth's turn to gasp. "But what do you mean? Why should a foreign . . . ?"

"Leave this to me," Nubar snapped, recovering somewhat from his exertion, but still not enough to rise to his feet.

"She's *my* daughter," Elizabeth protested, unwilling to be brushed aside so casually.

"And haven't I looked after her as though she were my own since she was a teenager? Leave this for Steddy and me to handle." Turning to Steddy, Nubar said: "Now tell me exactly what has happened. How much money does he want and when and where does he want it?"

"It isn't a question of money . . ."

"Not money. But then what *can* he want?"

"He wants a certain top secret document that Rollo got hold of before he disappeared."

"Rollo! Rollo is dead, god-dammit!"

"American, British and Israeli intelligence don't agree with you," Steddy answered, watching Nubar's face intently for any sign of reaction.

"Well, then, why don't they find him if it's so important? What could Thea possibly have to do with this – she hardly even knew Rollo?"

Suddenly Steddy's course of action became clear. He wondered that it had eluded him before. He had to play out the bluff.

"They know that you're hiding him and I've been elected to play middle man in the exchange," Steddy lied bluntly.

Nubar's face became livid.

"That's preposterous!" The 'r' rolled slightly as he spoke – a sure sign that he was nervous. "I haven't any idea where he is!"

"Then you admit that he's still alive?" Steddy pressed.

"Of course I don't – I thought he was dead, as everybody else did,"

Nubar answered, now clearly on the defensive. "And I don't know *now*, that he isn't," he added, regaining some control and standing up straight, albeit still leaning against the front wall of the butt.

Behind Nubar, on a distant ridge, Steddy saw a flash of crimson and white sparkling in the sun. One of the beater's flags, he thought. Nubar turned round to see what had captured Steddy's interest.

"It's the drive," Steddy said, and as he spoke, they could just hear the far-off calling of the beaters and the whacks of their sticks against the heather and bracken, echoing hollowly in the valley. Methodically, Steddy broke and loaded the pair of Bosses and leaned them back against the butt. "The birds won't be coming for a while yet, but keep well down so they don't spot you."

"Fuck the birds!" Elizabeth Harkonian shouted, abandoning her usual lady-like demeanour. "What about *my daughter*?"

"He will kill her unless he gets the documents. And if Nubar doesn't tell us how to find Rollo, we've got no chance at all," Steddy replied, as though he had heard none of Nubar's denials.

A small flight of birds had risen, flown towards the centre of the line and then landed in the heavy cover of the moor, beyond the effective range of the middle guns. Nubar watched them settle and then turned back to Steddy.

"You have evidently not understood a word I've been saying," he said, his composure now fully regained. "I know nothing more about Rollo than you do. Now let's leave that and discuss what measures we can take to get Thea back. Have you *tried* offering him money?"

The noise of the beaters became louder and now all the ghillies' flags could be seen describing a horseshoe far in front of the line – driving the grouse up and over the batteries to their natural alighting ground that lay behind them. There was a crack from one of the guns below them. "Here they come," Steddy said softly, handing Nubar one of the guns. "Now keep a sharp look-out. It we get any up here, they'll be crossing fast in front of you – trying to double back to the higher ground at the tops where they like to hide. Keep very still – they can spot movement long before they're in range."

Once Steddy had Nubar in position, he crouched behind him, holding the number two gun ready to pass to him when both barrels of the first were expended. While they waited, Steddy answered Nubar's question. He spoke very quietly, whether in deference of the birds or the gravity of the subject, one couldn't tell, but Elizabeth could hear clearly what he said over the sporadic, distant popping of gunfire.

"Believe me, I tried offering him money. He wants the documents and if he doesn't get them, he *will* kill her. It isn't an empty threat. I have personally witnessed him dispatch one of his previous victims. According to the C.I.A., he's the most ruthless operative in the Western world and I don't intend to stand by and watch Thea become another page in his Agency dossier."

Nubar neither moved, nor said a word. For all the world he was intently watching for birds. Suddenly there were three coming quickly towards them with the wind at their tails. "Someone down the line must have poked at them and made them jink," Steddy whispered. An old cock was in the lead, hugging the rippling terrain, with the other two lagging behind.

"Take the first with one barrel – shoot well ahead of him, then I'll pass you a full gun so you can get the other two with a right and a left."

Nubar killed the first one stone dead in the air and exchanged guns with Steddy rather smoothly, considering they had never worked as a team before. The second two, either spotting their movement or seeing the first bird fall in front of them, jinked into the wind as if to alight and almost floated in place, right in front of Nubar's gun. He took them easily with a right and a left, just as Steddy had orchestrated.

When Steddy moved to exchange the now empty gun that Nubar held for the one that he had freshly loaded, it was wrenched from his hands, but not by Nubar – by Elizabeth.

Her face was a frightening mask of hatred as she jammed the gun into the small of Nubar's back and held him thus against the front wall of the butt. The birds were in full flight now and the noise from the guns, up and down the line, was terrific.

"You loathsome coward!" she seethed. "You are going to tell Steddy where to find Rollo and you're going to tell him right this minute . . ."

"But dearest, I haven't the slightest . . ."

"I said right this minute," she repeated, twisting the barrel of the gun and working it down his spine so that there was never any lack of pressure against him. There was no reaction from Nubar.

"No one will give it a second thought," she said, jamming the barrel into him and twisting it. "Just another shooting accident, and what's more common on a grouse moor? Why I don't even think your loader will say anything other than it was an accident, will you Steddy?"

Steddy was more shocked by the loathing he saw in her face than by what she was about to do to Nubar. In a way, he admired her. She turned out to have more balls than either of them and, if she had her way with the gun, Nubar would be out of the competition. Steddy could never have carried the bluff this far without knowing for sure that Nubar *did* know where Rollo was.

"No," he answered.

Elizabeth renewed her invective.

"You rotten bastard! Using me and my family as social stepping-stones for your pompous, inflated ego, and now when my daughter needs you – when *I* need you – putting your twopenny social fantasies before *us*."

She turned to Steddy, and said almost conventionally: "Yesterday he bragged to me that after only five years on the waiting list, his name would come up on the list for White's. Who the hell do you think put him up? My uncle – that's who!" Turning back to Nubar: "A member of White's, ha! If you don't help us now, when I get finished with you, you'll be lucky if they let you into the men's room at the Royal Automobile Club!" She prodded again with the gun barrel until it was firmly lodged between his legs. "I have just removed the safety. And by God, Nubar, I'll shoot!"

"All right, all right. I'll tell you." Evidently the threat of losing his member worried him more than the thought of losing his long-awaited membership to White's, Steddy thought, suddenly full of contempt for Nubar.

"I didn't know anything about all this, but I would have handled it myself – got the papers back and worked out the transfer without you knowing a thing about it. I was simply trying to help an old friend; I would never have involved you in any of this, had I known . . . but how could I?"

"Oh, shut up, and tell Steddy where he is," Elizabeth snapped, still white with rage and racked with trembling, but holding the gun as firmly as ever.

He looked at her over his shoulder, his flabby jowls twisted by his position and the tight collar of the shirt Edith had lent him, and blubbered.

"He's in the Vumba."

"Vumba?" she roared back.

"Where's the hell's that?" Steddy asked as he took the gun from Elizabeth's shaking hands and reset the safety.

"It's on the border of Rhodesia and Mozambique."

"You mean Zimbabwe?" Steddy asked.

"That's right, Zimbabwe." Nubar was facing them now, his face running with perspiration. "Near a town called Umtali."

"Is it *in* Zimbabwe or in Mozambique?" Steddy asked.

"Zimbabwe. I own a coffee plantation there. Had it since the War. It was the idea of an old war buddy of mine who was from Rhodesia. He saved my life in Sicily when we were there with Monty – so I bought it for him to manage."

"No wonder no one could find him," Steddy said. "But how did you get him . . . ?" His words were interrupted by the nearing whistles of the pick-up boys working their dogs. None of them had noticed that the firing had long since stopped.

Steddy walked out on the moor and retrieved the three grouse Nubar had killed and placed them outside the butt where they would be found. Then he reached into one of the cartridge bags and withdrew the walkie-talkie. He and Wiley had set a pair of them on yet a third channel so that Wiley could warn him if there was trouble.

"Is that you Steddy?" Wiley answered the bleep of his machine that was on stand-by.

"It's me all right and we've found out everything we need to know. We're coming in right away – be prepared to travel."

"I'm afraid I've got a surprise for you too, old boy."

"What's the matter, should I stay away?" Steddy asked, his elation transformed to concern.

"No, come ahead as quick as you can. Over and out."

They followed the track down the steep incline, passing the pony men with their charges whose panniers were bursting with grouse. It wasn't necessary to make excuses when they reached the group already gathered at the road. Edith saw the state Elizabeth was in.

"My dear, whatever is the matter?" she asked.

Nubar, in full control of himself once again, said that she had been taken ill and that the sooner they got her home the better.

They piled into the waiting brake after brief goodbyes and a royal expression of concern and with a knowing wink from Karesin, were soon on their way back to the castle.

~ ~ ~

Steddy got back to the house and learned that Wiley had come clean with Allsloe. In the deal they had struck, Allsloe had agreed to withdraw all his men, save for Peter Holbrook who would stay as liaison. But Steddy's news that Rollo was in Africa set off a new round of negotiations with Allsloe and Holbrook conferring in the library while Wiley filled in Register by telephone. Register blew his top when he heard what had transpired, but eventually agreed that there was little else that Wiley could have done under the circumstances, and announced that he would fly up immediately.

The two men – Allsloe and Register – met later at the castle. No accusations of improprieties were made at the meeting by either party – too many rules had been broken by both sides to make it worthwhile.

The Harkonians kept to the bargain that Steddy had sworn them to and refused to reveal the exact location of Rollo's hideout to either Register or Allsloe. This was the only leverage Steddy had – the only way he could stay in the picture – the only way he could protect Thea's safety. He hadn't even told Wiley. The two department heads had balked, but they had little choice other than to let Steddy and Wiley handle the exchange.

They were all convened in the study when Steddy made his next scheduled radio contact with Chelak. He called for a meeting in an hour at the old keep. Steddy set out for the rendezvous, leaving Wiley behind to work out the details of their trip.

Elizabeth insisted they use Nubar's plane to save time and a chastened Nubar instructed the pilot to be ready for take-off at four p.m. Steddy didn't get back until much later. Chelak had kept him waiting a considerable time after he dropped the bomb that Rollo was in Africa. He evidently had to consult with others before consenting to Steddy's making the trip and outlining his own terms and conditions.

It was six in the evening when *Flying Cloud* touched down to refuel and discharge passengers at the private terminal outside Dublin. The plane would follow a flight plan not unlike the one it had flown just a fortnight before when Lord Rockford had been the sole passenger. The Harkonians left the plane in Dublin after Elizabeth had wished them a strained farewell and Nubar had once again pleaded his innocence of any knowledge of top-secret documents. Stedman and Wiley stayed on board during the refuelling. This was only the first leg of the long flight to Zimbabwe.

To the Bridge

Flying Cloud was still the crack ship that Steddy recalled from his two previous flights, but absent were the stewards and the crisp linen, the crystal and the smoked salmon, the old port and the waft of Havanas. She was stripped to her bare essentials to increase her range. Her only crew was Jellicoe, the same pilot who had flown Rollo out to Africa, one of Nubar's most trusted employees; he would have to handle the entire fourteen-hour flight, including paperwork and refuelling, unassisted.

When the aircraft reached its cruising altitude after take-off from Dublin, Wiley could no longer contain himself.

"Well, what the hell did the bastard say?"

"Which particular bastard do you mean? We're involved with quite a few on this outing – Register, Allsloe, Nubar . . ."

"Cut it out Steddy – you know I meant Chelak."

Steddy dropped the sarcasm. "He said that we were to go to the Victoria Falls Hotel when we had the documents and he would contact us there and that that's where the transfer would take place."

"Victoria Falls, is that in Zimbabwe?"

"How do I know? I've never been there – he wasn't exactly overflowing with information. I just listened and agreed."

"Well is it near where Rollo's hiding?"

"Wiley, I don't know where it is. I only know that he's as anxious to get the papers as we are to get Thea, so I imagine it shouldn't be too hard to find. It's one of the wonders of the world, and if Stanley or Livingstone found it, I guess we can, too. With a little help from our pilot friend. What did Register say?"

"He was furious that I wouldn't tell him where Rockford was hiding out."

"Didn't you tell him you didn't know?"

"Yeah, but after everything that's happened, you don't really think he believed me?"

Steddy unfastened his seat belt and got up to make them a drink.

"Might as well relax, it's gonna be a long flight." He poured out two whiskys from the spare remains of the drinks cabinet, added some ice and a little water and handed one to Wiley as he sank back into the deep leather club chair. "So what did he say when he calmed down?"

"He didn't calm down, but he did say that they'd fly someone in from Johannesburg to back us up – he'll contact us at Miekles Hotel in Harare tomorrow."

"That's effing marvellous, now we not only have to contend with Scotland Yard – or whoever the hell those fucking Brits really are – but we've got the C.I.A. to look out for as well. How the hell are we gonna shake an army like that and get to Rockford without them following us? Answer me that."

"Nubar said his friend would fly down in a plane and pick us up."

"Don't you think they have planes too? Didn't the C.I.A. teach you anything?"

"Hey Steddy. This set-up was your idea! Maybe you should have listened to Pete and played ball with the Company."

"Keep your shirt on and start thinking damn it – we're gonna have to lose them somehow. And fast."

After a few more drinks they slept and weren't even aware of the stopover in Rome. Steddy no longer had any qualms about his passport giving him away – anyone looking for him had already found him.

At ten in the morning, local time, they landed in Nairobi to refuel and were forced by the authorities to alight and wait in a minuscule, fly-filled unairconditioned transit lounge. There the politely curious Air Kenya people who ran it plied them with warm orange squash, and the heat of Africa suddenly enveloped them in its breathless embrace.

When the procedure took overlong and the pilot reported that they would not be able to take off until after lunch – a delay of almost four hours – Steddy became suspicious.

"Well, do you think it's the long arm of Uncle Sam, John Bull or a vengeful God who's engineered this convenient delay to catch up with us?" he asked Wiley, not really interested in the answer.

"You could be right, but they do break for lunch in countries like this. You know only 'Mad dogs and Englishmen . . .'" He stopped when he saw that Steddy wasn't paying attention, but had drifted off to where he had spotted an attractive stewardess and was attempting to charm her into getting him a large gin and tonic.

"Preferably *with* ice, but without will do . . ."

When finally the plane was allowed to depart, he bade goodbye to the stewardess who had only too happily been his supplier and promised to call her when next he passed through. Given the circumstances of their trip, Wiley found Steddy's attitude too cavalier for his liking.

*

Tired of Wiley's occasional disapproving glances, Steddy took the co-pilot's seat during take-off while Wiley rummaged in the space-age galley and somehow managed to produce a pot of black coffee to keep the pilot awake and Steddy flying straight and level.

Harare appeared at first as a lavender-blue cloud floating over the verdant plateau that stretched before them. As they flew closer they realised that the cloud was actually acres and acres of flowering jacaranda trees that lined the avenues of the residential section of the city, but by then the glass and granite skyscrapers of the modern African city beyond, dominated the horizon.

Customs was a breeze – the former Rhodesians seemed anxious to make a good impression on wealthy visitors with private planes, and as they had virtually no luggage, they were soon in a tiny cab speeding down the broad Samora Machel Avenue towards the centre of town.

Steddy had never before got off a plane and had the pilot ask if he wanted him to wait, but he was too tired to savour the new experience and merely told him to check into Miekles when he had secured the plane.

It was six o'clock when they pulled up in front of the legendary hotel – so far, nothing seemed like Africa – it was all too tame and civilised.

They ordered two double rooms for themselves and one for the pilot – handed in their passports and filled in the forms while an attractive, tall redhead, dressed and coiffed in a style that hadn't been seen in Europe or the States since the sixties, extolled the virtues of the five bars and the pool on the roof. Steddy perked up when he heard about the pool.

"That's exactly what I need – how about you Wiley?"

"Yeah, sure, but I wonder if there's any place we could buy some clothes. I don't think tweeds were really designed for the African bush?"

"There's quite a good men's shop across the lobby sir," the girl at the desk said, "but you'll have to hurry, it will be closing soon." She spoke with the curious formality that colonials impart to their mother tongue in an effort to get it right.

They bought a few shirts, trousers and swimsuits, Steddy dug into his money belt to pay for it all. When they parted in the corridor by their rooms, they agreed to meet at the pool half an hour later – at least for the moment, nothing seemed more important.

The hotel had three wings. The oldest had replaced the original structure that dated from the founding of Salisbury when Mr Miekles had manned the supply wagon of the Pioneer Column – Cecil Rhodes's private army that claimed the rich land for Queen and Empire. The second section had been built in the thirties and connected the oldest wing with the hotel's most modern wing, where Steddy's and Wiley's rooms were located. It had been completed just prior to independence and was handsomely constructed of rich Rhodesian woods, granite and marble that European technology had fashioned to offer every modern convenience.

Wiley found Steddy already wet from the pool, sprawled on a chaise on the roof of the new wing. It was open to the air and incongruously built of white marble to resemble a colonnaded Roman pavilion and had breathtaking views of Salisbury's plain. As he approached, a black servant, uniformed in white and wearing a fez, brought Steddy a long drink that looked as though a bush of mint was growing from it. Steddy looked up and noticed Wiley as he signed the chit.

"Could you bring another for the gentleman, please," he instructed the waiter. "Wiley, this is really a paradise – I can't imagine that there was ever any trouble here – no wonder Ian Smith held out for so long."

"Steddy, don't you think we should make some plans . . .?"

"Not a word until you've had a swim and a Mizilkasi or Kamakasi – whatever this is called," he said, holding up his drink. "I've already done some thinking . . . but have a swim and clear away the trip first – we can't do anything till tomorrow anyway."

Whether out of inclination, resignation or frustration, Wiley complied and jumped into the pool.

"We're going to have to hang on to *Flying Cloud* for a bit, I think," Steddy said after waiting for Wiley to settle down in the chaise next to him and watching him take a sip from his drink.

"I heard you say that to Jellicoe at the airport, but I don't remember that being part of the deal."

"I couldn't care less – as long as Jellicoe seems willing to go along with us. Anyway, he has to stay at least a day after that flight. I'm shot and *I* slept most of the way down."

"But we're supposed to call Nubar's friend to pick us up in his plane."

"I already told you – that's O. U. T. – out! Especially now that we lost our lead with that convenient delay in Nairobi. I checked, and the flight from London got in at 8:45 this morning, eight hours before we did, and there are lots of ways to connect through Johannesburg from anywhere in Europe or the States. We can't risk being followed to Rollo – they'd snatch White Star and we'd have no insurance that we'd get Thea back once they had what they wanted. I don't trust any of them!"

"So you want to use *Flying Cloud* to get us up there?"

"Jellicoe flew Rollo in in the first place – he must know the procedure."

"But no one was following him then. If they're really tailing us, they can track us on radar or just get our destination from the flight plan. I'm sure we'd have to file one before take-off."

"I don't know, but there must be some way to fiddle it. We'll have to level with Jellicoe – I'm sure he'll help. He's a good guy."

"Yeah, but don't forget he's Nubar's man first and foremost."

"And don't forget that Thea is Nubar's daughter – for all intents and purposes. I know Jellicoe will help us – I had a long talk with him while you were sleeping between Rome and Nairobi and . . ."

"Did he say he'd do it?"

"Hold on – I didn't ask him – we were in good shape with the time then. As it stands now, I'll bet that if we called the estate, before we even hung up the phone, one of those bastards would be on his way up there and pinch Rollo before Nubar's friend, this Bentley fellow, could even gets his plane warmed up."

"Well then what *did* he say?"

"Nothing in particular, only that he started as a bush pilot in Australia and then came to Europe with Quantas. He got into some sort of a jam and they fired him – he didn't say what – that's when Nubar hired him, and I get the feeling that he'd do anything for Nubar. He's devoted . . . Well, speak of the devil. We were just talking about you. Come and sit down and let us buy you a very well earned drink!"

Peter Jellicoe, a stocky, sandy-haired, athletic fellow who normally looked younger than his forty years, now looked every bit his age, after fourteen hours of straight flying and God knows how many hours without sleep. He hadn't even gone to his room when he checked in, but simply taken his swimsuit from his bag and come straight to the roof. In spite of his fatigue, he greeted them with a broad smile that showed up dozens of white lines in his deeply tanned and weathered face.

"See you chaps have the right idea," he said. "Don't mind telling you I wouldn't like to repeat that trip for at least twenty-four hours. Guess I'm not as young as I used to be. Ten years ago, I could have flown twice that long and still hit the town when I landed."

Steddy summoned the waiter.

"Have one of these won't you? Don't know what they're called, but they do work wonders on the old . . ."

"Just a lager if you don't mind," he said before jumping in the water.

199

While Jellicoe was in the pool, a banging gong called Wiley's attention to a young page carrying a blackboard with his name written on it. There was a phone call for him.

"Probably the C.I.A.," Steddy said. "They're so discreet."

Wiley took the call in his room and by the time he returned to the roof, Steddy had already laid out their problem to Jellicoe.

"So you see, anything you can do would be greatly appreciated." Then both men waited anxiously for the pilot's reply.

"I only flew Lord Rockford to Salisbury. Colonel Bentley picked him up in the Cessna. There is a grass strip on the property, though. I flew the boss up there once in a rented Twin Beech – but it isn't exactly a jet strip. Oh, it would probably do for length, but did you ever happen to notice the size of the nose wheel on *Flying Cloud*?"

"Very small, isn't it?"

"Small isn't the word! It'd suit a pram sooner than a jet aircraft – one good-sized gopher-hole would flip her."

"What about the airport in Umtali?" Wiley interjected.

"That's no good," Steddy answered. "A foreign jet drops out of the blue, and the first thing they'd do is get Salisbury on the radio."

"Wouldn't they pick us up on radar, even if we landed on the property?" Wiley pressed.

"That can be finessed," Jellicoe said. "Radar isn't exactly the all-seeing-genie it's cracked up to be. Sure, if you're looking for something to happen, you'll see it when it does, but a lot can happen on a radar screen without anyone noticing it. Those mountains in the Vumba are very steep and crowded together – so if you fly low, between them, the radar can't pick you up."

"You mean we could land at the plantation without being monitored?" Steddy asked.

"Theoretically. Of course, it would be better if we flew out to sea, beyond the range of their radar and then came back in low – trouble is that would mean crossing Mozambique air space unannounced – and with what's been going on there, we could get shot down."

"That sounds a little too risky. We don't want to start a war," Steddy commented.

"Listen, why don't you guys leave the flying to me – that's what I get paid to do."

"You mean you'll do it?"

"Hell, why not?"

"What about the wheel?"

"That Mystère's very sensitive to the controls. If the wind is steady and not gusting across the strip, I can keep her nose up almost until we stop . . . So when do we leave?"

Steddy looked at Wiley for his accord and when he got the nod, said: "First thing in the morning?"

"OK by me," Wiley said.

"What's first thing to you?" Jellicoe asked.

"About six."

"Suits me," Jellicoe said. "I'd better get back out to the airport and file a flight plan so we don't have any delays in the morning."

"Won't that be like announcing in advance where we're going?" Wiley asked.

"Yeah," Steddy said. "How do we do that without giving away the whole thing?"

"I told you to leave it to me, but what I'll probably do is file a flight plan for Durban or some town down the coast – I've got to check my maps first, but if I leave it till the morning, there's no way of telling how long we'll get held up."

"OK, you're the boss. Will you have dinner with us when you get back?"

"Thanks, but if I'm going to get any sleep at all, I'd better spend the night on board."

"You sure?" Wiley asked.

"Yeah, I need the sleep a lot more than three or four trips to and from the airport. Right," he said, standing. "Then I'll see you gents in the morning."

"OK, and thanks again. We both really appreciate what you're doing." They both stood and shook hands with him. When he'd gone, Steddy asked Wiley:

"Who was that on the phone?"

"'Fraid you were right."

"You mean it was the C.I.A?"

Wiley nodded bashfully in the affirmative.

"Good God – no wonder we lost Iran."

"I told him we'd meet him in the bar at seven."

"Will he be wearing a white sports coat and a pink carnation?"

"No, but you're close – a bush-jacket and a black moustache."

"That would just about describe half the people I saw in the lobby."

"Somehow, I don't think we'll have any trouble recognising him," Wiley said, grinning conspiratorially.

~ ~ ~

They hadn't needed the chloroform they had brought with them when they'd taken Thea – she was still unconscious. They had a back-up vehicle to replace the one that had been demolished, or Karesin would have come upon them when he went looking for Thea. As it was they'd just had time to use the other car to push the combined wrecks into the deep burn that ran parallel to the road and loosely replace the piled stones where the crash had pierced the wall. The rain took care of the rest.

Though her breathing was laboured, Thea was uninjured apart from a bruised eye. She had started to come to as they drove from the scene, which was when she had started fighting like a lioness, and when they had administered the first sedative by injection.

The first thing that she was truly conscious of was a sloe-eyed woman wearing glasses, who force-fed her coffee and gave her a capsule to swallow. Within half an hour, she was alert, aware of her surroundings, and mad as hell.

Periodically a gruff, moustachioed man with a gun stuffed into the top of his trousers would open the door and survey the scene as if checking on her jailer.

The room she found herself in was decorated in a feminine, French style. The walls were covered in pale pink toile de jouey that matched the curtains, and the bed was recessed in an alcove. The sloe-eyed woman was sitting at her side.

When she spoke, it was with a French accent.

"We will take a plane trip in a few hours. You must be awake and cooperate if you wish to see your friends again."

"Where are we?" Thea demanded, sitting up and for the first time feeling the pain in her chest where she had smashed into the steering column.

"That is not important, nor do you need to know who we are or why you are here. All you need to know is that if you behave yourself, there will be no trouble and you will be back with your friends in a few days. The tablet you just took was an amphetamine to counteract the sedative we have been giving you."

"I'm not going anywhere with you until you tell me where you're taking me!" Thea's voice rose, full of pent-up frustration.

"We are meeting your friends. If they keep their part of the bargain, you will be reunited with them in a few days. Do not worry – you are so pretty, I am sure that they would do nothing to endanger your life. Now please get up – we have to get you dressed."

Her head was awake – she wanted to strike out at her captors and escape – but her legs hadn't got the message yet.

"I have to go to the bathroom," she snarled.

"But of course – only please leave the door open." The woman nodded her head towards the man who had re-entered the room. "My friend would not like it if I leave you alone," she said sweetly; her sloe eyes, behind thick *Coca Cola* bottle lenses, told a different story.

Defiantly, Thea tried to pull the door closed behind her, but the burly guard who reeked of stale perspiration, forced it open, jamming her against the wall. She stood there wavering on her weakened legs until – at a signal from her wardress – he withdrew. When she had finished, the woman pointed at a chair in the corner.

"I have laid out some clothes for you to wear; they will be more suitable for the trip than what you had on when you came to us. But first, as you are not willing to cooperate, you must use this."

She unsnapped a small plastic case like a thermometer box and took out what looked like a tampon. She held it out to Thea.

"What is it?" Thea asked.

"It is like the Tampax, for the period."

"But I don't need one," Thea protested, still a little groggy and confused by the suggestion.

"It is not a *request*. You will use it or my friend will insert it for you."

"But I . . ."

"I will call him now?" she asked with the sweet manner she had used before – like a stage maid in a French farce.

Thea shook her head, took the small cotton-wrapped tampon from her and turned towards the bathroom.

"No, no – you will do it here – in front of me so that I can see that it is done correctly."

She sat on the bench by the bed and inserted the tampon. The string, she noticed, felt stiff and wiry. When she had finished to her keeper's satisfaction, she asked:

"But I don't understand? Why . . .?"

"If you had been nice with us it would not be necessary. But nothing in your behaviour indicates that we can trust you. So we have to take this small precaution." The woman spoke softly, just a sadistic smile played across her features – and sent a chill down Thea's spine. "It contains an explosive charge that can be detonated from this transmitter." She held up a small object that looked like a cigarette lighter and withdrew a two-inch aerial from the top. "It is a precaution that you cooperate while we are travelling. It would be most unpleasant – but I'm sure you will cause no trouble now – No?"

Thea shivered and slowly nodded her head. For the first time since her ambush she feared that she might not get out of this alive.

~ ~ ~

Flying Cloud took off at dawn as scheduled. Steddy and Wiley had arrived ten minutes before after slipping out of the hotel unseen, crossing the diagonal paths of Cecil Square, that were laid out in the pattern of the Union Jack, and making their way north by a circuitous route to the Monomatapa Hotel on Samora Machel Avenue where they found a taxi. It was still dark and, as far as they could tell, no one was following them. By the time they reached the airport, the great African sun was well above the horizon.

"Is this going to be a one-cigarette flight or do I have time to log a few Zees?" Steddy asked Jellicoe when they had levelled off.

"Normally, you'd barely have time to light up, but the route *we're* flying, I'd say you could have a good hour's kip – that is, if you don't mind missing the fun during the last half hour or so."

"Dare I ask where you've logged us to?"

"Antananarivo."

"Say again?"

"It's the capital of Madagascar – never been there?" he asked facetiously.

"Madagascar!" Wiley piped in from the co-pilot's seat. He had just removed the headset he was using to listen in to the tower.

"Don't get excited, we're not going there – but filing that as our flight plan puts us far enough out to sea to drop off both the Zimbabwe and Mozambique radars, without anyone noticing or caring."

"What then – or do I really want to know?" Steddy asked.

"We develop a little *trouble* with the cabin pressure, drop down to equalise it and head back low, towards the coast of Mozambique."

"What's low, about five thousand feet?" Wiley asked.

"Try about thirty."

"But you usually fly at thirty thousand feet," Steddy said.

"Not thirty thousand man – thirty – thirty feet."

"Holy shit!" Steddy said exhaling. Wiley just let out a low whistle.

"Isn't that kind of dangerous?" they echoed.

"Well, say thirty to sixty feet – depends on the swell."

"Christ! I guess you really know you're moving at that altitude," Steddy said.

"Too right, but there's really nothing to it – if you know what you're doing."

"And presumably you do?" Wiley said, smiling wanly.

"Yeah, do it all the time," he chuckled and rolled his eyes. "See, there's what's known as the 'surface effect' from the sea – put a lot of static on the radar receivers, and once they tune that out, they've tuned us out too, as long as we stay within it."

"Listen, I don't think I want to know any more about this, or *I* might develop a surface effect that would require a thorough cleaning of the rear cabin. I'm gonna lie down – wake me up when it's over." Steddy left the cockpit and headed aft to try to sleep.

"What's the matter with him?" Jellicoe asked Wiley, who remained forward.

"He gave his liver to science last night – all in a good cause, mind you, but he must be feeling like death warmed up."

"What did you guys get up to then?"

"Let's just say that we had to put someone out of action who could have got in our way today."

Steddy had really cleaned his clock, Wiley thought as he sat in the co-pilot seat, staring at the sun that was directly in their flight path.

They had met the C.I.A. man at the hotel's Can Can Bar. Steddy poked Wiley in the ribs when he singled out, *Our man in Harare*, as he put it. His name was Hegner and he stood at least a foot taller than anyone else there. Wiley greeted him like an old friend and introduced him to Steddy, who was jokingly watching to see if they used a secret handshake as a recognition signal. They ordered drinks from the bar and took them to a low cocktail table in a red-plush-draped window alcove. The whole place was lined in red plush with gilt wood trim and looked like a Hollywood rendition of a turn-of-the-century bordello – the hotel was amazing in that the general impression was conservative while the bars and the roof were like a hodge-podge of exotic, cast-off film sets.

When Steddy saw that Hegner was drinking a martini, he ordered the same, giving the fellow a fraternal wink as he did so. Before they had finished the ones they had, he went to the bar and signed for the next round. When Hegner excused himself and went to the men's room, Wiley said:

"Hell, Steddy, take it easy – we've got to keep our wits about us."

"Listen Wiley, I know what I'm doing. This guy's a boozer if I ever saw one and I've seen plenty. Just leave him to me. I'll fix him so he doesn't get up before tomorrow afternoon."

"I hope you know what you're doing – he's probably trying to do the same thing to you so you'll let something slip."

"We've got to play it real cosy, like we're all part of the same team –
get him off guard and relaxed."

Hegner returned to the table.

"Are you guys free for dinner?"

"Sure are," Steddy answered for both of them. "We can't do
anything but bide our time."

"I'd like to talk to you about that, but it can wait till we get to the
restaurant."

"Is there a good one here?" Wiley asked.

"Hell, yes, one of the best steak houses I've ever been to and it's not
far from here."

"Well let's have one for the road – it's early yet," Steddy volunteered.

They ended up having two for the road at Steddy's insistence and then
piled into Hegner's small rented car and headed for the outskirts of town
where the restaurant turned out to be everything he promised. It was
called Wombles and consisted of a series of joined, thatched rondavels.

He ordered the biggest steaks on the menu, which were at least two
pounds each, and when Steddy said that nothing went better with a
charred, bloody steak than a cold, dry martini, Hegner agreed and they
continued to drink them throughout dinner.

Hegner *did* think he was being clever and waited until Steddy had put
away three martinis at the restaurant before he thought him sufficiently
well-oiled to bring up the subject of the mission.

"We won't know a thing until the guy that owns the place Rockford's
staying at, calls us. There isn't any phone there so until he gets the cable
that was sent from England, there's nothing we can do but wait."
Steddy spoke with the most sincere expression he could muster.

"Well, he must have had it by now," Hegner commented casually.

"I don't think so – we were told that it takes three days to get a wire to
him where he is," Wiley answered, trying to sound as official C.I.A. as
possible.

"Didn't they give you any idea what part of the country he was in?"

"Nope."

The waitress came and asked them if they wanted any coffee. Steddy
was inspired and turned to Hegner.

"Ever had a Mulata?"

"What's that?"

"Just the only way to drink coffee that's all. Once you've had one,
you'll never drink it any other way. I'll see to it."

He rose from the table and headed to the bar in the adjacent
rondavel.

A Mulata was a drink of Steddy's own concoction that consisted of a triple measure of light Bacardi rum, iced coffee and just enough heavy cream to turn it the colour of its name, or more aptly the colour of the girl it was named after. It was served in the biggest glass available, preferably a cocktail-shaker filled with ice, and tasted like a coffee frosted. It was lethal. They had three of them and ended up singing "You're a grand old flag" and "I'm a yankee doodle dandy" at the top of their lungs, all the way back to town. Then, on Hegner's suggestion – he had finally gone over the top as Steddy had predicted – they went to a Greek discothèque on Baker Avenue where they started drinking Black Russians. It seemed like a good idea at the time. Hegner found a girl who was, as he must have said a hundred times, "like I like my coffee – hot, sweet and black." They left him there in the wee hours of the morning. Steddy threw up violently in Cecil Square on the way back to the hotel. Mission accomplished.

They noted Hegner's key was still in his box when they crept out of the hotel across the darkened lobby a few hours later on their way to the airport – but for Steddy it was a Pyrrhic victory.

When Wiley finished describing the high points of Steddy's sacrifice, Jellicoe said:

"Man, I'm glad I didn't come to dinner with you guys. Do you have any idea what a trembling hand can do when you're flying thirty feet over the drink at five hundred miles per hour?"

Steddy was sleeping in the cabin when, without any warning, the whisper of the jet engines changed to a shriek and the acute angle of the aircraft's dive forced his stomach into his mouth. With his face pressed against the port of the steeply banking aircraft, the blue-green water of the Indian Ocean looked close enough to touch. When they levelled off, he made his way forward to the cockpit where the sea racing under them looked like an arcade game gone mad.

Jellicoe was flushed and grinning – obviously enjoying himself while Wiley, in contrast, was pressed to the back of his seat, his face drained of colour.

"I thought you were sleeping," Jellicoe said to Steddy.

"Always ready with a joke I see. Was the aerobatics display for my benefit?"

"Nah – just the only way to do it. Listen, would one of you get my radar detector out of that bag on the deck." He nodded his head in the direction of his feet. "I don't like to take my hands off the controls if you know what I mean – it's about the size of a transistor radio."

Steddy saw that there was no way Wiley was going to release his death grip from the arm rests or lower his unblinking eyes from the horizon, so he crouched down and retrieved the small metal instrument from the bag at Jellicoe's feet and examined it.

"But this is just an automobile radar detector," he said, surprised.

"It's a trick I learned from some American Air Force boys. They use them when they're flying war games – the old jets they fly don't have sophisticated radar detectors – but they tell me that these are more reliable than the built-in ones on the new ships anyway."

"You mean you've never used it before?"

"Yeah, well, I've tried it out waiting for clearance to land and also in the car at home."

"That's just great!" Steddy said, with a note of disgust. "But how the hell do you expect a little thing like this to have the range to pick up coastal radar?"

"It doesn't need range," Jellicoe replied, eyes front. "All it has to do is detect radar that's reaching us – if it starts screaming, that means that they've locked onto us."

"Then what happens?"

"Let's get it going first. Turn it on and tune the control on the right until it squeals." Steddy did so – the high-pitched whistle was very shrill. "Now ease back on the control, very gently until it stops."

"Now what?" Steddy asked.

"Nothing, just sit tight and pray it doesn't go off."

"But what if it does?"

"Well, they'd probably try to raise us on the radio, but I've got that shut down and my radar as well – they could pick that up in a second. But really, don't worry – the Mozambicans aren't very well organised. By the time they scramble into their MIG 17s, we'll be out of their air space and over Zimbabwe. Mozambique's not even a hundred miles wide where we cross – shouldn't be in their air space for more than ten or twelve minutes max. Those MIGs of theirs are ground fighters anyway – no air-to-air missiles, just radar homing ones. That's one of the reasons our radar's shut down. Still a 23 millimetre cannon can do a real number on one of these babies – we're not exactly armoured. It's the Rhodesians we've got to look out for. If they get a visual on us, we'll have to follow them in to their base – their Hunters are armed with Sidewinders. If they let one of those fly at us, we'd just be dust in the sky."

"Not very encouraging," Steddy said.

Wiley was still rigid.

"I'm not really worried about the Rhos. By the time we're in their air space, we'll be in the mountains – and as long as we stay below the peaks, we'll be hidden from their radar in the ground clutter."

Steddy stopped talking to Jellicoe. They were flying so close to the water that every time Jellicoe turned round to see if he had heard what he was saying over the scream of the engines that reverberated off the sea, Steddy swallowed to keep his stomach down and had to restrain himself from shouting, *keep your eyes front damn you*!

The coast was under them almost before he realised they were nearing it. Jellicoe was rhythmically adjusting his altitude to match the gentle rise and fall of the blurred brown terrain. There was a brief squeal from the box in Steddy's hand – his guts went to jelly.

"Don't start worrying. If it doesn't become continuous, we're just part of the ground clutter," Jellicoe said, trying to reassure them.

The blur turned from brown to a pale green and Steddy could see the pointed peaks of what Jellicoe identified as the Vumba looming in front of them in the distance.

"Not long now," Jellicoe said, but every second was an excruciating eternity on a roller coaster for Steddy and his rigid companion.

Low hills were popping up on either side of them and the sun glinted off scattered pans of water that sparsely dotted the plain – only feet beneath them. As the channel between the hills grew narrower, Jellicoe gained some altitude.

"That's the Burma Valley," Jellicoe said. "When we pass those high rocky outcroppings ahead of us, we'll be in Zimbabwe."

But before Steddy could get a fix, they had jerked up and overflown them.

The box in his hand began to wail. Steddy's concentration on the terrain had been so intense that he dropped it – but it didn't stop this time. The Valley had widened out again and exposed them. It kept up its shrill shriek until they had gained the mountains and the shelter of their peaks. When it stopped, Jellicoe said:

"We're not five minutes from the plantation now; if the strip's clear and we can get down on the first pass, we'll be all right."

Steddy didn't answer him – all three of them were flying the plane now. Jellicoe had had to throttle back to manoeuvre between the peaks.

The house was the first thing Steddy saw of the coffee farm.

"Is that it?"

"That's Witches' Wood," Jellicoe answered between clenched teeth – obviously not happy at the prospect of taking a Sidewinder up the bum.

They overflew the house so low that Steddy could just about make out the headline of a newspaper on the terrace.

Jellicoe had to climb steeply to gain room to turn and come back. At the top of the turn, the box squealed again but only for a moment. He throttled back as they began their descent and said:

"OK, this is it – hang on."

Steddy was only able to distinguish the grass runway from the rest of the green at the back of the house by the single engine Cessna, tied down at the edge of the plateau. They seemed to be diving straight for it. Every muscle in Wiley's face showed in sharp relief, Steddy's knuckles were white too, gripping the back of Wiley's seat and the jamb of the cockpit's door.

Just when he thought they were going to hit the ground like a javelin, Jellicoe pulled up the nose until they could see nothing but sky, and cut the power. When they hit, Steddy's grip was wrenched free by the force of the impact, and he was sent flying back into the cabin – the angle was so steep that he couldn't regain his feet. Then the engines let out an unholy wail that sounded as though they would explode any second, and it was over. The nose fell level with a bang and they came to a stop. Steddy lay there on the thick carpet of the cabin, savouring the moment.

"Right. Everybody out and give me a hand – on the double!" Jellicoe shouted.

He was standing by the hatch, a bunch of chocks for the wheels slung over his shoulder, waiting for the softly whining motor to lower the stair to the ground. Steddy pulled himself together and when he reached Jellicoe's side, saw that behind the pilot, Wiley had returned to the land of the living and the colour was back in his cheeks.

"You never told me to fasten my seat belt!" Steddy quippped.

Jellicoe cut him off. "Can it! We've got to secure the plane and try to cover her somehow."

The pilot scrambled down the gangway before it was completely extended, with Steddy right behind him. A slight man with snow white hair and blue eyes that sparkled from his tanned, smiling face, was waiting for them. Behind him, keeping their distance, three black servants stood ogling the unfamiliar aeroplane and its occupants.

"You gave us quite a turn just then – thought you'd take the roof off the house, Jellicoe." He grasped the pilot's hand and pumped it enthusiastically, exuding the spry robust health typical of a certain brand of Englishman who thrives on colonial life in the sun, served up with copious amounts of pink gin. "Bentley's the name," he said exercising Steddy's arm with equal gusto. Steddy had only introduced himself when Jellicoe interrupted him.

"No time for that now. Got to find some way to camouflage the plane – we may have visitors any minute. Can you get some of your boys to help us?" he asked.

"You can have the old camouflage netting we used during the war. It's still stored in the shed."

He shouted an order to two black men who were hanging back by the house with the maids. They took off for the shed at a graceful African lope and soon returned dragging a corpse-shaped bundle of netting between them.

"It won't be big enough by a long shot, but it should do the job – had it made to protect the Cessna from the ZANLA raids."

Wiley joined them and the five of them man-handled the cover across the wings of the plane, and most of the fuselage.

While securing the netting to the outboard wing, Steddy was almost suspended over the edge of the plateau. From the air, he blessedly hadn't appreciated how sheer the drop was. It fell away almost vertically into the Burma Valley which formed the channel they had flown up between the *Mountains of the Mist*. Beyond, lay the plain of Mozambique and the Indian Ocean which he could see clearly from his perch on the wing.

Flying Cloud had come to a stop only a few yards from the edge.

"That's the best we can do. We'd better get into the house, out of sight, and keep our fingers crossed," Jellicoe said.

"We were quite a target here during the war. They used to take pot shots at us from those mountains over there, with rockets and anything else they could get their hands on. Fortunately for us they were lousy marksmen, though we did lose the stable and some beautiful beasts," Bentley said to Steddy and Wiley as he led them into the hall.

The house was cool and big. Made of stone and covered for the most part with ivy, it evoked no particular style. It just seemed to belong there. From the hall he led them down three or four steps into a large sunken living room that followed the fall of the land. An enormous multi-paned window dominated the far end of the room where, like a proscenium arch, it framed the spectacular view of the Burma Valley, the plain of Mozambique and the distant ocean.

The steps were flanked by a pair of elephant tusks that Steddy noted were taller than Jellicoe; another pair, equally tall, symmetrically flanked the window opposite. Big chintz overstuffed chairs were scattered over the highly polished floor that was paved with matching round slices, hewn from gum trees that Bentley said were indigenous to the forests of the Vumba.

They sat by the immense fireplace that was filled with plants and greenery.

"Where's Nubar?" their host asked Jellicoe.

"He's not with us this trip, but these chaps are friends of his come out to see Lord Rockford."

Bentley looked around furtively and then said in a lowered voice to Steddy: "You gave me quite a turn when you introduced yourself . . ."

"How's that?" Steddy asked.

"Well, the name he goes under here is Stedman Wright. Guess he didn't expect you to come calling."

"Where is he?" Steddy asked anxiously and then, noticing that the man hesitated: "Perhaps you should read this before we go on."

Bentley took the envelope that Steddy handed him and walked over to the big desk that stood before the wall of glass panes. He rustled through some papers until he found a pair of half-glasses, put them on the end of his nose and perched on the edge of the desk to read the letter that Nubar had penned over the Irish Sea aboard *Flying Cloud*. When he finished, he removed the glasses, and for a moment stared at them blankly in his hand as though they were somehow culpable for the news he'd just read.

"It's a nasty business," was all he said as he walked back to where they were seated.

"Very nasty, and the sooner it's over with the better," Wiley said, uttering his first words in more than two hours.

"Well he won't be back for a time yet." And then noticing the house boy standing at his elbow, Bentley said: "What am I thinking of – I haven't offered you a drink – you must think us completely lacking in hospitality up here. What can I give you?"

Jellicoe asked for a beer – Wiley and Steddy declined drinks, but said that they hadn't had any breakfast, if it wasn't too much trouble.

"Certainly not. I think I must still be rattled from your surprising, or should I say spectacular, arrival." He told the boy to have a full breakfast for three laid out on the terrace and to bring Jellicoe a beer and himself his usual. With the prospect of food to come, Steddy asked for a beer as well, "and my friend could use a brandy."

"I will have a beer – if the offer's still open," Wiley corrected.

They were feasting on a breakfast of mealie porridge, the African's staple made from white maize – and pan-fried steaks with grilled tomatoes, when Jellicoe was first to identify the faint but unmistakable drone of an approaching helicopter.

212

"Must be one of their Hawks, out of Umtali," he said. "That's the worst possible luck. If they spot *Flying Cloud*, they can just come right down for a closer look and catch us red-handed."

It was a single-engine British Aerospace Hawk, armed with Sidewinder missiles and a thirty-millimetre gun. None of them could continue with their breakfast while it poked around between the peaks of the Vumba that surrounded them. When at last it moved on and its drone had died away, Jellicoe said:

"That was close, but hell – we weren't on their screen long enough for them to be sure we were an aircraft."

"They patrol around here pretty regularly – might not be looking for you at all," Bentley said.

"Don't bloody bet on it," Jellicoe commented, frowning.

"Where is Rollo?" Steddy asked again.

"He tells me that he goes off camping, but I'm pretty sure he's involved with the South Africans in something."

"How do you mean?" Wiley asked.

"Well, it's only guessing, don't you know, but there's an ANC base somewhere across the frontier in Mozambique, and even though the South Africans made a treaty with Samora Machel a year or so before he died, I think he's spotting it for their Air Force, or at least doing something like that."

"The ANC are Mandela's people, no?" Steddy asked.

"That's right – African National Congress."

"And you think Rollo's spotting for the South Africans?" Wiley asked.

"He's in the perfect location to do it," Jellicoe piped in.

"Yeah, but how in hell would he have got mixed up with them?" Steddy asked.

"Oh that's not so hard to figure out," Bentley answered. "A lot of them come up here to Leopard's Rock for their holidays: it's a hotel about a mile from here, built by Italian prisoners during the War. Funny when you think I had to leave here to fight the Eities in Italy, and while I was gone, a whole flock of them were down here picking the coffee and tending the roses till we got back – upside down sort of world sometimes isn't it?" He noticed that Steddy was not interested in his digression and returned to the subject. "Anyway, I've seen him at the bar there, chatting them up more than once."

Jellicoe announced that he was going to have a nap and returned to the house. The colonel suggested that they finish their coffee inside as the terrace was getting warm and the bees had discovered the remains of breakfast.

They settled into the deep drawing room chairs again, and the boy was serving coffee. Calm had been restored after the harsh intrusive noise of the helicopter and the loudest sound in the room was the ever-present hum of flying insects and the coffee spoons stirring in the cups, when a booming voice from the doorway behind them shattered the quiet.

"Where the hell are you Nubar, you silly bastard? I long for the sight of your ugly mug – nearly killed myself running up the valley when I saw the plane come in!"

From where he stood on the landing, Rollo couldn't see Wiley or Steddy who were sunk deep in their chairs with their backs to him.

Steddy rose and faced him and was surprised by what he saw. There was nothing of the pallid fugitive about Rollo. He had lost his moustache, twenty pounds of bloat, and with them twenty years. He was wearing khaki shorts and a bush jacket with the sleeves rolled up and had a rifle slung over his shoulder, looking every bit the Hollywood version of an African white hunter.

"Christ Almighty! What the hell are you doing here?" he bellowed, good-naturedly. And when Wiley rose as well: "My God – the troops *have* landed; now we'll have some real fun." He noted their serious expressions as he descended the two steps into the room and strode towards them as if he owned the world. "If you've come to talk me into going back – don't even try – I wouldn't leave here if my father kicked the bucket and the queen granted me a full pardon."

"Not much chance of that," was the first thing Steddy said.

Rollo looked about the room. "Where is Nubar anyway?"

"He couldn't make it this trip," Steddy said.

"Don't tell me you're here for the sport – I bagged a leopard the other day that was six pounds under the record – the world record – not fifty miles from here – this place is a bloody paradise."

Steddy turned to Bentley and said: "Is there someplace I could talk with Rollo alone sir?"

"Call me Dereck, young man, and you may use my study. Stedman knows . . . oh dear, this is awkward having two Stedmans about the place . . ."

"I wouldn't worry – this one isn't planning to be around very long," Steddy said and made for the door. But Rollo stopped him.

"Half a minute – I've been out in the bush for two days and just run up the bloody mountain – you wouldn't begrudge a condemned man a drink?"

Steddy didn't comment as Rollo ordered a Pimm's from the servant who seemed always to wait just beyond the door. It was awkward facing him after everything that had happened – learning that an old friend is more than likely a traitor.

Wiley didn't know what to say either and when Bentley offered to show him round the coffee plantation, he seemed relieved for once to let Steddy carry the ball.

Rollo's initial joviality was dampened by Steddy's attitude and they both became painfully aware of the silence between them as they waited for the boy to finish serving the drink and leave. Eventually, Steddy was the first to speak. He had rehearsed the angry scene he would have with Rollo so often in his mind – lying in a bed of pain after almost being killed in Aberdeen – buried in sand to escape a trained killer, and most recently, every waking moment since Thea had been taken – but now it wouldn't come.

"I don't know where to begin, Rollo." It was a poor start.

"Steddy, old boy, you don't think for a minute that I killed her on purpose, do you?"

"Hell, no, I couldn't give less of a shit about your wife. I hope for your sake that you did do it on purpose – they've hung you for it anyway – but no, *I* don't think you did. That's not why I'm here."

"Well, then, what the hell is this all about? Something's bothering you, tell me what it is!"

"Bothering me! That's rich!" Steddy snarled. "You stole the Israeli war plan, and now Thea's been kidnapped because of you. Yes Rollo, something bloody well *is* bothering me!"

None of the colour left Rollo's well-tanned face and he barely seemed to notice the mention of the top-secret documents. He shifted agilely to the edge of his seat, exhibiting his newly won litheness, his face clouded with genuine concern, and he asked:

"What do you mean Thea's been kidnapped?"

"She was taken four days ago."

"But what have *I* got to do with it?"

"Rollo, she was taken by the Israelis and they won't give her back until I return the documents you stole from their Government."

"Hang on! I never stole anything from the Israelis or anybody else. Those plans were given to me. But how do they know I'm still alive?"

"That doesn't concern me because if you don't turn them over to me right now, you won't be alive much longer – and don't say you didn't steal them, because if you didn't steal them from the Israelis, then you stole them from the British – your own people – when you didn't turn them over to MI5 as you promised." Steddy could see he had touched a nerve; a flash of anger crossed Rollo's handsome face.

"We *have* been talking to a lot of people, haven't we?" he said sarcastically.

"But I never stole them – I simply haven't turned them over yet – they're sort of an insurance policy. I only got them the afternoon of the accident. I was going to meet with the boys at MI5 the next day, but then you know what happened. I panicked, to put it mildly, and I couldn't just leave them lying around – and then, well I just thought it wouldn't hurt to keep them for a while in case there was any big trouble."

"The only thing you insured was a pack of trouble for me and now maybe . . . God! If anything happens to Thea, I swear . . ."

"Hold on old boy, we'll get this thing straightened out. But how did you get involved anyway, or are you just acting as a messenger boy for Nubar?"

The anger Steddy had been unable to summon on cue now rose from inside him with a force of its own. Rollo's self-assured arrogance left no room for compassion where other people's welfare was concerned.

"God damn it – *old boy*, we *will* get this thing straightened out right this minute. Hand those papers over to me *now*!"

"Can't do it, I'm afraid . . ."

"What the hell do you mean?"

"Give me a chance to . . ."

"You've had nothing but chances. If you don't turn them over right now, I'll turn you over to the Israelis, and the Americans and the British and anyone else who wants a crack at you and let *them* pull you to pieces . . . I've only come here to prevent Thea from being . . ."

"Hold your horses, old boy – you'll get your ruddy papers, but I just can't do it now. You . . ."

"It's got to be now or Thea won't . . ."

"Let me finish! They're in the safe at Leopard's Rock. It's a hotel near . . ."

"I know all about it – that's where you hang out with your South African friends."

"Who told you that?" Rollo asked angrily.

"Never mind – you can start another Zulu war and then fight the Boers all over again, for all I care. All I want are the papers!"

"Look, Steddy, the safe over there is open from eight in the morning till nine and then from six in the evening until ten. So you see," he said, looking at his watch, "it doesn't reopen for eight hours."

"If you're stalling, so help me . . ."

"Calm down, Steddy, there's no way to get hold of Jock till he comes in, in the evening – oh, he might wander in sometime after five, if he finishes one sector of the coffee early, but not usually, and he's the only person with the key."

Steddy got up from his chair and stood in front of Rollo with his fists clenched and looked as though he would kill him. Rollo tried to mollify him.

"Look Steddy, there's just nothing we can do now, so let's make the best of it. Why don't you go up and have a shower and a rest and then we'll play a little backgammon before lunch – I haven't played since Austria and you owe me a game. Then we'll . . ."

Steddy grabbed the rifle that was leaning against Rollo's chair and with both arms, made as if to bash him with it. At the last moment, with the swing and the strength of a two hundred-yard drive, he propelled it into the fireplace where the stock broke and it went off with a terrific report in the confined space of the chimney. Rollo cowered in the chair. Steddy looked down at him and said:

"Fuck you, Rollo, you son of a bitch!" turned his back to him and strode from the room.

Steddy found the bedroom where Jellicoe was resting, and outlined the situation for him.

"We'd still have enough light after six, but the later it gets the easier it is for the radar to pick us up. I'd say we'd do best to make an early start of it in the morning," Jellicoe said.

"Can you get us into Victoria Falls directly?" Steddy asked.

"That's no problem, they've got a customs and immigration there – they get a lot of direct tourist flights from South Africa. I'll have to radio ahead once we enter Zimbabwean air space legally, but I don't think they'll make us go through Harare."

"How long will it take us?"

"Well if we leave at seven, and I wouldn't want to leave any earlier because of the radar, and if we go out the same way we came in, which we'll have to do in order to re-enter legally, we should get into Vic Falls by nine or nine-thirty."

"OK – let's plan on doing that." Steddy started to leave the room and then turned back. "Have you got enough room out there to take off?"

"I told you to leave the flying to me. Lucky I used to fly off an aircraft-carrier. What we lack in runway length, we pick up in altitude; the drop from the plateau to the plain is almost four thousand feet –

we'll make it." And then he added jokingly, "But this time I think your friend Wiley ought to take a seat in the rear."

Steddy slept through lunch – Wiley told them not to wake him – but he came down on his own just in time for tea which was laid on the sofa table in the drawing room. By the time he had finished, it was almost five and a chastened Rollo sheepishly suggested they set out for Leopard's Rock.

They walked over back roads that were still deeply rutted from the rainy season, through broken security fences topped with barbed wire that were left over from the war and finally through a forest of gum trees that grew straight and tall, and led onto the eighteenth green of the hotel's golf course where six native boys on their knees were weeding by hand.

Beyond the green and an ornamental pond filled with white swans, stood the hotel at the top of a hill. Like Witches' Wood, it was built of weathered stone covered here and there with moss and ivy. It was two storeys high with a slate-shingled roof, the ground floor had tall French doors with rounded tops that also pierced the four romantic turrets. The overall effect was that of a nineteenth-century French château – not a grand château, but the kind more associated with a working estate or a vineyard. Nevertheless, it was very impressive, finding it there as if by accident, amid a primeval forest in the shadows of the *Mountains of the Mist*, commanding the highest point in the Vumba.

"It must have been very grand once upon a time," Rollo commented as they climbed the hill. "Even the queen stayed here as a princess with her mother and sister, just after the War. Goes to show what can be accomplished with the unlimited use of slave labour – talented Italian slave labour at that – prisoners of war, you know – must have had a few stone masons among them. Pity about the hits it took during *this* war."

As they drew nearer, Steddy could see the great pits in the stonework that Rollo had referred to. Leopard's Rock was the highest point in the area and rockets in the hands of the ZANLA forces had found their mark in the stone turrets and outer wings of the hotel.

The war had been for seven bloody years an out-and-out civil war between the white Rhodesians and the blacks. Moreover, the blacks were divided amongst themselves into warring factions by historic tribal feuds that went back long before the white settlers ever drew a boundary around their tribes and formed a nation called Rhodesia, and would no doubt continue long after they were gone, or until one tribe succeeded in annihilating or enslaving the other.

The whites were out of the fray – the Lancaster House Agreement had ended white rule – and now, since Lord Soames had turned over the keys, those who remained sat on the sidelines and watched the resumption of the age-old tribal wars.

The young men, who had grown to manhood to fight through the eight years of war, and who consequently had known nothing *but* fighting all their adult lives, could get no work with the new government's "hire blacks first" policy. They felt betrayed – it was their country too – many of their families had settled the land almost a hundred years before. Disillusioned, they literally drank themselves senseless in city bars till they killed themselves or one another, or emigrated to South Africa with nothing but the shirts on their backs and joined the South African Forces to do the only thing they knew how – fight – fight guerrillas.

All this Steddy learned from Rollo as they had made their way from Witches' Wood to Leopard's Rock.

Rollo had been swept up in the great saga of the white man's role in Africa a century too late, just as it drew to its inevitable close. The heroic ideals and sympathies that welled within him belonged in the Victorian era and the age of Cecil Rhodes.

Steddy felt sorry for his friend who had spent his life as a wayfarer, searching for his place in the world, and now when he thought he had found it, it was in a world that had ceased to exist.

Jock, the manager of the hotel, had not returned when they checked at the small counter in the circular hall that served as the desk, so Rollo steered Steddy into the bar where he poured them each a pink gin and filled out a chit that was left at the corner of the bar for the use of guests and local planters, on the honour system. They had the place to themselves and sat down on stools covered, aptly, with leopard skin.

The gin bottle looked exactly like Gordon's; it was the identical shape and bore the identical label – but on close examination Steddy noticed that the name was Garden's, and the bitters bottle that he had taken to be Angostura, turned out to be Angus Stewart. He asked Rollo to explain.

"We had UN sanctions here for eight years." (Steddy noted that although Rollo had only been in Zimbabwe for a few weeks, he was already referring to himself as a Zimbabwean.) "It wasn't easy. The only thing they could get from outside was arms from South Africa. The intrepid bloody Rhodesians really rose to the challenge – produced everything right here – ersatz, mind you, but you can't tell the difference – down to the wrapping on candy bars – really incredible."

"But the UN lifted the sanctions years ago, didn't they?" Steddy asked, drawn into the story.

"Right, but by then there wasn't any foreign exchange for anything but vital necessities."

They talked for a while longer – like the old friends that they had been. Steddy was impressed at how quickly Rollo had grasped the political and economic situation in present-day Zimbabwe. He seemed to have a mission and appeared to be genuinely happy for the first time in all the years Steddy had known him.

"Of course, I'll miss the boys – it would be grand to have them out here with me – raise them here . . ."

"Well couldn't you do that?" Steddy said, warming.

"Apart from the fact that I'm a wanted man with no visible means of support, Father would never let them out of his sight as long as he lives, and to be perfectly honest, I haven't set them a very good example, have I Steddy?" he asked morosely.

"They're still very young – they won't remember any of this – and if everything works out with the documents and all, I'll have a word with Allsloe the chap from Scotland Yard. I'm sure that when I tell them that you turned over the papers to me without any problem, they won't want to prosecute you for that – then if you'd just face the music about Jackie – well we'd all testify that it was an accident and I can't imagine that they'd hold you."

"You don't know my father. They wouldn't let me off if *he* had anything to say about it. Oh, there's Jock now."

A stout red-faced man with curly blond hair and a beard, made his way to the table where he clapped Rollo on the shoulder and shook Steddy's hand warmly when Rollo introduced him as an old friend.

"Here to do some shooting, are you?" he asked Steddy. "He got a marvellous leopard the other day."

"Not this trip unfortunately, but I hope so next time."

"He's just here for the day on business, but now that he's been, we'll get him back soon . . . I need those papers I gave you to lock up for me, Jock – something in them I've got to return to him."

"Surely he's got time for me to join you for a beer first?"

"By all means," Steddy answered.

Jock drank his beer and between telling Steddy about the great variety of game in the area, he asked dozens of questions about America and how Zimbabwe was being perceived there – like all the local whites, he seemed starved for news. When he finished his drink, he excused himself and returned a few minutes later with a brown paper accordion file tied with ribbon which he handed to Rollo and excused himself to go and "wash up".

Rollo opened the folder and rummaged through the few possessions he had managed to gather before his hasty departure from England. He withdrew a flat pale yellow eight-by-ten envelope that couldn't have held more than a few sheets of paper and handed it to Steddy. It had no title on the front, but was sealed on the back with three blobs of sky-blue sealing wax that were incised with a clear impression of a seven-light candelabrum surrounded by branches – the arms of the state of Israel. Steddy marvelled at how so small a thing could be the cause of so much trouble and pain. Then he examined the seals closely for, as Chelak had explained, Thea's survival depended on their condition.

"Never touched it," Rollo said when he noticed Steddy's scrutiny. "I figured that if the seals were broken, no one would believe I hadn't peddled a copy or two."

"Thank God for once you figured right," Steddy said, breathing a sigh of relief. "I can't tell you what holding this intact in my hand means to me."

"I'm glad to do it. I'm only desperately sorry that you – and Thea of course, too – got involved in all of this in the first place – I had no idea . . ."

Steddy let out a gasp of frustration. "Rollo do you know the story about the fellow at a London club who posted a notice on the board that said, *Would the peer who stole my umbrella please have the decency to return it?*" Rollo shook his head. "Well a friend of his passed and after reading it asked the chap: 'How do you know it was a *peer* who took it?'

"The fellow replied, 'No *gentleman* would ever do a thing like that!' "

Rollo started to laugh, but then hung his head sheepishly.

"You know Rollo I realise that you didn't mean to involve us, but you can't blame me for having cursed you on a daily basis ever since this nightmare started. If you only had stayed to face the music."

"I wonder. I was on a suicide course, living in Europe – something had to give and if I hadn't run, I never would have come here. At least I'm doing something useful now – something I believe in. It makes a world of difference you know . . ." And then, on the verge of proselytising to Steddy like a true convert, he stopped, as though he had already said too much and, flashing one of his movie-star smiles, changed the subject.

They had one more drink as the bar started to fill with an assortment

of men who were dressed like Rollo and all seemed to know him well.
Steddy couldn't help but feel that he was an intruder and the cause of
their reticent behaviour – they all seemed bursting to discuss something
but reluctant to do so in front of him. When he suggested to Rollo that
they get back to the house so that he could make plans for the following
day, Rollo seemed happy to go, but when the other men pressed him
to stay, and Steddy said he could follow the track back to the house
without any trouble by himself, Rollo agreed immediately and walked
Steddy to the clump of gum trees where the trail began.

"Tell Dereck and Pamela I'll be back in time for dinner," he said as
he saluted Steddy in farewell. "We'll have a good old jaw; I've got a lot
of catching up to do, and then maybe you'll give me a few games of
backgammon after dinner – you *do* owe me a few you know!"

~ ~ ~

Steddy was in the co-pilot's seat for the take-off. Jellicoe had spent the
early morning hours examining the length of the strip with a fine tooth
comb, and with the help of two African boys had filled and levelled
every furrow and pothole he could find. With Wiley safely in the aft
cabin, he carefully manoeuvred the aircraft to the furthest extremity of
the runway and then, with the brakes locked, ran her up to full power.

"It's lucky we don't have to try this with a full load of fuel!" he
commented drily.

"Have we got enough to get to Victoria Falls?" Steddy asked.

"That and then some," Jellicoe said as he eased off the brakes.

It felt to Steddy as though they were being ejected from a cannon.
The ground sped by at a terrific rate as they bumped and lurched over
the uneven terrain towards the edge of the plateau.

"We just passed the point of no return," Jellicoe said through
clenched teeth, adding little to Steddy's confidence.

When they crossed the edge, the plane bellied out sickeningly as
Jellicoe fought to hold the nose up into the updraught off the
mountains, but it soon became evident that they were holding their
own and were airborne.

The radar detector that Steddy held never went off once, though it
was of little consolation to him with Jellicoe continuing to cling to the
side of the sloping hills to avoid contact as they swept down the valley –
manoeuvring the slalom course between the mountains that led to the
plain of Mozambique and the Indian Ocean. Eventually Steddy
relaxed; Jellicoe was clearly the master of his plane – gently effecting

the banking turns to the right and left, with only the deftest movement of his strong, rough hands that held the controls as steadily as a diamond-cutter wields his wedge.

When they passed the shoreline, and tore out over the open sea, causing the water to boil, Jellicoe's face relaxed, and he said:

"Piece of cake."

"Then I'm going on a diet!" Steddy said, laughing loudly with the release of pent-up nervous tension. "But seriously, apart from all the white hair I've sprouted in the last five minutes, you know that was really fun. I took up flying once – nothing fancy, just single-engine machines to learn how, but it was *so* boring, there was no sensation of speed. Now this was really exciting – makes me want to take it up all over again."

"Don't get too excited, you won't get many opportunities to play with a six million pound aircraft the way we just did."

They reached approximately the same point in the open ocean where they had dropped off the radar the previous day – made a low-level turn back towards the African coast and ascended to thirty thousand feet.

When they crossed over Beira on the Mozambique coast, Jellicoe was on the radio to them announcing his destination as Victoria Falls. The Umtali tower in Zimbabwe picked them up five minutes later; he repeated the same procedure, giving them an approximate ETA of 1100 hours.

"Sorry, we're gonna be a little late, but I had to make sure about the runway – taking a chance with it once was risky, but twice would have been plain crazy – especially at full power," Jellicoe said.

"Don't sweat it. Listen, I never thought we'd get what we needed so quickly – we're in good shape."

Steddy was still amazed at the ease with which Rollo had turned over the documents – he seemed so changed, so purposeful, Steddy thought; not at all the man pursued by demons he had come to know over the last few years when gambling and feminine conquest had lost their real pleasure for him, and had become instead a habit that he was driven to feed, like an addiction.

He was awakened by Jellicoe poking him in the ribs. Wiley was standing between them leaning on the backs of their two seats.

"Christ, Steddy, wake up! You can't miss this!" Wiley almost shouted at him.

About five miles ahead of them in the middle of the lush green, deeply channelled plateau, was a tremendous column of smoke that looked like a brush fire extending in a line about a mile wide.

"What is it?" Steddy sked.

"The smoke that thunders," Jellicoe intoned in an accent imitative of the local Africans.

"Of course, the Falls! I never thought – I mean I knew we were going to Victoria Falls, but I guess I wasn't thinking. Christ, you could put a half a dozen Niagaras in there."

"That's the spray the Falls throws up – it's about a thousand feet high – want to go in for a closer look? The plane could do with a wash!"

"Never mind that!" Wiley cut in. "I've done enough low-level flying to last me a lifetime."

Peter Jellicoe and Steddy laughed as the plane began its descent through a right-hand banking turn in preparation to land at the small airport of Victoria Falls, not far from where David Livingstone had landed in a very different manner 125 years before.

~ ~ ~

For two and a half days, Thea had eaten, moved and slept more or less in a trance that was as much due to the difficulty she was having in grasping the reality of her situation, as to the periodic doses of Valium her captors injected her with. She was vaguely aware that they had taken off from one of the Paris airports, and that they had subsequently changed planes in Rome for a seemingly endless flight that she passed in a half-sleep-half-waking state filled with grotesque nightmares made all the worse by the utter confusion of her emotions. She loved Steddy, or did she? Where was he? How could he allow this to happen to her? If it hadn't been for him she would never have got into this mess at all. But then he *had* tried to stop her – he *had* warned her not even to come to Scotland . . . the plan *had* been entirely *her* idea. But where was he *now*! The words screamed through the cotton wool in her brain. The battle of her conflicting emotions – logic, irrationality and just plain fear – raged back and forth continually. She read the name of the airport as they descended the gangway into the hot steamy climate of sub-Equatorial Africa – the sign over the terminal read Lusaka, but for the life of her she couldn't match the name of the city to a country.

They were separated from the line of people at passport control and politely escorted to a small waiting room. On one wall hung a coloured photograph of a black man, flanked by portraits of Marx and Engels. She thought it odd at the time – that something wasn't quite right – and for a fleeting moment almost had it, but as a dream vanishes with the morning, the solution was just beyond her grasp.

224

After a brief wait they were again courteously escorted back to the apron where a small, white, twin-engine plane awaited them. Not a word was said during the flight that lasted a little over an hour until they landed on a deserted stretch of road in the middle of what looked like a residential development gone to seed – all the infrastructure had been put in, but no one had ever built any houses, and the signs were so weather-beaten that they were illegible, but for one that clearly indicated a school crossing where no school had ever been erected. The only things that stood out in her memory were the smoke that filled the sky just before they landed, and then as they got out of the car in front of the hotel that proved to be their destination, and she heard it for the first time, a low, constant, rumbling noise that betokened some great force – like an active volcano or a giant dynamo.

Ironically, the hotel was an American Inter-Continental, although it resembled more a series of bungalows that appeared to be deserted, so that Thea was surprised when they were greeted at the door by a blue-black, giant King Kong of a man dressed, in spite of the appalling heat and humidity, in an American-cut tuxedo with shawl lapels, that must have been put together from the cannibalised parts of at least two suits of normal size. Cannibal was the operative word – all he lacked was a bone in his nose, a leopard skin loin cloth and a giant cauldron to be a casting agent's dream.

She was confused by everything – she knew that she must be in a Marxist country from the pictures at the airport, but *how was it that an American Inter-Continental Hotel was there? And since when did Marxists extend airport courtesies to Israeli agents?* She remembered only too well the Israeli raid into Uganda. How could she not, when the man who welcomed them to the hotel looked like Idi Amin's double?

When they were installed in a sparsely furnished bungalow that passed as a suite, she learned from looking through the tourist paraphernalia on the desk that they were in Livingstone – the Zambian side of Victoria Falls. The two countries – Zambia and Zimbabwe (formerly Northern Rhodesia and Southern Rhodesia) were divided by the great Zambezi River with half the Falls in the Zambian town of Livingstone and half in the town of Victoria Falls in Zimbabwe.

Why had they brought her here? she wondered. *And why had they been officially received at the airport?*

It didn't make any sense to her at all.

~ ~ ~

The Victoria Falls Hotel was the usual cream-coloured Colonial pile that one finds, in various states of repair, scattered throughout Queen Victoria's former Empire, with one exception. It was perched on a rise not a thousand feet from the edge of the Zambezi Gorge where the millions of gallons of water that spilled every second over the mile-wide Falls converged and were compressed into the narrow 350 foot-deep channel where, still boiling, they reunited into the Great Zambezi that roared by the hotel on its way to the Kariba Dam, 300 miles away.

Wiley and Steddy couldn't hear the continuous rumble of the Falls over the clatter and wheeze of the antediluvian air-conditioner in their small double room on the fourth floor. Steddy tried shutting off the machine, but the temperature was well into the nineties – much warmer than in the highlands of the Vumba, and he quickly turned it on again.

They had arrived an hour before and after some coaxing, were given the hotel's last available room, and not until they had reached it were they brought the one message that had been waiting for them. It was from Thea, and said that she would call again at six. They didn't know whether she had got free, or, more probably, that Chelak was simply using her to make the call. They would have to wait to find out.

"What the hell are we supposed to do – sit here all day and wait?" Steddy said, pacing the small room like an animal while Wiley reclined on the bed.

"What else do you want to do? I told you to go for a swim and I'll hold the fort here," Wiley replied, not terribly interested whether he did or didn't.

"Screw this! The message said six and six is what they meant. If Thea was free, she would be here."

"Maybe, maybe not," Wiley answered, not bothering to open his eyes.

"Well, I'm not going to sit in this fucking room for five fucking hours. I'll go fucking nuts!"

"Do what you like," Wiley said, now leafing casually through a guide to the Falls. "You're acting as though you didn't give a damn for Thea."

"For God's sake, I love her," Steddy answered somewhat defensively.

"Oh really? Your amorous behaviour can only be described as erratic, to put it mildly."

"Listen you son-of-a-bitch!" Steddy paused and looked out the window for a time, obviously trying to control himself, then turned to his friend. "I'm sorry Wiley – we've been on top of each other a lot the

226

past few days, under a lot of pressure – if Chelak said he'd call again at six, you can bet he'll call at six, not five to or five after. What say we take a look at the Falls and grab something to eat? We'll leave a message that we'll be back by five, just in case. That way at least we'll have a chance to calm down and clear our heads. We'll need all our wits about us if we're gonna pull this one off on our own."

Wiley saw the sense in what Steddy said. He knew that he wouldn't go without him and he also knew that after five more hours cooped up like this, if they didn't kill each other, they certainly wouldn't be in any shape to orchestrate the delicate exchange.

He agreed to go with Steddy and the minute he did, he saw his friend visibly relax. Steddy was like a destroyer, or a terrier – not designed to operate at slow speed. Perhaps that was one of the reasons he was good at games; he always had to be worrying something whether a game, a girl or a puzzle. Wiley thought that it didn't really matter which – as long as he was doing something.

Neither of them was ready to face the fact that Thea had come between them – so in a way, the compromise to see the Falls was a silent accord to put off the inevitable confrontation until after she was safely returned.

They told the desk that they'd be back at five and following the clerk's instructions, left the hotel through the French doors that led to the terrace. The sight that awaited them was a surprise – they hadn't realised that they were literally within spitting distance of the Falls. Following the lawned terraces down to the edge of the gorge, they could see the iron bridge that spanned it, shrouded in glistening, technicolor mists that rose from the Boiling Pot where the waters converged; beyond that, all that was discernible of the Falls were the great clouds of spray that hung above them and the deep rumble that resonated in their bellies.

They followed the narrow, dirt path along the edge of the gorge that – aside from the discreet wooden arrows marking the trail – was devoid of the more obvious signs of civilisation, that is concrete and Coke bottles. In fact, apart from the narrow track, little had changed since Livingstone's day.

"The mid-stream of the Zambezi is the border between Zambia and Zimbabwe." Wiley was reading from the guide book. "I wonder which side the frontier is on?"

As they continued along the path, nearing the Falls, the trees and undergrowth thickened and the moisture that hung in the air turned into an English mist that little by little increased into a fine shower until when they reached a small clearing where there was a simple, but larger-than-life bronze statue of Livingstone, they were in a veritable deluge that fell from a clear blue sky.

Soaked to the skin, they took off their shirts, Wiley using his to protect the guide book.

"That's the 'Devil's Cataract'," he said pointing in the direction of Livingstone's imperious gaze.

They scrambled down the crude, steep steps cut from the stone side of the cliff until they were just a few yards from the point where tons of sun-white water raged past them in great tangible, foaming clumps, to the shadowy bottom of the narrow cut that was hidden in the mist. The flimsy wooden rail offered little protection against sliding from the wet muddy ledge into the staggering vortex beneath them. Steddy clung to one of the woody creepers that grew along the face of the cliff and tried to peer out along the length of the Falls – the roar of the water was deafening and when he shook his head to clear the water from his eyes, he noticed a family of baboons had followed them down half-way and seemed to be screaming at them, but their shrieks couldn't reach them. There was a moment when he lost his footing and thought, *this isn't supposed to be happening in one of the world's greatest tourist attractions*, but that was the wonder of the place; for a brief moment, he was the discoverer of the Falls, there *was* no one else. The moment was quickly over, but the memory lingered long after they had regained Livingstone's statue with the baboons scampering in front of them.

"We'll have to buy some more clothes," he said to Wiley.

"I guess so – I lost my shirt climbing up, but I managed to salvage this," he said, holding the sodden guide book aloft. He was standing by the statue trying to get a bearing on the map in the book. When the baboons saw that they were soaked and almost as naked as they were – with no possibility of any food to offer, they took their leave.

"I just want to get to the Danger Point," he said, pointing in the book. "If we make our way through the rain forest along the south cliff for about half a mile . . ."

"You mean there's something more dangerous than this?" Steddy shouted to be heard. "I almost bought it down there."

"It's at the point where all the water from both sides rejoins at the Boiling Pot and becomes the Zambezi again. We should be able to see the bridge from this side, from there."

"I don't imagine it's any different on this side than the side we saw from the hotel," Steddy said good-naturedly.

"Come on, there's something I want to check out." Wiley took off his soggy shoes and set out purposefully down the winding track. Steddy also removed his and plodded after him.

They followed the trail around the corner of the Devil's Cataract and then along the top of the cliff at the edge of the rain forest that ran parallel to the Falls – two hundred yards across the cut. Even so, the Falls were not always visible through the clouds of spray, but when they were, the sight of them, in all their breadth, was staggering.

During the entire walk along the opposite cliff – about three quarters of a mile – they passed not one tourist, only a few African women, and they, like Wiley and Steddy, had taken off their tops and put them under their skirts to protect them from the heavy rain of spray. Their brilliant smiles and slippery, naked breasts added to the time warp of Steddy's fantasy that they were the first white men there.

At Danger Point, the rain forest thinned to grassland and across it they could see the bridge, shrouded in spray and rainbows, spanning the narrow gorge, 350 feet above the Boiling Pot.

"That's where he'll do it – I'd bet anything."

"What are you talking about?" Steddy shouted back at Wiley.

"The exchange. That's where he'll make it."

"Isn't that a little melodramatic?"

"Listen, I *do* know a little bit about this sort of thing, and I'm telling you that that is where he'll set up the exchange."

"But why the hell do it on the bridge?" Steddy asked, humouring Wiley.

"Come on, I'll show you," he said cutting across the grassland of the point towards the bridge. "It's the frontier – that has to be it."

"What do you mean?" Steddy asked, hurrying to keep up with him.

"It's in the guide book, the mid-stream of the Zambezi is the frontier between Zambia and Rhodesia."

"Zimbabwe," Steddy corrected him.

"It's an old guide book – anyway the frontier is on the bridge – it's a natural – why else would he drag us to Victoria Falls if it wasn't so that he could have a bolt hole across the frontier into Zambia at his back? The only thing I can't figure is that Zambia is Marxist – no ally of Israel's."

When they reached the narrow approaches to the bridge, they were back in civilisation. A line of trucks and smaller vehicles crawled in the lane towards the Zambia side and a line of Africans carrying bulging bundles clogged the footpath.

"They come over here to buy – Zambia's bankrupt of food and everything else you can think of," Wiley said.

"How do you know that?" Steddy asked.

"I read the papers," Wiley smirked. "Not everything's classified you know."

They crossed the railroad track and joined the line of Africans – interspersed with a few tourists – and shuffled towards the customs and police control that was housed in a small single-storey building, constructed about ten yards along the six hundred foot span. Wiley had given Steddy his passport to put with his in his money belt to keep it dry.

"I've got the passports – do you want to go across?" Steddy asked him. "We could see the Falls on the Zambia side."

"It might be a good idea to check out the control points," Wiley said, still thinking about the frontier. "Let's see how the line goes."

The rain of spray from the Boiling Pot got stronger as they neared the span so that Wiley had to put the guide book in his hip pocket.

"It says that Cecil Rhodes personally picked the location of the bridge so that people crossing on the train could see and hear the Falls and feel the spray. Must have been quite an engineering feat, seventy-five years ago."

When they reached the first building and entered through the "In" door, they found themselves in a typical British bureaucratic office, painted the same pale hospital green as its counterparts in London, Delhi or Hong Kong. But here in Zimbabwe, as in Delhi, they seemed to have run out of paint and the walls were peeling.

There was a special place at the counter for tourists and with only a family from Belgium and a couple from Germany in front of them, it didn't take long to get exit stamps on their passports.

The five hundred feet of the span between check-points was no-man's land and one was free to cross at one's own pace, presumably because it was one of the best views of the Falls. When they got to the mid-point, they crossed the railroad tracks that bracketed the roadway on either side and climbed onto the big pipes or electrical conduits, to reach the railing for the view.

"Don't you see he has to do it here?" Wiley shouted at Steddy who was looking straight ahead at the Falls, shielding his eyes from the spray.

"You mean in no-man's land? But what's the advantage to him?"

"Maybe he's made some sort of arrangement so he can slip back across the border and be away before we could get across."

"But even if you're right – I don't have any interest in catching him – all I want is to get Thea back safely."

"But you know the man is homicidal. If she's got a look at him, and I think we have to assume that she has, he'll kill her. With all this noise from the Falls, you could shoot someone and no one would even hear it."

"Someone would see the body if he did."

"Yeah, but not right away, and even if they did, you could yell your head off and nobody'd hear you – at least he'd have enough time to get clear. I'm not saying he set it up this way to kill one or all of us, but you can see he's left himself the option, and at the very least a way to escape."

"But not before he gets the file," Steddy interrupted.

"You're right, but don't you see, if the exchange is made here, he'll be able to get the file and then take a shot at her before she reaches us . . ."

"If you're right, what the hell can we do about it?"

"Forewarned is forearmed."

"But we're not armed at all!" Steddy cut him off.

"Come on, let's see what the control is like on the Zambia side."

They continued across the bridge – still barefoot and naked to the waist. The Zambian check-point was embellished with a lot of Marxist trappings, but the paint job was no better. There was no special line for tourists and Wiley and Steddy had to stand in line for some time before they were given visa application forms. When they had them filled out, they were told to wait until, eventually, they were sent into a small office where a black man in uniform sat at a desk.

"You should have applied for a visa in advance, you know," he said, frowning over their applications.

They were embarrassed to sit down in their sodden state and stood in front of him, making puddles on the raw concrete floor.

"We're just here for a few days and want to see the Falls from your side and have lunch; we've heard they're much more impressive on the Zambia side," Steddy flattered him unashamedly.

"Oh yes, much bigger – much bigger. Are you bringing any currency in with you?"

"We have money for the fee and to buy lunch," Steddy replied. "That is, if it's all right to pay in American dollars?" he said, having a sneaking suspicion that it would be.

"How much money are you bringing across with you?"

"Only two hundred dollars," Steddy volunteered. "But we would like to come back again tomorrow if we could get a visa that would be good for two days." Steddy pulled the two hundred dollar bills from his pocket, careful not to push his trousers down and, in so doing, reveal the money belt that was tied at his waist. He put the wet, but still negotiable bills on the desk.

"The fee is twenty-five dollars per person – it would have been less if you had made arrangements in advance."

"That's all right – we're sorry to have caused the inconvenience . . ."

"That's twenty-five dollars per person, per day," he added, trying to get as much of the money as he could. "How many days will you wish to cross?"

"Just today and tomorrow would be fine," Steddy answered.

The officer filled out two flimsy slips of paper from a pad, stamped each of them twice and handed them to Steddy, who pushed one of the hundred dollar bills towards him – it left a wet trail on the linoleum top of his desk.

"Enjoy the Falls," he said, unsmiling.

"Can you recommend any place in walking distance where we could have lunch?" Steddy asked.

"Inter-Continental Hotel – very good – very American." The officer grinned for the first time showing at least thirty-eight white teeth. "Just follow the road – you won't miss it."

"Christ, Steddy, that was clever of you to get a pass for tomorrow too," Wiley said admiringly. "You handled that really well."

"I'm not a double-dyed idiot, and I do listen occasionally," Steddy replied as they walked barefoot off the bridge into Zambia.

~ ~ ~

The marriage of Register of the C.I.A. and Allsloe of Scotland Yard, now seconded to British Intelligence, was not made in heaven. It was more in the mould of a shotgun wedding, a marriage of inconvenience. In Scotland once they had realised what they were up against, they had come clean with each other and decided to pool their resources and any information they eventually got. The issue was entirely too hot politically for them not to cooperate. Apart from the very real intelligence value of the material at stake, the British had set up an American citizen and put his life and that of his American girlfriend, in jeopardy, and the Americans had been caught hands down with C.I.A. operatives actively pursuing their craft on British soil. It was a first-class mess and neither country wanted any of it to see the light of day.

Register and Allsloe, with Holbrook in tow, took the direct flight to Zimbabwe, the day after Steddy and Wiley left on *Flying Cloud*. Allsloe had arranged with his opposite number in Nairobi to hold up their plane so that Register's man in Johannesburg would have time to get on the ground in Harare, before Steddy and Wiley arrived.

When they got there to find that "the idiots" as they were now referring to them, had given Register's man the slip, they were both incensed – Register, doubly so, as Wiley was supposed to be one of his men.

The chief inspector refrained from comment while Register read Hegner – his bleary-eyed subordinate – the Riot Act and sent him back to South Africa. They decided that Holbrook, Allsloe's assistant, would be all the help they needed, if they ever succeeded in relocating their quarry.

Their break came when *Flying Cloud* was spotted landing at Harare Airport. (Steddy had sent Jellicoe back there after he dropped them off at the Falls, thinking the plane would be less conspicuous in a big airport.) Allsloe had no trouble finding out from the tower that it had come in from Victoria Falls and, during a few minutes of private conversation with Jellicoe, was able to persuade him to fly them back – only a twenty-minute flight in *Flying Cloud*.

The Victoria Falls Hotel was the first place they went to from the airport. The man on duty at the desk was very helpful and told them that Mr Wright and Mr Travis had gone out to see the Falls and would be back by five. "Are you the gentlemen they're expecting to hear from?"

"That's right, but don't say we've been here – we wanted to surprise them," Allsloe told the man, and then quietly said to Register:

"That must mean that we're in time and they haven't made contact yet."

The clerk said he was sorry, but there were no rooms available and directed them down the road where they checked into the Elephant Hills Country Club, left their things, and set out on the trail to the Falls to try and find "the idiots" before they contacted Chelak.

They were even less prepared for the wet than Steddy and Wiley had been, and it wasn't long before they were sliding around in the mud in their city shoes, and weighed down by their soggy tweeds. After an unsuccessful hour, they were about to give up and go back to the hotel to wait, when they came upon the bridge – the first place Allsloe could act like a policeman and ask someone if they'd seen them. He strode ahead of the line into the check-point and showed a limp picture of Steddy to the man on duty at the tourist desk. He recognised him and volunteered that he had been in the company of a blond man, equally as tall.

Half-way across the bridge, looking like survivors of the wreck of the *African Queen*, they ran into Wiley and Steddy on their way back. They were barefoot and bare-chested, had rolled up their trousers à la Huckleberry Finn, and looked a great deal more comfortable than the three men who confronted them. Allsloe kept trying to wipe his glasses to see clearly, but there was nothing dry to wipe them on and Register's seersucker Brooks Brothers suit was glued to him, showing off all the bulges in his pockets. Holbrook, in contrast, looked surprisingly composed, as if he did this sort of thing every day.

The noise from the Falls played to Steddy's and Wiley's advantage in the conversation that followed.

"You bloody idiots!" was all Register could manage to splutter.

"What's that?" Steddy yelled at him, one hand cupped at his mouth and the other around his ear.

"You were supposed to stay in touch with Hegner – not get him silly assed drunk! We had a deal!" Register bellowed.

"We couldn't find him the morning after we had dinner and we had to leave," Steddy's reply was yelled back.

"Did you get the documents?" The rough timbre of Allsloe's voice boomed out clearly. Nevertheless, Wiley pretended not to hear.

"Better wait till we get back," he said, gesturing towards the Zimbabwe side of the bridge. Allsloe gave up for the moment; he could see they weren't hiding any documents about their persons.

They made their way back to the Zimbabwe frontier in a group and entering from the other side of the building, found themselves on the opposite side of the counter that they had so recently been processed through. Without talking, Register prodded them to go first at the opening marked for tourists. After a brief examination of their papers, the official stamped them and reached for the three passports Register slid across the counter. He examined them a little more carefully than he had Wiley's and Steddy's and then looked up and addressed Register.

"I do not find your exit stamp from Zambia. As a matter of fact, I do not find your entrance stamp to Zambia."

"That's because we haven't been to Zambia," Register replied politely. "We changed our minds."

"But I am not permitted to enter you into Zimbabwe unless you have legally exited from another country . . ."

"But we did legally exit from Zimbabwe," Register said, pointing to the Zimbabwe exit stamp. He was beginning to get annoyed.

"But that does not tell me where you have been in the meantime."

"It was only stamped five minutes ago," Register was red-faced and steaming now.

"I cannot help that. You must have a legal exit stamp from another country – we must follow the rules."

Register was apoplectic – it was the last straw after a generally unsatisfactory, uncomfortable day. Allsloe saw that he was about to explode and grabbed him firmly by the elbow, muttering under his breath.

"We don't need any trouble here just now." He manoeuvred Register from in front of the window and spoke to the clerk. "If we were to enter Zambia and exit it with a stamp, would that be all right?"

"Oh, perfectly, sir."

"Then that is what we'll do. Thank you very much," Allsloe said politely.

"Oh, thank you sir – and have a nice trip."

Steddy and Wiley were standing off in a corner, roaring with laughter – the C.I.A. and Scotland Yard had met their match at the hands of an African bureaucrat who had probably been trained by the British in the first place. They called to the sodden threesome from the door that exited into Zimbabwe.

"We'll see you back at the hotel – we've just got to get into some dry clothes." They laughed most of the way along the paved road to town, where they bought some rather bizarre looking shirts and trousers – all that was available – before returning to the hotel to await the call from Chelak.

Earlier, Steddy and Wiley had been unaware that as they ate lunch by the empty pool in the run-down, quasi-deserted Inter-Continental Hotel compound, they were just yards away from the bungalow where Thea was being held. They had walked all the way from the bridge. As they left the spray of the Falls behind them, the heat became terrific, so that by the time they got there, and were ushered to a table by the same giant in black tie who had greeted Thea and her group – all they really wanted was a beer. He informed them that Zambia was out of beer that week. Steddy said: "You mean *the hotel* is out of beer?"

"No, sir, the country is out of beer."

What Rollo had told Steddy of the plight of the formerly white-run nations, suddenly hit home. They ordered the simplest thing on the menu, a Croque Monsieur, and the fellow said he would see if there was any cheese. When it finally came, it did have a sort of cheese on it, but it looked as though they had simply scraped the clotted top off six-day-old sour milk and slathered it on the ham. Steddy found it revolting and wouldn't touch it, but Wiley was so famished that he tried to salvage the bread. In disgust, Steddy turned his chair into the sun and his back to Wiley, until he heard Wiley screaming, "Get away! Get away!" accompanied by outraged shrieks. He turned to see that a large baboon with bared teeth had jumped on the table and was having a vicious tug of war with Wiley over the last crust of bread. Poor Wiley, who must have been starving even to think of eating the revolting thing, lost it and the baboon jumped off to join his fellows who had formed a rooting section under a nearby tree during the fray. It seemed everyone in Zambia was hungry.

"So much for Socialism or Marxism or whatever," Steddy said, laughing as he paid the outrageous bill. Wiley was not amused at having lost out to a baboon and even less at having lost his lunch, but he didn't say very much about it until they had had a good laugh together after their encounter with Allsloe and Register on the bridge on the way back.

It was five when they got to the hotel, and Wiley announced in the lobby that the first thing he was going to do was order a sandwich from Room Service.

"Order me one too," Steddy said. "I'm going to have a look around down here to get the lie of the land, as it were – and I'll try to find a plastic bag for the documents. If you're right and we do meet on the bridge, they'll want to see the envelope, so I'd better get it wrapped in something transparent and waterproof or it'll get soaked."

"Good thinking but don't be long, the call may come any minute."

Steddy was back in the room in less than half an hour.

"You know they've got a casino in the hotel?"

"Well I'm glad you had the fortitude to resist it, for a change."

"Come on, Wiley, I'm very upset about all this – we just react in different ways," he said, picking up half of the ham sandwich Wiley had ordered for him.

"We'd better talk about this Steddy – you know it's OK to play cat and mouse with Register and Allsloe, but as you yourself pointed out, when push comes to shove, neither of us are armed and if they pull any funny business – we may have the visas to follow them back over the bridge, but there's precious little we can do about it. We're going to need all the back-up we can get."

"Yeah, you're right, but we can't just turn over the documents to them and lose control of the whole thing – you know that's all they care about. Thea's of secondary importance as far as they're concerned."

"I agree with that, but we'll have to play our cards very close to our chests – not tell them about the arrangements until the last minute and hang onto the papers . . ."

"So how much do we tell them?" Steddy interrupted.

"Let's see what Chelak says first, then we can . . ."

The phone rang. They looked at each other. It rang a second time before Wiley uncradled the receiver and handed it to Steddy.

"Hello," Steddy said.

"Steddy, it's you . . ." It was Thea, but her words were cut off.

"It's Thea, but . . ." Steddy started to say to Wiley, when another voice came on the line.

"Mr Wright." It was a woman's voice with an accent. "I will give you the instructions for tomorrow's meeting on behalf of our mutual friend. Can you hear me clearly?"

"Yes," Steddy replied, the phone half on his ear and half on Wiley's who was crouched next to him – head to head.

"Good, for I will only say this once. You will be on the bridge over the Zambezi, with the documents, at eleven o'clock. You will stop half way to admire the view of the Falls and you will be approached. You may bring your friend, Monsieur Travis, with you to effect the transfer, but no one else. Until tomorrow then."

"She rang off as though she was making a date for tea," Steddy said to Wiley after he had hung up the phone. "Well, you sure called that one right," he said, patting Wiley on the shoulder.

"Wouldn't have been able to if you hadn't forced me to go to the Falls today – and they sure were punctual," he said, pointing at his watch. "Two minutes after six."

There was an urgent knock on the door.

"Right on cue wouldn't you say?" Steddy said as he opened the door and let in the three bedraggled, hot-shot, super-spies.

~ ~ ~

Steddy adamantly refused even to let them have a look at the envelope that contained the documents. Wiley backed him up all the way. A serious argument followed, but when Allsloe and Register realised that further efforts to sway them were futile, they agreed to give back-up on the exchange. They had little choice given the predicament they were in, and they didn't want to miss their opportunity to be in at the kill.

They synchronised their watches at dinner in the vast dining room of the hotel, that had seated a thousand people in its heyday, and were serenaded by a "Continental" orchestra that alternated with a chamber music ensemble throughout the meal.

Wiley went straight to bed after dinner, but Steddy had a nightcap at the bar with Register, Allsloe and Holbrook, and, when at ten o'clock Allsloe said he would retire, Register agreed to look in on the casino with Steddy for a few hands of blackjack.

The casino was a makeshift affair, the original one having been destroyed during the war by rockets fired by the ZIPRA forces from Zambia across the Zambezi. The crowd consisted mostly of white Rhodesians who, it appeared, were wild gamblers, no doubt because they couldn't take any funds out of the country, and didn't know how long they would be allowed to keep what they had.

The two men played a few hands, but couldn't really get into the game as their minds were elsewhere, so they quit and had one for the ditch at the small bar in the gaming room. Register again tried to persuade him to be more cooperative.

"Don't you see that levelling with us is the best thing for the girl? We can't be really effective if we're dancing in the dark."

"I just can't take the chance. I'm responsible for getting her into this in the first place, and then none of it would have happened if it hadn't been for that limey bastard setting me up. In spite of the fact that *you're* a nice guy, you're both cut from the same mould and our priorities in this thing are in no way the same. Nothing you can say or do will change my mind."

"You're just too damn close to the situation . . ."

"What the hell should I be?" Steddy interrupted.

"Look, I *do* understand, but you don't – you don't have any idea what you're up against and there's no way I can convince you. It might have been different if you were working for me . . ."

"Say again?"

"Just that, in spite of our difference, I have to say that for an amateur you've really been thinking on your feet – given all of us a merry chase – I think Allsloe would agree with me. We all underestimated you."

"Flattery will get you nowhere."

"No, I mean it. If you weren't involved with this girl, I think you could have been a big help. As it is, well, if you'd ever like to do something useful for your Uncle Sam when this is over . . ."

"Gosh, there's no limit to how far you people will go to . . ."

"No, I mean it, but let it be. We'll play it your way tomorrow."

They parted in the lobby at the foot of the stairs leading from the casino. Steddy went to his darkened room to join Wiley in pretending to sleep, and Register walked down the road to his hotel to do what spies do before an operation.

~ ~ ~

Steddy and Wiley set out on foot for the bridge, fifteen minutes ahead of Register and Allsloe. Holbrook was already in position somewhere on the span. They took the footpath again at the back of the hotel and looked as though they had gone native, dressed in the local shirts and trousers they had bought the day before. Register and Allsloe had managed to procure disposable Hong Kong raincoats and walked by the main road to the bridge from the Elephant Hills Country Club.

It was quarter to eleven when they cleared customs on the Zimbabwe side and set out across the bridge. When they reached mid-span, they traversed the railroad track, climbed up on the big conduit pipe and leaned over the rail – looking for all the world like tourists hypnotised by the panorama of the Falls.

They were already soaked to the skin, but the broad-brim, woven-hemp, native hats they had bought protected their vision from the warm downpour. The documents were safely encased in the clear-plastic bag Steddy had got from the desk, and were tucked in his belt, under his shirt. Holbrook, they noticed, was stationed on the same rail, about forty yards further along towards the Zambia side. They alternated straining to see in either direction for any sign of Thea, and Steddy spotted Register and Allsloe – equipped with cameras – as they entered the passport hut on the Zimbabwe side. It was almost eleven and there was still no sign of Thea or her captors.

By ten minutes past, Steddy was getting agitated.

"You don't suppose he's spotted those assholes, do you?" he shouted to Wiley.

"I doubt it. Just try to relax; he's probably just checking the terrain."

"I don't like it. He's always done everything he said he would do almost to the second."

"Just relax, Steddy!" he barked, revealing the state of his own nerves.

"We're here unfortunately at his convenience, not vice versa. Relax!"

"Yes Mr Wright, you must listen to your friend and relax. This will all be quite painless if we all keep our heads."

The voice came from Steddy's left elbow. It startled him as he had not noticed anyone approach, so intent was his gaze to the right

239

towards the Zambia frontier. When he spun around, he saw a small wiry black man, wearing a hat that was, like the rest of his clothes, shabby. But there could be no mistaking the voice, its timbre was identical to the first time he heard it on the Scottish moors. Chelak had arrived.

"Do not stare at me but continue to observe the Falls – they are most majestic, are they not?"

Steddy poked Wiley in the ribs with his elbow, so hard that he doubled over; the roar of the Falls had prevented him from hearing Chelak's words and he was still staring off to the right. Wiley swore at Steddy, but Steddy cut him short with a stage whisper that could have been heard at the Victoria Falls Hotel, had it not been for the vortex of rushing water in the Boiling Pot below them.

"It's him – it's him!" he said, fiercely.

"Have you got the documents with you?" Chelak asked.

For some reason, in his nervousness, Steddy fumbled in his trouser pockets.

"I believe you'll find them under your shirt," Chelak said, politely. "And I already know my disguise is most effective, so please ask your friend not to stare at me. Just act normally – as if you're showing me a map to ask a question."

"Don't look at him, Wiley," Steddy rasped as he unbuttoned his shirt to get at the envelope.

"It isn't necessary to disrobe," Chelak said in the same even lilting voice. His remark made Steddy realise how rattled he was and he tried to pull himself together.

"Where is Thea – I don't see her?"

"First, I will examine the seals on the documents, and if all is in order I will signal for her to be brought into view, then the exchange can be made."

"I will want her to be safely in the hands of my friend, before I turn them over to you," Steddy said, repeating the plans they had rehearsed the night before.

"That is agreeable, but come, come – the documents."

Steddy removed the plastic sheath from under his belt and, holding it firmly in two hands, showed it to Chelak in the manner he had suggested – as though they were consulting over a map. When Chelak made a move to hold the envelope, Steddy withdrew it and cautioned him.

"You may look – but don't touch," he said, unemotionally – more in control of himself now.

240

Chelak bent over the envelope – studying the seals, through the plastic – periodically wiping the rain from it with his hand. Steddy let him touch the package only because he was unwilling to loosen the death grip with which he held it in both hands.

"Not the best conditions for the sort of examination required wouldn't you say Mr Wright? You will have to be patient and bear with me. Clever of you to think of the plastic wrapper. Have you been here before?" His conversation was casual, but throughout his eyes were scanning the seals on the back of the envelope.

"We had a look around yesterday while we were waiting for your call."

"Well, at least you've had some pleasure from your journey. Please turn it over."

Steddy brought the plastic to his chest to execute the reversal, tried to wipe it dry on his shirt, and then returned it to its position under Chelak's nose. He examined the blank side of the envelope with as much care as he had the side with the seals and then closely eyed the edges.

"Come on. Let's get on with this. It's not in my interest to have fiddled with the damn thing – all I want is Thea back. Now!"

"Just the last edge, Mr Wright." Chelak continued eyeing it as he spoke, until his straightened shoulders indicated that he had finished to his satisfaction and then said: "If you will watch by the customs house on the Zambia side, please . . ."

Steddy replaced the envelope under his belt, but continued to hold it to him with one hand as he turned to his right and peered at the crowd of people coming towards them from the Zambia customs building. Chelak bent over as if to pick up something he had dropped.

It must be a signal, Steddy thought.

He noticed a heavy-set European peel off the opposite rail and head towards the building. A few minutes later he reappeared with a smallish European woman and Thea between them. It had to be Thea. She towered over both of them, and even with her hair hidden under a scarf and wearing an unfamiliar cotton dress that was glued to her in the rain, there could be no mistake. Steddy instinctively moved to go to her, but Chelak held him back.

"That would be very unwise – we must do this as planned."

"All right. All right," he said, turning back towards the wiry, little man.

"Your friend will cross to the pedestrian way on the other side of the bridge where Miss Boulton will advance to meet him. When they are together, you will turn over the documents to me. It is very simple but don't think you can try anything. She will be killed instantly if you make one false step before I am safely back over the Zambian frontier." The casualness had gone from his voice, replaced by a savage quality that Steddy knew to be more genuinely representative of his character.

Steddy turned to Wiley and repeated Chelak's instructions with a few of his own.

"He means business. For God's sake, don't get any patriotic notions about absolving your sins in the eyes of your employer," Steddy hissed at him.

"Fuck you, Steddy – I love her too!" It was out and he didn't care, moments later he was sliding across the tracks and the roadway to the footpath on the other side – to Thea, who was advancing on her own, slowly and shakily, but with an obvious determination, to meet him.

Steddy stood with his back to the Falls – counting each footstep that brought Wiley and Thea closer together. He didn't have the time or inclination to wrestle with Wiley's confession – he didn't even allow it to enter his consciousness – that was already filled with thoughts of Chelak and what he would and could do, and visions of Thea with her face blown away by a silent gunshot.

Wiley reached the point on the footpath opposite them and stood perfectly still, waiting for Thea to reach him. She did, and he put an arm around her – she seemed to go limp against him as if in a dead faint.

"All right, Mr Wright, the documents please." Chelak was closer now, at his elbow.

Steddy pulled the envelope from where it rested against his belly – never for an instant taking his eyes from Thea's distant figure.

All of a sudden all hell broke loose.

In the corner of the frame of his vision he saw Holbrook running towards Wiley and Thea – at the same moment Chelak tried to wrest the envelope from his grip. He struggled with him and noticed from behind Chelak's back that Register and Allsloe were racing towards them – but someone was closer.

Thea started screaming – a piercing wail that could be heard over the rush of the Falls, and Holbrook was on one knee, holding a gun in front of him with both hands, firing at the man and woman who were running towards her.

Steddy was holding off Chelak's arm with one hand when he noticed the deathly glint of white metal flash dully in his other and had to drop the envelope in order to try to fight off the lethal platinum spike that he already knew by reputation.

His purchase on that arm was awkward as he had stepped off the pipe and Chelak had the advantage of height over him. He felt the thing scratch the back of his neck and knew he couldn't hold him off much longer, when suddenly Chelak went limp in his arms and collapsed in a heap at his feet. There was a figure behind him, but to Steddy it was just a blur, as he whipped around to see Thea who was still screaming. He was just in time to see the man fall dead, under Holbrook's gun – the woman already lay writhing on the ground.

Thea pushed Wiley away from her with a violence that two minutes before he wouldn't have thought her capable of. She hiked up her skirt and squatted in the path for a moment as though defecating – then vaulted the tracks and pitched something out over the water. There was a flash of light and then a pressure in Steddy's eardrums that he felt more than heard.

He started to run to her, when a hand restrained him. When he looked around it was a perfect stranger – the man he owed his life to.

"Could I just trouble you for the envelope please, Mr Wright?" he asked with the greatest courtesy.

"Who the devil are you?" Steddy asked, still registering shock and surprise.

"The man who saved your life – wouldn't you say that's enough of an introduction?"

Steddy was very confused – too much had happened too quickly for his brain to compute it all, and on top of that he saw Register and Allsloe casually strolling back towards the Zimbabwe control point and Holbrook running for his life in the same direction . . .

"I must have dropped it when we were fighting, " Steddy said to the stocky man in the raincoat who faced him.

Out of the corner of his eye, he saw Wiley supporting Thea on the other side of the bridge – walking slowly towards Zimbabwe.

Steddy looked down at the ground to find the envelope and for the first time focused on Chelak. He was lying on his back, his body contorted in death. His lips were drawn back from his teeth and his shirt front had torn open, revealing a green-white, hairless chest that contrasted sharply with the dyed black skin of his arms and face.

There was no sign of the envelope.

The stranger stood over him motionless, watching.

Steddy gingerly tried to shift the body to see if it was under him, but the weight was more than he would have guessed and he had to get down on his hands and knees to move it.

The envelope lay in a pool of blood that had formed from the deep knife wound in Chelak's back. Steddy grasped it between two fingers and tugged it out from under the lifeless form – it was slathered with blood. He rose to his feet.

"It's a bit messy, I'm afraid," he said, and held it up into the rain, over the rail, to get the full benefit of the spray from the Boiling Pot.

"Be careful, Mr Wright."

He knows my name, Steddy thought, and noted his harsh, but unidentifiable accent.

Then, holding the plastic sheath by its edge and shaking it – ostensibly to wash away the blood – he allowed the pale yellow envelope to slide from it – into the Boiling Pot – 350 feet below them.

The man made a move to grab for it, but then threw up his hands and smiled. "It doesn't matter – the original is in safe keeping. You have done my government a great service, Mr Wright."

Now Steddy was completely baffled.

"But it was an Israeli document, wasn't it? – I saw the seals myself!"

"That is correct – but I haven't introduced myself – the name is Lev Ginsberg, Israeli State Security."

"But you killed him," Steddy said, pointing at Chelak's body.

"He was a traitor – a fanatic – working for the Syrians. We've known for some time. It would have been very bad if *they'd* got hold of that," he said, pointing down to the river. "But he was good at his work, and I knew that if he would accept the exchange, then the seals were not broken and, how do you say, we have a happy ending, no?"

Happy ending, brought Thea to Steddy's mind and he looked back to where she had been, but she and Wiley were gone. *They must have got back into Zimbabwe*, he thought. There was commotion around the two bodies on the opposite side of the bridge, with frontier police from both countries and crowds of people gathered round. The sound of an ambulance could be heard getting nearer. Then Lev interrupted his thoughts.

"We'd better be getting out of here before they notice there are three bodies on this bridge."

Steddy concurred. He didn't fancy being held indefinitely in an African lock-up while they tried to sort out the mess.

They walked together from the bridge, into the customs' hut and out the door on the other side into Zimbabwe – there was so much confusion that no one even bothered to stamp their passports. They were just waved through.

At the fork in the road, Ginsberg shook Steddy's hand heartily, as if to make up for the words he couldn't express in his poor English.

"I say goodbye, my work is done. Thank you – shalom – thank you."

"Thank you," Steddy said, a sense of lightheaded elation creeping over him. They waved again as Ginsberg turned to take the road to town and Steddy the road to the hotel.

~ ~ ~

Allsloe and Register were huddled in the lobby when Steddy arrived at the hotel. They separated, and bracketed him on either side.

"Where's Thea? Is she all right?" It was the first thing Steddy asked them.

"She's in your room – the doctor's with her." And then, seeing the concern on Steddy's face: "She's all right – just very badly shaken."

"Where's Wiley?" Steddy growled.

"He took the doctor up to her for an injection; let her be now, she'll sleep for quite a while. The doc's one of ours – had him on call, just in case . . ."

"Just in case! Just in case! It's only sheer fucking luck that we weren't killed with the stunt that asshole pulled – where is that son of a bitch Holbrook?"

"He's in custody for the moment, but not for very long. We should have him out in a day or two – the administration here is more cooperative with Her Majesty's Government than the newspapers would lead one to believe," Allsloe said.

"Don't go off half-cocked about Holbrook, Stedman," Register interjected. "Those people on the bridge were about to detonate a bomb that was wired to Thea – Allsloe will explain it – I have to make a call."

Register left them to telephone from the booth by the desk. Steddy and Allsloe wandered into the bar, where the Englishman explained in some detail how Thea had been booby-trapped and how only Holbrook's quick action had saved her life.

"I hope you will bear that in mind if you're thinking about making any trouble for Her Majesty's Government."

"Don't bring Her Majesty into this – she didn't have a goddamned thing to do with the way you set me up!" Steddy replied angrily.

"Certainly not, just a figure of speech," Allsloe countered, taking Steddy at his word.

"We never planned it to go this far, but I'm afraid I rather misjudged your – how shall I say – resourcefulness."

"What the hell did you expect me to do?"

"That, in essence was the problem – you never did what we expected you to do. Are you sure that you've never had a run in with the law before?" Allsloe said, half in jest, trying to heal the situation with a little humour.

"Now you're making me angrier," Steddy said, and then cut off Allsloe's objections with another question.

"What will happen to Rollo now?"

"Ah, yes, Lord Rockford," he sighed. "Well, now that we know at least what country he's in, it shouldn't be much of a job finding him. Of course, if you'd like to cooperate . . ."

"Screw that! What'll you do to him once you get him – his wife's death was accidental, you won't be able to pin that on him . . ."

"His wife's death is the least of his problems. He has seriously breached the Official Secrets Act, and I'm not sure but that he isn't guilty of high treason . . ."

"You mean, 'hanged by the neck until dead' on the old silk cord?"

"Hanging peers by a silk cord was voted out by the House of Lords, ten or twenty years ago."

"You know what I mean," Steddy insisted.

"I should think he'll be sent away for quite a time."

"He didn't really do anything – he told me that he was going to turn the documents over to you the next day, but then the accident happened, and I guess he got scared and ran – he was drunk and thought that he might be able to buy his way out of the mess with the documents."

"I doubt if they would have helped, but they are no longer an issue. You saw to that!"

"Just one fucking minute. That guy you let follow me around for a month was a fucking Syrian agent – he would have killed me on the bridge if it hadn't been for the Israeli – and where were you guys, by the way? My protection, ha!"

"We saw that Mr Ginsberg had matters well in hand and thought it best to withdraw."

"Would you have rather had the Syrians get the papers?"

"None of this is any longer germane, I'm afraid. I don't see where all this is leading."

"Then I'll tell you. If you don't let Rollo off, I'm going to scream bloody murder all over your lousy British tabloids."

"I don't see how that would help you, and if you think it could make the slightest difference in a case where a peer has committed high treason, you're very much mistaken," Allsloe said, rising in his chair indignantly – feathers ruffled.

"Well, if you'll wait here just a minute, I'll show you something that might make a difference."

Without waiting for an answer, Steddy strode from the bar, through the big hall and out into the lobby – Register was still on the phone in the booth as Steddy passed on his way to the desk. He took a small silver key from his trouser pocket and flashed it at the clerk as he walked behind the counter into the vault where the safe-deposit boxes were located. The clerk followed him in, took his key, found the corresponding box and with Steddy's key and the one that he had on a chain, opened it and left the room.

"Let me know when you're through."

Steddy lifted the lid, pushed his money belt aside, and took out one of the two envelopes that lay beneath it. He reclosed the box and turned the lock that still had his key in it, put it in his pocket and told the chap at the desk that he'd already locked his side as he passed him on the way back to the bar.

Allsloe was still sipping his whisky and soda when Steddy returned. He took his seat, undid the fastener at the back of the envelope and withdrew a copy of the four sheets of paper that had caused so much trouble.

He held the first sheet – the letterhead bore the shield with the candelabrum – under Allsloe's nose and gloated at the reaction it produced. The bright red, permanently surprised eyebrows turned into circumflex accent marks, and his tiny red mouth opened, forming a perfect O.

When he had regained enough of his composure to speak, he said:

"Mr Wright, you do amaze me. But this is a Xerox copy, how did you get it? Chelak examined the seals!"

"I never broke the seals. I cut the envelope open at the edge with a razor blade and made the copy for fifty pence at the desk – they let me do it myself. As far as Chelak noticing through the plastic cover, and with all that spray – well, even seasoned spies sometimes see only what they want to, wouldn't you agree?"

"Touché," was all that Allsloe could say in response.

"I assume you intend to exact your pound of flesh for those," he said, pointing at the papers that still remained in Steddy's hand.

"You bet your British ass I do," Steddy replied, restacking the papers and relaxing back into the big, comfortable chair.

"And what would that be?"

"Withdraw all charges against Rollo – in effect, think of me as his messenger, delivering your ill-gotten goods as promised."

"And if not?" Allsloe asked with little hope of being given quarter.

"If not, I'll release them to the papers – and the United Nations – and raise the most unholy diplomatic stink that's been seen since the Zimmermann telegram."

"Say no more – you have a deal." He paused pensively. "I doubt if Lord Rockford deserves your loyalty . . ." Allsloe looked up from under his startling eyebrows, his gaze directed at Steddy. "On the other hand, perhaps you deserve each other!"

He took the papers from Steddy's extended hand and left him to ponder his words.

~ ~ ~

The room was darkened when Steddy was finally allowed in to see Thea at ten o'clock that evening.

She didn't say anything as he approached the bed, so he didn't either. He didn't know what he could say or do. He was overwhelmed by the horror of what had happened to her, the hideous violation of her body . . .

They had treated their love carelessly, the way some people treat their clothes – taking for granted it would be there when they needed it.

He needed her, but could think of no dialogue that could now bring them together.

He gently lowered himself to the bed beside her and took her hand that lay lifeless on top of the sheet.

"I'm so very sorry, darling," he said tenderly.

She didn't open her mouth, but the corners wrinkled down, ackowledging what he had said.

"I guess you don't want to talk about it?"

Her head moved slightly to the right and then to the left.

"Would you rather rest some more?" he asked.

She squinted her eyes and moved her head up and down. He bent over and kissed her tenderly on the nose.

~ ~ ~

The nurse was standing out in the hall talking in hushed tones with Wiley. Steddy must have looked crestfallen, for she volunteered:

"I wouldn't worry, sir, the doctor gave her a very strong sedative and

I'm just going to give her another injection now – sleep's what she needs. Mark my word, by tomorrow she'll be fit as a fiddle."

Her accent was pure British, and Steddy wondered what branch of the service Allsloe had drawn her from – they seemed better prepared for the mopping up than for the actual dirty work.

Wiley followed Steddy who had taken the stairs down, rather than wait for the lift.

Steddy was depressed and he didn't know why – certainly he was worried and upset over Thea, but the underlying source of his depression eluded him.

Wiley, on the other hand, was walking on air, in spite of the dressing down Register had given him. But he sensed Steddy's mood and said:

"Want to have a drink?"

"Sure. Why not?" Steddy answered, without enthusiasm.

"Oh, by the way, Allsloe's got us a room at the Elephant Hills – he couldn't send our things over, 'cause we don't have any," Wiley said, trying to raise Steddy's spirits, or at least get a reaction out of him.

"Bully," was all he got in return.

They were on their second drink. Wiley was carrying on a one-sided conversation, with Steddy's only remarks being an occasional "Uh huh," when Steddy suddenly asked him:

"What's going to happen between you and Register?"

"Not much – you can't fire someone who was never on the payroll," he said, trying to make light of his breach with "the Company".

"Come on, Wiley – don't tell me you don't care about it – just a little?"

"Well, I guess I do. I've been working with him a long time and now, well, I blew the first real operation I've ever been involved in – at least in their eyes anyway."

"Well, not in mine!" Steddy affirmed. "I owe you one. You really stood by me when it counted."

"Don't be so morose, Steddy. You sound like Napoleon saying farewell to his generals – it's not really a big deal."

"Yes it is, and I know what it means to you in spite of what you say. If I hadn't made you stick by me, you probably would have ended up a hero. Here," Steddy said, tossing the small key to the vault over the table. "This should go a long way towards fixing things up."

"What is it?" Wiley asked perplexed.

"The key to my safe deposit box at the desk."

"I don't want any money, Steddy," Wiley said, insulted by the gesture.

"It's not money, but you should find it of greater value – but don't get it if Allsloe is still around."

"He went back to the Elephant Hills," Wiley answered, still puzzled.

"Then go and get it, and bring my money belt back while you're at it. I'll order us another drink, and then maybe we'll stop in at the casino before we move out of here."

Wiley returned with the opened envelope in his hand while Steddy was signing the chit for the fresh drinks.

"Steddy, I don't know what to say. How could you have taken a chance like that with Thea's life at stake?"

"Isn't that what you wanted from the beginning?"

"Well yes, but not . . ."

"Oh, can it, Wiley," Steddy said, moving to leave.

Wiley answered with a trace of bitterness.

"Maybe you're the one who should give this to Register – you obviously have more of a stomach for this sort of work than I do, it seems."

"Oh just keep it and shut up!" Steddy told him, stuffing the papers in Wiley's breast pocket. "Maybe tomorrow everything will look a little different." Steddy strode from the bar towards the casino.

"And maybe it won't, Steddy, maybe it won't," Wiley muttered.

A Saving Grace

The holding lounge at Nairobi airport was as hot and fly-ridden as it had been when Stedman was stuck there with Wiley on the way down, only now, perhaps because it was Sunday, there was no stewardess serving up iced gins – not that anything would have lightened the weight of confused emotions he carried with him.

He had been waiting an hour for the flight to London – as good a place as any – when the twangy tones of Peter Jellicoe's Australian accent cut through the heat and the flies and the haze of his self-centred mental meanderings. He was speaking to the flight attendant at the door to the lounge.

"If Mr Wright's in here, would you tell him that we're ready to take off whenever he is."

"What the hell are you doing here?" Steddy called across the room. "I'm booked on British Airways!"

Jellicoe, spotting Steddy for the first time, replied: "Well I'm still responsible for getting you back in one piece and I don't appreciate having to chase you down all over Africa."

Steddy's initial anger melted. The man had gone beyond the bounds of his duties for them and Steddy realised that he'd never even thanked him.

"I'm sorry, I guess it all finally got to me."

"What's that then – a week's vacation in sunny Zimbabwe?"

Steddy was unable to suppress the smile that came to his face.

"My flight to London's due to be called any minute."

"Your flight is ready whenever you are – I don't like losing passengers even if they try to lose me."

"I've got my ticket," Steddy said lamely, holding out his boarding pass as proof.

"You don't need one to fly with me."

"But . . ."

"Hey, we came together, we'll go back the same way if it's all the same to you. I don't like ten-hour solo legs any more and besides, I've got used to your lousy coffee."

Steddy laughed and, symbolically tearing his boarding pass in two, followed Jellicoe out onto the steamy tarmac where the water puddles from the earlier rain hissed and boiled in the hot sun.

She was at the foot of *Flying Cloud*'s stair and broke into a run when she saw him, stopping half-way while a Cessna taxied between them.

Even from afar, the impact of seeing her hit him with the force of a physical blow that took the wind out of him, and when he glanced accusingly at the pilot, he realised there were tears in his eyes and quickly turned away – back towards Thea.

The Cessna had broken her run. When it had passed, she closed the gap between them more slowly, until she saw the sun glint off the wetness on his cheeks and began to run again. They were both laughing by the time their tears mingled and her body moulded to his with a perfection that told the world they'd been made for each other.

He'd got a full pardon at the last minute. Life and joy overfilled him and he had to keep laughing to relieve the pressure.

"Let's go home," he said as they walked towards the plane in an awkward tangle.

"Where's that?" she laughed.

"Wherever you are."

They never even heard Jellicoe start the engines.